Two Steps from Heaven

Serpent's Bane

by

J. S. Robinson

Published by New Generation Publishing in 2024

First Edition

Paperback ISBN: 9781835635070
Hardback ISBN: 9781835635087

New Generation Publishing
www.newgeneration-publishing.com

For Katrin

Prologue

That night had been an especially cold one in The Most Serene Republic. Thick mist hung over the nation's capital while ice-tipped winds battered the homes below. Open windows which were not hurriedly closed, found themselves slammed shut by the freezing gale which blew through the narrow streets. Those unlucky enough to still be wandering so late at night kept their shady business hidden beneath thick hoods and cloaks, clutched tightly against their shivering bodies as they stalked the alleyways like shadows. Yet this offered little comfort. This winter had been harsh. Not one easily kept at bay by mere rags and wringing hands. Some days even fire did little to push out the chill which quickly set into one's bones.

Within one small home, illuminated by the strained flames of an aged fire, lay a man, fast asleep on an uncomfortable red sofa which had gone out of fashion a decade ago. Yet these were not the times to be concerning oneself with such matters. Around him lay many papers and letters, beginning their night as organised stacks in multicoloured folders. Now, however, they were scattered like leaves by a heedless wind, both on and around where the man had been working. Many resting upon the man himself as, despite his best efforts, tiredness overcame him. His chest rose and fell steadily, his breath rising into the chilling air even here.

In the adjacent room lay his wife, and despite being wrapped in a thick duvet, she was still not spared from the cold and her feet felt like ice. Yet still she slept, uncomfortable and alone. He had promised to join her as soon as he had finished his work. While she may have believed such a promise once, she was under no such illusion now and generally resigned to her solitary slumbers. She could not remember the last time the pair had shared their bed together. The last time they had walked through the city streets hand in hand, stopping leisurely to peruse whatever took their fancy from the city's countless exotic merchants, intimately delighting over inconsequential things with one another. Even meals were now spent separately, the man hunched over his desk, a quill glued to one hand while he shovelled in food with the other, not once lifting his eyes.

The position of an administrative assistant within the vast bureaucratic network which formed the nexus of the Republic's fragile and inept government, was a thankless one at the best of times. Overworked, undervalued, and underpaid, it was no wonder that few lasted more than a month in this job. But times were tough in the Republic. A floundering economy only made worse by the constant meddling of the oligarchs, each time confident that their latest scheme would revive the country's fortunes before inevitably and predictably failing, plunging the people even further into desperation and poverty.

If only from their marble towers, their country homes and island retreats could they see the havoc and misery they caused. Rows of people lined the city streets from end to end, their heads bowed in shame, dirty hands outstretched, their only remaining option if they did not wish to starve. No matter how many missions were established, no matter how many altruistic philanthropists made it their hobby to temporarily alleviate the sufferings of the masses, misery was always in surplus.

The truth was that the man had been extremely lucky to keep this job at all, and so he worked night and day to ensure he could provide for his family. But even then, the uncertainty of what the next day would bring ate away at any spare moment of peace. Somewhere, buried deep beneath the piles of papers, hidden away from the gaze of his wife was a letter from the bank. The Servants of the God of Man had seen it fit to drastically increase the interest rate, and now he was barely six months from being unable to pay his mortgage.

The thought of his beloved wife, out on the streets, begging for charity filled him with rage. Not just at the heartless bank and the useless government for which he worked, but at himself also. He had promised to protect her, to care and provide for her, and yet he could not even do that. '*What sort of man cannot provide for those he loves?*' he would often ask himself in his increasingly recurrent moments of self-deprecation.

His wife never gave in to worry or despair though. She would never berate her husband for not working hard enough, like the wives of many of his colleagues. She could see the stresses of the world eating away at him. With each day that passed he became more frayed and worn, soon there would be nothing left of him at all. She tried to convince him to quit, to take her by the hand and run off into the world in search of a better life. Despite wishing for nothing more, his pride would not allow him to just up and run. '*The only thing worse than a man who cannot provide, is one who runs away from his responsibilities*' he would say whenever she suggested it.

So, for now, they were trapped in an ever-tightening noose. A noose that was slowly strangling the life and love from them both. As the last embers of the fire went cold and the small living room was enveloped in darkness, the man felt something. Even in the depths of his exhausted and dreamless slumber it had been enough to wake him. It had felt like a presence, perhaps it was his wife, come at last to drag him to bed? No, this was something else entirely. Perhaps a break-in? They were becoming increasingly common these days as the people of the city became more desperate.

He kept his eyes closed, taking a deep breath, preparing for whatever confrontation was to come, adrenaline now coursing through his veins. He was no fighter, but he would do what he could to defend his home. Then, from beneath his eyelids he saw a light, so pure and white it dazzled him even now. Realising he could wait no longer, his eyes flicked open, jumping to his feet, fists at the ready.

But this was no break-in, and the man's stance immediately shifted from one of violence to a mixture of awe and terror. Just a few feet away, hovering above the ground in the centre of the tiny living room, was a man. At least, he thought it was a man. The figure's features seemed to be carved from marble, a square jaw, wide, muscular shoulders and large, strong hands. And yet they were fair beyond compare. The figure's skin was without a single blemish, their long hair seemed so pure, so healthy that its colour was beyond description. Lastly were their eyes, burning with a white light so fierce it illuminated the room, making them impossible to look upon.

The being, whatever it was, seemed to wear robes made of light itself. But as time passed, the light began to shift and bend until it had transformed into armour the likes of which had never been seen by mortal men. Beyond words was the quality of its craftsmanship, the intricacies of its adornments, and the power which radiated from it.

The man fell to his knees as his legs lost the strength to support him. The being remained, floating just off the ground, silent and yet their presence was like a hurricane, an indomitable force of nature. The man tried to call out to his wife, to urge her to run and not look back. But he was unable. A will, far greater than this own forced his silence, commanding his body as if it were a puppet on a string. All he could do was stare in disbelief and pray he would not be harmed.

At last, after what felt like an age of silence, the being spoke. And its voice was one of music. Of the deafening crash of the tide against the shore. Of the vastness of the stars and the lofty majesty of unconquered mountain ranges. Its words rocked the very foundations of creation.

"Be not afraid!" it boomed as the very ground beneath them shook and the walls of the house trembled. Yet nobody came to investigate the source of this demand, for beyond that room the world was still. All of creation had halted, seemingly to pay homage to this being's presence. Rivers had ceased their flow, leaves freshly roused by the wind remained inanimate in the air, the very blood in men's veins froze.

The man tried to say something, but the being spoke first. "Rejoice! Rejoice! For I bring the will!" At last, the being looked directly into the man's eyes which remained undamaged from their brilliant light. "Thou art blessed amongst men, for thou art favoured by the Lord!." The man felt a shift within him, as if a great weight had been removed from his stomach and he spoke, bowing his head so that it was level with the floor.

"Of which Lord do you speak, oh great enchanter? As there are many in these lands." The man spoke with the expected ignorance of a world too long left to its own devices. He still believed that the being before him was something as meagre as a powerful sorcerer, in the service of a noble Lord. The being became visibly angered by the question and responded in turn.

"Fool!" it said, its voice like the roaring of a star threatening to burn the world to ash. "There is but one who holds the title of Lord! All others are usurpers and false!"

The man was trembling now, like a dog he cowered and begged for mercy from a being far greater than himself. "Forgive me" he pleaded, "I do not understand." The being agreed.

"No! You do not. You cannot. You are but dust, and to dust you shall return, but even dust must play its part." Whatever this creature was, it was not making sense and the man began to sob, fearful for his life and that of his wife. The being held out its hand and the man felt his head begin to lift against the command of his own mind, until he was gazing upon those burning eyes once more.

"You kneel before the Great Captain and servant of the Lord. Rejoice! As the Lord has chosen thee as an instrument of his divine will."

'*This must be a dream*' the man thought, there was no

way this could actually be happening to him of all people, the most mundane and uninteresting man in the world.

"This is no dream!" the being boomed once more. "Now stand!" it commanded. The man did as he was ordered, still trembling but glad to have control of his body returned to him. Without warning, the being reached for its side and withdrew a sword from its scabbard. The instant the blade contacted the open air it erupted into flames. A pure, orange flame that burned away the chill of the night air.

"Behold!" the being bellowed triumphantly. "Serpent's Bane! The testament of thine heavenly mission." The being held the sword aloft so the man could fully appreciate its majesty. He was transfixed, the flames were more than mere earthly or magical fire. They were something else entirely, holy beyond measure, he could feel evil retreat from its heat. "Go now! Be released upon the world like a heavenly flood until the mercy of the Lord is known to all!"

Without warning the being vanished, the world outside returned to action and the man was left alone once more. Darkness reclaimed the room where the man stood, his legs shaking, in his hands a sword resting within its scabbard. He had been chosen, of that there could be no doubt. But why, and for what, he did not know. All he knew for certain, was that destiny was not finished with him yet.

Chapter 1

Nate crouched low and pressed himself against the wall so that he was one with the gloominess of the den. His bow at the ready, an arrow already nocked, he waited for his target. All around him scenes of carnage lay. Scattered bodies, broken spears, and seemingly endless streaks of dried blood. The stench of death hung heavy in the air like smog, a thick, noxious cloud of stale, dying breaths from those who had come before. Some attempting the very same feat Nate nervously prepared himself for now. Unfortunately, this was a scent Nate had become familiar with, and it no longer bothered him as it once had. The den was a hollow in the side of a hill, dark and moist, it could easily have been mistaken for belonging to a bear. A mistake which would have been proven excruciatingly wrong.

A safe distance from the entrance to the dank hollow stood three examiners. They were there to grade Nate's performance and, if he did well, allow him entrance into the monster hunting Guild, Flintlock & Co. Stood beneath the safety of an invisibility barrier, they watched on, clipboards in hand. They would be grading not only Nate's ability to kill his target quickly, but also his skill and resolve when facing danger alone. There were of course extra marks for ingenuity and style, but Nate was more concerned with making it out of this alive than how many tick-boxes he filled.

Watching on alongside the examiners were Chen and Marcus, both of whom had already passed their own entrance exams weeks ago. Now, with nothing better to do, they watched Nate with opposing thoughts running through their minds. Marcus was nervously chewing his nails and mumbling incoherently. Trying his best to convince himself that Nate would be fine, while being ready to rush to his aid when it all inevitably went wrong. Chen, however, stood with folded arms and pursed lips. Of course, Nate would go and choose the most dangerous creature he could for his exam. Anything to rub success in her face at the slightest opportunity. What a knob.

As the last echoes of the day faded into night, all those present readied themselves. It would not be long now. The soft, gentle rays of sunlight slowly retreated. The golden carpet laid out before them receding like the tide until it was pulled over their tense bodies like a blanket, leaving them exposed to the cold gloom of night. Nate made one final check of his surroundings as he ran his strategy through his mind one last time.

The Epinae he had opted to slay was a species of flightless bird, as tall as two storeys and with talons the length of a man's arm. Rather than offering a quick death with their talons, they would instead use them to pin their victim in place while picking at their flesh with their pointed beaks. Always taking the upmost care to avoid damaging any major organs, this kept the meat fresher for longer and was universally agreed upon to be one of the most unpleasant ways to die. For a place like Purgatory, with all its infinite possibilities, that was saying something.

Nate's plan was to use his bow to bring the creature down, one good shot into its eye should be enough. Their feathers were thick and more akin to scales, meaning a bladed weapon would be useless. Just as he made his final preparations and readied himself for the ribbing Death would give him when he was inevitably eaten alive, he noticed something. A ledge, difficult to see in the darkness, jutting out from the wall about three meters above where Nate was crouched, extending out to just a few feet ahead of him. If he could get up there, he would have the perfect shot. Nate's heart was pounding as he wrestled with himself over whether to change positions. Finally, after a few minutes he pulled himself from the safety of his shadowy hiding place and began to climb.

"What the hell is he doing?" Marcus whispered in despair.

"Getting himself killed." Chen gasped, her earlier sourness replaced by apprehension as she gripped the shaft of her spear ever more tightly.

Just as Nate had reached roughly halfway between the ground and the ledge, the air was pierced by a terrible squawk that made the blood in even the examiner's veins run cold. Suddenly from among the thick brush came the epinae, its body close to the ground, its dull, silvery feathers reflecting the growing moonlight, its darting pink eyes scanning the vicinity of its home for danger. "Shit," Nate whispered. There was no time to continue his climb and so he simply let go and hoped the fall would kill him before the epinae did. He landed with a crunch on a pile of old bones which splintered beneath him.

Nate winced as his ankle twisted under his weight but did not dare make another sound or movement. The creature, having heard the noise, quickly turned its head in the direction of the den. However, its eyes wide, devoid of any intelligent thought, quickly moved on. Nate quietly allowed himself a sigh of relief, there was still a chance he could do this. But then, a second squawk of a lower timber came, causing Nate's heart to drop into the pit of his stomach as it echoed through the den.

Emerging from the opposite side of the dense vegetation to the first epinae, arrived a second, much larger one. It's dark purple plumage indicating it to be a male, its talons much longer, its beak like the tip of a bronze spear. A mating pair, Nate had unknowingly selected a pair of mating epinae as his entrance exam. He was definitely going to die.

The exact science behind how animals were able to reproduce in Purgatory while humans and other intelligent beings were not, had been a hotly debated topic among scholars for millennia. That is until the late empress of the Imperium had solved it. She had found that the female always gave birth to twins, one male, one female, with no exceptions. These twins were discovered to be exact genetic copies of their parents. This halted the evolutionary process entirely, with no new genetic traits being passed to the new infants. As to why this was the case, theologians continued to argue, and there did not seem to be any end in sight to their bickering.

Such things were of no interest to Nate at this present moment, however. Instead, he was desperately trying to avoid becoming a romantic meal for two. The male epinae bowed its head to the female in a sign of affection, before turning back to the brush and retrieving a fresh carcass. Thankfully it was not human and appeared to be some sort of bovine Nate did not recognise. Lifting what was left of the beast, which even in pieces looked to weigh nearly a tonne like it was barely a pebble, the male epinae entered the den followed closely by the female.

Marcus, unable to stand by and watch as his apprentice was torn to pieces, reached for his sword. A hand suddenly shot out from one of the examiners and took hold of his wrist. Their eyes met and a wordless exchange was had, they could not interfere under any circumstances. Gritting his teeth, Marcus withdrew his arm and turned back to the den where Nate was alone with two of the most dangerous creatures this side of the Borderlands.

Nate lay as still and silent as stone while the creatures just meters away tore into their prey. They celebrated the kill with sickening shrills and mouths full of blood and meat. The wet tearing of flesh and sloshing of blood multiplied as their mastication bounced around the walls. Thankfully Nate had not been noticed amongst the darkness and piles of discarded corpses. Although he had no idea how he was going to get himself out of this, and the epinae's meal would only last so long, even if he was somehow able to reposition without being noticed and get a lucky shot, that still meant dealing with the other unexpected guest.

It was only at this late moment, this proverbial eleventh hour that Nate regretted not bothering to learn the invisibility spell which could probably come in handy right about now. Then he realised, as if a key had been turned in his mind granting access to previously locked avenues of thought

– magic. He could use magic to even the odds. He steadied his racing heart and whispered into the void. His words barely audible, even to himself. But that was the point. Suddenly, from outside the den came the sound of laughter and shouting as if a large group were passing by. The epinae both immediately raised their heads, looking at one another with beaks dripping with viscera. The examiners could hear it too and, from the safety of their position, looked around to see what could possibly be going on now. They were in the middle of nowhere after all.

The male cautiously left the den, its eyes darting from place to place, its head tilted to better discern the direction of the noise. As it rounded the corner and out of sight Nate smiled to himself, his hastily conceived plan had worked. This was one of his favourite spells, one he had learned quite by accident while trying to swear at Chen behind her back. It had resulted in what they thought was an entire angry mob screaming obscenities aimed at her from right outside their barracks. Yet when they went to investigate, there had been nothing there.

Kyle had decided to christen the spell 'Ethereal Whisper', quite useless for anything other than as a distraction. Yet Nate had immensely enjoyed using it to drive his roommate to near insanity. That was until he had climbed into bed one night to find it full of cow shit. Considering there was not a single cow of any kind to be found anywhere in the Vanguard, Nate could not help but be both impressed and disturbed by the tenacity required to transport that amount of shit past the guards. Now, with greater control, he mainly just used the spell to order drinks at the bar without having to leave his seat.

With the male gone, Nate had to quickly deal with the female. Luckily, its head was still turned in the direction of the noise, leaving its huge pink eye a clear target hanging high in the darkness. Silently, he drew back his bow and prayed for a perfect shot. The twang of the bowstring as the arrow left it reverberated around the den, to which the female immediately turned its attention. The arrow glanced off the steel-like cheek, the pink eyes burning with hunger now looking directly at the intruder.

"Shit!" Nate said, not bothering now to whisper. The female let out a piercing shriek as it charged forward, its still bloody beak like an arrow of its own. Thinking fast, Nate dropped his bow and threw out his left arm in a sweeping arc. From his hand erupted a bright flame that set the earth between them ablaze, momentarily halting the creature in its tracks. From outside Nate could hear the male rushing back and knew his job was about to become much harder.

With the female still momentarily held at bay by the magical fire, which was quickly diminishing with nothing but damp earth to consume, Nate reached out his other hand. Shooting forth from his palm came a spear of what looked like blue glass. It raced towards the female and struck it on the side of its beak, snapping the upper part off entirely. The epinae fell back with an ear-splitting cry, its long, thin legs buckling as it crashed into the male which had just entered the mouth of the den. The pair fell against the wall in a chaotic ball of feathers and claws. The whole structure shook violently as its flimsy foundations came under assault by the huge creatures' writhing.

As the two monsters frantically thrashed to free themselves from one another's tangled appendages, the entrance of the den continued to shake, loose chunks of stone falling by the wayside. With a sudden thought, Nate placed both his hands out in front of him, using every spare bit of strength he had to grip the loose rocks with telekinetic force. Telekinesis he had discovered, was not so simple as using one's mind to move objects rather than one's muscles. It took a mental effort just as great as a physical one would have done. Now, trying to dislodge tonnes of rock put a pressure on Nate's mind so forceful that the corners of his eyes began to bleed.

Nevertheless, with a great cry of exhaustion and pain, Nate wrenched the stone free which came crashing down onto the still sprawling creatures. The female was instantly slain as a huge chunk of rock crushed its head, its legs and wings still writhing frantically for a few seconds before becoming still. The male, however, had avoided most of Nate's attempt to bring about an abrupt end to this debacle, and now stood to its full height, full of animalistic rage. The den was pitch black now as the falling rubble had totally blocked the entrance, and Nate found himself trapped with a still very much alive, and extremely enraged epinae.

He tried not to pant, despite the tiredness overwhelming him from such a concentrated effort. Doing so would only alert the enraged monster to his location. Instead, he silently withdrew a potion from a small pouch at his side. From its ridged texture he knew it was the correct one and removed the cork, pouring the contents into his mouth. The taste was vile, like a lime cough medicine, and Nate had to do his best not to gag. Despite the taste, however, the potion immediately began to take effect. The crushing blackness of the cave began to give way and Nate could soon make out the shape of its walls, the bodies on the floor and, most importantly, the epinae which was only meters away, sniffing at the now scorched earth.

When preparing for his exam, Nate had wondered whether he should bother bringing any potions with him at all. Assuming he would make a single, heroic shot and then skip back home. Thankful now for his previous caution he began to formulate a new plan. Luckily for him, epinae could see no better in darkness than humans. Their superior sense of smell was also now negated thanks to the remnant whisps of smoke which, with no means of escape, began to fill the den.

Still, Nate would need to be careful. One wrong move would still see him devoured. With one hand he used a small amount of telekinetic force to displace loose bones at the other end of the den, knocking them against the walls and scraping them along the floor. With the monster's attention successfully diverted, albeit temporarily, Nate used his other hand to once again begin climbing up to the ledge he had seen earlier. After successfully scaling the wall and now perched upon the edge of the ledge, Nate could see the epinae was still following his trail of misdirection.

Despite his advantages, Nate felt unsteady. His head was pounding worse than any migraine, and the vile potion in his stomach threatened to make him sick. He had always assumed the various potions one could purchase around the Vanguard would taste as pleasant as fruit juice, instead you were counted lucky if they did not make you ill for days afterwards. Nevertheless, he still had a very dangerous job to complete before he could return home and feel sorry for himself. Slowly, he used his magic to drag a free lump of flesh from the creature's earlier meal towards him. Sensing the movement, the epinae turned and followed it.

Slowly, Nate lifted the bloody and still dripping carcass from the ground, pulling it up through the air until it was about a foot above his head. The epinae followed obediently, and Nate finally had his chance. The monster, sensing the cessation of movement, struck out at the suspended flesh. Its mouth opened wide, thrusting out its thick, spiked tongue, reeking of rotten meat and blood. Rapidly pulling his sword free, Nate stabbed into the creature's open mouth, hoping to pierce its brain. Unfortunately, he was too slow and caught the tongue instead. The creature recoiled and shrieked in pain before whipping around one of its wings, its talons at the ready.

In the darkness the furious creature missed its target, yet Nate was still caught by the trailing wing and fell from the ledge once again, crashing hard onto the ground, the wind knocked out of him. Dazed, Nate looked up to see the bronze beak ready to come down and impale him where he lay. With a final effort he rolled away just as the tip of the beak pierced the ground where he had been just seconds ago. Extending his arm once more, another glass spear raced forth from his palm towards the epinae's eye. There was a sickening squelch as the spear found its mark and burst from the opposite side of the creature's skull in a shower of brain matter and bone.

At last, the task was complete and the final epinae fell to the floor with a crash. Nate allowed himself a moment to lie on his back, panting, trying desperately not to be sick. When a small amount of strength had returned to him, he pulled himself to his feet. His boots quickly making vile, sticky, tearing sounds as they traversed the pool of blood emerging from his vanquished foe.

Outside, the others had waited with bated breath for any sign of life since the collapse of the den's entrance. They had heard bestial cries and seen trails of smoke, but now all was silent. Chen gripped Marcus' arm so tightly he could feel it through the steel gauntlets which were rarely absent. With great relief and an even greater degree of surprise, they watched the fallen stone blocking the entrance be blasted away and a triumphant, if not a bloody and bruised Nate come stumbling towards them.

They all immediately rushed forwards from the safety of their invisibility barrier. Chen did not even give Nate a chance to speak before throwing her arms around him in relief, quickly pulling herself free to chastise him.

"You stupid idiot, do you have any idea how lucky you are? You should be chicken feed by now."

But when Nate spoke in response, his words sounded like infantile babble. His eyes were dripping with blood, and he walked with a gait like that of someone with a serious injury, yet none that could be seen. Nate tried to speak again but his words were incomprehensible, like a baby he spluttered and swayed from side to side. Chen took a cautionary step back.

"What's wrong with him?" She asked the crowd that had gathered. One of the examiners stepped forwards, tucking her clipboard under her arm, she took Nate's chin in her hand and examined him. After a few moments of silence, interrupted only by Nate's insane gibberish, she removed her hand and smiled, withdrawing a white vial from her own pouch.

"Just gave himself a little bit of brain damage using all that magic," she smirked, pouring the clear liquid into Nate's mouth. Nate's face puckered as the sour potion passed his lips but was then almost instantly back to normal. His eyes had stopped bleeding, his bruises and scrapes were gone, and he could at last form a coherent sentence.

"Well, that was easy," Nate sighed, stretching his arms above his head as if he had just rolled out of bed.

"That's a shame, I thought brain damage suited you," Marcus grinned before grasping his apprentice's hand firmly, beaming like a proud parent. Nate smiled triumphantly before turning his attention to Chen.

"Makes your exam look like a piece of piss," he winked. Chen shook her head, folding her arms to show her displeasure.

"You know, you'd be a nice person if you weren't such a twat," she replied with a tired sigh. The day's mix of excitement and fear finally taking their toll. Nate brushed the comment aside with a smirk and finally turned his attention to the examiners.

"So, how was that?" he beamed with all the enthusiasm of a four-year-old going a full day without injuring themselves, something which Nate had not yet managed to do since arriving in Purgatory nearly a year earlier. Although the examiners looked less than impressed, they wore scowls as they ran their fingers down their clipboards, either ticking or crossing boxes to determine Nate's future. After a few moments of tense silence, broken only by the scratching of quills, the examiners compared notes before finally offering their Judgment.

It was the woman who had provided Nate with the healing potion that spoke. She was short and plump, with straw-coloured hair and rounded cheeks upon which rested a pair of spherical spectacles. "Well, the main issue is that we did not actually see how you completed the assignment, and we can't really grade what we didn't see." There was a pause as Nate and his friends despaired, each silently examining their racing thoughts for what the examiner's words could mean. Had he really gone through all of that just to be failed on a technicality?

The woman continued, removing her spectacles and wiping them with her sleeve. "Nevertheless, I do believe you are the first and only member of Flintlock & Co. to slay two epinae at once, and alone at that." It took a moment for her words to register, but once they had, Nate could barely remain upright from the shock.

"Wait, member? So, I passed?" he whispered, as if asking any louder would change their minds. Now all three examiners were grinning and the one to their left spoke. He was tall and thin, with a long white moustache which swayed level with his collar yet did not meet beneath his nose.

"I don't think denying Flintlock & Co. of someone with your clear aptitude at slaying monsters would benefit anyone." Nate stood frozen and wide-eyed as there was an eruption of cheers from behind, as Marcus and Chen threw themselves at him, almost crushing him to death with their embrace. From her pocket the examiner withdrew the patch which would denote Nate's membership and handed it to him with a smile. The image upon the patch was that of a ship, one of the many longships which had delivered Arda Tinelia to their lands. The ship was embroidered in gold, with the blue of the sea beneath it and a handful of silver stars on the backdrop of a dark sky.

There were many different patches to denote ranks within the Guild. The one Nate would from now on proudly display upon his upper arm was the patch of a new initiate. Many ranks above him was that of master monster slayer and, with it the most coveted patch of all - two crossed flintlock pistols upon a background of red and black. Even with Nate's obvious proficiency at killing monsters, he was still a few centuries away from obtaining such an exalted position.

"You're one of us now, make the Guild proud," the examiner said with hints of both pride and expectation in her voice.

"Thank you," Nate gasped as he took the patch and examined it, perhaps the first thing he had ever truly earned.

A burly, metal-clad arm soon wrapped itself around his shoulders as Marcus' grinning face came parallel with Nate's.

"Drinks on you when we get home." Nate was flabbergasted at the very thought. Knowing full well how much mead his friends could consume during a single evening.

"I think you may be misunderstanding your role as a friend celebrating my glorious achievement," Nate asserted. Marcus could only laugh at Nate's naivety.

"Do you have any idea how much a single epinae is worth, let alone two? Let's just say we're opening a tab with your name on it." Truthfully, Nate had not given a single thought to the bounty he would be paid for completing his exam, but now he could not help but punch the air with glee. As they made the long journey back to the city of Tinelia, all Nate could think of was the comfy new bed he was going to buy himself. One with plenty of space and a nice thick duvet, but most importantly one that did not stink of shit.

The party were a good week away from the city, having had to travel into the countryside to find their target. The nearest village was almost six miles by horse, which thankfully, they had been permitted to take. As Bob calmly trotted through the leaves which carpeted the forest floor, Nate could not help but feel a mixture of excitement and pride. Not only had he successfully joined a Guild but had done so without anyone there to aid him. At last overcoming one of his most pervasive doubts, that he was nothing without someone there to guide him. He had proven to his detractors, and more importantly to himself, that he was more than capable of making it out here. Now the next stage of his new life could begin. He could at last commence the work to atone for his sins in earnest.

The journey back was relatively uneventful. There had been the odd scrap with a wandering monster, but none had proven a match for six well-trained monster hunters. Nate generously avoided any killing blows, giving his companions a chance to improve their finances somewhat. It was only fair, considering a single epinae was worth anywhere in the region of three to six thousand gold. Although this was a poultry amount in the grand scheme of things, Nate found it sadly amusing how immortality had affected the market. He would need to kill a few hundred more epinae before he could even think about owning a house.

Nevertheless, he did not allow such matters to dampen his spirits. After all, he had plenty of time to build his fortune, plus he did not mind his current living situation. Nobody had been able to tolerate living with him and Chen for more than a month, so the pair enjoyed the luxury of having the barracks to themselves. While this did lead to the pair arguing like an old married couple over who's turn it was to do the washing, it was preferable to sharing their space with eight other people.

As the party passed under the Vanguard's gate they were met with the welcoming sights and sounds of home. It was roughly mid-day and, as usual, the streets were twenty deep, flowing like a river in all directions. It was here that Nate and his friends bid farewell to the examiners. He would expect to meet them again tomorrow at the Guild Hall, where he would be officially inducted into the Guild. The only logical conclusion to this month's long ordeal was a well-deserved pint or five at Pedan's.

The aura which permeated from Pedan's Inn was one of homeliness. The stench of stale beer, old sweat and whatever was cooking in the kitchens felt like a loving embrace as Nate stepped inside. It was relatively quiet, so the trio sat themselves around the firepit. The warm, crackling tongues of amiable flames a welcome relief after so long on the road. Marcus stretched out his legs and reclined as far as the chair would allow, letting out a contented sigh as he tilted his head back and shut his eyes.

"What are you so tired for? Pretty sure I'm the one who did all the work the last few weeks," Nate scolded in a joking manner. One of Marcus' eyes forced itself open and stared at his apprentice.

"Wouldn't have made it very far without me helping with

the tracking though, would you?" he said with another sigh, placing his hands behind his head.

"Or me mixing that potion before we left," Chen added.

"Would be an awful shame if the Guild found out you had help on your exam," Marcus grinned, shutting his eyes once more.

Nate narrowed his own eyes at his companions. He knew neither would seriously out him, but he played along.

"I hate you both," he smiled, fluttering his eyelashes. A look which prompted a spluttering laugh from Chen, no matter how many times she saw it. Out of nowhere Pedan appeared beside them, his arms laden with drinks and plates of food. Taking them gratefully, the companions thanked him and set about correcting their stomachs after weeks of travel rations.

"A fitting reward for my triumphant return, I suppose," Nate grinned as he took a bite out of his steak.

"Of course, and a hero's bill to go with it," Pedan replied with a mischievous grin of his own. It was plain that Marcus had not been joking when declaring that Nate would be the one treating them tonight.

Many hours and drinks later, the three giggling and wobbly friends made for home. The bill had been better than Nate had expected, but still required alcohol to lessen the emotional blow. The next day would see Nate formally welcomed into the Guild, an auspicious day they would not want to miss by being hungover. So the merry trio friends made their way to their respective beds before the sun had fully completed its transition.

Bob was pleased to be back in her favourite spot. A makeshift stables Nate had painstakingly constructed for her, jutting out from the side of the barracks like a boil. The planks were askew, each decorated with half a dozen bent nails, and the roof leaked occasionally. But it was warm and comfy, filled with straw and as many blankets as Nate could get his hands on. Chen had considered informing Nate that horses usually slept standing up. However, seeing the love and effort he was throwing into the project, she didn't see the need to ruin it for him. As Bob settled down for the night, Nate and Chen wearily unlocked the barracks door and shuffled inside. The pair instantly threw their arms around themselves as the chill locked within rushed to escape.

With an exhausted grunt Nate set about making a fire. His magic could have completed the task in an instant, but only Chen would be able to feel its warmth, and he'd be damned if he did something altruistic for once. While he fiddled with logs and flint, Chen set about preparing for bed. She had recently saved up enough to buy herself a rather luxurious double bed which was the envy of the barracks. Too often though would she return from her latest Guild duty to find Nate already asleep in it.

Sure enough, for the split second her back was turned, Nate seized his chance and dove onto the soft mattress, wrapping his arms and legs around the duvet like a spider trapping its prey.

"Absolutely fucking not," Chen fumed, her mouth foaming with toothpaste and a pointed finger aimed at Nate. Nate didn't reply, instead tightening his grip on the duvet as Chen tried to wrench it free, to no avail. Spitting the contents of her mouth into the fire, she stared at Nate with rage-filled eyes and presented her ultimatum.

"I'm going for a piss, if you're still there when I get back, I'll sew that patch to your head."

Nate had no desire to wake the next morning. The warm, soft embrace of the duvet outweighed anything the outside world could offer at this moment. Without opening his eyes, he ran his hand up and down the delicate, silky surface. It was pleasant to the touch, and he smiled to himself as he imagined what he hoped would be many more hours before necessity forced him away from this bliss.

But then an unexpected noise forced his eyes open. It had been like a gentle rush of air, very much in fact, like a sigh. As Nate's eyes shot open, he immediately found the source of the disturbance. Lying next to him, so close that their faces were almost touching, was Chen. He looked down and saw that his hand was still slowly caressing her bare arm. With a racing heart Nate pulled back, beyond relieved to find that they were both fully clothed. Alcohol had not betrayed him beyond redemption quite yet.

Nevertheless, he scrambled from the bed in a panic, somehow not waking Chen in the process. Steadying himself, he took a moment to pace around the barracks until his heart had stopped trying to rip its way out of his chest. At last, he tentatively looked back to Chen. Her jet-black hair covered most of her face, which was pleasantly relaxed. One leg remained uncovered by the duvet, sticking out at an angle, while her right arm was wrapped around one of her pillows, hugging it tightly.

For a moment, Nate could not help but admire his roommate's soft, delicate features. Her small nose currently squashed against the pillow; her rosy lips parted slightly as she quietly mumbled to some imaginary character in her subconscious. And of course, her petite, child-like hands for which Nate teased her constantly. One was hidden beneath her pillow, the other, free, reaching out longingly, desperate to intertwine its thin appendages with another.

However, Nate quickly and violently shook these thoughts from his head. He would not allow intrusive ideas scrambling from the back of his still sleepy mind, like insects trapped for so long under a rock scurrying into the light of day to become actions. Taking advantage of Chen's unconscious state, Nate drew himself a bath and allowed himself to relax. The hot water a soothing remedy to the blisters on his feet and sore thighs after so much riding over the last few weeks. As he sunk low into the water, staring at his toes which clung to the edge of the bath like a marooned sailor clinging for dear life onto the hull of his sinking ship, Nate could not help but feel a mixture of emotions.

On the one hand, he had finally achieved his goal of joining a Guild. It had taken all the effort and strength he had to pass the gruelling tests, both physical and written. Now he could theoretically relax, the hardest part was over with. Now was the time at last to make some real money. The fact that he would no longer need to fear for his life at the very mention of the name Captain Ardell was a most welcome added bonus.

But then, even after going through the dozens of benefits joining the Guild would afford him, there was still a weight in his stomach, like stone butterflies. Lifting their cumbersome wings, each beat pushed him further into unknown water. Guilds could be far less forgiving than even the most neurotic of captains. The army's main aim was usually to keep their soldiers alive. Guilds, and the people in them however, only cared about one thing. While in the army you would never expect a company to abandon or turn on their own. In the Guilds however, this was an all too common occurrence. Especially when big game was involved. Nate knew that he would need to watch his back from now on, well, more than usual anyway.

Nate allowed himself to sink further into the water, his nose now nearly level with the rippling surface. He was going to be careful, no unnecessarily dangerous adventures for now, and only with those people he trusted utterly. Yes, he thought as he breathed a contented sigh, everything was going to be fine. After his lengthy and relaxing bath, Nate was donning his new armour by the time Chen awoke.

He had bought this new set not long after returning from their mission last year as a reward for managing to survive. It was not too dissimilar from his previous set, deciding he liked the manoeuvrability leather allowed, rather than being weighed down in steel. The main difference between this and his old armour being that the newer one was studded. The breastplate was divided into squares, each one containing a metal stud in each corner. Very similar to a brigandine, although extending no lower than the waist. His gauntlets and boots, which doubled up as greaves were the same, dotted with studs although lacking the squared pattern.

This set was also noticeably lighter in colour to the last.

A gentle brown that blended in well with the forest for most of the year. Overall Nate could not have been happier with his purchase. It had not been cheap and had eaten most of the reward gained for the mission. But the difference in quality was tangible, he felt safer just looking at it. He still stubbornly went without a helmet despite the obvious danger. Even Chen with her tiny body went around with the equivalent of a bucket on her head. Nevertheless, Nate could not be swayed and everyone had simply given up trying.

Nate ventured outside while Chen bathed. Feeling uncomfortable enough, he didn't need anything adding to it. He found Bob impatiently awaiting his arrival, stomping her foot in demand of food as he approached. He could not help but laugh as he filled up her food and water buckets respectively, stroking her soft neck as he stared into the distance. It was a beautiful morning, the sun was warm, yet the air retained its fresh crispness from a cold night. Filling his lungs Nate allowed himself a moment to simply stand and admire the world around him. A world which would be forever changed after today, for him at least.

Once Chen had dressed, she and Nate set off in the direction of the Guild. Annoyingly, it was rather out of the way, on the very edge of the grassy sea which divided the Vanguard between interior and exterior. Thankfully, however, it was on their side, so there would not be as much trekking involved. Marcus met them part way, still nursing a sore head and with a hefty set of bags under his eyes. But from the stupid grin on his face and swagger in his walk, Nate assumed he had gone to see Jenna, or maybe one of his many other lady friends after parting ways the previous night.

"Nervous?" he teased, throwing a friendly albeit anvil-like arm around Nate's shoulders. He did not bother waiting for Nate to respond before continuing. "Can't believe my little disciple is joining a Guild. They grow up so fast," he said, wiping away an imaginary tear while throwing a smug grin at Chen who too could not help but smile. Nate however rolled his eyes, by now tired of still being regarded as a novice.

"Don't worry, I'll remember all the times the two of you kicked my arse when I'm living it up in the Warrens." Chen and Marcus both produced a mixture of scoffs and raspberries, not the reaction Nate had been hoping for.

After roughly two hours of walking, the trio arrived. The Guild was a gated compound rather than a single building, the three showed their patches to the guards who allowed them to pass through. Sitting on the very edge of the city, while annoying, did allow for more development than the more conveniently located Guilds. Upon passing through the gates, you were immediately met by a path of white bricks, flanked by saplings barely taller than the people they were supposed to shade. This path continued uninterrupted and without deviation for another hundred meters before bringing you to the Guild Hall, a five-storey structure made from sandstone which gave off a reddish-brown glow over the surrounding area.

This building was where most Guildmembers spent their time when not out on missions. Within was everything a professional monster hunter would need to hone and perfect their craft. A library filled to the brim with knowledge of every creature known to science, and how best to slay them. Laboratories where one could practice their alchemy, supplied by the two greenhouses which sat some way behind the Guild Hall, out of the reach of its imposing shadow. Then of course there was the lounge, without a doubt the most utilised room in the building. Here members could drink and relax on expensive chaise sofas and settees, trading stories and details of missions old and new.

There was much more to the Guild Hall, but Nate had seen very little of it being only a prospective member. The rest of the compound was taken up by whatever was needed, but for which there was no room within the Guild Hall itself. This meant its own blacksmith, stables, and storehouse. In the end, it was essentially a private fort, albeit newer and better funded than those belonging to the state. The Guild's latest addition, on the very edge of the compound near a small river, was a bathhouse which also functioned as a sauna in the winter. Usually Nate would not have been interested in sweating for fun, but after seeing the number of beautiful women making use of it, he couldn't wait to give it a try.

Chen and Marcus had not been members for long, but already they were greeted as if they had been there since the beginning. Nevertheless, the pair still struggled to guide Nate down to the initiation chamber once inside, having only been there once themselves. The main entrance of the building was like that of a palace, with chequered red and white marble flooring, tall sandstone pillars which raced to the ceiling, meeting a large glass dome surrounded by images of cherubin and various other flying creatures looking down upon them. In place of art or sculptures were instead various weapons and trophies, usually in the form of preserved monster heads mounted on the walls.

Strategically mounted directly across from the entrance so that they were the first thing anyone saw, was the Guild's namesake - two very old, very battle-scarred flintlock pistols, crossed over one another and fastened upon a wooden board overlaid with red velvet which had been hammered to the wall. It was said that these were the very pistols used by their mysterious and anonymous founder during their own monster slaying career. Although, considering every Guild chapter had the very same pistols nailed to their own walls, this claim was at best unlikely.

This was not the sort of place Nate ever expected to end up when he first arrived in Purgatory. To be honest, even a year later, he still felt out of place surrounded by ardent monster hunters. He had to keep reminding himself that he had earned his place here. He was no less deserving of respect than anyone else. Still, it would take some getting used to, no longer being on any schedule other than his own. Never needing to worry when Ardell was next going to slam his head into a table. He was sure he would enjoy his time here. A good thing too. He was here forever, after all.

Nate was almost disappointed to find that the initiation

chamber was more like an office than the dark and menacing chamber beneath the bank. Looking at the room you would never have guessed they were all in the profession of hunting monsters. There was a collection of desks all pushed against the walls and a medium sized open space between them. There were various bookshelves and drawers which held important Guild information, all immaculately neat and organised. It was all rather mundane.

Nate approached the only occupied desk and stood there for a moment in silence as the attendant read what looked like a newspaper. The headline, in big bold letters reading, '*Peace in our Time?*' While in slightly smaller print beneath, *Nine months later, where is The Emperor?*' Despite being no more than a metre away, the man at the desk continued to ignore Nate as if he were invisible. Only after Nate rang the tiny decorative bell on the desk did the Guild's bureaucrat reluctantly and firmly throw down his paper and sit upright.

"What?" The attendant asked impatiently, glaring at Nate as if he had just interrupted some urgent task. Taken aback, Nate stammered his response. This was not how he had expected his initiation to go, there didn't seem to be a cake in sight. Noticing the patch in Nate's hand, the attendant snatched it from him before rising from his chair to sew it onto Nate's armour high up the left arm. The process took only a few minutes. Painful, silent minutes as Nate dared not utter a word of conversation lest the needle miss its mark.

When he was done, the attendant returned to his chair, picking up his paper once more and resting his feet upon the desk.

"Is that it?" Nate asked bewildered, surely there was more to it than that? The attendant tilted his head back in frustration and took a deep breath, loudly slapping the paper against his thighs to show his frustration.

Raising his left hand into the air while keeping his eyes on the article he had been reading, he unceremoniously and sarcastically welcomed Nate into the Guild. "By the power generously given to me by a lack of anyone else being in the room, I now declare you a member of Flintlock & Co. Go now and do something or other, as long as it's not in here." Nate was unsure of the legality of this statement, but left nevertheless, not wanting to antagonise this new colleague any further.

Marcus and Chen were waiting for him outside the door, sniggering. Nate was now certain that the whole thing had been a joke. That is until Marcus slapped him hard on the shoulder while wearing a beaming smile.

"And there we have it. Nate the monster slayer."

Chen folded her arms and leaned against the wall, her voice thick with friendly mockery.

"Let's not go that far, it's not like he's done anything even remotely impressive yet."

Once they had finished their congratulations and Nate had taken in the moment, the three all stood there, as if waiting for something to happen. They were still not used to the idea that they no longer had any orders to follow other than their own and were slightly lost without someone to point them in the direction of a task. Nate looked around at the building which was to be his new place of work with a smile, there was no time to waste.

Chapter 2

Nate stood within the Guild's stateroom, utterly overwhelmed by the choices before him. This large, rectangular room which neighboured the lounge was where members would come to choose their latest assignments. Each wall, many dozens of meters long, was overlaid with cork boards where thousands of flyers and notices had been pinned. Each one was a request for aid in some venture or another. As Nate slowly shuffled across the room in search of what would be his first assignment, he made mental notes of the apparent order of the room. Despite the seeming chaos of thousands of overlapping sheets of parchment and paper, there was in fact a method to the madness.

The wall immediately opposite to the only door in or out of the stateroom held the most banal and tedious of assignments. All were some variations of: go to location, retrieve specific item, return item. Although this puzzled Nate, if the person requesting help knew exactly where the item they sought was, why didn't they just get it themselves? Unable to understand this logic, he moved on. The further along he went, the more varied and dangerous the assignments became. There were scouting requests for the army, guards for merchant caravans and even sorcerers offering generous amounts of gold for 'research assistants'. Nate didn't quite buy it, however, and judging from the lack of interest those notices had received, neither did anyone else.

Then there were, of course, the monster hunting requests. The bread and butter of the monster slaying industry. These were slightly different to most of the other requests, as they required more than one participant. These therefore had removable tabs to indicate how many people had already shown interest. As Nate perused further, he saw that many of these contracts concerned extremely dangerous creatures, sometimes thousands of miles from home. While the rewards for such a job would be bountiful, Nate didn't think he should choose one of these as his very first mission.

Instead, he hovered around nearer to the entrance, looking over the forest-worth of requests until one caught his eye. Edging closer he re-examined it to make sure he had not missed some hidden, deadly detail. Some villagers a few days from the city had reported seeing strange lights at night, coming from an abandoned mine on the village outskirts. The parchment then went on to explain that an unusual number of Husks and other varieties of undead had been seen congregating there. Remembering his last encounter with Husks Nate shuddered, but reminded himself that the one responsible was dead. These would just be your average run of the mill mindless drones.

Deciding this would be the perfect introduction to his career, he took the last remaining tab. This contract only requested two individuals and Nate was glad to see he would not need to wait around for someone else to take an interest. Returning to the lounge where dozens of other Guild members sat talking and relaxing, Nate presented the tab to the archivist whose job it was to record and document all assignments and contracts, both incoming and outgoing.

Today the position was taken by Marathel, a rather meek and quiet woman who did not at all seem well placed amongst loud and violent monster hunters. She wore a plain, copper coloured dress and a pair of huge, round glasses that sat on her face like globes. Amusingly, the glasses contained no lenses and Marathel only wore them because she thought they made her look cute. Despite her nervous disposition, she was extremely well loved by the other members of the Guild, and there seemed to be an unspoken agreement about not giving her any trouble.

Marathel's glasses rose about two inches above her eyebrows as her round cheeks formed into a wide smile upon seeing Nate approach.

"Finally found one you liked the look of?" she asked, receiving the tag. Nate was not sure how to respond, and so he just smiled awkwardly as Marathel went about noting down the details of the contract before giving Nate his instructions.

"Be back here tomorrow at seven, you and your new companion can meet and discuss the contract then," she smiled warmly as she handed Nate a receipt.

"Will do boss," Nate nodded as he headed for the dojo. He wanted to get a few practice swings in before he was out on the road. The dojo was located on the third floor of the Guild Hall and was usually empty. It was not as large or well-equipped as the training grounds on the western side of the compound, but this suited Nate just fine. Fewer people around meant there was less chance he would be called out for his form or bullied for not being as accomplished as other members of the Guild.

As expected, the dojo was almost empty. Only a single person lay within, and they were in the process of tidying up after their session. Nate exchanged a courteous nod as they passed before making his way towards the practice dummies. These were no straw dummies one would find the army training with, however. These were animatronic, capable of basic movements in their arms, allowing for a more realistic training experience. Although, admittedly not by much as the dummies would stand perfectly still. Nevertheless, Nate enjoyed using them and set about positioning them as he liked.

He would warm up with one. Adjusting the rudimentary speed settings on the dummy to *standard*. There were a few seconds filled with the sounds of ticking and whirring as the machinery in the dummy got working before it was ready for action. Once it was ready, its hands which held a shield and sword, began to strike at Nate. It was nothing like fighting an actual person, the dummy could only move its arms in straight lines, but it was better than nothing. Nate warmed up by easily dodging the attacks and half-heartedly striking back with his own sword.

Once his muscles were awake, Nate dodged around the back of the dummy and upped the speed to *fast*. Immediately, the machine began striking at around twice the speed it had done previously. Occasionally swinging both arms at once, aiming to catch Nate out, he ducked under the swinging shield and struck the dummy in the midriff. After about five minutes of this, Nate was really starting to get into it, and he decided to up the tempo even more. He first switched the dummy off, not wanting to catch a wooden sword to the back of his head while he was setting up. He then dragged over a second, also armed with a sword and shield, positioning it on his left flank, just visible in his peripheral vision.

Setting the first dummy back to *standard* he then set the second to *slow*. He began deflecting and defending blows from two directions, dodging and ducking without striking back. Once he was familiar with the movements on both sides, he began to fight back, taking great pleasure in being able to strike both his mechanical opponents without being hit once. The effort was starting to take its toll, however, and before long Nate was dripping with sweat, although he was by no means wanting to give up yet.

Filled with hubris, Nate pulled over yet another animatron, this one armed with a spear. He then set all three to *standard* speed before taking a step back and observing them from a distance. They relentlessly stabbed and slashed at the spot directly before them, Nate eyeing their every move, timing their swings and thrusts. After giving himself a few minutes to rest and observe, he stepped between the three dummies. Which then proceeded to beat the absolute shit out of him. He dodged two blows well enough, but it was the spear-wielding opponent which caught him out. It struck the back of his knee, forcing him to kneel which was quickly followed by a sudden shield to the face. Lying on his back with a bloody nose, Nate looked up at the dummies furiously stabbing at the air just inches above him. Carefully rolling out of their range, he righted himself and went straight back in. Although he fared no better the second time around.

Paying too much attention to the dummy with the spear, Nate did not see a sword coming at him from his right. It struck him in the side which caused him to spasm off balance. With his sword now out of position, the dummy before him caught him across the face, spinning Nate around one hundred and eighty degrees. He was them immediately punched in the ribs by the tip of a wooden spear, before all three dummies began a synchronised barrage of blows against their doubled over victim. Falling to the ground in a heap, the bruised and battered Nate dragged himself away from the incoming blows until he was safely out of reach.

He lay there for a good while, listening to the continuous whirring and striking of the machines, every inch of him aching and sore. It was at this moment he found himself thinking back to the battle at the smuggler's camp. He had watched Captain Ardell take on, what was it, ten opponents without a scratch? Yet here he was unable to take on three with only slightly less intelligence than himself. Nate groaned in a mixture of both frustration and pain as he pulled himself back up. Turning off the dummies and returning them to their resting place, there was at least one benefit to this beatdown. He now had an excellent excuse to use the bathhouse.

To Nate's utter dismay, he found that the baths were completely segregated. Not a buxom blonde or fiery ginger in sight. Only sweaty and hairy men with chiselled physiques that made Nate feel like he was little more than spaghetti with sleeves in comparison. Nevertheless, overcoming his initial disappointment, Nate soon found the hot water and hanging steam a welcome relief to his pain. Naturally, he sat in a corner, as far as physically possible from any other man, just taking in the room around him.

The bathhouse looked to be pulled straight from the heart of Rome itself. Marble walls and columns, beautiful mosaics beneath his feet, and lifelike statues of nymphs and goddesses, from whom fresh, hot water poured. For once, Nate allowed himself to relax, stretching out his legs and leaving only his head above the water. What he thought to be only a few minutes quickly turned into hours, and by the time he reluctantly pulled himself from the water's warm embrace he was a walking prune. He was glad for it, however, as the pain which had earlier racked his body was not but a dull ache. Present, but much like listening to Chen explain whatever book she was reading, just slightly annoying.

The day was still far from done and he found himself at a loss deciding what to do next. Chen was at a lecture at one of the many theatres across the great green divide in the other half of the Vanguard, and Marcus was on a mission of his own, not expected to return for a few more days. Joel had literally disappeared into thin air a few weeks ago, nobody having sight nor sound of him since. Marcus had said that was common of Joel though. He had many connections in both the highest highs and lowest lows of society and would often get involved in schemes for one faction or another.

Then there was Kyle, who had demanded Nate take part in secret magic training every few days. They usually did this out in the divide where few prying eyes would be watching. Truth be told, Nate had learned a lot and come a long way in his magical abilities since beginning this training. It was just a shame Kyle was the one leading it. Unable to stomach the thought of listening to Kyle explain the complexities of magic yet again, he decided food was his next best option.

While wandering the streets one day, now that he had nothing better to do, Nate had stumbled upon a wonderful family run restaurant. Not family in the literal sense, of course. In Purgatory it was quite common for those with wealth, power or businesses to 'adopt' a son or daughter. Of course there was no way to tell if the person you were adopting was one thousand years older than you, but such things mattered little. It was instead the most significant act of friendship one could commit in the afterlife. Two people who shared such a strong bond that they pledged all their titles and possessions to the other should they die. In a way it was like a marriage, but platonic and ending in fewer murders.

The restaurant was located about forty-five minutes from

the Guild, closer to the centre of the city. He could never let Pedan know, of course, but this place was superior in practically every way. Crucially, though, they cleaned their cloths between uses, and not with spit either. As he walked without haste, enjoying the journey, Nate looked around at the people passing by. He saw many soldiers, their basic armour, usually old and muddy, giving them away. It was not long ago that he was one of them. Gazing jealously at those who could afford to take their time, to enjoy the city around them, and not worry about the whims of their sadistic captain.

It felt like a lifetime ago that he was stood before Captain Ardell for the first time, shaking in his boots before having his head slammed into her desk. *'Good times,'* he smiled to himself; glad he would never have to repeat them. As he arrived at the restaurant, a strange thought occurred to him. It had been nearly a year since the attack against the Imperium, since the death of the empress. Yet seemingly nothing had come of it. In the immediate months following, there had been ceaseless talk and preparation for the war which was bound to follow. Yet as time passed and not so much as a whisper came out of the Imperial Palace, life had slowly returned to normal, as if nothing had happened at all. By all rights he should be out there right now, engaged in a desperate struggle against the most powerful nation in the world.

Instead, he was eating lobster and chips in a cosy seat beside an art-covered wall. Something about this didn't feel right, not in the slightest. But Nate was content to let the good times continue. He was in no rush to have his guts spilled on some muddy field in the middle of nowhere. After his pleasant meal Nate returned home, excited yet nervous at the coming day. He thought about the companion he would be undertaking this mission with and prayed they would be, at the very least, not a complete arsehole.

"No, no, no, absolutely fucking not!" Cassandra fumed as she was introduced to her companion. Nate too was not exactly thrilled, although some of that came from his new companion's over the top reaction.

"Find me someone else," Cassandra said, folding her arms and glowering at Marathel who shrank meekly in her seat. She peered over her desk at Nate who stood a few feet from Cassandra, arms also crossed and aiming a scowl at the back of her head.

"I…I'm sorry, Cassandra," Marathel began. "But once the places have been filled and the contract logged, the mission fulfils its legal obligations and must now be completed."

"Bollocks!" Cassandra shouted, slamming her palm onto the desk causing Marathel to jump in surprise. The commotion immediately caught the attention of the few other Guild members in the room who gravitated over towards the noise. Another woman of similar height but much stockier build approached Cassandra. She had dyed silver hair dotted with dozens of golden clasps which rested just below her shoulders. Her eyes burned with a fierceness accentuated by the black war paint which surrounded them and spread like wings to meet her hairline.

"Oi, you're not upsetting Marathel are you?" she grumbled in a very deep, very impatient voice. Confronted by this new opponent, Cassandra immediately adopted a more apologetic, conciliatory stance, one Nate had never expected her to even be capable of. Like a puppy, she was almost cowering, stooping her shoulders and not making eye contact, speaking instead to the floor.

"Speak up," the woman said raising her own voice, clearly not in the mood for whatever nonsense was going on.

"It's nothing," Cassandra mumbled at last. The woman with the silver hair scowled, leaning in close to Cassandra but speaking loudly enough that others could hear.

"Good, sounds like you'd best fuck off then," Cassandra nodded sheepishly before spinning around and hastily exiting the room, barging past Nate as she did so.

"You didn't need to be so nasty," Marathel complained to the woman in her sweet, squeaky voice. The woman simply turned and flashed Marathel a sly smile before walking off without a word. Nate had remained in place throughout the entire ordeal and was glad that, for once, it wasn't him at risk of having his head kicked in.

"Is there really nothing you can do?" Nate asked approaching the desk. Marathel raised her hands in admission of defeat, rubbing her left eye through the empty lens of her glasses.

"Sorry, Nate Rules are rules. We wouldn't be in business long if we didn't stick to them," Nate shook his head in frustration, already exhausted at the thought of the next few weeks. Alas, there was nothing that could be done. He thanked Marathel for her help and set out in search of his new best friend. Hopefully the two could reach a point of not wanting to kill each other before they were meant to set out.

Nate caught up with Cassandra as she travelled the long path out of the compound and back into the city. Hearing someone approaching quickly from behind, she turned her head before rolling her eyes and picking up the pace. Noting her response, Nate muttered to himself, '*for fuck's sake,*' as he ran to catch up with her.

"Cassandra, wait!" he called out just as she reached the gate. She stopped abruptly, clenching her fists into balls. Should she hit him before he spoke, or give him the chance to say something stupid first? These were the kind of thoughts currently being contemplated in Cassandra's mind as Nate finally reached her, conveniently within striking distance.

"What?" she growled. At first Nate said nothing, instead wincing and doubling over, desperately trying to catch his breath. His short jog had taken far more out of him than it should have, and he was already imagining what words of disapproval Marcus would impart should he see him now. After a few excruciating seconds Nate straightened himself, doing his best to control his breathing.

"Listen," he began, before noticing the condescending tone he had chosen and changing tack entirely. "I'm sorry," he said, raising his hands. Cassandra said nothing, her eyes narrowed but she decided to allow Nate to continue, at least until he pissed her off.

"I'm sorry for what I did. I was new, I was stupid, I was scared more than anything and I let my emotions get the better of me. I promise, you can count on me. I won't fuck this up."

Cassandra took a deep breath as she looked Nate up and down. The two had had virtually no contact since their last mission together, but Nate had clearly changed. Physically he was far stronger, and he could clearly hold his own in a fight considering what he did to get into the Guild. But that was not what concerned Cassandra. A strong body cannot make up for an immature and ill-prepared mind. If Nate was still ruled by his emotions, then this mission would be a disaster. Yet his apology seemed to indicate at least some small modicum of change. Perhaps working with him would prove to be not so impossible as she first thought.

"Fuck off," she growled as she turned and left the confines of the compound. Just as Nate dropped his shoulders and let out a disappointed sigh, Cassandra turned back to face him.

"I'll see you tomorrow," she said at last, through narrowed eyes.

"Think she likes you," one of the gate guards chuckled as Nate returned to the Guild, rubbing his head in confusion.

The next day Nate met Cassandra at Pedan's Inn during the early morning. The Guild would have been a far more suitable meeting place considering all its assets, but Cassandra was loath to go back until her embarrassment had waned. Instead, she lay out a set of maps upon a large empty table on the third floor for the pair to inspect. The village they would be travelling to would take them on a similar route to the one they had travelled on their previous mission. This time, however, they would not get as far as Sundered Crown. Instead, they would head north into a more wetland area for two days before arriving at their destination.

"Theoretically, this should be easy. With fewer Husks wandering the forests nowadays, it should be a straight shot to the town with minimal disturbances," Cassandra explained.

"Surely there's more to worry about than Husks?" Nate replied. Cassandra shook her head dismissively as she took a sip of her ale, it was only seven o'clock.

"It's unlikely there's anything too dangerous this close to the city. Consider how far you had to go to find those Epinae, and even they aren't supposed to be anywhere near here," Cassandra added. Nate was unconvinced by Cassandra's dismissive attitude to danger and examined the map more closely. Even if she were right, there would only be two of them. Meaning any danger would be magnified tenfold compared to a large party.

"Could we use the river?" Nate asked, tracing his finger along a thin blue line which ran to within only a few dozen miles from their destination.

"I can't swim," Cassandra admitted casually.

"You can't swim?" Nate scoffed in disbelief.

"No, I can't," Cassandra confirmed venomously. "By the way, would you happen to have a boat we could use? Do you know how to sail? Not to mention the whole journey would be upriver." Nate didn't say a word in reply, silently admitting defeat.

"Dickhead," Cassandra muttered, while Nate resisted the urge to smack her head into the table. With there only being two of them, there was very little to prepare for. Cassandra marked out every twist and turn of their journey on the map, and their objectives were clear. All that remained now was to gather supplies and head out.

"Have you got spare underwear? Warm socks? Plenty of food?" Chen fussed as Nate went over the last checks of his gear. He could not help but roll his eyes at Chen's overprotectiveness.

"Yes, mother, I've got spare underwear. Anything else you want to smother me with? I've got a bruise somewhere you could kiss better" he teased.

Chen scowled as Nate dismissed her fretting, placing her

hands on her hips and furrowing her brow as she watched him pack.

"I'm just trying to make sure you don't starve to death before you even get there," she said crossly.

"I'll be fine," he said, hauling his backpack across his shoulders. "It's not like this is my first rodeo," he grinned, although behind it hid a great sense of unease and uncertainty. But he couldn't let Chen know that, of course. As Nate pulled the barracks door open, he was hit by a torrential gust of rain and wind which threw him off balance momentarily. "Shit!" he said to himself, now dreading the ride to the outer gate.

"Wait!" Chen said, just as Nate was about to step over the threshold into the steel-coloured downpour. He turned around, expecting to see a puppy-eyed Chen wishing him safe travels while worrying every moment for his safety. Instead, she stood with her arm outstretched, in her hand, Nate's bow.

"Ah, yes, might need that," he said taking it from her gratefully before wrapping it in a green fabric to keep it dry. Attaching it to the top of his pack so that it rested across his shoulders, Nate was now fully prepared for his journey. Although, he was surprised to see, despite his earlier joking, that Chen looked genuinely nervous. Her foot was tapping against the floor, seemingly out of her control, and she held her left arm in apprehension.

This was the first time in a long time that Nate would be going into danger without Chen to back him up. Considering his penchant for making a mess of practically every situation, it was probably right of her to worry. Nate thought about comforting her, but that wasn't really his style. Instead, he continued to be himself, totally ignoring social ques.

"Still waiting for that kiss," he grinned mischievously. Chen immediately lost all her feelings of inner turmoil and rolled her eyes. She approached Nate who, for one small moment, believed his devilish charm to have at last borne fruit. Instead, however, she placed her foot on his stomach and launched him out the door into the freezing rain, slamming it shut behind him.

Thinking nothing of it, Nate rolled onto his front and pulled himself from the muddy ground. He could barely see a few meters ahead and pulled up his hood to protect himself from the stinging rain. It took almost all the treats Nate could spare to coax Bob out of her warm and cosy stable, and into the unforgiving cold of the outside world. Although Nate had done her a kindness and purchased her a warm tarpaulin-like coat to protect her from the worst of the weather. Nevertheless, even the relatively short journey to the Vanguard's main gate was extremely unpleasant. Water spouted from the tips of his nose like a fountain piece, and he was already soaked through to the bone.

Cassandra had been waiting under the outstretched roof of a nearby building. Her own horse, a beautiful, milky-white mare with a mane the colour of sand, at least four hands taller than Bob. Both looked equally as dissatisfied with the weather and Cassandra said nothing as Nate approached, although there was some brief conversation between Bob and her counterpart. This focused mainly upon the jealousy of Cassandra's mare over Bob's coat, and frustration at being pulled from the stable to go traipsing around in the wet and cold.

Even despite the horrendous weather, the line of people waiting to enter the Vanguard had not diminished in the slightest. Thousands of people would rather subject themselves to the elements than seek temporary shelter and risk losing their place in line. A decision which could set them back weeks.

In the early days after the attack on the Imperium, there had been a huge influx of refugees. None had been attacked or displaced but instead had come expecting war to break out at any moment. The Citadel had been reluctant to take them in at first but had ultimately decided that a capable body inside the walls was better than one outside. However, as time had gone on and the great war never materialised, the

Citadel had cracked down hard on any new arrivals. Even those many thousands, which had already made it past the first two levels of the city, had no guarantee of making it into the next.

Nate could not help but feel sorry for them, no matter how many times he passed by. Many were, of course, just merchants or mercenaries, hoping to profit off whatever crisis happened to be ongoing at the time. Many others, though, were simple people, trying their best to limit the suffering caused by the whims of those in power. As Nate looked out for as far as the fog and rain would let him, at the countless people waiting for their chance at safety, he could not help but think that if this was peace, he hoped never to witness war.

The journey out of the city was uneventful, as expected. The only highlight on their first day was when they stopped at a certain excessively French boarding house. Marie and Edgar had been characteristically overjoyed to see Nate again before bombarding him with questions firstly, about Marcus, and then whether Cassandra was Nate's wife. One awkward dinner and restful night later, the pair were back on the road with instructions to have Marcus visit before the pair seemingly died of heartache.

The rain had not for one moment ceased its assault in the days since the pair had set out. Now as they stood before the main gate separating them from the outside world, it still showed no sign of abating. In one last reminder of the horrors of bureaucracy, Nate and Cassandra were forced to leave their steeds behind in a nearby stable until they returned. With war still a possibility, the Citadel didn't want to lose any potential assets.

As Cassandra wiped rain from her nose and squeezed out a bath-full of water from her hair, Nate turned to her. "Ready?" He asked, with an unmistakeable quiver in his voice, of someone who couldn't decide if they were scared or excited.

"Let's get this over with," Cassandra sighed in response, as they started on down the long path into the wilderness.

Chapter 3

The Emperor lay inanimate as the members of the Righteous Congregation were milling around the bedchamber. For almost a year they had repeated the same ritual. Each day they would arrive at his bedside at the break of dawn, desperately hoping to find him awake and undamaged. When it was clear that no change had come over him, they would pace about the room for as long as their duties allowed, arguing, debating, desperately trying to fathom how to keep the country running for another day without The Emperor to guide them.

This new reality benefited some more than others. Over the past nine months, Elias had expanded the office of the Grand Seeker to encompass almost all The Emperor's royal duties. Lords and ladies now lobbied him for support, sent him gifts and invitations to social events in the hope of currying favour. Indeed, there were now few areas of Imperial society where the reach of the Seekers did not extend. Armed mobs of zealots roamed the streets, harassing and abusing anyone they deemed to not be living by their holy laws. Often in full view of the city guard, who were powerless to stop them. Temple attendance was now mandatory, and a hefty tax claimed to be for the rebuilding of the city had been raised. Yes, truth be told, while Elias had been inconsolable at first by the sudden incapacitation of his imperator, he had grown comfortable with the weight of the crown upon his head.

His only real opponent in what remained of the Congregation came in the form of Nestor. Sir Bryce was too busy preparing for a war, which could not begin without The Emperor's express instruction to bother with courtly matters. Rohm had been imprisoned the day after the attack on the Imperial City, either for ineptitude or treachery. It made no difference. He currently rotted away in the bowels of the palace dungeon. Adeneus and the Empress Sarah were of course both dead, meanwhile Cardinal Praxus was still trapesing around the middle of bum-fuck-nowhere. Yes, Nestor, with his juvenile optimism and infuriating defiance of whatever Elias suggested, had held up any real political progress for the last nine months. That, however, could all change today.

In a few moments, Elias' candidate for the position of Arch-Sorcerer of the Imperial University would arrive. A certain Philip Thorn, a former Lord and master of the arcane. He had appeared in Elias' office one evening, bringing news of the fracturing of the Battlemages and pledges of support for the Imperium. While all rather conveniently timed for Thorn, his loyal backing in the Congregation would finally end the deadlock, allowing Elias to take almost full control of the country. Everything was finally looking positive, and Elias could not help but fail to supress a thin smirk as he watched Nestor fretting over some documents from his position by the fire. He would need Sir Bryce to be the deciding vote in the appointment, of course, but that was easily bought with a few barrels of mead and the transferring of some minor, inconsequential titles and lands.

Elias was not looking at the chamber door when the knock came, but it brought a smile to his face as he folded his arms, pretending to admire the portrait of the late empress hanging above the fireplace. His mouth twisted into a cruel sneer as he heard the door open, looking directly into the portrait's photo-realistic eyes, they were like shining emeralds as he spoke quietly to it.

"I'll take things from here" he whispered, turning around at last to see with his own eyes his genius and ambition realised. Yet his smirk and air of confidence quickly faltered and faded away as he saw not one, but two people entering the room. One was Philip Thorn, as expected. Dressed smartly in Lordly regalia and his old professor's cap, he looked to be the very personification of the office of Arch-Sorcerer itself. The woman beside him was, therefore, his complete antithesis.

Dressed in scruffy and stained black robes, she looked to be more used to the inside of a stable than the illustrious setting she now found herself in. The two stepped forward as the Congregation gathered around them. Philip spoke first, removing his cap and bowing before the unconscious Emperor, before turning and smiling to those around him, revealing his many silver teeth.

"My Lords, it is an honour to be called to serve in such desperate times." He then proceeded to shake each man's hand in turn before positioning them behind his back. It was Nestor who spoke next.

"I'm sorry, in which capacity do you serve sir?" Philip's eyes darted quickly to Elias before meeting Nestor's, a look of puzzlement on his face.

"My apologies my Lords, I had assumed the Grand Seeker had already informed you of my appointment to the position of Arch-Sorcerer." A smile quickly came to Nestor's face, a smile which indicated he was in no way surprised by the information he had just received.

"Yes," Elias blurted out, his attention until now having been focused entirely upon the grubby woman sullying the room with her presence. He quickly tried to regain his composure, shrugging nonchalantly.

"I simply thought it was about time we filled Adeneus' position. I didn't think it was worth bothering either of you with this appointment, considering how busy you are," he directed at Nestor and Sir Bryce.

"Good plan," Sir Bryce grunted. Half his mind was still hard at work trying to figure out a way to invade Tinelia without needing to declare war. For a moment Elias hoped his casual demeanour and almost disinterested attitude would mask the serious political implications this appointment would have. Yet this hope was dashed by the faux shock Nestor draped over his words, a smugness so thick Elias could have plastered the walls with it.

"Well, isn't this a funny coincidence?" Nestor lied. He knew exactly what Elias had been up to, and for weeks had been searching for a way to counter him. And now she stood directly before them. He raised his hand in a pointed gesture at the woman in black.

"This is Catarah, she was Adeneus' second. I was planning on appointing her to the position myself." Elias bit his lip in anger. '*That bastard! I can't believe he's done this. And a woman too!*' Regaining his composure, Elias gave a shallow laugh.

"Well, we can't have two Arch-Sorcerers, can we?" he said as the two candidates exchanged rival glances.

"Indeed not," Nestor smiled back. What followed was the most tense and awkward silence any of them had ever experienced, as Nestor and Elias fought a titanic battle with nothing but piercing stares and dagger-filled smiles. Sir Bryce, who had been bored by the seemingly rehearsed scene, raised his hand and huffed.

"Well, I suppose we should hear what they have to say before we vote."

"Brilliant idea, Sir Bryce," Elias smiled, clicking his fingers in agreement. As if such a trial would guarantee his candidate's success. Nestor could try all the dirty tricks he wanted, but pulling some urchin off the street and trying to appoint them to one of the most powerful positions in the country was just plain pathetic.

"Please Philip, would you mind sharing your credentials with us?" Elias asked, amused by the idea that Nestor believed his own candidate could in any way compare.

"Certainly, my Lord," Philip bowed before removing his cap and puffing out his chest at his own self-importance.

"As some of you may already know, I was once a professor at the Imperial University. My specialities were in offensive and transmutory magics, although I have in the last few decades also become a specialist in warding. I also have extensive knowledge of magical artefacts and a wealth of experience in practical field work spanning centuries."

Nestor gave a nod, as if he were genuinely considering anything Philip was saying, while Sir Bryce did the same, although he had absolutely no idea what Thorn had just said. Nestor then narrowed his eyes and folded his arms, as if he were pondering a question which he had not planned on asking since he had discovered Elias' plan weeks ago.

"Now that you mention it, I do recall a former Lord by the name of Thorn who deserted the Imperium for the Battlemages. Could you perhaps be one and the same?" Thorn's stance stiffened, while Elias bit the end of his thumb to refrain from going ballistic. Why did Nestor have to be this way, a constant nuisance and meddler? Could he not see that better men than he were busy achieving greatness?

Sir Bryce meanwhile also stiffened at the question. He had a deep hatred for the Battlemages who had killed hundreds, if not thousands, of his men over the years with their dishonourable and cowardly spells. The others could hear his armour tighten as his muscles tensed, as he stared at Thorn with a newfound enmity.

"Ahem," Thorn began, clearing his throat and hoping this little detail could have been ignored. Elias, however, came to his defence.

"He is indeed the very same, my Lords" he began. Sensing Sir Bryce's temper rising beside him, he quickly continued before he had the chance to pull Thorn's head off with his bare hands. "However, Philip and I have had a very long and thorough conversation. I believe he is no more a threat to the Imperium than any of us in this room."

Nestor, now playing off the situation, stepped back in theatrical shock. "Elias, you truly believe we can trust a man who has for centuries sworn loyalty to an organisation bent on destroying us?" He had hoped this would only antagonise Sir Bryce further, yet he appeared to be strangely calm given the circumstances. His hand was wrapped tightly around his sword now, his breathing heavy, but this soon subsided as he allowed himself to take some calming breaths. Sir Bryce may have lacked the necessary traits to partake in the schemes and plots of court, but this provided him with a more clear and balanced view on things. He had no interest in courtly politics as long as his Emperor was served faithfully. He had no reason, therefore, to suspect that Elias had anything other than the best of intentions at heart.

He spoke at last. "I must admit I don't like the idea of a former sworn enemy being privy to The Emperor's inner circle. But Elias must have a good reason to suggest him. Come let us hear it so we may make a decision." Elias and Nestor were both shocked by Sir Bryce's logical and emotionless approach. Elias could not help but smile and even gently bowed in thanks, while Nestor stood wide-eyed. The one time Sir Bryce had kept his emotions in check, and it just had to be now.

"Thank you, Sir Bryce," Elias smiled with a renewed sense of triumph. He turned now to Thorn. "Philip, would you like to tell the Congregation what you told me?" Thorn bowed, relieved he still had his head on his shoulders.

"I admit, my Lords, that I did indeed betray the Imperium by joining the Battlemages. However, it was not out of hate for this great nation or our beloved Emperor," he said looking in the direction of the inanimate monarch. "I was young and foolish, drawn in by the promise of mastering new and forbidden magics. I never once believed their lies and slanderous propaganda. I also never took part in any violence against our troops," he directed at Sir Bryce, hoping to placate him. "Instead, I spent all my time at research. But when I heard of the murder of the empress, and the attack on the city, I knew I must return to defend my homeland. There were many within the Battlemages who shared the same grief and longing for home. So, we banded together, forsaking the Battlemages and pledging our full support to The Emperor whom we love so dearly."

Nestor offered nothing but a piercing stare. Sir Bryce too was loath to believe the story. However, duty came before all, and even he recognised the benefit of a contingent of battle-hardened sorcerers within their ranks.

"How many men do you have?" he asked.

"Roughly two thousand, my Lord," Thorn responded. Sir

Bryce was dumbstruck. He had no time for poncy spells, but two-thousand former Battlemages was not the kind of offer one could refuse. Nestor bit his lip in worry and frustration at Sir Bryce's reaction. This was not at all going how he had hoped.

"Good Lord!" Sir Bryce exclaimed, bringing a thin smile to Elias' lips. He folded his hands beneath his robe, a wave of ecstatic victory washing over him.

"I suppose it's settled then," Elias stated. Sir Bryce seemed to nod in agreement. But then Catarah, who everyone including Nestor had forgotten about, spoke.

"Is nobody going to ask me anything?" she said with a huff, as if she were bored out of her mind, which she was. The others looked to her in astonishment, as if she had just materialised out of thin air. Nestor, suddenly remembering his entire plan, stammered and spluttered as he tried to get a sentence out.

At last, he was able to say. "Yes, of course, we have yet to hear from my own candidate." Already filled with the sweet taste of victory, Elias rolled his eyes.

"Come now Nestor, let's not drag this out. We both know the office of Arch-Sorcerer is held only for the greatest of magic wielders, not Adeneus' former lovers. Let's be honest, if that were the case half the city would have the job. No offense," Elias said, giving Catarah a half-bow. Nestor was red in the face on Catarah's behalf. Catarah herself, however, could not care less what Elias said or thought about her. She was beyond the skill of anyone in the Imperium, Adeneus had known this, and she had nothing left to prove to anyone. But she'd be damned if she was robbed of her rightful position due to one man's ignorance.

"I suppose we are going to just abandon Adeneus' research into the Husks then, in defiance of The Emperor himself?" she asked slyly. Elias looked at Thorn, whose facial expression conveyed that he knew absolutely nothing about the matter. Turning back to Catarah, he gave an awkward half-laugh and shrugged his shoulders as if admitting some shared defeat.

"I'm sorry my dear, but Adeneus' research was a failure, one that cost him his life. I doubt anyone would be able to perform such dark magic with any success." Thorn nodded and hummed in agreement. Whatever Adeneus had been working on, it was probably a colossal waste of time. Unlike his own research. Research which would greatly benefit the office of Arch-Sorcerer

Catarah too nodded, "Indeed, not just anyone has the skill to master this kind of magic. But I do. And I have."

Elias scoffed at the claim, but he could see in Catarah's eyes that she meant what she said. But before he could attempt to belittle her claims further, she spoke again, this time addressing Sir Bryce.

"Which would you prefer, my Lord? Two-thousand men whom for the last millennia have wanted nothing more than to gain access to this very council, to destroy the empire you helped build, or one-hundred million expendable meat-shields that swear unwavering loyalty to you and The Emperor?"

A sweat formed across Sir Bryce's brow as he pictured the thought. An army beyond count washing over their enemies until only the Imperium remained. Crossing the Borderlands and beyond into lands unknown like the unstoppable tide of night. His heart quickened. Yes, he thought, as he imagined the glory to come. Nestor at last felt cause for optimism as he saw the light in Sir Bryce's eyes shimmer excitedly. Elias, however, desperate to quash any challenge to his own candidate, laughed, far louder than the situation warranted.

"One-hundred million? Ha!" he said, placing his hands on his hips and shaking his head. "Clearly maths is not considered a worthwhile subject at the University these days. How exactly do you plan to capture that many Husks? Never mind control them, which, as we have seen, cannot be done without great harm befalling the controller."

Even Nestor had to admit, it sounded far-fetched. But Catarah had a glint in her eye, which only materialised when she knew something others did not. It was therefore an almost permanent feature. Her mouth turned into a smirk as she withdrew a parchment from her dirty robes, allowing it to unfurl so each man could see what was etched upon it.

There was a drawing. No, these were blueprints for a tower, tall and dark with an eight-pointed spire. Etched between the points were visualisations of magical energy, sharp and barbed like lightning. Neatly arranged across the page were figures and notes. Everything that would be needed to construct such a structure down to the final stone and stair. Elias, still unimpressed, waved his hand dismissively.

"And what is this supposed to be?" he asked without caring for an answer. Catarah could not help but smile.

"This, my Lords, is how we control every Husk from here to the end of the known world. All we need is to build it." Everyone in the room looked at one another in disbelief, even Nestor. Surely this could not be true. Sensing the opportunity in the air, Catarah spoke again.

"I have also solved the issue of the spell killing its host."

"How?" Sir Bryce gasped, now desperate to make his fantasy a reality.

Catarah placed the parchment back within her robes, allowing the men to hang in silence, waiting with trepidation for what she would say next. Even Thorn could not help but eagerly hang upon her every word, never in all his years having heard such unimaginable claims be made with such certainty.

"Adeneus' only mistake was believing the potency of the spell depended on the magical ability of the wielder. While in truth, the greatest sorcerer in the world would not be able to cast this spell with any greater success. No, the only vessels able to contain and control so much magic without it killing them, are prophets." There was a collective sigh of disappointment at her admission. There were no known prophets or oracles anywhere in the Imperium since the purges. A testament to the ardour with which the Seekers carried out their missions.

But that disappointment did not last long. Each man slowly turned his attention to Sir Bryce. They all knew exactly where they could find a particularly powerful oracle, and they would need his skills to retrieve her. Sir Bryce's eyes once again lit up as the realisation dawned upon him. He puffed out his chest and grinned to himself, a tight grip on the pommel of his sword. At last, he would have the chance to take the fight to Tinelia, and what better way to start than with their most beloved oracle.

It seemed the choice for the position had been made without a vote being necessary. Elias had been beaten at his own game. Both he and Thorn stood there, a shared look of shock and defeat across their faces. For a moment, Nestor allowed himself to inwardly celebrate his victory, drinking in the dissatisfaction radiating from his opponents. But then, Sir Bryce decided to snatch this short-lived victory from his grasp, much to Elias' relief. While Catarah was the obvious choice for the position of Arch-Sorcerer, there was another which needed to be filled. One for which he felt two battalions of Battlemages would be well suited.

Rohm, the former spymaster, may be rotting away in a cell but there was still an army of informants across the breadth of the world waiting for orders. If there was one thing the Battlemages were known for, other than their ability to be a pain in his arse, it was their skill as spies and sleeper agents. After some rather limp attempts by Nestor to conjure objections to the idea, Philip Thorn was proclaimed Lord Spymaster of the Imperium. Catarah took the title of Arch-Sorceress and the political deadlock, it seemed, would remain in place for some time.

It seemed that Sir Bryce, for all his lack of subtlety and intrigue, had come away the biggest winner from their meeting. Each member of the Congregation left The Emperor's bedchamber with very different thoughts and schemes running through their minds. For some, the day had been a great success. For Philip Thorn, the day had proven only a minor setback. With the Grand Seeker on his side, along with his new position on the Righteous Congregation, there was still much he could do to achieve his goal.

Nestor could not help but feel frustrated with the day's events, however. For all his planning and success, he had still come away without a victory. After a long day of bureaucracy and paperwork he settled down for the night in his chambers, the candle already burning low, and he began to think. To think about his opponent, about Elias. What drove him? Beneath all the zealotry and spite, what made the man think the way he did, and what could Nestor hope to do to counteract it? He lay there for an hour, pondering, guessing, drawing imaginary lines between causes and goals he believed Elias may have some stake in. By the time the candle had burned itself out and only the faint light of the moon remained, lapping against the corners of his room, did he have an idea. Why not just ask the man himself?

At first the thought seemed foolish, filling his stomach with butterflies that he tried to swat away. But the longer he lay there in the pale light, the more restless his legs became, the more the idea seemed to make sense. At last, unable to cease his curious mind and jittering legs, he threw off the bedcovers and lit a fresh candle. Adorning his favourite green dressing gown, he left his chambers and traversed the palace, headed for Elias' office.

The palace was an eery sight after dark since the attack. While it had once been referred to as *the world within the world* and *that which never sleeps*, it was now uncomfortably quiet. The Seekers had implemented a curfew from nightfall until dawn, and only those with special privileges were allowed to wander the palace after dark. A privilege which, as it so happens, the Seekers themselves enjoyed. Nestor thought it ridiculous as he walked the empty halls and corridors, the ghostly whisps of smoke from so many lamps racing one another to the ceiling. The attack had not come from within but from the sky.

Clearly this measure was all Elias could do to implement his will upon others in retaliation. Nestor would love to see him try passing a curfew on the stars themselves, although he was positive that if Elias thought he could do such a thing, he would. None of the guards who now guarded almost every stairway and door confronted Nestor asking about his business. This would likely have been the case even if he had not been The Emperor's right-hand man. As Nestor had such a gentle and kind-hearted manner with all those he met, none would likely have the heart to tell him no. Even many of the Seekers, the less insane ones anyway, had more positive things to say about him than their own pontiff. Although these truths were kept very private, as it was impossible to know who could be trusted, even within their own order.

Fear and suspicion of even one's closest friends, that was how Elias preferred to rule. While effective for now, Nestor often wondered how long it would be before such tactics came back to bite their master. Elias had an official residence within the palace, the same as all other members of the Righteous Congregation. But he often preferred to sleep in his office, working into the early hours of the morning. His office was in the northern section of the palace. From here he could look out over the unspoiled beauty of the countryside where it was illegal to develop. He had chosen this room specifically for the view of the Forked Rivers. That natural barrier which protected the Imperial City in almost all directions. From his desk he could look out and see the waterfall from which the river flowed before finally splitting in two, like two great loving arms around the city.

Elias was surprised to hear a gentle rapping upon his door so late into the night. He looked up from his work and was silent for a moment, wondering who could possibly have business with him at this hour. He was even more surprised to see Nestor enter, carrying a candle and dressed in his sickly green dressing gown. In his century of residence, this was the first time another member of the Congregation had visited his office. He rose from his chair and beckoned Nestor to enter. Having been caught off guard, his usual gruff meanness replaced by an almost reassuring pleasantness.

"Nestor, I didn't expect to see you up so late, and here of all places," he said as Nestor slowly crossed to the chair opposite the desk, taking in the room around him as he approached. The office was mostly a mix of brown and grey due to the hundreds of old books and parchments organised in neat stacks in almost every corner. Otherwise, there was little much else to say about the room. It was rather plain and boring by all accounts, although, there was a rather fascinating wooden ornament which Nestor first thought to be a desk.

Upon closer inspection he could see that it had been carved to show a detailed account of the known world. From the tallest mountaintops to the rivers that flowed from the far north. Most impressive, however, were the finely detailed replicas of the world's cities. From the pointed spires of Tinelia's Citadel and the mighty Imperial Palace to the fiery pits of the south where Vendaag's molten fury spilled out upon the world.

Elias noticed Nestor's interest and he too turned his attention to the map.

"Got a feeling I'll need a bigger one once Praxus returns," he said, clasping his hands upon his desk, admiring the handiwork he had commissioned. Nestor gave a hum of acknowledgement before sitting opposite his colleague.

"So, what can I do for you, my friend? It is not often we have made opportunity to speak to one another like this."

Nestor waited for a moment before replying, wringing his hands together slowly, wondering whether entering the den of the beast was such a good idea. For a century Elias had not once given any indication that he was open to so much as a friendly chat, let alone potentially working with someone. Nevertheless, he had come this far, he may as well take the plunge.

"Well," he began, no longer sure what he wanted to gain from this meeting. He already felt uncomfortable, like the eyes of a thousand-headed monster were upon him, analysing his every move for some slight indication of his motives, desperate for him to make a mistake which it could exploit. But then a new feeling came over him, one of protection, like a warm and heavy blanket. He may not have an army of psychotic militants at his back, but he had the rule of law, laws he himself had written. And as long as he lived, the free and fair would not be overcome by the cruel and ambitious.

Nestor relaxed a little, leaning back in his chair slightly.

"I'll be frank with you, Elias. The last nine months have not been easy. And I cannot help but think it has been made all the more difficult by our constant skirmishing. I was hoping my coming here would allow me to better understand you, so that the bitter struggle of the past may be avoided in future."

Elias tipped his head to the side in a sort of amused confusion. He stood and made his way over to the wooden map they had both been admiring earlier. Pulling the two ends apart, a small platform upon which a pair of glasses and a bottle of some alcoholic concoction rested, rose from the centre.

"I must admit I appreciate your candour, Nestor" he said, while pouring two glasses roughly to the halfway point before passing one to his guest. The liquid, just like the rest of the room was brown. Nestor took a sip to be polite and found the taste utterly revolting. Elias chuckled at Nestor's screwed up expression.

"Awful, isn't it?"

"Why drink it at all?" Nestor asked, putting the glass upon the desk. Elias drained the glass, shaking his head in disgust before replying.

"It's a reminder, my pencil-pushing friend. A reminder that no matter how high we climb, no matter what titles and privileges we enjoy, our cosy lives only remain so through our own efforts. If we were to just for a moment relax the reins we hold so tightly, our worlds could collapse. Then we'd be drinking this same shit as the rest of the scum out there and calling ourselves lucky that it's not any worse."

Nestor nodded slowly in understanding, although his brow was furrowed as he began to at last gain glimpses of the inner workings of Elias' mind. Elias too was intrigued by Nestor. Until now he had seen him as nothing more than an infuriating busybody, desperate to keep the status quo out of a fear of change or lack of ambition. But now he was unsure. The very act of this unannounced and unofficial visit confused all of Elias' assumptions about the man. Clearly there was something more going on behind his otherwise dull and uninteresting eyes.

More than anything it was the sudden honesty, this abrupt break in their until now uninterrupted game of lies and backstabbing. Whatever this new tactic Nestor was attempting, it had been entirely unexpected, and it made Elias question whether their potential coming to some sort of agreement was as impossible as it had first seemed. He thought for a moment, resting his hands on his stomach and gazing off into the distance. Both men sat in silence for a while as they tried to decide what they wanted from their meeting.

It was Elias who spoke first.

"I'm going to do something, Nestor, something I have always advocated against. Sitting here now, I feel we may finally be able to come to some kind of understanding."

"And what would that be?" Nestor asked, tensing slightly.

"I'm going to be honest," Elias smiled.

Nestor raised an eyebrow with suspicion.

"Did I ever tell you about my own world, the one I was born into?"

Nestor shook his head.

"I don't believe so, no," he replied, folding his arms, unsure where this was going and how it could possibly help either of them.

"Well, you see," Elias began, sighing deeply as he tried to recall the memories and lessons from so long ago.

"My world was for the longest time, a shithole, to be frank. Thousands of years of nothing but tribal warLords and asinine kings waging war for the sake of something to do."

"Sounds somewhat familiar," Nestor grinned, prompting the same reaction from Elias.

"Anyway," Elias continued, "one day, practically out of nowhere, a woman arrived at one of the old provincial capitals. Preaching some nonsense about our shared destiny as a species. At first nobody paid her any heed, hysterical women screaming in town squares was nothing new after all. But eventually, some people began to take stock in what she was saying. A merchant here, a lowly Lord there. Eventually kings themselves began to listen to her preaching, no longer with ridicule in their minds. Why they did so is beyond me. Perhaps they were drawn in by the promise of a better world? After all, who in their hearts doesn't want that?"

"What was she preaching exactly?" Nestor interrupted. "It must have been quite fantastical by the sounds of it."

"Oh, fantastical indeed," Elias replied with a forced laugh as he recalled the stories. "She claimed the gods had spoken to her, you see. Allegedly they had told her that out amongst the stars were innumerable races and species just waiting for us to discover. Claimed it was our ordained destiny, written by the gods themselves, to create a great community which spanned the cosmos."

"Interesting," Nestor added. "And how did that play out exactly?" he asked, expecting an unpleasant answer he was positive Elias would thoroughly enjoy detailing.

"Far better than you would expect actually," Elias replied, much to Nestor's surprise. He could not imagine such a claim to gain much traction in a world as backwards as Elias had described.

"The kings and warLords lay down their arms, coming together to fulfil the prophetess' vision. For the first time since our people had crawled out from under their rocks, there was peace. Swords were beaten into ploughs, engines of war turned into instruments of industry. Technology advanced at an unprecedented rate. Within two centuries the last disease had been eradicated from the world. And while the prophetess may have died long before, another always took her place.

To press on, to drive the vision of this brotherhood amongst the stars forward."

Nestor shifted in his seat as Elias continued recounting his peoples' history. "Eventually, my people succeeded in mastering spaceflight, and it felt like our destiny was finally at hand. Every man, woman and child were boarded onto great arks designed to carry us across the darkness of space, into the bosom of the family we had been told for centuries awaited our arrival. It was during this time, while we prepared to make our final journey, leaving our home world behind, that I was born. I was a child when the final ark departed from our world. I even remember the trees swaying in the gust from our engines, as if they were waving goodbye to those with whom they had shared that planet for so long. There was not a single ounce of sadness, not a single tear shed across our entire race, as we left the only home we had ever known. Only joy. Joy and a barely contained frenzy of passion as we raced at great speed towards our destiny."

"As we breached the confines of our solar system there was a definite sense of disappointment as no welcoming party came to greet us. Although no heed was paid to this, as we had waited so long for the day of contact to come, what was a few more days or weeks? But then, as the years went by, we passed cosmic milestone after cosmic milestone, system after system, dead world after dead world. We began to feel something new, an emotion which had not reared its head amongst our people for centuries. We began to doubt."

Nestor, completely enthralled, had not noticed himself leaning forwards, now almost halfway across the table, desperate not to miss a word of Elias' tale.

"I was in my sixties when a final, desperate decision was made by the commanders of our arks. Our engine's power was accumulated and re-routed to a long-range communication device and a final, desperate plea was blast out into the cosmos. For weeks we waited, then months, and the months turned into years. With no power we sat idle in the darkness, hoping, praying that someone would come to our rescue.

One day, after our food had run out and after our candles had burned away, a voice came over the ship's speaker system. And what it said has remained with me to this very moment, sitting here with you, Nestor."

"Wh... what did it say?" Nestor asked, his voice trembling, so engrossed in the tale he had forgotten all about his own reason for coming here. Elias leaned across the desk, which creaked under his weight as he did so.

With a menacing whisper, he replied.

"We. Are. Alone."

Elias returned to a more relaxed position, resting his hands on his stomach as he let Nestor stew on his words. Although, despite his best efforts, he was unable to keep his mind from wandering back to those final moments. Witnessing an entire species die was not the sort of thing one could forget, no matter how many years passed. He could still feel the biting coldness trapped within those great metal coffins. He could still taste the thirst upon his lips after so many days without water. Could still feel the tugging of his shirt as his young daughter clung on desperately for warmth, fully believing her father would make everything right. He found himself pinching his hand beneath the table, the pain keeping his grief at bay.

Nestor shook his head slowly. Never could he have imagined the pain Elias must have gone through in those final agonising days. Nevertheless, while it went some way in explaining Elias' general attitude, there was something that did not make sense to him.

"Yet here you are, the leader of a religious order that suffers no detractors, no criticism or reform. I would think given your own experiences, this would not be the case."

Elias could not help but smile. Nestor was right of course, but he could not possibly understand. He had not been there, had not seen the unity and brotherhood with which his people had lived, even at the very end.

"Faith," Elias began before pausing. This one-word answer clearly did nothing for Nestor. He repeated it, in case saying it aloud may impart some hidden knowledge. Elias nodded his head slowly.

"The ignorant believe faith is a tool of oppression, designed to control others. The vindictive see it as a weapon, capable only of destruction. They are all wrong. Faith is a candle in the darkness. A soothing call in the screaming silence of the nothingness that surrounds us. Faith is freedom from despair. Faith is all we have."

At last Nestor began to understand. As he looked into Elias' calculating eyes, he could feel the fires of faith burning cold beneath them. Elias did not believe a word of what he preached. Or maybe he did. Maybe he was the most fanatical of them all. In truth, it was irrelevant. All that truly mattered is that others believed him.

"I suppose The Emperor's illness has made it difficult to keep faith with the people then. It can't be easy, after all, to preach the divinity of a man who lies helpless and sickly in his bed."

"Well, as you can see, I have been hard at work trying to remedy that. Work, I daresay, would have a far greater chance of success if you did not seek to block me at every turn." There was a touch of venom in Elias' voice as his eyebrows knit into a scowl.

Nestor intertwined his fingers and looked at Elias through narrowed eyes. He took a deep breath, as if to indicate this thought had only now occurred to him.

"And how may, I ask, would you keep the faith should The Emperor not recover? After all, a society based on his divinity would struggle to function without him."

"Careful, Nestor," Elias said abruptly. "Your words are edging close to blasphemy." His own eyes narrowed now. He knew what Nestor was asking, knew exactly what he was hoping to hear. But whether it be hubris or ignorance, Elias could not help but answer. He chose his words carefully and spoke slowly.

"Continuity, Nestor. Continuity is what matters, what

keeps the faith alive. No matter what happens, we shall always have an emperor."

The two sat there staring at one another for a few moments longer, digesting all that had been said and learned. Abruptly Nestor rose and offered Elias a bow, something he had not done for many years.

"Good night, my Lord. Thank you for entertaining an old man's curiosity," he smiled thinly. Elias nodded with a tinge of suspicion but said nothing as Nestor left the room. He may not have looked it, but Nestor had meant what he said. He felt his years in his bones. How long had he wandered Purgatory now, two millennia, three, perhaps more? Each day mimicking the thumping of his heart, rapid and meaningless.

Nestor shuffled to his bedchamber and dragged himself to bed, his shoulders heavy under the weight of the empire kept alive by his efforts alone. That was not to say the night had been wasted, however. Elias had given away far more than he should have and, for the first time in a year, Nestor felt confident. As he rolled under the covers once more a plan began to formulate. Much would need to happen, a lot of it beyond his control, but the Imperium could be saved. But before it could be put into motion, The Emperor needed to wake up.

A few days later Nestor found himself making the usual early morning journey to The Emperor's quarters. His robe billowed closely behind him as he walked with a faster pace than normal. He was late. There had been the Lord's state allowances to sign off, not the sort of thing that could be left to the last minute, not if he wanted to keep his friends. The guards outside The Emperor's quarters were unusually strict today. They demanded to see Nestor's identification papers, despite the fact they had been allowing him access every day for the past year without so much as a glance. Upon entering the chambers, however, he understood why. Sitting upright in his bed being examined by his physician was The Emperor, very much alive and answering the physician's questions. A great air of joy and relief filled Nestor like a deep, revitalising breath. That was until he saw that he had not been the first to arrive. Already standing by The Emperor's bedside was Elias. Nestor cursed his luck, wondering how long Elias had been there already, filling The Emperor's mind with falsehoods.

Catarah and Sir Bryce were also already present, Lord Thorn being the only absent member of the congregation. Nestor quickly rushed to The Emperor's side.

"Your Holiness," he exclaimed with a great breath of relief as he surged towards The Emperor's side. Immediately Elias shot out his arm, halting Nestor from getting any closer. The last few days had seen almost a thawing in the pair's relations, but now, with The Emperor awake, all that seemed to have been forgotten. With viperous eyes Elias spoke softly.

"Please allow the royal physician to assess his Holiness before you start clambering all over him."

Nestor bit his tongue in anger, his jaw becoming tense as he replied with hateful eyes of his own but said nothing. Catarah and Sir Bryce watched the exchange with varying degrees of discomfort. Sir Bryce was used to the constant bickering and snarkiness. Catarah, though, could not help but feel as if she were planted in a schoolyard amongst poorly behaved children. The Congregation stood in silence as the physician completed the last of his tests. He closed his bag of tools and handed The Emperor a peach-coloured potion.

"You seem to be in perfect health, Your Holiness, although your body will take time to readjust after so long at rest. Take one drop of this potion with each meal until none remains, this should help your muscles to recover more quickly."

"Thank you, doctor" The Emperor replied, his first words in almost a year. The sound as sweet as birdsong to those who had for so long relied upon them each day. As the physician left, the others in the room closed in on The Emperor. Each was eager to be the first to speak, but none had the courage. Instead, they all stared in silence as The Emperor's eyes fell over them one by one. He said nothing at first, that was until he faced someone he had never seen before. A woman, with hair as black as a raven's wing and eyes the colour of the sunset. She stood dressed in a white and purple robe, the robe of the Arch-Sorcerer. His eyes narrowed, which caused the woman to squirm under his inquisitive gaze.

"And who is this lovely creature, Elias?" The Emperor asked at last.

Nestor had been about to jump in to answer, overjoyed to converse with his imperator at last. But the addition of Elias' name caused him to freeze while a sickly, cold feeling settling in his stomach. Elias bowed low, practically vomiting out words of praise and thanks before at last introducing Catarah, far more pleasantly than had been expected. Clearly, her appointment mattered little to him now. All that mattered was that The Emperor was awake, and his plans could at last be put into motion.

After her introduction Catarah bowed before The Emperor, speaking in a soft voice, finding herself to be uncharacteristically both intimidated and enthralled.

"It is good to finally meet you, Your Holiness. I am honoured to be here at your waking as your Arch-Sorceress."

The Emperor raised an eyebrow. "As I recall Adeneus was my last Arch-Sorcerer, so I must ask, who appointed you?"

There was an awkward silence as The Emperor's question filled the room. Each member of the Congregation looked at one another, all thinking the same thought. All these months they had been so desperate for The Emperor to wake, not once had they considered where his memories may lie. None wanted to be the one to deliver the news that had resulted in his illness to begin with. But summoning her courage, Catarah spoke.

"A…Adeneus was murdered, Your Holiness, by the Tinelians. Lord Nestor asked me to fill the position."

The Emperor nodded gently as the memories which, to him, had only occurred days previously flooded back.

"Yes," he whispered. "Sarah, she's gone too," he added, but none had the heart to confirm it. It was at this point that Sir Bryce decided that enough time had been wasted already.

Sparing no ceremony, he spoke bluntly and to the point as only a seasoned military man does.

"Your armies are ready Your Holiness, we await your order to launch the counterattack against the Tinelian dogs." The others shot him foul looks.

"Sir Bryce, this is hardly the time," Nestor hissed. The Emperor, however, seemed to be ignoring them all and spoke softly, staring towards the window wistfully, as if recalling some ancient memory.

"I had a dream," he whispered. The others immediately halted their chastisement of the impatient knight and turned their attention back to The Emperor. None, not even Sir Bryce, would ever again dismiss The Emperor's dreams as just that. They were warnings, ones that had they been heeded in the past, would have saved their nation much grief and anguish. None spoke as they waited for The Emperor to recount what he had seen.

"I saw a great river. It flowed like water but was made from flame. It met the sea where it produced a great mist which covered the land. Nothing grew there, all was black and dead. And the ringing of steel rang out with a roar like it had come from the bowels of the world itself."

The Emperor finished and Nestor immediately spoke. "It sounds like Ifritus. Is that what you saw, Your Holiness?" He asked while the others nodded in agreement at his conclusion.

The Emperor at last turned his attention from the window back to his servants who eyed him with varying degrees of concern.

"Yes," he whispered. "I must meet with the Lord of Embers at once," The Emperor said suddenly, throwing off his bedcovers and trying to stand. The other members of the Congregation reacted in horror, and all rushed to ease him back into bed. Yet he would have none of it. Pushing them away, he steadied himself on the edge of the bed before pushing off. He was wobbly at first, as his legs tried to remember their function, but soon stood to his full height.

Nestor, almost tearful, begged The Emperor to return to

bed. The realm could not afford its imperator to suffer any more injury or illness, not after all it had already suffered. But The Emperor placed his strong yet reassuring hands upon Nestor's shoulders. Looking deep into his eyes he smiled for he had good reason to be filled with happiness.

"He can bring her back, Nestor. The Lord of Embers can bring Sarah back."

Chapter 4

This was the first time Nate had stayed in the large, unnamed town beyond the city walls. Usually, he would pass straight through on the way to whatever task lay ahead. This time, however, Cassandra wanted to spend the night on the edge of the town before continuing their journey. In truth, it differed little from the Vanguard. Hundreds of people lined the streets in search of one comfort or another, while guards patrolled the high wooden walls around them. It was funny, Nate thought, the difference a certain material could have on his state of mind. These wooden walls which protected him now seemed little more than a child's attempt at emulating the sense of security the city's thick stone provided. It would take little effort to breach them and put the inhabitants to the sword in comparison. Unsurprisingly, this did little to help ease him off to sleep. Nevertheless, it was still infinitely better than being outside.

The pair had found themselves rooms at a modestly priced inn. The food left a lot to be desired and the beds were little more than thin mattresses placed on the floor, but it was the closest they could get to the wilderness without spending the night beneath the stars. One last night of comfort, sort of. As Nate lay in the dark doing his best to bore himself to sleep, he found his mind naturally gravitating towards their mission. In truth, this was the first time he had given it any thought whatsoever since signing up for it.

There had not been a great level of detail provided. The locals had been too afraid to approach the strange lights they had seen due to the undead which seemed to be patrolling the area. This did not give Nate much to go on, but he had a few ideas. It was entirely possible that the lights were something natural. Perhaps some escaping gas from the mine, the smell of which had attracted some undead. As he tried to come up with an explanation he began to drift from the mundane to the terrifying.

He imagined stepping into a dark cave, lit only by the faint glow of crackling magical energy. Within, a man, strapped to a chair, the skin falling from his bones. His hollow eye sockets staring back, his mouth open, whispering incoherently at first, then screaming as Nate approached. Nate shot up in his poor excuse for a bed. The image of the twisted man clear in his mind, so clear Nate feared him to be hiding just inches away in the darkness. He immediately threw out an orb of light which illuminated the tiny room and revealed that he was indeed alone.

Breathing heavily after successfully scaring himself, Nate lay back down as the orb burned itself out. Back in the darkness he did nothing but listen to the sound of his own breathing. He was still a newcomer to this world, had barely tasted a fraction of what it could throw at him if it wanted, yet already it was affecting him. In more ways than he ever expected. As he finally shut his eyes and gave sleep a serious attempt, he wondered if the others felt the way he did? Somehow, he doubted it. He found it difficult to imagine Marcus, Cassandra or Ardell unable to sleep at night out of fear or regret. He was still so weak.

Nate awoke early the next morning and decided to use the time alone wisely. Ordering some bacon and eggs with a side of hujo, Nate examined the map of the area they would be travelling today. There was no real reason for this, it was still the same journey as before. Nevertheless, he felt he should at least try to look like he knew what he was doing. But as he was tracing his finger over the path Cassandra had marked, something caught his eye. There was a much shorter, narrower road which veered off to the west before turning north at a right angle. The road in question would take them much closer to the village and, by the looks of it, far sooner than their current trajectory. Nate decided he would raise it with Cassandra once she was awake. In the meantime, he hoovered down his bacon and reluctantly finished the rest of the hujo which he still couldn't stand.

He didn't have to wait long. Soon Cassandra appeared, descending the staircase to the ground floor like an angel, the sun at her back, her golden curls bouncing upon her shoulders. Nate could not help his male brain from being transfixed as she walked towards him, the hypnotic movement of her hips erasing all but one thought from his mind. It was clear that Cassandra was not in the best of moods as she sat opposite Nate. She had dark rings under her eyes and had already yawned thrice on that short journey. She had barely sat down when a full breakfast of cooked meats, fresh fruit and a variety of bread was placed before her by the smiling innkeeper.

"Compliments of the house. It's not often we get such beautiful guests." Cassandra gave the same smile she had been forced to practice since she was a teenager. The kind of smile that gave the man what he thought he wanted but without any obligation behind it on Cassandra's part.

"Must be so tough being a beautiful woman," Nate teased gently.

"Saves on the food bill," Cassandra replied with a hint of humour in her voice as she stabbed at a piece of pre-cut melon. "What are you up to?" she asked, pushing back her hair so she could see the map Nate had laid out across the table.

Suddenly remembering what he had spent the morning doing, Nate flipped the map around so Cassandra could see. Pointing to the road he had found and tracing it with his finger, he offered his suggestion that they take this path instead. He was disappointed though when Cassandra immediately began shaking her head.

"Too dangerous," was her only response as she tore a chunk from one of her bread rolls.

Nate turned his palms upwards in confusion but said nothing. Surely each road through the forest could be no more dangerous than the last, it wasn't as if they were patrolled.

Slightly annoyed that she would need to explain such a basic concept to someone who had already been in Purgatory for a year, Cassandra grunted before offering her explanation.

"Narrow roads mean not much traffic. No traffic means more chance for bandits or monsters."

Nate could not help but lean back in his chair and smirk. "Shame we don't know any monster hunters," he replied.

Cassandra, however, was in no mood for jokes. She was exhausted and had no interest in having her arms ripped off by something she wasn't being hired to kill. Nate's cavalier attitude was also a source of frustration, something she was hoping he would have at the very least suppressed somewhat. It wouldn't be so bad if he could just make up his mind. One moment he was a quivering wreck at the thought of being out of the city, the next he was gleefully advocating putting them both in unnecessary danger. It was exhausting to try and keep up with.

She shot him the kind of stare Ardell would have given if he had said something she disapproved of. It was enough to shut him up immediately, although this look was still nowhere near as terrifying as the original. Nevertheless, it got the reaction Cassandra had hoped for. All that time practicing in front of the mirror, desperately trying to capture that same level of respect that Ardell commanded, was slowly paying off.

"Sorry," Nate replied. Really, he should have known the flaw in his plan and now felt stupid for suggesting it in the first place. While at first finding Nate's look of dejection rather satisfying, Cassandra soon could not help but feel pity at his sad, pathetic face.

"It's good that you're looking out for these things," she said, hoping it would sound casual and not something uttered out of kindness. "Just make sure you raise anything with me, this will work best if we are a team," she added. Nate could not help but smile at Cassandra's clear attempt to cheer him up. She thought she was playing it off as part of the job, but she wasn't fooling anyone.

After finishing their breakfast, the pair walked for a few minutes before they were once again faced with another gate. This time there would be no beds or fresh mead on their travels until they reached their destination in a few days' time. Checking the straps on his backpack were tight, Nate finished his preparation by stringing his bow. Cassandra meanwhile donned her helmet. It was a typical hoplite design, bronze with pointed cheek and nose guards. The only modification, of Cassandra's own design, was a pair of ear guards in the shape of snakes which encircled roughly four inches around the back of her head.

With their final preparations complete, the pair nodded to one another to indicate they were ready and set off into the wilderness. This journey, however, was nothing like the last they had taken along the same route. Usually, the road would be almost empty, refugees and travellers only appearing every few days in large groups. Now, as the gate opened and they stepped out, it was as if they had not left the city at all. Thousands of people continued to line the road out of the town for miles. Both Nate and Cassandra were in shock at such a sight, throngs of people in such numbers neither of them had seen before.

They passed rows of dirty, ragged tents made from whatever fabric was to hand, within which even dirtier and more ragged people lay, waiting their turn to enter the town. The entire road was taken up by the makeshift camps of the desperate. The nearby forest too teemed with those unable to find a place on the road itself. Countless small campfires burned, and it seemed that a good portion of the forest had succumbed to the axes of those seeking warmth.

"What the hell is this?" Cassandra whispered to herself as she stepped over bundles of rags and other junk which littered the road. Nate remained silent, trying his best to avoid the thousands of eyes which followed his every movement. He could not help but both pity and fear those around him. They were desperate and in need of aid. But to what lengths would they go to ease their plight, especially when two such tempting targets were walking right into their midst? He tightened his grip on his bow and placed his other hand on the hilt of his sword. He wouldn't stand a chance against an angry mob, but this was all he could do to bring himself a little reassurance.

The mob did not bother with them though. They had far more pressing concerns than causing trouble and allowed them to pass with nothing more than envious stares. What had started out as a mild morning gradually turned bitterly cold and rain was not too far behind. Nate wrapped his cloak around him more tightly and decided to put away his bow as his hands were becoming numb. Resting it over his shoulder he caught the attention of Cassandra.

"Don't do that."

"What?" Nate replied looking up from under his hood.

"If you leave your bow strung it will lose its elasticity."

"Really? Didn't know that," Nate said taking the bow from his shoulder and removing the string. He then wrapped it up and placed it across the top of his backpack once more. Cassandra rolled her eyes at her companion's cluelessness. How he had managed to slay two epinae was beyond her understanding.

The pair walked for six solid hours in the cold and rain, and not once did the queue of people that had begun outside the town begin to diminish.

"This is insane," Nate whispered as they came across a collection of four carriages which had been arranged in a circle, their owners huddled around a large campfire in the centre between them. Pulling up her drooping hood, weighed down by the weight of water it had absorbed, Cassandra could not help but agree at the bizarreness of their surroundings.

"You'd think there was a war on," she muttered.

"Maybe they know something we don't," Nate replied, as the two shared a look of increasing unease. Despite the soreness of their feet and numbness of their extremities, neither wanted to make camp yet. It was still light for one, but most of all they did not want to be anywhere near these desperate people while their guard was down. The pair soldiered on, ignoring the pleas of their bodies to rest.

They continued for another three hours before finally deciding to call it a day. Thankfully, the seemingly endless line of refugees had trickled off around two hours previously. However, the pair decided to play it safe and give themselves some more distance before settling down for the night. Unlike the previous journey, the pair went further into the woods instead of finding a camp by the roadside. This made them less likely to be discovered by anyone traversing the road late at night. Although it came at the price of making them more susceptible to any wandering monsters.

"I can't believe you never learned that invisibility spell," Cassandra huffed as she threw down a collection of blankets which would act as her bed for the night. "That means no fire, which means I spend the night freezing my tits off."

Nate had been busy rummaging through his pack in search of something to eat but could not resist an opportunity to be crude. "Guess we will have to snuggle up to keep warm then."

Cassandra ignored him and rubbed her hands together before placing them under her arms. "Haven't you got an invisibility potion that lasts for a few hours or something?"

Nate pulled back his head as one does when imparted with new and surprising information he could not quite believe.

"Are invisibility potions even a thing?" he asked. He had never heard Kyle mention them or seen any for sale. Such a thing would be incredibly handy, however, and save him from unknown hours being bored to death during his magic lessons.

"I was hoping you'd tell me," Cassandra said, the disappointment evident in her voice.

"You're the one who came out here dressed for a frolic in a wheat field," Nate said rather unsympathetically. It was true that Cassandra's armour offered little in the way of insulation. Her thighs and arms were almost completely without protection from the elements and Nate could see the goosebumps covering her exposed skin from where he sat. He was cold too, his hands had been practically without sensation for hours, but his thicker leather armour did go some way in keeping the rest of him somewhat warm.

Stomping over to where Nate was crouched, still in search of food, Cassandra held out her hand. Looking up and unsure what she was after, he gave Cassandra a half-hearted low five, admittedly confused why she seemed so serious about it.

"No, you idiot, give me your blankets," she fumed, pulling her hand away from Nate's touch before extending it again.

"Excuse me?" Nate replied, not quite a fan of the rudeness he was being subjected to due to his companion's own choice of attire.

"You're the reason we can't have a fire, so you get to have first watch," Cassandra explained through now chattering teeth. Reluctantly, Nate handed over his blankets and bedroll, which Cassandra hastily snatched before finding a suitable place to sleep.

"Don't see you learning any invisibility spells," Nate whispered to himself.

"SHHH!" Cassandra scolded as she wrapped herself in as many layers as possible before curling up near the base of a tree. Nate could not help but smile to himself as he watched Cassandra, who now looked like a fat, angry caterpillar, shivering herself to sleep.

The night only grew colder from there, and Nate soon found himself envious of all the blankets Casandra had rolled herself into a cocoon with. He tried to keep his mind busy instead of focusing on how cold he was. The best way to do this, he had found, was to practice new spells. The hardest part about his lessons with Kyle, other than them being with Kyle, was the different way in which Nate learned magic. Normal people had to physically and mentally tune themselves into the magic energy that surrounded them. Only then could they manipulate it into the spell they wished to invoke with great difficulty and effort.

Nate on the other hand, due to being a prophet, had no

such issues. His connection to magical energy was constant and uninterrupted. As a result, he spent more time trying not to accidentally blow himself up than practicing new spells. He also found it incredibly easy to manipulate magic as he wished. He was still unable to duplicate leaves or summon food out of thin air, much to Kyle's disappointment, but he had been able to create a few spells that were entirely unique and never seen before.

The downside was that these unique spells were utterly useless unless he wanted to entertain some small children. Considering there were no children in Purgatory, Nate settled on entertaining himself. With his back against a tree and Cassandra sleeping soundly nearby, Nate positioned himself. He pulled up his legs until his knees were just below eye level and touching one another. He then began to concentrate, not too hard, but enough that the sounds of buzzing and chirping insects were drowned out.

Before long, the spell took effect. Standing upon his knees were two small figures made of light. One a soft blue, the other muted yellow. They were in the shapes of men, but had no features whatsoever, only the basics of arms, legs and heads. Smiling to himself, Nate then continued concentrating while the two magical beings stared up at him from their perches on his kneecaps. Suddenly, the two little creatures found themselves armed. The blue one with a sword made from the same light blue colour, as him, the other a long yellow spear.

The two immediately began to duel one another. With great skill and poise for creatures which stood only two inches tall and had existed for all of five seconds, they fought one another across Nate's knees. Before long the fight spilled onto the ground where the little men used blades of grass and broken twigs as weapons. Nate was thoroughly enjoying being immersed in the tiny battle and had entirely forgotten that his job was to be alert and on the watch for danger. The two beings continued to fight for a few more minutes before the duel came to an abrupt halt. The blue creature hurled a tiny pebble which the other dodged but struck Cassandra on the ear.

The moment Nate had diverted his attention from the little men they had evaporated into nothingness. He was therefore left awkwardly smiling as Cassandra rolled over to face him. She held her now stinging ear in her hand, while shooting Nate a look which conveyed the pain he would be in if she were not confined by so many blankets. As Cassandra rolled back over, this time making sure her ears were protected, Nate returned to boredom.

As the hours ticked by, Nate wanted nothing more than to light a fire. The limited warmth provided by his armour had proved not enough to ward off the chill of the deep night, yet he knew a fire would expose them both to danger. Although he found it deeply unfair that he was unaffected by his own magic, a tiny flame hidden in his hands would do wonders right now. Nevertheless, this was not the way of the world and Nate would simply have to suffer until it was his turn to hog all the blankets.

Thankfully, Nate's shift was uneventful. The chittering and clicking of nocturnal wildlife being the only evidence that the forest was not entirely empty. After checking his watch for the billionth time, (a gift from Chen for the anniversary of his death day and arrival in Purgatory), Nate was relieved that it was his turn to sleep at last. When he turned to wake Cassandra, he found that she was already in the process of untangling herself from the web of blankets she had spun.

"I'm keeping this one," she grumbled, holding onto an especially thick, woolly blanket. Nate's blanket. Nate said nothing and crawled over to where Cassandra had been, eager to take advantage of the already warm bedroll. It did not take long for sleep to come. The soft, warm material acting like a soothing salve over his aching body. Unfortunately for Nate, however, this would not be a peaceful night.

Whether it had been hours or mere seconds since he fell asleep, Nate did not know. The only certainty was that he was afraid. He was in a cavern or some sort of underground structure. The walls did not seem natural, they were too smooth, too uniform to be so. Someone, or something, had clearly spent a great deal of time building this place. Whatever it was. The only source of light came from a pair of torches in the distance. While every instinct told Nate not to approach, he did so regardless.

As he walked, each tentative step echoed across the room. Each footfall lasting many seconds, indicating that the structure was far more massive than what Nate could see in the limited light. All around him the darkness stalked like a predator, eagerly awaiting the moment the torches would extinguish and Nate would be at its mercy. A moment Nate felt was sure to come. However, as he came to within only a few meters of the torches, something unexpected happened. More lights sprang into life from the desolate darkness, lining the way before him. With this new pathway Nate could see more clearly now, although blackness still prevailed over much of the room, leaving only this thin trail of light for him to follow.

Nevertheless, Nate could see something new. Beyond him in neat, endless rows were tall, wooden columns. No, not columns. Bookshelves. Row after row of gargantuan bookshelves which reached up beyond his sight and continued into the abyss above. As Nate continued down the path which had been laid before him, he noticed that not a single inch of the shelves were empty. Countless books forced their way into every available space. While those that could not find accommodation on the shelves, lined the floor with their pages, like the scattered leaves of an Autumn forest.

Despite the change of scenery, Nate felt no more at ease than before. The rustling of pages as his boots passed over them, the sound as they wafted through the air like the diseased, dying breath of some long-forgotten age. It was only now, after travelling for some distance along this identical, literary lined path, did Nate begin to question himself. Why was he following a path someone else had paved for him, to a destination he did not know?

As the thought came to his mind, he stopped with the intent of turning back the way he had come. As soon as his feet no longer carried him forward, however, the lights went out. It was as if the room itself had known Nate's intentions. Now, alone in the darkness, Nate began to fill with fear. His heartbeat like a war drum, echoing across the stone walls. His breaths deep yet panicked. But wait, there was something else. He had thought wrongly, he could feel it now. It was like an iron maiden, this crushing pressure coming at him from all sides until he felt he would suffocate.

He was not alone.

At the very moment this realisation entered his mind, it was confirmed. A voice, deep and terrible, echoed throughout the structure, making the very foundations shake at its might.

"Who are you, come to this place beyond time and the waking mind?"

Nate remained silent, partly out of shock, but also in the hopes that doing so would trick the voice into thinking it was alone. It was useless, however, the voice had sensed Nate the moment he had arrived, there was no hiding from it.

"Speak!" it bellowed. "I am no foe," it claimed somewhat unconvincingly.

"I...I...I'm just a traveller.... lost," Nate stammered. He was met by silence but could sense movement nearby. Something was circling him.

"Not lost," the voice hissed in reply. "One cannot merely stumble upon this place," it continued from somewhere behind Nate. Or at least, what he thought was behind. The discombobulating darkness having done away with his sense of direction.

"Believe me when I say I had no intention of coming here, and I would very much like to leave," Nate replied. He held his arms outstretched in the darkness, as if that would have been any protection from what lay in the shadows.

"Wait," the voice replied, its former hostility replaced by what sounded like curiosity. "I would very much like to speak with you. Come, step into the light." With that, two torches erupted either side of Nate, fully illuminating him but without allowing him to see his interrogator. Nate remained perfectly still, terrified out of his mind as he felt a pair of huge, ravenous eyes examining him.

"Why have you come and what is it you seek?" the voice asked curiously. Nate shook his head nervously, not wanting to give the wrong answer but also not wanting to lie.

"I…I promise that I have no idea how I got here. I don't even know where 'here' is."

"Hmm," the voice grumbled in response, not entirely sure it believed what it was being told. It would be highly unusual if true.

"You have come to a place of knowledge. A hidden place. A place which can only be found should something you seek be contained within," the voice explained. "So, tell me, what ancient power, what forgotten memories of a dead age do you desire? Do not fear, for I shall help you in your search."

Whatever this voice belonged to, it clearly wasn't getting the message Nate was trying to convey. He began to back away slowly, hoping that somehow he would be able to outrun whatever incomprehensible nightmare studied him from the dark.

"I…I'm sorry," Nate breathed as his heart threatened to burst. "You have the wrong person, I'm not looking for anything." As he stepped from the safety of the light into the shadows behind him, two more torches erupted. Clearly, quietly slipping away unnoticed was not going to be an option. The voice grumbled once again, clearly agitated.

"You came to me," it stated, filled with suspicion. What followed was without a doubt the most terrifying sound Nate had ever heard. A vicious, animalistic growl which rolled like thunder. It reverberated around the room and shook Nate's very bones as he quaked in fear.

"You enter my home uninvited, are treated with courtesy and offered assistance, yet you will not reveal your motives."

At first it sounded as if Nate was about to either receive a stern dressing-down or be ripped to shreds, but the tone of the mysterious voice quickly changed, as if struck with a sudden thought.

"Unless," it began, as if talking now to itself, "unless you speak the truth." Nate quickly nodded his head in agreement as he sensed a way out of this without being torn apart. "Perhaps that which you seek has not yet been revealed?" it asked rhetorically. Nate could feel the body to which this voice was attached step closer until he could barely make out an outline in the darkness. A huge, monstrous figure which filled the space between the bookshelves with ease.

"What is your name?" it asked.

As much as Nate hated the idea of letting this thing know literally anything about him, he could not help but answer out of fear should he not. "Nate," he replied shakily.

The room was suddenly filled with a gust of foul air which whipped Nate's cloak around him as the creature exhaled ponderously. Suddenly the voice spoke once more, but it was more a whisper which seemed to slither along Nate's very skin.

"I offer you council now, Nathan," the creature said, refusing to use the shortened version of Nate's name. "Be wary of the path that you tread. Think carefully, act honestly, for you do not know the consequences your actions may bring." The voice began to recede as the creature retreated into the depths of the structure.

"I sense much within you, a great conflict within your soul. Beware," it whispered now, its voice gliding across the aisle like the wind. "Your hatred may just doom us all."

With that, the torches extinguished themselves, leaving Nate in darkness once again. But before he could panic, a distant light arose in the darkness, accompanied by a faint noise. Taking a step towards it, Nate dared to hope for a way out. Yet before he could take another step, the light began to grow, and so too did the noise which came with it. What had started out as little more than the flame of a candle quickly became a bonfire. The soft crackle of scorched dust now a shout.

Nate took a step back, but it was too late. The fire was out of control. He turned to run, sprinting as fast as his legs would carry him, tripping on the slippery, loose pages which carpeted the floor. All the while the fire grew and grew until it was a raging inferno beyond all control. The deafening roar which followed was like that of an enraged beast on the hunt, and Nate was the prey. There was no escape. It did not matter how hard he ran, the flames were faster.

Before long they had caught up with him, their hot tongues licking at his heels. Nate let out a cry, hoping to urge himself on, to push harder, but it was no use. He tripped, a lopsided pile of books his assailant which he had not noticed jutting out into his path, so blind was his panic. He turned onto his back at the last moment to see the scorching wave engulf him, searing the skin from his bones, reducing him to naught but ash as he let out one last agonised scream.

Nate awoke in a flailing panic, panting as if having run a great distance. Staring down at him with a scowl was Cassandra.

"Bad dream," he panted, before Cassandra had chance to speak.

"You sure?"

"What do you mean?" Nate asked as he pulled himself to his feet, still breathing hard from his nightmare.

"Well, you're a prophet. Dreams are rarely just that," Cassandra stated matter-of-factly.

"How did you…" Nate began before cutting himself off. "Marcus," he sighed, shaking his head. It had been Marcus who told him to keep his identity a secret, now here he was telling everyone.

"To be fair, he was very drunk," Cassandra added, as if that would help matters. Now Nate could not help but wonder who else knew, and what might they want from him?

"It doesn't matter," Nate said taking a few steps followed by some deep, calming breaths. It had just been another stupid dream; it hadn't meant anything. How could it? Just another product of being endlessly subjected to a constant state of fear and angst.

"If you say so," Cassandra replied as she turned to pack up her things. It was starting to get light and the pair would need to be on the move soon. Glad that she had decided not to pry further, Nate joined his companion for a rather bleak breakfast of plain porridge. They were more thankful for the fire which they could at last afford to build now that daylight was on its way.

The temperature had begun to steadily rise from its depths during the night. However, the air was still cold and a dampness hung around them that clung to any exposed skin, saturating their clothes. After eating and warming themselves as best they could, the pair packed up their belongings and prepared for another long day of walking.

"So, tell me," Nate piped up, attempting to fill the silence between them broken only by the sound of their boots upon the dirt road. "You got anyone special in your life?" he asked in what had to be the worst attempt at small talk Cassandra had ever heard.

"Nope," she replied without turning her head, keeping her eyes instead focused upon the road. Nate was surprised, a woman as beautiful and capable as Cassandra was sure to be in high demand.

"Got to say I'm surprised," he added. "You're not exactly unfortunate looking." Cassandra could not help but smile slightly at Nate's weak attempt at a compliment, although she made sure not to let him see it.

"What about you?" she asked, deflecting the question back. "I've noticed you seem to be joined at the hip with that roommate of yours."

"Pfft," Nate scoffed. "No thanks, not even if you paid me," he replied, quite rudely in Cassandra's opinion.

"Guess that settles that then," Cassandra said sternly, clearly indicating she had preferred the silence. Nate, however, could not stand the thought of spending the next week or so in total silence and continued badgering Cassandra with whatever idiotic thought entered his mind.

At first Cassandra had resisted Nate's attempts at getting to know her, but after a while, he wore her down. The two ended up talking at great length about whatever topic came to mind. Nate had been especially interested to learn that Cassandra had already died twice since arriving in Purgatory. This was naturally of great interest to Nate, as he wished to know exactly what to expect when the inevitable happened.

As it transpired, dying in Purgatory did not send you back to the meeting room with Death as Nate had expected. Instead, Cassandra said both times she had woken on the outskirts of a town. The first time, in a farmer's field. The second, in a hollowed-out tree. Both times she had been wearing whatever clothing she had died in. Of course she could not have returned to these places even if she had wished. The places she had lived were so far from Tinelia that no one here had ever heard of them and they appeared on no maps. She would not have known even which direction to follow.

Funnily, it was not being dumped in an entirely new place, far from her old life, that bothered Cassandra the most. She had become used to it after the first go round. No, it was that each death meant the raiding of her account by the Servants of the God of Man, leaving her without even a single coin to her name to begin her new life with. The lesson Nate learned from this was that it was best to try not to die at all. Easier said than done though.

After a few more hours, the pair came across a familiar sight - a junction splitting out in half a dozen different directions. The first major intersection which would take them in any direction they wished to go. They would not be taking the smaller, eastern road to Sundered Crown this time, however. They continued straight ahead, taking the widest and most travelled road.

For the most part, it was a rather pleasant journey. The sun had finally beaten back the worst of the cold so Nate could feel his hands again, and even Cassandra seemed to be in a good mood. The pair, feeling more relaxed upon such a wide and open road, were happy to chat and let their guard down a little. Nate even went so far as to summon a small flame in his hands which he used to warm a grateful Cassandra. Yes, it was all going swimmingly. Until it wasn't.

After many hours' travel with only a few short stops to rest and eat, the pair came across another, smaller intersection with four possible paths. This had been where Nate had recommended back at the inn they take the alternate, quicker road which would bring them much closer to their destination. They passed by it, however, continuing their current route until it started to get dark and only one path remained. This, however, is where problems began to emerge.

After another hour, when the sun had finally decided to call it a day and was in its last transformative stages, the weary pair heard a strange noise. Coming not far from up the road was a loud collaboration of shouting and metallic ringing, only growing ever more deafening as the pair cautiously approached. It also became noticeably brighter the further up the road the pair travelled, until the edges of the forest were illuminated as if it were still daytime and the stars themselves were hidden behind the glow of thousands of lights.

The pair decided not to approach the source of the noise head on and slunk into the forest instead, approaching from the flank. Weapons drawn they edged closer, neither daring to make a sound should they be discovered. When they were finally close enough to see the commotion with their own eyes, and the noise had become almost unbearable, their hearts sank into their stomachs.

Ahead of them was a refugee train. Thousands of people all heading towards Tinelia in a single, massive entity. This would have been a serious problem even with all else being well, but this was not the case. Anarchy seemed to have broken out amongst the refugees. Nate and Cassandra had no idea who had started it or how, but the refugees had turned on one another. The metallic ringing they had heard had in fact been the clashing of swords; the shouting, the cries of battle and death throes of the wounded.

"Shit," Cassandra whispered as she hid herself behind a tree.

"We can't go that way," Nate said unhelpfully.

"No shit, idiot," Cassandra spat venomously, as she wracked her brain in search of a plan. Nate continued to peer out from behind cover at the violent scenes before him before turning back to Cassandra.

"We have to go the other way."

"What other way? This is the only way," Cassandra hissed angrily through gritted teeth as she too looked back at the carnage unfolding only meters away.

"My way, the one I showed you at the inn," Nate explained.

"It's too dangerous," Cassandra replied, trying her hardest not to be convinced.

"What, more dangerous than this?" Nate whispered angrily. He understood his option was not preferable in optimal conditions, but what lay before them was in no way optimal.

"Fuck," Cassandra cursed as she admitted defeat. "Fine, let's get the hell out of here," she said, leading them back the way they had come, away from the massacre unfolding behind them.

By the time the pair arrived back at the crossroads it was almost pitch black. Only the moon offered the slightest reprieve from being enveloped in the cold, suffocating dark. The limited vision meant the pair could not see further than a few meters down the road at a time. Whatever was in their path, be it obstacle or enemy, they would not have much time to react to it.

"Ok, we find somewhere to hide, we keep quiet, and we stick together no matter what. Understood?" Cassandra asked breathlessly as her nerves got the better of her.

"Understood," Nate replied equally as nervous as they took their first, wary steps into this new unknown.

Chapter 5

"Damn it," The Emperor cursed, fighting to raise himself from his bed. His body was still recovering from its near yearlong rest and struggled to perform the most basic tasks. Seeing him try to move on his own, his attendants rushed to aid him.

"Please, Your Holiness, you must be careful," cooed one particularly beautiful brunette with rosy cheeks and wild, burgundy eyes which seemed to him like a tempestuous ocean of blood, within which the dark stones of her pupils weathered. She placed her hand gently beneath The Emperor's arm and eased him into a sitting position.

"If there's one place I think I'm safe from causing myself too much harm, it will be my own bed!" he replied, clearly agitated. It was not the help's fault that The Emperor was in this situation, but he had nobody else to vent his frustration to.

"Apologies, Your Holiness, of course," the brunette replied with a tinge of hurt in her voice. The Emperor could not help but immediately feel guilty and apologised. After all, these women were the only ones ensuring he was not spending each day lying in his own filth. He must thank Elias for that, they had come at his orders, directly from the seeker's headquarters many hundreds of miles away. It was funny, The Emperor thought. For an organisation which detested women so, he could not help but notice that none of those in their employ were anything less than stunningly beautiful.

As he was aided in swinging his legs over the side of the bed, another attendant, this one with bright indigo hair, helped with his trousers and slippers. The pair's eyes met for a moment as her hand gently brushed against The Emperor's thigh. An accident? Possibly. She looked away quickly, doing a poor job of concealing an embarrassed smile. The Emperor too felt a small rush but tried his best to suppress it.

Once he was fully dressed and aided with a cane in one hand and two attendants no less than a step behind, The Emperor made for the Congregation Chamber. There was much to discuss and little time, each passing moment potentially lengthening the distance between him and his goal of locating Sarah. What had once been a quick walk, taking no more than a few minutes, now felt like a marathon. The Emperor's legs began to ache mere seconds after leaving the confines of his chambers and he was already beginning to tire. Half a dozen times did he need to stop and rest, using the balcony for support before he could continue.

The damage he had witnessed the last time he had taken this route had by now been repaired. Not so much as a crack remained to show where the bombs had fallen. Nevertheless, he could not help but see the events of that night clearly in his mind as he looked over the balcony once again. He could see the people running, screaming for help as they were either crushed or burned alive. He remembered the desperate looks on the faces of the rescuers the following day, trying in vain to locate survivors amongst the rubble. He turned away from these painful visions and back towards the Congregation Chamber. Dragging his feet as the weight of his body began to overtake the little strength he had, he was helped the rest of the way by his attendants.

I must be a sad sight, he thought. For such a once great man to be spared the indignity of lying face first on the floor, helpless and pathetic, by nothing more than two ordinary women. All rose as The Emperor entered the Congregation Chamber. His aides were immediately sent away while Sir Bryce helped The Emperor to his throne. Nestor and Elias buzzed around him trying to look helpful but ended up being nothing more than obstacles to overcome. At last, and with an exhausted gasp, The Emperor lowered himself into his seat, resting his head against a quickly provided cushion and taking deep breaths. The rest of the Congregation remained silent and took their seats as they waited to be addressed. The Emperor looked around for a moment, taking in the room. At his right side sat the empty throne of his empress. Its ghostly whiteness haunting him with painful memories. What had once been so familiar to him now felt alien and barely recognisable. So many missing faces, replaced so soon by ones he did not know.

These new faces were of course the new Arch-Sorceress Catarah, and spymaster Phillip Thorn. Thorn had seemingly adapted very well to his new position, dressed in an elegant suit and plumed hat dotted with small rubies. Catarah, on the other hand, wore what seemed to be the same dark, stained robe as when she had been given the job. Personally, she found no need for fancy robes. It was not by her sense of fashion that she achieved her position, but by her unmatched magical prowess. That is not to be said, however, that she did not recognise the benefits of dressing up for certain situations. But every man present had now already become acquainted with her ways and paid no heed to her scruffy appearance. Both new appointees shared one thing in common - they were both filled with pride and awe at how far they had come. Starting at the bottom of society, both had managed to climb and claw their way to the very top. An opportunity neither would squander.

While Catarah, much like her predecessor and mentor before her, tried her best to concentrate on the matter at hand. She could not help her mind wandering back to her latest project. Every day she was pushing the boundaries of what had once been considered impossible. Already in her few short weeks as Arch-sorceress, she had disproven and re-written magical theories which long predated herself. Yet she was still missing the most critical ingredient which would catapult her to new realms of magic entirely. She still needed a prophet. This meeting, she hoped, would remedy that.

Thorn too found himself distracted. He cared not that he was sat in the presence of The Emperor, or that he was partaking in the most vital and consequential matters of statecraft. No, Thorn cared only for that which he believed, lay hidden somewhere in this very room. All his scheming, all his plotting and planning which had begun even before he joined the Battlemages, it had all been to gain access to this very room. His goal was so close he could taste it, could feel the hairs on his arms tingle at the mere thought of what may lie only a few feet from where he now sat.

At last The Emperor spoke, and whatever thoughts and schemes the rest of the Congregation were concocting would need to be placed on hold for now.

"What's first?" The Emperor sighed. He already had an unpleasant feeling in his stomach that he knew the answer, but he would have to hear it from the Congregation's own mouths before he could deny them. At first the room was silent, each member looking at one another in agreement, a rare thing indeed. It was Sir Bryce who broke that silence.

"War, Your Holiness, of course."

"Of course," The Emperor replied, resigned, his suspicions confirmed.

"We have roughly one million men already, but our spies indicate the Tinelian's have already mobilised four times that number. If we wish to catch up, we will need to do the same and do so aggressively," Sir Bryce continued. He began to spread out a collection of maps across the table for The Emperor to inspect.

"It will take us at least half a year to reach a parity of forces. That is why I have come up with a strategy to see us through this time while maintaining an advantage." The Emperor decided not to interject while Sir Bryce was of this frame of mind, knowing it would be a wasted effort. It was best to let him ramble on for the time being.

"I believe if we strike first, attacking these two axis, we can cut the Tinelian force into three," Sir Bryce continued, excitedly tracing along the map with the point of his quill. "Also, if we are able to cross this river in the south and establish a foothold, we should be able to maintain a defensive line until our forces are fully mobilised." At last Sir Bryce halted his barrage of military jargon and looked to the rest of the Congregation for support. They all nodded in agreement, having all been subjected to the same speech multiple times before.

The Emperor too nodded, for a moment giving Sir Bryce the gratification he had been so desperately craving. But his hopes were soon dashed.

"There will be no war," The Emperor declared, as disinterested as if he were being asked to choose wallpaper. The rest of the Congregation were shocked into silence. None more so than Sir Bryce who stood like a statue, his mouth open, unable to make sense of what he had just heard.

"No war, Your Holiness?" Elias asked inquisitively, as if he were questioning The Emperor's lucidity. For what a shame it would be if The Emperor was still unfit to rule and Elias were forced to retain all the powers he had adopted during these last months.

"No war," The Emperor repeated. Noticing the shared looks of concern and confusion amongst his council, he elaborated further.

"War will gain us nothing, only take away valuable resources from our goal of locating the empress."

"We were attacked, Your Holiness, hundreds were killed, and you wish us to do nothing?" Sir Bryce asked with a questionable hint of dissent. He could not fathom how anyone, let alone his own monarch, could allow their country to be ravaged without repercussion.

"War would kill thousands more, hundreds of thousands. It would destroy the economy and push millions to the brink of starvation. So do not pretend to me, good Sir, that you are moved by death," The Emperor replied angrily. Sir Bryce stepped back slightly, not used to being the target of his Emperor's anger. He bowed and returned to his seat, unsure of why he had been permitted to promote his strategies at all.

"I must admit, Your Holiness I am surprised by your decision," Elias began. "While it is a noble thing of course to maintain peace, even in such circumstances, I believe it to be a mistake in the long term."

The Emperor drummed his fingers on the arm of his throne but motioned for Elias to continue. They could try all they liked; they would not convince him. But he must be seen to give them their fair chance, especially while he was still so frail. Even more so while the Seekers still roamed the streets and the palace halls, outnumbering his own guards three to one. Oh yes, The Emperor had been made well-aware of the steps Elias had taken these past months to expand his influence. Influence which The Emperor's sudden recovery had reined in like an unruly beast.

Elias stood, fidgeting with his glasses as he spoke. The Grand Seeker had no trouble with his eyesight, and even if he did, the palace physician could easily produce a remedy. No, Elias was yet another victim of fashion, believing this small accessory projected intellect and authority well beyond the limits of their thin and delicate design. It seemed even a man as powerful as he could not resist or deny the difference one small change could make to one's character. He addressed the room, appealing to each member of the Congregation for their continued support with heavy glances.

"As I say, it is a noble thing to preserve peace even in the face of aggression. Yet, if others misinterpret our pious stoicism as weakness, we may end up inviting more destruction upon ourselves." There were murmurs of agreement from the others around the table. All feared an imminent invasion by a powerful coalition, so appearing weak now would only make this outcome more likely.

The Emperor sighed once more, his head felt heavy, resting it upon his fist as he waved Elias' concerns away.

"If we were to be attacked, then why has it not yet happened, hmm? Why did our enemies not strike while the iron was hot, while I was unable to rally and lead our people? They fear war as much as we. Their attempt on my life and the murder of the empress must be punished, yes, but not now. All that matters at this time is finding my wife."

There was a sudden bang as a fist was slammed against the table. Looking up The Emperor expected to see Sir Bryce or maybe Elias venting their frustration. The last thing he expected, however, was to see Nestor standing hunched over the table, his eyes shimmering with fury.

"Sarah is dead, Your Holiness," Nestor cried angrily. "She was murdered under this very roof. Yet you want to waste your time in a hopeless search, which we all know will never succeed, rather than bringing justice to those responsible."

Nestor's outburst had been completely unexpected and totally out of character. Even Sir Bryce had flinched at his striking the table. Yet he had simply said what they had all been thinking, and he commanded newfound respect for this. Even Elias had to admire the courage it had taken to make such a stand, nodding to indicate his respect and approval.

The Emperor, however, was furious. His deep, stuttering breaths audible as he tried to suppress his emotions. He looked at each member of the Congregation, each returning his gaze with nervous or awkward expressions. Even Nestor had slunk back into his seat looking sheepish as the adrenaline of his outburst was wearing off.

"This is what you wish then, all of you? To make war rather than, as you say, a hopeless endeavour to locate my wife, your Empress?" The Emperor said, throwing a bitter glance at Nestor. He was met by silence, but this was an answer unto itself. "Fine," he snapped. "You may do as you wish, you have my full approval. But I shall have no part in it," he groaned, struggling to rise to his feet.

Sir Bryce moved in to help support his imperator, but The Emperor swatted him away and struggled to the door alone. As the door to the chamber slammed shut and the Congregation was left without its leader, all the authority to act as it wished granted, Catarah spoke for the first time. Throwing her feet up on the table and keeling back on her chair she smiled, barely able to contain a childish laugh.

"And here I was worried this was going to be boring." The other members of the Congregation were not so jovial, at least not outwardly. Each of them now had a year's worth of work to suddenly catch up on and they could waste no time.

Nestor was the last to leave, still in shock at himself for his outburst. He had not once spoken against The Emperor like that in all his years of service. Now he could not help but wonder if his coming years were numbered.

Nestor found himself working late that night. The rest of the palace had retreated to the safety of sleep, but he still had too much left to do. He was busy signing edicts which would rapidly move the economy onto a war footing. This meant new taxes, re-allocation of labour, prioritising armament production and so on. He had already burned through two candles, and was halfway through a third, when an unexpected knock on his door shifted his tired eyes away from his work.

"Enter," he said cautiously, not knowing who could be visiting at this hour. Even now he refused to force his army of administrators to work so late into the night, preferring to shoulder the burden himself. Yet for all his guessing, he never would have expected to see Elias of all people stepping into his office.

"My Lord," he said in a surprised, almost suspicious tone. Elias stepped into the dim light in only his night-clothes. These consisted of a red shirt and matching long johns, and a bright purple night cap complete with a fluffy bobble on the end. It was such a surreal sight that Nestor wondered if sleep had got the best of him after all. He was, however, very much awake and the Grand Seeker it appeared really was stood at the end of his desk in his pyjamas.

"I was going to apologise for waking you, but I see that won't be necessary," Elias smiled as he pulled up a nearby chair and sat opposite his colleague.

"No, I, er, still have a lot of work left to do," Nestor replied looking down at his collection of unfinished papers, then back at Elias.

"Oh yes indeed," Elias smiled, gently intertwining his fingers. "So much work to do, so much to be excited about."

Nestor did not respond, instead eyeing Elias with disapproval. They may have momentarily agreed war to be the correct course of action, but he was hardly looking forward to what was to come. There was a brief silence while Elias shifted in his seat to a more comfortable position and spent a few seconds studying the room.

"No fancy maps in here I'm afraid," Nestor joked which was met with a brief, thin smile from his colleague.

"I was hoping that after our chat some time ago that we could once again count on one another," Elias said softly. Nestor at last lay down the quill which had been glued to his hand all day and gave Elias his full attention. He leaned in slightly so that he may better hear his guest's hushed tone.

"That will of course depend on the nature of the problem," Nestor replied. While working with Elias rather than against him would be more pivotal than ever, he would refuse any scheme which slid them backwards into tyranny.

"We need to do this war properly," Elias began. "That rock-noggin Bryce wants to attack now, tonight if he could." Nestor could not help but be taken aback in what seemed to be such a deviation from Elias' usual way of thinking.

"And you disagree?" He asked tentatively, certain he had misunderstood Elias' intention.

"Of course!" he replied, sitting up in his chair to express his sincerity. "We want to win this war, don't we? If we stage a full-on invasion of our neighbour now, with no warning, the whole world will turn on us."

"Then what do you propose?" Nestor asked, intrigued to examine this new, more rational side of the Grand Seeker. Elias leaned back in his chair once more. Truthfully, he detested the idea of using the international justice system, but he was also no fool. He could see clearly that the Imperium's greatest chance at success came from playing the role of the victim, and they had an airtight case.

"We make our case before the Judges," he stated. Nestor immediately straightened his posture at a suggestion he never once expected to hear come from Elias' mouth. His eyes grew wide in surprise, but he said nothing.

"If we gather the international community and prove to them that we have a just cause for war, we can rally the world to our side and crush the Tinelian's."

"You really think it will be that simple?" Nestor asked. While he harboured great respect and admiration for the international legal frameworks established after the last great war, he knew better than anyone that bureaucracy had a habit of becoming more inefficient the larger it grew.

Elias shrugged his shoulders in response.

"Tinelia's allies will surely try to oppose us and most likely join the war on their side. But if we can convince the Eastern powers that Tinelia is indeed the aggressor, we can roll over them in no more than a year. The best part," Elias said with a grin and hunching his shoulders slightly, "we're not even lying."

Nestor leaned back in his own chair, his hands pressed together beneath his nose as he processed Elias' plan.

"I admit, I did not expect such a, may I say, logical, suggestion to come from you Elias. On this matter at least. I expected to have to fight you at every turn."

Elias smiled foxily at the comment.

"I'm full of surprises, my friend."

"So it would seem," Nestor agreed before offering out his hand to Elias. "I will help you on this. We shall win this war, and we shall win it justly."

Elias took the offer gladly, shaking Nestor's hand to cement their new friendship.

"I knew I could count on you, my Lord," Elias smiled as he rose from his chair and headed for the door. Just as he was about to leave however, he stopped. Holding the door open with one hand he turned back to face Nestor as a gust of cold wind raced through this new breach.

"See if you can't convince his Holiness to abandon this idea of travelling south. No good can come of it," Elias stated, sounding rather more serious than he had done all night. Nestor nodded in response. While The Emperor had not raised the issue at the meeting of the Congregation, it had otherwise been the only topic he would entertain for more than a few moments. With that, Elias left, leaving the tired bureaucrat alone once again in the dying light of his third candle.

The Emperor was another of the few in the palace who could find no solace in sleep that night. While his body begged for it, his mind would not cease its tormenting visions of days past. Days spent with Sarah where all their troubles seemed so far away, so trivial compared to now. Instead, he found himself standing in what had once been a cavern below the palace. Now, however, it was more akin to a great cathedral. The white stone would not be outdone in its brilliance, in the way it shone with its own light despite being so far from the sun.

The Seekers and the palace architects had tried their best though. The once smooth and empty stone floor was now lined with rows of marble pews. A finely carved lectern stood on the raised platform above the pool of sapphire water below. It was here that Elias would stand and deliver his sermons to the gathered congregation. That was the plan at least. This new place of worship would not be opened to the public for another year or so. There was much renovation still to be done. Renovation which would display the true supremacy of their faith.

The Emperor was not interested in the faith of others, however. What the smallfolk needed to feel some small degree of comfort in this unforgiving existence. His connection to the Lord was direct. He did not need faith, for he had proof. Yet this edifice which all men had sought since time immemorial, brought to him no comfort. Instead, it was like a knife in his side, constantly twisting, bringing about new, bitter wounds in his mind and heart.

He had seen paradise and he had seen destruction. He knew he must prevent one to achieve the other. But how? The key was Sarah, and she was gone. She could be further from him now than the most distant reaches of the universe, farther than the mind could comprehend. Worst of all, he did not know where to even begin his search. He had been assured by the greatest minds in the Imperium that his wish was an impossible one. The most capable sorcerers, the most learned and eccentric scientists all said the same thing - the distance was insurmountable. Sarah was gone, she may as well be dead for good.

He would not listen, of course. He did not care how educated these men claimed to be, how many awards and auspicious titles they held. He knew Sarah could be found. And he would be the one to do it. The Lord of Embers was the key, he would be able to find her. The thought had come as The Emperor lay immobile, a prisoner in his own body for those long months after Sarah's death.

Had it been a vision, or just a dream? A product of a damaged mind which knew neither waking nor sleeping? It did not matter. He had seen a great mountain of fire belching black ash into the sky. Rivers of flame, which met a dark sea in a clash of boiling silver steam. Upon those very shores had been a man, great in stature and power. Like a conductor, he bent the elements to his will. Throwing up his arms he summoned great pillars of blinding fire and crashed them against the blanketing darkness of the ocean.

It had ended there, with this violent meeting of opposites, but the meaning had been clear. The Lord of Embers was an enemy, but a powerful one. One that even The Emperor had been unable to subdue. If anyone could offer him insight, point him in the right direction, it would be him. The journey south would be a long and arduous one, however. One which The Emperor's body was still not ready to undergo. He gritted his teeth in frustration at his own weakness, at how much he resembled the men around him - weak, vulnerable, unworthy of the charge bestowed upon him.

He slowly shuffled up the stairs and towards the door in the right palm of the carving which had remained unchanged since his last visit. The Seekers believed this to be a depiction of the Lord himself and would not dare to try to amend it. Not that they could have marked its impeccable surface even had they tried. With a heavy and desperate heart, which already knew the outcome of the events to come, The Emperor attempted to open the door. It did not budge; it was still firmly locked.

With a sad sigh he rested his head against the flawless glass, so clear that one could almost see the sadness draped over him in its reflection. As he was about to return to his chambers, descending the slippery stone steps with trepidation, a sudden urge overcame him. He did not know why, but he turned his attention to the pool beneath the platform. The clear waters lying undisturbed and tranquil. The longer he stared, the stronger the urge became until it was impossible to resist.

Limping over to the pool's edge, The Emperor undressed slowly. Grunting as he struggled with his clothes, which seemed so heavy and cumbersome. At last, after much great effort he stood at the edge of the pool, naked, and breathing heavily from the strain of so much movement. With no small amount of hesitation, The Emperor dipped his foot into the water, expecting it to be painfully cold. He was surprised to find the opposite to be true. The water was quite literally perfect. Not too hot or too cold, but like stepping into the most relaxing bath he had ever experienced.

The moment his legs were fully submerged they felt different, stronger. He no longer limped into the water and took steady, even strides until he stood up to his waist. He now felt like two different people entirely. His lower half felt like that of a young man, strong and capable. His upper body, however, like that of an ancient, withered by time and trial. The Emperor looked down at the water, staring at his own reflection. His eyes were sunken and surrounded by dark rings. His hair seemed thinner, his skin looser and wrecked with wrinkles. He no longer recognised this visage of himself staring back at him.

With a sudden rush of energy and determination, he

plunged into the waters. When he re-emerged a few moments later, he was not the same man as before. He was tall and strong, his body glowed with renewed strength, and he felt new energised life flowing through him. He held out his arms and examined them. The muscles he had lost during his months of inactivity had returned, he flexed them while smiling giddily, unable to believe what was happening. He then turned back to the carving which stared down at him from its lofty position. Still half submerged he bowed until his nose was almost touching the water.

There could be no doubt in his mind now. The Lord himself had spoken, had offered his blessing and support on this endeavour. This was no longer the desperate quest of a grieving husband, but a divinely ordained mission.

The next morning it was hard for the members of the Congregation to disagree after witnessing The Emperor's miraculous recovery. A man who only a day previously had seemed so frail and helpless, now stood as strong and mighty as the day he took his throne. At first, they had fretted that he would reverse his decision regarding the war, but only one purpose filled his mind.

The Emperor immediately set about ordering preparations be made for his journey to meet with the Lord of Embers. Unable to refuse him, the Congregation begrudgingly complied. He would travel with a retinue of one hundred of his Chosen, the greatest warriors the Imperium had to offer. Nestor would join him, at his own request. The others found this a strange decision considering all that remained to be done in preparation for the war, but he was adamant.

Two days later all was prepared. The Emperor stood in the courtyard outside the palace, which still bore scars of its previous, bloody vocation. Before him were gathered one hundred of his Chosen, hand-picked by Phalon, the leader of The Emperor's personal guard and responsible for training and recruiting new Chosen. He was a stout and serious man, as one would expect of the one responsible for The Emperor's safety. In many ways he was like Sir Bryce, although considerably less hot-headed and did not revel in battle. Phalon considered himself to be unlucky in that he had no taste for violence but was nevertheless exceptionally good at it.

It had long ago been a contest between himself and Sir Bryce as candidates to head The Emperor's armies. Sir Bryce only edging ahead because The Emperor had preferred Phalon's sense of humour and attitude. He had therefore appointed Phalon to a position of much greater importance and prestige, which thankfully Sir Bryce did not realise. It had been Phalon who had sparred daily with The Emperor since his ascension, creating the man most considered to be the greatest swordsman who had ever lived.

Now Phalon stood before The Emperor like a proud parent as he inspected the gathered Chosen, passing in front of them, occasionally nodding his approval.

The Chosen were without a doubt, the most well-drilled fighting force in the known world. Even the Imperium's enemies could not deny the fear the mere mention of their name spread amongst their own forces. There were several differences which set them apart from the regular armed forces of the Imperium. Differences which made them instantly recognisable on the battlefield.

Firstly, no women were permitted within their ranks. This had, in some part, been influenced by Elias who had declared women incapable of possessing the physical and spiritual strength for the task of protecting The Emperor. Secondly, all were ordained members of the clergy. Each having to pass a series of rigorous theological written exams before their application would even be considered. This requirement had, surprisingly, not been opposed but rather supported by Phalon. While he had little love for the Seekers, he admitted that a host of fanatically loyal protectors would be far less inclined to stab their imperator in the back.

What truly separated the Chosen, however, other than their extensive and brutal training, was their appearance. The standard uniform for Imperial soldiers was leather overlaid with steel, a spear and shield at their side. This was in line with almost every other modern army and considered the most cost-effective way of equipping a somewhat capable fighting force. The only exception being the desert nomads in the far west across the Shrouded Sea, who preferred loose garbs and sabres.

The Chosen, however, were walking hulks of steel. Every inch of their body covered in thick armour, usually in a variety of bright and vibrant colours. The Chosen had no wish to remain camouflaged, instead desiring to be in the very heart of battle, their valour and splendour on display for all to witness. Indeed, many of those who stood before The Emperor now were adorned in bright red, blue and orange. Although black was also a popular choice and made up about a third of their number.

These men wanted to be seen. To be feared.

At their sides, whatever they felt was best suited to inflict death on an apocalyptic scale. Most carried swords finely decorated but in no way ornamental. Others carried axes, maces and half a dozen other instruments of pain which would not be found in any other army. The Emperor could not help but grin beneath his mask at the clear zealotry of an individual a few rows back. At his side he held a scythe taller than himself, a vision of death itself.

"You've selected well, my friend. These are fine men you've brought me," The Emperor said cheerily so as to give his men an early morale boost.

"I would offer you nothing less, sir," Phalon responded. Phalon also enjoyed the unique privilege of being allowed to address The Emperor as anything other than *'Your Holiness'*. Something that irked Elias greatly, although only out of jealousy.

As The Emperor completed his inspection he was approached by the Master of Horse. Following closely behind him, the most beautiful animal any of those gathered had ever seen. A jet-black stallion with eyes like rubies and a mane of silk. A gift from the late Empress many years ago. Legacy. A fitting name, The Emperor had always thought. The creature approached The Emperor with a friendliness reserved only for its master. No other, not even the Master of Horse himself, could command the beast. Its will was its own, and to this day only The Emperor had earned its respect.

Legacy was, however, only one half of a pair. His mate, Tempest, had been the Empress' horse. A mare whose purity was matched only by its rider. As white as milk and with the temperament of a saint, she was the polar opposite of her companion. Yet the two would rarely leave one another's side and had borne many beautiful children, often given as gifts to the rich and powerful.

The Empress had always maintained that the horses had come to her in a dream. She had seen two clouds racing across the sky on a clear day. One white and aloof, the other dark and foreboding. Upon her waking she had found a storm raging outside, and for reasons unknown even to her, had travelled barefoot into the palace gardens. Whipped ragged by the wind and lashed by rain she had heard a crying. The source of which had been these two creatures, seemingly materialising out of thin air as the gardens were surrounded by high stone walls.

Back then even Elias had been more than happy to declare this a miracle. A gift from the Lord which further cemented The Emperor's divine right to rule. That had been a happy time. A time when The Emperor and Empress would ride madly through the countryside, laughing as they took turns besting one another in their races. Things were different now. Since Sarah's death, Tempest had refused to leave her stable. She would spend the days pacing back and forth, her head swaying as she cried out for her master who would never come.

This mournfulness had seemingly passed in some part to Legacy also. While he approached The Emperor, he was uncharacteristically skittish, pulling back slightly as The Emperor reached out to stroke him. The Emperor acknowledged this with a sad dip of his head as he took the reins.

"I know, boy," he whispered, resting his head against his dark companion. As The Emperor climbed into the saddle, Phalon and Nestor followed suit. The Chosen would travel on foot, led by Phalon they would flank The Emperor on all sides. The journey would be long, and no chances would be taken that would compromise The Emperor's safety. As final checks were completed, Nestor came up beside The Emperor and spoke, hoping to convince him to abandon this folly before it began.

"Are you sure about this, Your Holiness? The Lord of Embers is not likely to want to help us, even at the best of times."

The Emperor replied sternly. "He will help us. Or he will spend the rest of eternity trapped in that fiery hell." With that, Phalon gave the signal and the heavily armoured column began to move.

Chapter 6

Nate and Cassandra could not help but feel on edge as they traversed the dark, winding path ahead of them. Nate was certain it had looked far straighter on the map, but that did nothing for him now.

"Fuck's sake," Nate cursed quietly as he tripped over a hidden branch which extended over his part of the road. It was not quiet enough for Cassandra, however, who immediately shushed him.

"Your shushing is louder than my swearing," Nate retorted. All he got for his efforts was another aggressive shush. Despite having backtracked for over an hour and then followed this diverging path, the pair could still hear the distant commotion they had sought to avoid. Risking exposure, Cassandra stopped and ordered Nate to produce a dim ball of light. Glad for a moment of rest, however brief, Nate obliged. The small orb he produced was no brighter than a candle, but in a dark forest they may as well have rung a dinner bell.

Cassandra used this time to re-examine her map, getting frustrated as she tried to locate the path they were on. Then getting even more frustrated after Nate pointed it out.

"It'll be another two nights before we reach anywhere even remotely habitable," Cassandra whispered. "No point carrying on anymore, let's find somewhere to rest," she concluded much to Nate's relief. The pair exited the road and carefully navigated the dense vegetation which flanked them on all sides.

It took a few minutes of fumbling around in the dark, but they managed to find a small modicum of shelter in the form of a large, jagged rock formation. Placing their bedrolls behind two said rocks, the pair prepared to rest at last. Despite their overbearing exhaustion, neither could force themselves into sleep. The constant pumping of adrenaline and stress of the day had yet to wear off. Instead, Nate lay in his bedroll staring up at the starry sky, chewing on some dried mystery meat while Cassandra did something similar.

They really should have set up a watch, but ultimately decided against it due to them both being on the verge of collapse. Ardell would have been furious to see them sleeping out in the open without so much as a keen eye to protect them. But Ardell wasn't here, and what Captain Ardell didn't know was probably a danger to everyone involved. Nevertheless, the hours began to tick by, and sleep welcomed them into its embrace like an old friend at last.

For so long had the pair tried to avoid the battle between the refugees that not much of night remained when they finally settled down. It was not long before the first creeping rays of day began to crawl over their rocky cover, illuminating the two sleeping travellers. Nate was the first to wake, reluctantly forcing his eyes open after feeling the warm sun upon his eyelids. He lay still for a moment, staring up at the brightening sky wondering if he could sneak a few more hours.

He rolled over to see if Cassandra was already awake and if his plan could be put into action. Thankfully, just a few meters away, Cassandra remained inanimate, wrapped in her bedroll and blankets. Nate smiled to himself as he relished the thought of the sleep to come and began to turn back over, out of the light. But then something caught his eye. Something he had not seen the previous night.

Slightly ahead of him, visible just over the tip of a nearby rock, was what appeared to be a giant mushroom. It was a deep crimson red, dotted with bright white spots, and seemed to shiver slightly in the wind. Interested but not concerned, Nate once again prepared to roll over before spotting two more mushrooms separated from Cassandra only by the rock which she slept under. Except these two were green, dripping with some sickly brown mucus, also shivering.

Judging by the distance and size of the surrounding rocks, Nate guessed that these mushrooms must be at least as tall as him, if not slightly smaller. Now thinking only with his empty stomach, Nate licked his lips at the novelty of a freshly foraged breakfast. Having skimmed over the foraging section of the army's survival textbook, Nate was confident they would be safe to eat. Well, maybe not confident, but he had a fifty-fifty chance of being right.

Crawling from under his rock, a small knife in hand, Nate approached the red and white mushroom. As he placed his foot on the rock separating him from his breakfast, he could not help but notice that there was not so much as a breath of wind. Yet the mushroom continued to shiver even more vigorously than before. Upon mounting the rock and looking down at his prey, Nate froze in shock, his knife clattering against the stone as he dropped it.

This mushroom, or what he had assumed was a mushroom, had a face. It was little more than a collection of vertical slits arranged in parallel lines of varying elevations, but it was recognisable. Not only that, but it also had two spindly arms that sprouted from its thin white stalk. Arms which ended in vicious, spear-like points. Arms that were soon aimed at Nate. He gasped as the first blow landed, sending him flying backwards from his perch, crashing hard into the rocky ground below. Luckily for him, the blow had not come from the tip of the monster's appendages but rather its forearm. Otherwise, Nate would have found himself sucking air through his chest.

"What the hell are you doing now?!" Cassandra fumed, furious that her brief rest had been disturbed. When no answer came, she rolled over to see Nate crumpled on the ground, struggling to breathe after having had the wind knocked out of him.

"What the-?" she gasped before she was cut short. Flanking from either side came two green and mucus covered giant mushrooms, their uncanny faces arranged in what looked a lot like murderous rage. She rolled back against the rocks as these two struck out with pincered limbs, their two points dripping with sticky, foul smelling slime.

By now Nate had recovered and managed to retrieve his sword. Coming from behind he plunged his blade deep into the back of one of the green monsters.

The creature barely noticed, showing no indication it was even aware it had been impaled, save from quickly bringing its arm out and catching Nate in the face. Stumbling back with a bloody lip, Nate was quickly set upon by his original opponent who dived down at him from a rocky peak. His actions, while inconsequential, did provide Cassandra enough time to untangle herself from her bedroll and retrieve her spear.

She struck out, the tip of her spear piercing through one of the many slits she assumed were eyes, causing the creature to stumble back. Although this was only a momentary reprieve as they came at her again, the monster's arms swinging like motor blades. Now locked in a battle with a foe of extraordinary strength that didn't mind being stabbed, Nate was unsure what to do. He swung his sword without any real plan, just hoping he would get lucky. And for a moment, he thought he had.

Ducking under a striking arm, Nate sprung back up and put all his strength into a blow aimed at where the creature's elbow should be. The arm came free from the body with unexpected ease, like it was made of, well, mushroom.

"Ah ha!" Nate cried in triumph as the creature fell back. His glee was short lived, however. Within moments, and while Nate watched on in stunned horror, the creature's arm quickly regrew. Thin, fluffy veins sprouting from its stump before turning thick, filling out the space its arm had previously taken. In only a few short seconds, the creature had done what would take a sorcerer many hours, or even days. What made the situation even worse, fascinating nonetheless but still noticeably problematic, was that its new arm had taken a different form. No longer was it a thin, sharp blade. Now it was wide and thick, the end being a hardened club with the consistency of tree bark.

"Shit," Nate said as the creature swung at him again, missing by mere inches and instead pulverising a nearby rock into dust.

"What do we do!?" Nate shouted to Cassandra over the shrill cries of the creatures which assaulted his ears like nails down a chalkboard. Cassandra was too busy with her own problems to answer Nate's question. Each successful strike from her spear was repaired almost instantaneously, the creatures not deterred at all by pain. That is, if they could even feel pain. She had managed to reach the relative safety of a small peak and was stabbing down at her assailants with little to no effect. In contrast, Nate was forced to throw himself around like a ragdoll, although between the sharp rocks and wrecking ball like force of the creature's fist, he knew which he preferred.

As the fight dragged on with no conclusion in sight, Nate and Cassandra began to tire. As their weariness fought against them like yet another foe, they began to make mistakes. Cassandra had lost her footing and caught the tip of her assailant's blow. The creature's pincer tore through her calf, forcing her to stumble back with a cry of pain as the blood began to flow. This only caused her to lose her footing more seriously, and this time tumbled down from her relatively safe position. Crashing into and rolling over dozens of sharp, protruding rocks in her descent, she hit the ground with a violent crash as her bronze armour rang against the stone around her.

Seeing Cassandra fall, Nate became suddenly filled with a fresh boost of adrenaline. Lashing out with his left arm he hit his opponent with a blast of telekinetic force, casting the creature against the rocks with a mighty crash. Fragments of stone and dust rained down around them. The creature at last seemed to be still, its torso bent inwards from the force of the spell. Not surprisingly, once again it was only moments before the creature had righted itself, its body returning to its previous, undamaged state.

In his left ear Nate heard Cassandra cry out in fresh pain. One of the creatures stood over her, pushing its blood-soaked pincer against her stomach. Cassandra gripped the pincer with both hands, abandoning her weapon, pushing back with all her remaining strength. It was not enough however. Slowly the creature was gaining ground. It was not long before the point of its claw had broken through Cassandra's armour like it were made of dried leaves. Cassandra groaned in pain through gritted, bloody teeth as the claw slowly entered her body.

Knowing he did not have much time, Nate needed to end this fight now. But how? As he dodged yet another attack, a sudden thought came to him.

'They're just fucking plants'; he thought as a lightbulb lit up in his brain. Holding out his left hand again, Nate launched a fresh spell, one that would this time surely turn the tide. From his palm erupted a column of flame that engulfed his opponent. The screeching, which had earlier been painful, was now unbearable as the monster went up in flames. They could feel pain after all.

"Grow your way out of that," Nate smirked triumphantly as he turned around just in time to catch a pincer to the hip. The blow had luckily not broken anything or cut very deep, but the force threw him hard in the opposite direction of Cassandra, who was now crying out for all she was worth. She was still on the ground, the tip of the monster's claw now roughly three inches into her body. She still pushed back, but her strength was rapidly failing as blood poured from the wound and began rising in her throat.

Help was close at hand, however. Recovering from the surprise attack, Nate turned to face his new opponent. This time, there was no intense duel. Instead, he launched a fireball which struck its target dead centre, blasting it into smouldering pieces. Rushing over to where Cassandra lay, still struggling despite her injuries, Nate first used telekinesis to rip the creature away before immolating it at a safe distance. Its piercing shrieks quickly dying away into silence.

There was no time to celebrate their victory, as Nate rushed to Cassandra's side. There was now a substantial bloody pool beneath them. Her armour, once immaculately polished, was now torn and slippery with blood. Cassandra could not speak, each word coming out as nothing more than a choking bubble of blood and froth as she went into shock.

"Shit," Nate panicked as he gently cradled her head in his right hand and tried to summon a healing spell with his left. It took a few panicked, stressful seconds before the spell took hold. Seconds filled with the sickening sounds of Cassandra drowning in her own blood, scratching against the stony floor as she went into a series of fits. Despite the emotions swirling around Nate's heart, fear and guilt, quickly spiralling into hopelessness, the spell did its work.

Cassandra's wounds sealed themselves, the blood no longer pouring between Nate's fingers. Her breaths went from struggled gurgles to normal, albeit shallow and laboured. Tentatively removing his hand Nate could see that he had done it, he had saved her. Where a gaping wound had once been was now nothing but smooth, soft skin which trembled with each frantic heartbeat. Gently, Nate shifted so that Cassandra's head was resting in his lap. She had passed out, and Nate didn't blame her. He positioned himself against the nearest rock, trying his best not to disturb his companion and shut his eyes for a moment, relieved the madness was over.

A few hours later Nate awoke once again, this time thankfully with no murderous mushrooms in sight. He looked down expecting to see Cassandra still unconscious, but she had moved from his lap and now struggled a few meters away, trying to pull her backpack across her shoulders.

"What are you doing?" Nate gasped, "You should be resting."

"We need to keep moving," Cassandra grunted, doubling over as the backpack's weight pressed upon where her injury had been. Her body may have been healed, but the mind was not so easily convinced. It would be a few days before she felt truly recovered. Nevertheless, she was adamant they get moving again.

"Let's just give it another day," Nate pleaded. Not for himself, but for the sake of his companion who would be nothing more than a liability travelling in such a state. Cassandra turned to him at last, still bearing the colours of their battle. Her chin and neck were a deep crimson, her hair and back of her legs the same, from where she had lain in her own blood.

She shook her head slowly, holding onto the nearest rock for support.

"The blood will attract monsters, the smoke, people. We need to get out of here," she explained. Nate cursed her logic, but she was right. He packed up his own belongings before attempting to offer Cassandra his body to lean on. He tried placing her arm over his shoulders to take some of her weight and make moving easier, but she pushed him away. Confused, Nate was about to scold her for being stubborn before Cassandra beat him to it.

"One of us needs to be on guard, just give me some time," she whispered through the lingering pain in her stomach. Nate gritted his teeth but once again admitted Cassandra was right. He drew his sword and led his injured companion back towards the road, keeping close in case she suddenly needed his support.

"You're right," Nate said just as they cleared the rocky area and were once again surrounded by trees.

"About what?" Cassandra asked as she stumbled between the overgrown and cluttered forest floor, surprised Nate would ever make such an admission.

Nate lifted his head and took a long sniff.

"It smells bloody delicious round here."

Cassandra didn't dare laugh; she didn't want to give him the satisfaction and so grunted as they made their way back onto the road at last. What followed was without a doubt the most frustrating and exhausting journey either of them had ever undertaken. Cassandra could only walk almost entirely doubled over, and then only for a few dozen meters at a time before needing to stop. As a result, they kept to the edge of the road where Cassandra could more easily rest against a tree when she became tired. Nate on the other hand was stressed out of his mind, trying to keep one eye on his companion while simultaneously watching out for danger.

They managed to make it just over two miles before Cassandra could not physically continue. Much further than Nate had expected when they began earlier. However, she had increasingly grown on Nate's nerves and was testing the limits of his patience by the time they set down that evening. Every time he had offered to help carry her pack, or even asked how she felt, she had become gradually more aggressive. What had started as a snarky comment or silence in response to Nate's concern had turned into outright insults and nastiness.

Nate understood she was still in pain, but he had thought maybe she would show even the slightest hint of gratitude to the person who had saved her life. To make matters worse, Nate was dealing with a horrendous migraine. The inside of his skull feeling like a rumbling storm deep out to sea, a world away from any source of relief. A reward for his strenuous magic use. It was cruel, he thought, that such a life-saving tool extracted such a painful price. Like a surgeon being expected to slam their head against a wall after each surgery. Nevertheless, there was nothing Nate could do about it now, and he moved on, trying his best to ignore the pain.

That night turned out not to be as bad as either of them had expected. Neither were in serious amounts of pain anymore and Cassandra now found herself able to stand without doubling over. Even so, they took things slowly. Ever the gentleman, Nate allowed Cassandra to eat first while he went on watch. However, as he set himself down on a grassy verge there was a sudden shout from behind.

"Shit!" Cassandra cried. Nate instinctively rushed back, his hand on the hilt of his sword. Thankfully, there seemed to be no monsters in sight and Nate allowed himself to relax slightly. Instead, he focused on Cassandra, her face showing a look of horror and panic. In her hands, her food pack.

"What's wrong?" Nate asked as he continued to quickly scan the forest around them. Cassandra did not say a word, instead, extending her arm for Nate to examine her pack. Peering over the rim Nate noticed what looked like mouldy green shoots. At first thinking it to be nothing more than Cassandra's food having gone off, he quickly recoiled as the realisation hit him. Mushrooms. Every single piece of food in Cassandra's pack had sprouted thick, white mould. From the furry base sprouted thick green stalks topped with wide green heads and dripping with brown mucus.

He instantly rushed over to his own pack and fell back, coughing violently as opening it released an explosive cloud of spores. He too had not been spared. Covering his mouth with one hand and using the other to turn the pack upside down, he watched in horror as he realised nothing could be salvaged.

"What do we do?" He asked exasperated, looking to Cassandra for guidance as his stomach cried out in anguish.

"Starve," was her response, kicking her pack which flew into the dark thicket and out of sight. A rather less helpful solution than Nate would have liked at this present moment. After some quick foraging, Nate was able to find a decent haul of berries which he proudly presented to his companion. It was not much, but it was still better than nothing. After Cassandra removed those which would have certainly killed them, they were left with only half a dozen each. Only a few of which would cause them to shit themselves into next week if they were overripe. Both scowled at their meagre meal before eating them all at once.

"I'll take first watch," Cassandra grumbled. Her stomach causing her renewed grief again, the addition of hunger an unwelcome burden.

"You sure?" Nate asked. Truthfully, he desperately wanted to sleep after the day's exhausting events. However, he felt guilty at denying Cassandra the rest which she so surely needed. Not answering, Cassandra positioned herself with her back against a mound of raised earth which offered a decent view of their rather sad looking camp. While at first wrestling with his inner decency, considering demanding that Cassandra gets some rest, Nate's inner scumbag prevailed. Laying his bedroll down within a pair of thick arching roots, Nate at last shut his eyes after what had felt like a week without so much as a breather.

Nate awoke suddenly from nightmares filled with blood, screaming and the sound of tearing flesh. These dreams had been a regular occurrence since his time in the wailing pits, and yet they were only growing more vivid with time, not diminishing. Aching and tired, he pulled himself into a sitting position and surveyed the camp. Cassandra was leaning against the same mound of earth not too far away, her back to him. He checked his watch, it would be his turn to take over soon, so he decided to grant Cassandra an extra hour of sleep by taking his shift early. There was no point in trying to go back to sleep now anyway, the nightmares always came back worse if he tried.

He approached Cassandra from the side and noticed that she had dozed off. Such a thing was an extremely dangerous mistake to make, easily earning her a whipping had they been in the army. Watching her Nate felt only empathy, it had been a more tiring journey than they had expected and he could not fault her for needing rest. He just wished Cassandra's stubbornness had allowed her to surrender the first watch.

"Cassandra," he called softly, hoping to gently ease her out of sleep. After all, he knew how unpleasant it was to be suddenly awoken against your wishes. She would not rouse, however, and so Nate gently shook her shoulder, calling out her name once more. Cassandra's eyes immediately shot open at his touch, she leapt to her feet, swatting Nate's hand away as if it had been a snake.

"Don't fucking touch me," she fumed, her fists balled at

her side. Nate was taken aback at this unwarranted aggression and responded equally as harshly.

"What the fuck is your problem?" he growled, able to feel his blood pressure rising and a stinging heat on his neck.

"You're my problem, you little creep," Cassandra spat, coming closer and jabbing Nate in the chest with her finger. "Keep your disgusting little paws to yourself," she added.

"You were asleep, on watch," Nate replied, his teeth barred. He could not believe this reaction when Cassandra was in the wrong. Cassandra, unable to wrest control of her emotions, pushed past Nate.

"Gods only know what you put your poor roommate through," she spat venomously.

Unable to let such a comment slide, Nate roughly grabbed hold of Cassandra's bicep as she tried to move past. "What the hell does that mean?" He spat furiously.

Cassandra was not listening and just stared back at Nate with burning anger, her face clearly communicating disbelief that Nate's hand was on her arm.

"Let go!" she growled.

Nate too refused to listen and questioned Cassandra further. "Why are you such a bitch all the time?" He was genuinely curious.

Cassandra didn't answer and instead pushed Nate away with her other hand, freeing her from his grip.

Nate wasn't sure why he struck her. Perhaps it was the lack of sleep, perhaps hunger, or maybe just being fed up with people being rude to him without cause. Probably a mixture of all three. Regardless of the reason, as Cassandra freed herself, he followed up by slapping her hard across the face.

Cassandra stumbled back in shock, clutching her stinging jaw and cheek. Nate was immediately overcome with guilt and tried to apologise. This attempt was abruptly halted as Cassandra reached for her sword.

"Stop!" was all Nate had time to say before Cassandra was swinging her blade at him with unchecked fury. Dodging and diving to the floor, Nate retrieved his own weapon and the two crossed blades in anger for the first time. The pair panted heavily as they stared at one another through the gap between their swords. Neither said anything, training and instinct had instead kicked in, overcoming any logic or sense of fellowship.

Pushing his opponent off, Nate followed up with blows aimed at Cassandra's hands and legs, hoping to incapacitate rather than kill. Cassandra, however, had no such strategy. Aiming instead for Nate's most vital regions, almost felling a tree with one swing as she narrowly missed his head. The two fought for many minutes, spreading carnage across their camp as they trampled over bedrolls and the remnants of the fire. Neither seemed ready to give up. Nate for fear of his life, Cassandra out of animalistic rage.

If Nate had the time to think about it, he would have been impressed at his form thus far. The last time the two came to blows Cassandra had literally wiped the floor with him. Now, his countless gruelling training sessions were proving their worth. With a deft swipe Nate was able to catch the cross guard of Cassandra's sword and fling it from her grip. Assuming the fight to be won, he relaxed. It was only by a fraction, but it was enough for Cassandra to capitalise on. She rushed forward, taking hold of Nate's breastplate with both hands and rammed him into a tree.

As she felt the point of Nate's sword in her ribs, she was forced to accept defeat. She did not release her victorious opponent though. Instead, she remained in place, her hands still gripped tightly around his armour, pressing him into the sharp bark.

"You want to know why I'm this way?" she asked, moving her face closer to Nate so that he could hear her words which were now barely a whisper. Nate did not answer, too confused by the sudden change in situation and wisely remained silent.

"I was eighteen when I was murdered," Cassandra whispered, her eyes becoming wet and her voice already beginning to croak. "I had a husband and two beautiful children," she sniffed, tears now freely flowing down her still red and stinging cheek.

"My husband was a merchant, but more than anything he was a good man, a good father. But of course, his success offended the egos of lesser men." Cassandra sniffed again as a fresh teardrop fell from her cheek onto the point of Nate's blade, still pressing against her ribs.

"One day while he was away, some such men came to our home. They claimed my husband was putting them out of business and demanded payment." Still Cassandra did not loosen her grip as she recounted her sad tale, staring deep into Nate's eyes, her own unblinking and filled with madness.

"I begged them to leave, stating that we had no money, that my husband would pay them on his return. Of course, they had no interest in money, they wanted an altogether different payment," she said, pressing Nate even harder into the tree, her face inching closer, her lips quivering. "They made me watch as they shattered my son's head beneath their boots. He was such a good boy, always smiling and laughing. But now," she said through gritted teeth, "Now whenever I try to remember his laugh, all I hear is theirs as his blood painted the floor of our home."

Nate could not speak, nor could he any longer feel the bark cutting into the back of his neck and scalp. Never could he have imagined the horrors that lay behind Cassandra's bright eyes, and yet she was still not finished. Every few words were now followed by stifled sobs as she tried to finish her tale, despite the physical pain it caused her. Pain worse than the bite of any blade.

"Then my baby girl," she whined as Nate watched her eyes focus away from him, and back to these horrific memories. "My baby girl, they smashed her against the wall. Taking turns as if it were a sport," she raged through barred teeth, bubbles of spit forming in the corners of her mouth. Never had Nate seen something so beautiful be warped into something of such repulsiveness. It terrified him.

"Then it was my turn," she sobbed, her grip tightening

into something superhuman. Her eyes focused back on Nate now. She wanted him to see what she carried in her mind every moment of every day, for the rest of eternity.

"They beat me and raped me, until I knew nothing of the passing of time. Until one day was like a thousand. Until I could think not of the faces of my own children, but only of the pain. Of the endless violation of my body until nothing else remained. Even as I bled to death they continued, and I remember my last thought as the darkness came for me was one of thanks. Thanks, that the pain was finally at an end." There was a brief pause as Cassandra looked away from Nate and shook her head, sniffing loudly before turning back to him, speaking slowly and clearly, her anger palpable through the still flowing tears.

"Do you know what it feels like to have someone force themselves upon you?" She asked rhetorically, pressing her right hand hard into Nate's groin so that a sharp, stabbing pain quickly raced up through his body, causing him instinctively to try and pull away, such escaped blocked by the tree behind him. Cassandra kept her hand in place, despite the growing sharpness of Nate's sword in her side. "Do you know what it's like to have all that you are reduced to an object, to something of such little value that your screams of pain and pleas of mercy are worth nothing but laughter?"

"I was a good wife, a good mother who loved her children more than anything." She inched closer so that their noses were almost touching. Nate barely dared to breathe, the heat of Cassandra's hate radiating from her so fiercely that he was sweating. With trembling, furious words Cassandra whispered. "I. Shouldn't. Fucking. Be here."

At last she released Nate from her grip and stumbled back before falling to the forest floor sobbing. Before Nate could react, Cassandra put her forearm to her lips and bit down as hard as she could. Nate watched in horror as bright red blood began to flow, filling Cassandra's mouth and dripping onto the ground. This was how she dealt with her memories, new pain to block out the old. Instinctively, Nate crouched down and reached out a consoling hand. Sense took over and he quickly withdrew it before making contact.

Instead, he remained there, still and silent, listening to the sound of his companion's heart wrenching crying. As it happened, that was the best thing he could have done. Once Cassandra had released her emotions, she silently held out her arm. She looked away from Nate who immediately understood and gently healed her, keeping his hand hovering over her flesh rather than touching it.

"Cassandra, I…" he began before he was cut off.

"I don't need your sympathy," she said rather calmly, all things considered. She looked back at Nate, her eyes still red but the tears at long last dried up.

"Let's just get this mission over with. Then we never have to see each other again." At first, this sounded like a great deal, but Nate could not shake the images Cassandra had planted in his mind. She may be a bitch, but she had a hell of a good reason to be and he could not hold it against her. Even if it had culminated in her trying to kill him.

"You sure? I felt we were just starting to become friends," Nate grinned reassuringly. Cassandra looked at him confused.

"You mean you don't want to bash my brains in?"

"I wouldn't go that far," Nate scoffed jokily. "But that's pretty standard for friends, in my experience." He looked up at the still dark sky and then at his watch.

"You'd better be off to bed. Having your arse handed to you can be tiring. Believe me, I know."

Cassandra could not help but smile thinly at Nate's moving on from the events of the last few minutes so casually. He was a lot of things. An idiot mostly, but perhaps he was not all bad. As she slithered into her bedroll, she looked up into the night sky and could not help but think the same thought she always did. Her children may not be here in Purgatory, but maybe, just maybe, her husband was. She would give anything to see him again. Anything.

Chapter 7

The journey from the Imperial City to its vassal state on the southern coast was a long and unpleasant one, taking some weeks. Situated on a peninsula, which took up almost the entire Imperial coastline, Ifritus was an inhospitable wasteland of molten rock and noxious fumes belched from the depths of the world. While an excellent natural barrier with Tinelia, it was not the sort of place one would expect to find a soul, let alone an entire society. Yet this was the beating industrial heart of the Imperium.

From a craggy overlook The Emperor and his retinue examined the land below. Nothing grew here. Black ash suffocated the landscape to the horizon and beyond. The sky choked by the endless spewing of debris from the land's dozens of active volcanoes. This shadow, which hung over the world, was only occasionally illuminated by flashes of jagged, furious lightning that wrestled within the ascending pillars of black death. It was not the sort of place one would visit without the upmost need.

Ahead of the party stood Vendaag, the largest volcano in the known world. Its endless roaring shaking the ground like the Devil trying to break free from the depths of hell. This is where they would find the Lord of Embers. As they descended from their overlook towards the fiery mountain, they came upon the capital of their client state. This city had no name. Such monikers were trivial excesses which the people of this land had no time for. Indeed, many of them did not even bother with names of their own. It was not names which mattered, but the quality of their steel.

The city had been built over the great rivers of lava which ran down Vendaag's slopes. Made of a resilient stone, the hundreds of buildings stood many meters above the banks of these fiery rivers which met the ocean in a clash of boiling steam. The Emperor and his followers were received by no one as they stepped foot within the city. This lack of fanfare irked Nestor greatly. Did these people not know their conquerors when they saw them? As a result of this diplomatic slight, the visitors had to navigate the many treacherous walkways and bridges which hung over the ravenous, flowing fire alone.

It was by these thousands of deployable bridges that allowed the people to traverse safely throughout the city. Operated via a simple crank handle, anyone could raise, adjust, and move said bridges to reach different areas. The Emperor and his men, however, found the task both arduous and tedious as they were forced to repeat it dozens of times before they were within reach of their destination. While never once having been interested in visiting until now, Nestor found Ifritus a fascinating place due to the structure of both its politics and economy.

As agriculture was impossible, all the land's food was delivered via lengthy caravans which the royal party had avoided on their own journey. The endless ash clouds and boiling waters making travel by any sort of ship an impossibility. A fact which many of the party had bemoaned before setting out. Long ago it had been believed that these lands were in fact the most fertile of all. The failure to grow even a single crop to this day, had dashed the hopes of many in a food basket for the empire. Even the water, scarce as it was, required extensive treating before being safe enough to drink. As a result, there was a dedicated detachment of sorcerers stationed here to ensure the water never ran dry or foul.

With almost all other vocations rendered impossible by the terrain, nearly everyone in Ifritus was some form of metal worker. Every home had its own smithy, and it was from the ever-flowing inferno beneath their feet that came the materials of their craft. Coughed from their deadly mountains came masses of rock and minerals. Flowing down the burning orange streams like demonic vessels, they ranged in sizes from that of a fist, to small mountains of their own. Using rudimentary cranes or even fire-resistant buckets, the people would haul these worldly foundations into their workshops to be broken down and made into something greater.

Here, an individual's wealth was not counted in gold or land, but in the quality of their work. Those who produced anything considered below the Ifriti standard would find themselves residing near the sea, at the bottom of the mountain's slopes. Those who were true masters of their craft, would find themselves closer to the source of these volcanic veins. From here they would have privileged access to new materials, allowing only the dregs to trickle below.

The Emperor and the rest of his retinue, however, could not have cared less for this unique socio-economic structure as they struggled through the city. The ferocious heat attacked them on all sides, their heavy armour and cloaks in no way appropriate for such conditions. Many of the locals went about in nothing at all, while others preserved their dignity with sweat-soaked and soot-stained loincloths. Nevertheless, they soldiered on until they stood at the base of Vendaag itself. Doubled over from the heat, many at risk of collapse as they were on the verge of being cooked alive within their own armour, which encasement acted like ovens.

Situated near the summit of the mountain was a door, which led to the Lord of Embers' own forge. The same place The Emperor had trapped him nearly a thousand years ago. It was unlikely to be a happy reunion, but nonetheless a necessary one. Thankfully, there was an alternative to the tens of thousands of stairs which lined the path to the great forge. An old and worn steam-powered carriage carried The Emperor and a select few of his men to the top in only a few minutes.

As the six men ascended the mountainside they looked out at the surrounding country. If one could call it that. No matter how high they climbed the scene never changed. Nothing but a dead and cursed land in which man was never meant to dwell. Nature had done all within its power to keep life from this place. But even this had not been enough to stifle man's greed. Nothing good had ever come of this place and many assumed never would. The Emperor prayed that maybe this black and wicked place could redeem itself.

As they departed the rickety contraption, which at any moment felt that it may fall apart, the door to the heart of the mountain was visible. It was open, and through it little could be seen. Only an orange glow was barely visible, muted by the wall of ash and smoke before it. The Emperor took a moment to compose himself. It had been a long time since he had stood here as an invader. Now he came to his old enemy in search of aid only he could give. He hoped with all his heart that the years had mellowed the old bastard out.

Nestor too was visibly nervous. Having removed his signature green robe, he now stood in only a white undershirt and brown trousers. Not for a few seconds had his shirt been exposed to the thick, polluted air before it had become irrevocably grey. Sweating profusely, he wiped his face with the back of his hand. The Lord of Embers had once been the greatest threat to the Imperium. That had been when he was still a free man, not confined to this blazing prison. He'd had over one thousand years to stew in his hatred and all Nestor could do was pray that the spell still held.

Bracing against the rushing wind, which buffeted them from the forge's entrance, The Emperor and his retinue made their way forwards. Into the very heart of Vendaag, the very last place in the world they would be welcome. Holding out his hand to shield his face from the wall of burning ash which separated him from the volcano's interior, The Emperor passed through and found himself faced with a familiar sight.

The forge was a large, circular construction which took up most of the chamber. A wide ring of magma encircled the room save for where The Emperor stood, the only entrance or exit. Within was all that one would expect. Hundreds of tools for every vocation within the realm of metallurgy. A crane, much like those used by those city-dwellers below, and finally, the magmatic wellspring. A circular hole cut into the very centre of the island upon which the forge sat, from which the Lord of Embers would pull forth the most exquisite ores Gaia could offer. From this origin flowed the dozen molten rivers which spilled from breaches in the mountainside. The very lifeblood of the city below endlessly pumped by its raging heart.

The more unexpected details of the forge included a four-poster bed, large stone bath, and a stone bookshelf, upon which many blackened and scorched tomes and almanacs lay. None of these conveniences had been present at The Emperor's last visit.

The final element, which made this mountain the prison it had become, was the shimmering barrier which encircled the room, halting just inches from where The Emperor stood. Created in a last, desperate attempt to save himself from the Lord of Ember's killing blow. It had stood the test of time it seemed, being as strong as the day it had been created. For all his ingenuity, the trapped Lord had not yet found a way to break the spell confining him to this vision of hell.

The Lord himself was stood with his back to the entrance, hammering away at some new project. He was naked, as one could expect from someone perpetually trapped in a volcano. His monstrous muscles glistening with sweat as he brought down the hammer with great force again and again. Sparks flew in every direction and the chamber itself shook with each new blow. With one final swing, the Lord was done. Wiping his brow with a cloth which he then wrapped around his waist, he turned to greet the company he had sensed entered.

A monster of a man, the Lord of Embers sauntered over to meet his uninvited and unwelcome guests. With the bearing of a god and hair as orange and wild as the molten fire which surrounded him, the self-proclaimed world-smith would strike fear into even the most gallant of heroes. The Emperor, however, was not afraid. It had been a long time since their duel amidst the smoke and flame of Vendaag's heart, and he was stronger now. Stronger than the arrogant Lord before him could ever dare to imagine.

He was, however, taken aback by the Lord's appearance. He was not at all as The Emperor remembered him. He still carried that wild, unhinged look in his eyes. However, it was his body that was different. As he neared, finally standing but a few inches away and separated only by the magical barrier, The Emperor saw the Lord's upper body was riddled with hundreds of gemstones. Each was a different size and shape from the last, fused into his flesh which had grown around them. The Lord noticed The Emperor's stare and laughed, a deep, bellowing laugh which mimicked the ceaseless roar of his prison.

"Admiring my handiwork?" he asked, never becoming bored by the reactions of those who could never possibly fathom his skill or genius. The Emperor said nothing. Instead, the Lord extended his arm, pointing to the gems which protruded from it with glee. "Each stone is infused with a spell, each allowing me to reach new heights in my craft, each bringing me closer to godhood."

"Well, it's nice to have a hobby," The Emperor replied flippantly. He cared not for the Lord's boasting, even the slightest hint of respect or admiration would only further inflate his already overstretched ego and make getting anything out of him even more arduous. The Lord's lips curled into a snarl at the refusal by this man to recognise his greatness, a man who had only defeated him through dishonour and trickery.

Nevertheless, he curtailed the viciousness of his reaction. There was no sense in losing his temper now, not when liberation was so tantalisingly close.

"Come then, reverse your work and be off. I have no wish to spend my first moments of freedom in your presence," the Lord demanded. The Emperor, however, raised an eyebrow beneath his mask.

"I have not travelled all this way to release you. As I recall you have yet to fulfil your end of our deal," The Emperor replied. The Lord's eyes grew wide, his chest puffing out and his muscles tensing in rage. He could not control himself any longer. He knew The Emperor would try to weasel his way out of their deal from the moment it had been agreed.

"Do not try to trick me boy!" the Lord spat. "The dagger was sent to you months ago. That's your three requests all used up. Now set me free!" he raged. The Emperor remained calm although he was now admittedly, thoroughly confused.

"What dagger?" he asked. With that, the furious Lord turned his back and stomped his way over to a desk, so blackened and charred it had been invisible against the ashy backdrop of the chamber. From it he retrieved a parchment, burned at the edges but still legible. He pressed it against the barrier which allowed the scroll through, leaving the Lord's hand pressed against the glassy, purple surface.

The Emperor took the parchment and passed it immediately to Nestor, who quickly began to read. Meanwhile, The Emperor and his rival stared at one another, unblinking, filled with visions of violence.

"It's a commission for a dagger, Your Holiness. To be delivered to the Imperial Palace."

"A divinite dagger," the Lord of Embers interrupted. "The last of the three divinite creations you agreed upon in our deal," the Lord continued. He refused to believe The Emperor's apparent ignorance was anything more than another dishonourable trick. A trick to keep him confined to this prison and from posing a threat to the Imperium.

"Well, clearly you've been tricked, as this letter did not come from me," The Emperor replied, slightly amused that the Lord could be so easily fooled.

"It bears your seal!" the Lord bellowed, pounding his fist against the barrier, his rage building up like the chamber beneath him. The Emperor turned to Nestor, who replied with wide eyes and a shocked nod of his head. Suddenly The Emperor's whole demeanour changed. Turning back to his furious prisoner, he demanded to know who had sent the letter and when. This time, however, it was the Lord's turn to claim ignorance.

"It came via pigeon. I did not bother to doubt its validity as the Imperial Seal was proof enough. Could have been a year ago, could have been yesterday, for all I know. Time has a funny way of merging when you're being held against your will."

The Emperor's mind was now swimming in dark and paranoid waters. Only members of the Righteous Congregation had permission to use the Imperial Seal. Why would one of them use it for such a niche purpose considering the power it held?

As much as the Lord of Embers enjoyed the sense of panic running through The Emperor's mind and body, he had more pressing concerns.

"Listen, I don't give a bloody fuck who sent the letter. It bears the Imperial Seal. The work was done, the dagger delivered. Now let me go!" he fumed. His entire body was shaking with anger as he realised his enemy would certainly now try to renege on their deal. The Emperor was looking over at Nestor who was re-reading the letter for the third time. Suspicion filled him as he examined the creases of Nestor's face, clearly as confused as he. A divinite dagger would be fit for only one purpose - piercing divinite armour, of which The Emperor had two sets.

Filled with new urgency, The Emperor turned back, ignoring the continuing outbursts of his captive.

"I need you to make something for me, and I need it now." The stress in his voice clearly emphasising the importance of the matter. The Lord of Embers, however, was incensed.

"You dare?" he whispered. Afraid that should he speak any louder and his rage released, the mountain would be brought down upon them. "I will create nothing for you. You are a liar, and I would rather remain here for the rest of eternity than suffer the indignity of your demands again."

There was a tense silence as the two parties stared at one another, waiting for the others' next move.

"A man who does not keep his word, hiding behind his spells, is not deserving of my help," the Lord of Embers said at last, turning away from his old foe. Now it was The Emperor's turn to lose his temper. He had neither the time nor energy to entertain his prisoner's delusions and stepped forward without hesitation, passing through the barrier as if it were mist. For far too long had the Lord of Embers believed himself to be The Emperor's equal. That would end today.

Nestor and the few Chosen immediately cried out in shock, unable to comprehend what madness had overcome their master. While they believed in The Emperor's divinity with all their hearts, even they could not help but be fearful of the Lord of Embers' might.

This was a moment the captive Lord had dreamed of for a millennium. The moment his new power would tear down The Emperor, and his spell with him. And yet, the Lord felt not at all as he had so often expected he would, if ever he found himself face to face with The Emperor. The dauntless way in which The Emperor had approached, as if he feared the Lord no more than an insect, caused him to falter. Stepping back gingerly, he could sense something was different. A feeling which had been suppressed by the magic of the barrier which had only moments before separated them. But now he could almost taste the power which radiated from his enemy. It hung in the air, thicker than the ash which surrounded them. Looking into The Emperor's cold, spiritless eyes, the Lord felt a shiver up his spine, a warning of imminent danger. This was not the same man he had faced before; no, this was something else entirely.

The Emperor at first thought of striking the Lord, or perhaps taking hold of him by the throat. Nothing too serious or mortifying, but enough for the Lord to know his place. Yet both acts were quickly shown to be unnecessary. The Lord had stopped retreating and now stood with wide, quivering eyes. The Emperor was no taller than he, but his presence felt like that of a god, bearing down upon the insignificant mortals below. Even with all his enchantments, the Lord knew he was no match for the raw power The Emperor now possessed.

Sensing the intimidation his opponent now felt, The Emperor shifted back to the matter at hand.

"My wife is dead," he breathed, as if all the pain had suddenly come rushing back as the words passed his lips. "Help me get her back, and I'll consider your end of the bargain fulfilled."

There was no trace of a lie in The Emperor's heart as he made this promise. The Lord of Embers, eternally suspicious, felt his guard drop at the pain in his enemy's words. However, while for the first time he may have believed The Emperor's promises, that did not make his request anything less than insanity.

"I'm sorry," he apologised, his words genuine. "But what you ask is impossible. The distances involved, the precise magic you would need. Even given a thousand years, I could not build you a ship fast enough to find her. We would all be lifted to paradise before you were anywhere close."

The Emperor refused to accept this and took another step forward. His very presence a threat.

"I don't need a ship. A trinket, a spell, just something to point me in the right direction. You claim to be a world-smith for God's sake. Prove it now." Desperation and exhaustion were clear in his voice, and for the first time, the Lord of Embers felt what may have been pity for his old foe. Never had he seen a man so broken behind his eyes. But even then, it did nothing to change the reality of the situation. Even with all his skill, locating a single person in a world with no end was an impossible task. Like being asked to find a teardrop in a bottomless ocean.

"I'm sorry," he repeated in a tone far gentler than one would expect from a man of his temperament. The Emperor suddenly felt a great pain in his heart. As if each valve and vein were filled with broken glass. As the Lord of Embers watched The Emperor, and perhaps his only chance at freedom, turn away, a thought came to him. It was improbable, even bordering on the impossible. Risky too, for them both. For should The Emperor fall in the process, the Lord could remain trapped for all eternity. But it was the only solution which had even the slightest chance of success.

Just as The Emperor was about to accept that this was a task beyond even the Lord of Embers, the Lord spoke. The softness and distance in his voice made it abundantly clear that what he was suggesting had little chance of success.

"In the north, deep into the Great Wastes, there is a library. The entrance has most likely long since disappeared. But should you locate it, within you may find what you need."

"A library?" The Emperor whispered, grasping this sliver of hope with all his heart. The Lord nodded.

"Built during the Age of Subjugation. It is of the old gods."

"Where exactly? The Great Wastes are so named for a reason." The Emperor asked, not caring how desperate he sounded. The already pessimistic Lord shook his head.

"I do not know. I have only ever visited in my dreams. The place may not even exist," the Lord admitted, folding his arms. The Emperor's heart once again sank at his words. "But nothing I learned there has ever proven false, which leads me to believe it does exist. The Battlemages may know, they used to keep records of that sort of thing." The Emperor's eyes widened upon hearing this. What fortune to have such a resource at his command after all these years. Clearly, Heaven was smiling upon him, paving the way for him to be reunited with Sarah once again.

"You have my deepest gratitude. When I return, successful or not, I shall release you," The Emperor said, returning the way he had come. The Lord of Embers remained where he stood, watching his guests depart, already questioning whether he had just doomed himself to eternal captivity. As he was once again left alone, the Lord returned to his previous work at the forge.

Delicately, he placed a gemstone as blue and pure as ice upon his great anvil. Striking it thrice with his hammer he channelled the magic stored within his body. A great gust of wind suddenly materialised, enveloping him as he strained to direct this raw magical energy. At last, he was successful. He took the gem gently between his thumb and forefinger, taking a moment to admire his work. The intense light of the room reflecting off its surface in an array of colours.

With a menacing smile the Lord pressed the stone into his skin, finding an unoccupied spot upon his right breast. Immediately he was filled with a burst of power, feeling the electric energy coursing through his veins and across his skin like lightning. He fell back at the force of the magical release and quickly rose to stand. Whatever The Emperor had become, the Lord of Embers would need more than this to defeat him. Luckily for him, he wasn't going anywhere.

As The Emperor began his journey to the base of the mountain via the carriage, his head was filled with thoughts of hope and betrayal. Noticing this sense of tumult upon him, Nestor spoke up, hoping to distract his master from whatever heavy thoughts currently occupied his mind.

"You called him a world-smith, Your Holiness. What does that mean? I've never heard of such a title before."

Distracted from his contemplation, The Emperor answered Nestor's question with a sigh, resting himself against the railings of the carriage after such an exhausting journey.

"It's an old term. One used by the dragons and their servants. In essence, it's a being with the skill and power to be able to create an entirely new world, using nothing but magic and metal."

Nestor could not help but scoff at the idea.

"How ridiculous," he smirked, folding his arms and looking out once again at the wasteland which surrounded them. The Emperor, however, was not so quick to dismiss the claim. In those dark, early days of his reign he had studied meticulously all the ancient texts the republic had kept hidden. He knew how close the dragons had come to achieving their goal. But he was not interested in a new world. What he wanted, was waiting for him in this one.

"What do you suggest now, Your Holiness?" Nestor asked once they were finally free from the suffocating heat of the city.

"Home," The Emperor replied with a sense of urgency. "We must prepare for a long journey north, and I would rather be well away before those fools start their war."

Nestor, of course, was one of those fools. And The Emperor knew it. However, he could not help but release some of his frustration at his supposed servants who had opposed him at every turn.

"Very good, Your Holiness," Nestor responded with an audible lack of enthusiasm for The Emperor's plan. He humoured his master because it was his job to do so. But despite the love he still held for the late Empress, he was not so blind to believe she would be returned. There were some things which were simply hopeless. The sooner The Emperor understood that, the better.

"Would you like me to accompany you on this journey also?"

The Emperor shook his head.

"I have something else I need you to do, something more important."

"Anything," Nestor replied, his tone one of slight suspicion.

"Find out who requested that dagger. I fear one of our friends at court may be hiding it behind their smile."

Nestor's brow furrowed at the request.

"Would it not be best to have this matter investigated by the guard, Your Holiness? After all, I had access to the Imperial Seal during your illness. It could have been me who requested it."

The Emperor chuckled slightly.

"The thought had crossed my mind," he admitted. "But believe me, Nestor, I hold you in high enough regard to know you would kill a bed-ridden man in a less moronically conspicuous manner."

"I'm not so sure, Your Holiness," Nestor smirked.

"Sometimes I do get the sudden urge to beat you over the head with a rock." This comment turned the heads of a few nearby Chosen, but The Emperor gave a hearty laugh as they rode away from the heat at their backs and in the direction of home. Although Nestor could not help but dread the task at hand, having to investigate the most powerful and influential people in the Imperium, all while playing politics, threatened to undo everything he had worked so hard to achieve. This would not be an easy exercise, and he did not even know where to begin.

Killing The Emperor would have done nothing but throw the country into chaos, benefiting nobody at court. But then a thought came to him. There was one member of the Congregation who, until very recently, had been a sworn enemy of the Imperium. Recommended by someone who had thoroughly enjoyed the brief taste of power The Emperor's illness had brought, this would not be pleasant, but it was a good place to start.

Chapter 8

The last two days of travel were undoubtedly the worst. Able to eat only what they could scavenge, which soon became very little as they crossed into marshland, Nate and Cassandra were ready to give up before their mission had truly begun. The pair sat on a tall mound of soaking wet moss, hungry and tired. Nate had built a campfire and had at least attempted to look for something to eat but had come away with nothing. Cassandra, meanwhile, remained where she was, poking at the body of an everglade dryad who had picked on the wrong hungry woman. These dryads were sadly not the helpful kind, the kind that took on the forms of beautiful women and aided travellers lost in the forest.

Everglade dryads had pale blue skin which helped them lurk unseen in the murky waters. Their hair, thick and easily mistaken for watergrass. Their sharp horns and blade-like claws, however, were unmistakeable. Although, if you could see these, it was probably already too late. In this instance at least, Cassandra had been too angry to even entertain the thought of dying and was glad for something to take her frustration out on.

"How long before we reach the town?" Nate asked, returning from yet another failed search for sustenance.

"Another day," Cassandra replied. "If we live that long," she mumbled to herself as she used the tip of her spear to push the dryad back into the water from whence it came.

"God I'm…"

"If you say you're hungry, I'm going to beat you," Cassandra quickly snapped before Nate could finish speaking. Puffing out his cheeks, Nate took a seat next to Cassandra on the wet mound before immediately standing again. The pain in his stomach simply wouldn't allow for him to give up yet. He started to slowly make his way around the banks of the thousands of islets, keenly scanning the murky waters.

"What are you doing?" Cassandra sighed with that unmistakeable tinge of annoyance at seeing another human being whilst hungry. Nate did not reply, instead holding out his hand in an obvious shushing position while leaning dangerously far over a particularly disgusting patch of water. There was a moment of silence where it seemed the whole world was still before Nate's face lit up with glee.

He reached out his hand before quickly yanking it back. Suspended in the air by his magic, flopped a rather meagre looking fish. Judging by the looks on Nate's and Cassandra's faces, you would have assumed him to have caught a whale.

"Oh my God, you're actually useful," Cassandra practically squealed as she rushed over. Over the next hour the pair worked together to catch four more fish. Nate doing all the catching, while Cassandra took care of the messy bits he didn't like. When they were done, not only were their bellies full, but they had enough left over for breakfast.

"Don't say I never do anything for you," Nate smiled smugly as he lay atop his bedroll, his arms behind his head. Unable to help but be in a much better mood, Cassandra responded.

"You're right. I'll tell the girls back home I was only mostly right about you."

"What girls?" Nate replied immediately, sitting up from his makeshift bed. "What girls!?" He called out again as Cassandra just laughed and went in search of this barren wilderness' version of a lady's room.

Sensing that the pair had a heightened mood for once, mother nature decided she was having none of it. That night they had to contend with a veritable tsunami of rain from which they had no protection. There was not a single tree for miles, and the pair soon found themselves having to search for higher ground as the water around them began to rise. Luckily, they were able to retreat to the safety of a nearby hill. The ceaseless torrent of rain had them both considering just letting the waters take them at this point, as clearly someone didn't want them completing their mission.

Soaked to the bone and shivering, Nate was able to light a magical fire once the rain had stopped, which unfortunately was of no benefit to himself. While Cassandra warmed herself by the flames, Nate wrapped himself in all the blankets he could, trying his best to get some warmth back into his body. Unsurprisingly, neither of them got much sleep that night. Things only got worse once dawn approached. The water below them had receded somewhat, but not so much that the path they had been following the day before was visible. This meant they spent the entire next day trying to find a way through the marsh instead of arriving at their destination.

To make matters worse, it seemed every fish in the area had caught wind of the two's antics the day before and buggered off. So, by the time Nate and Cassandra finally exited the marsh, they were once again starving. As the sky began to turn a bright shade of orange, they could see ahead of them neat fields of crops stretching into the horizon. They were close, therefore, the pair decided to continue, despite their chattering teeth and boots which squelched with each step.

It was just after ten o'clock when the pair arrived, bedraggled and sopping wet, at the entrance of the village. Although, calling these huddled abodes a village was pushing it. A dozen houses, three empty market stalls, a track which led back out of town down a narrow, winding path which they assumed led to the mine, was all there was. More of a hamlet really, by Nate's reckoning. Although, Cassandra, disinterested in his expertise in rural planning, pushed them on towards the only building not enveloped in darkness.

A pub, by all the gods, a pub. The pair practically broke down in tears when they saw it. Cold mead, hot food, soft beds. All so tantalisingly close. They dragged themselves as fast as their aching legs would allow until at last they entered the golden glow of civilisation. As the pub door swung open, revealing the two intrepid monster slayers, they did not get the reception they expected. The pub was quite full, literally appearing as if the whole village was there, and they all stopped and turned to see who had arrived so late in the day.

In the doorway stood a man and a woman, caked in mud, soaked to the bone, and dripping all over the floor. Nate and Cassandra, their wide eyes stared around the room in wonder, like a pair of neolithic tribespeople who had taken a wrong turn and found themselves in Buckingham Palace. There was a long, awkward silence as the two parties stared at one another before a shout came up from the barman.

"You poor devils!" he said, quickly making his way over with a pair of fresh blankets he had just been about to spread over his own bed. The man was obscenely large, with a stomach that hung almost to his knees and arms like battering rams. It was a wonder why the village needed monster hunters at all. If anything nasty came knocking, this fellow could just eat the damn things. With his cry the whole pub sprang into action, fetching fresh beers, stoking the fire, and leading Nate and Cassandra to the seats closest to the inviting flames so they could dry off.

The pair barely had a moment to get a word in as they were whisked off their feet by hospitality. Once the two were sat by the fire, blankets wrapped around their shoulders and drinks placed in their hands, the barman spoke again. Although it was about his new guests rather than to them.

"Poor sods, they must be refugees on the way to Tinelia and took a wrong turn," he said to another man while he placed new logs by the fire.

"Surprised they made it this far, must have been one hell of a journey," said another. As the village people went about doing everything they could to make their guests comfortable, Nate being Nate, went and ruined it. Lifting his face from the bottom of his mug with a foam moustache, he felt compelled to correct his hosts.

"We're monster hunters, actually." The whole building immediately stopped, Cassandra too froze, feeling dozens of eyes suddenly harden upon her.

"You're what?" The barman asked. Sensing the mood to have shifted, Nate was more timid the next time he spoke.

"We're…. monster hunters…. The ones you asked for?" he asked, wondering now if they had ended up in the wrong place after all.

"Oh… oh," the barman replied. In truth, that notice had been posted so long ago that the villagers had entirely forgotten about it. Now, at last faced with the help they had so desperately sought, they seemed less than enthused by their presence.

"It's all been sorted," the barman said rather suddenly. "No need for no monster hunters here, I'm afraid. Sorry to have wasted your time and make you come out all this way," he chuckled nervously. Cassandra sank into her seat, defeated at this revelation, all that trouble for nothing. Nate, however, was not so convinced.

"What was it in the end?" He asked.

"What was what?" the barman replied.

"In the mine, the lights, the undead. What was it?"

"Oh… erm," the barman stammered, looking around the room for assistance.

"Gas," came a voice from amongst the crowd. Based on the looks on the faces of the other patrons, this was news to them.

"Aye, gas," the barman repeated, looking at Nate with less than certainty in his own words.

"And the undead?" Nate pressed, raising his eyebrow to show how unconvinced he was by the barman's story. The barman, however, did not even attempt to explain this away, instead waving his hand dismissively.

"As I said, all sorted now. No need for you to trouble yourselves." He quickly turned to a woman near the bar and snapped his fingers. She immediately understood and brought over a quarter keg of wine which she placed between Nate's feet.

"Our way of an apology. Take this with you and feel welcome to stay the night, free of charge," the barman smiled nervously. You didn't need to be a genius to realise there was something strange going on. Nate and Cassandra shared a look which outwardly seemed like grateful acceptance and nodded, throwing in smiles for good measure.

"Sounds like a plan," Cassandra said, slapping her thighs.

"Wonderful," the barman sighed in relief, clapping his own hands together loudly.

A room was quickly prepared for them and the two were enthusiastically shepherded inside. Alone at last, they shared a suspicious look.

"Something's going on," Nate asserted.

"Obviously," Cassandra replied. She was still sopping wet and hungry. She really didn't have the energy to play detective. She just wanted to kill something and go home. As she looked over at the double bed they had been provided, she wondered if it would end up being Nate.

Despite being eagerly hidden away, the barman had been more than happy to provide the now defunct monster hunters with a free meal, so long as they stayed in their room. Warm, dry, and fed at last, the pair lay in the darkness formulating a plan. Cassandra of course lay in the bed, the soft duvet heaven in comparison to what she had become accustomed these last few days. Nate was less fortunate, taking the floor just in front of the door.

"I'm guessing we're checking out the mine first thing in the morning?" Nate asked.

"You're starting to get the hang of this," Cassandra replied sleepily, indicating she was not at all interested in continuing this conversation. The room returned to silence for a few minutes before Nate spoke again.

"If someone opens this door, they're going to take my head off."

"Don't threaten me with a good time," Cassandra yawned.

True to their word, Nate and Cassandra were up at the crack of dawn. Leaving the generous gift of wine behind, they returned the way they had come the previous day, watched carefully by the entire village who had turned out to see them depart. Making a show of waving goodbye, Nate and Cassandra followed the path out of the village until only the thin wisps of smoke from distant chimneys were visible. They then left the beaten path and travelled in the rough direction of the road which they assumed led to the mine, which the villagers were apparently so eagerly protecting.

They cut through fields of tall, green crops which were unfamiliar to Nate, despite the fact he'd spent the last year eating them. Thankfully, it didn't take long before they had circled around and could see the smoke from the village on their left side. Taking care not to be seen while they crossed the farm tracks between fields, they came upon a more overgrown path about twenty minutes later. Checking they had not been discovered, the pair stepped onto the dirt track and continued along it, away from the town.

It was only a few minutes before the landscape changed entirely. What had been neat, flat fields soon became littered with large boulders. The soil itself no longer rich and fertile, but chalky and dying.

"Must be getting close," Cassandra said as she picked up the pace, Nate following closely behind. Suddenly, Cassandra stopped dead in her tracks, staring down at the ground. Nate did the same, immediately seeing a plethora of footprints leading to and from the mine. Some were less than a day old, others nearly a week. All of them, however, were normal, as if the creator had no trouble walking whatsoever. It was this normalcy which drew their confusion and concern. The undead were notoriously clumsy, the uniform neatness of the prints indicated their owners were not of the undead persuasion.

Neither Nate nor Cassandra liked the picture that was being painted by the evidence before them. They had been hired to deal with undead but, so far, they had seen no evidence any had been here at all.

"Maybe they were telling the truth," Nate proposed. Cassandra, however, shook her head.

"I don't smell any gas. Even then, If they're telling the

truth, why are they still visiting the mine and why so often?" She said pointing at the tracks.

"Hmm," Nate said without following it up with any actual thoughts.

"Let's keep going. If we smell any gas, we take their word for it and turn back," Cassandra decided. Nate said nothing and followed obediently until they came upon the mouth of the mine. The initial excavations were not very wide, a welcome relief as both had expected to have to descend an entire quarry. They immediately noticed the distinct lack of any gassy smell and an even greater collection of footprints by the mine's entrance. These, however, were more of what they had expected to see at this point.

Feet which seemed to point in different directions, which dragged behind or in one case were missing entirely, replaced by long troughs where presumably a husk had dragged itself. These were intermixed with the more usual, fresh tracks they had been following.

"Now that," Nate stated, pointing, "that is weird," Nate stated. Cassandra stood in silence for a moment, staring at the tracks with her hands on her hips. At last, she let out a sigh and drew her sword, placing her spear against a beam which supported the mine's entrance.

"Why is nothing ever simple?" She asked rhetorically as she pushed the rickety wooden door open and descended into the dark.

"Bloody hell," Nate complained as he followed his companion.

Guided by one of Nate's magical orbs, the pair slowly traversed the narrow mine. The walls were lined with torches which showed no signs of having been used recently. The floor was wet and slippery, meaning they had to take extra care as they made their descent. All in all, the mine did not look to have been used in decades, let alone as recently as the previous day. They continued nevertheless, the passage becoming wider and taller, in some cases branching off in different directions to new chambers.

Nate and Cassandra continued along the main tunnel. If anything was down here after all, it made sense it would be in the deepest, darkest, scariest part of the mine. As they continued, hearing nothing but the sound of their own heavy breaths and wet footfalls, they became increasingly convinced that there was nothing down here after all. But if there was nothing, why were the villagers acting so strangely? That question is what kept them going.

Suddenly, and without warning, a sensation came over Nate. Something he had felt before and immediately recognised.

"Wait," he whispered. Cassandra stopped immediately, not in the habit of ignoring warnings whilst in the belly of a mine, potentially surrounded by undead.

"What is it?" she whispered back, stress clear in her voice. Nate looked at the walls around him but could see nothing beyond their shiny, earthy surface.

"We just passed through an invisibility barrier," he stated, not entirely confident he believed his own claim. He could not ignore the sudden magical shift he had felt course through his body. Seeing as he had not been either vaporised or turned into a toad, he went with the next most likely option.

"You sure?" Cassandra pressed, hoping Nate was wrong. Undead were one thing, sorcerers another entirely.

"No," Nate replied, which did nothing but stress them out even more.

"Let's keep going," Cassandra whispered, hoping Nate was just being overly sensitive. Unfortunately, however, the passage before them immediately began to change, indicating that they were indeed not alone and that their company wasn't the brainless type. Light began to fill the tunnel. Not the warm orange glow of torchlight though, ghostly blue light, identical to the one which had guided them thus far.

As they pressed on, their fears were realised. Lining the ceiling of the passage were small magical orbs which lit their way. These orbs continued down only a single passage, giving Nate and Cassandra a clear path to follow. Their steps were slower than ever, neither wanting to come face to face with a repeat of their last misadventure. After another ten minutes of quaking boots upon soggy ground, they encountered a horrific yet familiar stench - the smell of unburied corpses which intensified as they entered the main chamber.

It was a large, shapeless room, dozens of meters wide but only about eight feet high. The floor was lined with rugs and the rest of the room filled with the amenities of daily life. It looked to all the world that someone was living down here. Off in one corner was a magical, smokeless fire, many days old Nate Judged by the way it struggled to maintain itself. There were tables and chairs, and remnants of a previous meal. The aspect which caught their attention and alarmed them the most, however, was the pair of beds placed next to one another at the back of the chamber, separated by a wooden screen.

One sorcerer was reason enough to worry, two were as good as a death sentence. Silently, Nate and Cassandra moved forward, approaching a section of wall that protruded out near the centre of the room, obstructing a view of whatever lay around it. Just as they prepared to round this corner, they were shocked out of their skin as a woman appeared before them. She too had been unaware of her visitor's presence and was equally as surprised.

"Fucking hell!" she cried, stumbling back but managing to remain upright. Nate and Cassandra too had fallen back but quickly regained their composure. Cassandra lunged forward, taking hold of the woman by the front of her robe, forcing her down onto her knees at the edge of her sword. Nate meanwhile rounded the corner, weapon at the ready.

"Jesus Christ," he exclaimed, covering his mouth.

"What is it?" Cassandra gasped as she tried to keep her prisoner still. Nate didn't reply, however, instead waving his free hand to indicate this was something Cassandra needed to see for herself. Swapping places, with Nate now taking charge over the prisoner, Cassandra rounded the corner to see what had elicited such a reaction from her companion.

The view which greeted her should have been expected but did not disappoint.

A mound of corpses were piled on the left side of the cavernous room. A mixture of rotten, grey and brown bodies unceremoniously dumped in a grotesque heap of flesh. Their mouths hung open, screaming silently, eternally, while their soulless eyes stared back in anguish. Across from them, three human-sized cages which were currently occupied with the bodies of what looked to be husks.

"Not again," Cassandra groaned as she tried not to heave from the stench.

"It's not what you think," the prisoner panicked, speaking for the first time since the unexpected encounter had begun. Nate yanked her back by the scruff of her neck, his sword at her throat. Cassandra turned to her with furious eyes, storming over with clear murderous intent.

"Where's your partner?!" she demanded. In the heat of the moment, Nate had totally forgotten that there was likely another necromancer lurking somewhere nearby.

"Gone," the prisoner gasped throwing up her hands in fresh surrender as Nate's sword kissed her skin.

"Bullshit," Cassandra growled.

"He was injured. I had to send him a few towns over for a healer," the woman winced, terrified that at any moment she would be killed, all her progress lost in an instant. She pointed towards one of the beds. Upon it lay many bloody bandages and empty vials, proof of her claim. Cassandra did another search of the chamber before considering her captive to be telling the truth, although this did nothing to change her opinion of what would come next.

"Fucking necromancers," she breathed as she approached with her weapon at the ready.

"Please!" The woman begged, her eyes swelling with tears. She knew exactly how the situation looked, and it wasn't good. But did she really want to admit what she was truly doing here; would it be better just to let these goons kill her rather than know the shameful truth? But as she felt the tip of Cassandra's sword pressing into her breast, she could not help but blurt out a confession.

"I'm not dangerous, I swear! I'm not really even a necromancer. We're farmers!" The woman sobbed in desperation.

"I think it's a bit late for that," Nate laughed. Cassandra, however, stopped in her tracks, as if the necromancer had been able to cast a spell after all. She stared intently at the woman at first, at her unwashed hair, her terrified eyes, and the bloodstained apron she wore over her robe. She then looked back at the cages and the pile of dead which lay rotting only a few feet away.

"We?" She asked. Grasping at this diversion from her imminent end, the necromancer could no longer help but spill all her secrets.

"My partner and I. We never hurt anyone, all the undead are husks, we just use them for farming." She looked around as much as Nate's blade, still pressed against her neck, would allow. "Why do you think there are no guards? Why we keep the undead in cages? I swear, we're no danger to anyone!"

With her case argued, it was now up to the court of Cassandra to decide her fate.

"Shit," Cassandra sighed. At last, it all made sense. "Nate, let her up," she ordered reluctantly.

"What?" Nate gasped, unable to follow Cassandra's thought process.

"Just do it!" She barked, at which Nate hastily complied.

"Thank you," the woman sobbed with relief as Nate helped her to her feet.

"Can someone please explain to me what the hell is going on?" Nate shouted. Cassandra's face looked as if she had just swallowed a lemon, answering him with no small amount of frustration.

"She farms the undead," she explained. Nate, however, was still none the wiser and replied with clear frustration of his own.

"Okay, let's for a second pretend I'm a fucking idiot who has no idea what that means. Care to dumb it down for me?"

"You explain it," Cassandra sighed angrily at the necromancer as she took a seat in a nearby chair. The necromancer looked at her feet, her hands still trembling as she wrang them together. Her voice was shaky at first as the adrenaline still flowed through her system, but she was eventually able to explain herself.

"I bring the dead back to life… so that I can kill them myself," she admitted guiltily. Nate squinted his eyes at this confession, things were somehow making even less sense than before.

"What's the point in that?" He asked, more exhausted by this painful conversation than he had been all day.

"Come on, Nate, even you're not that dense," Cassandra goaded before the necromancer could answer. The cogs in Nate's brain began to turn, he wasn't used to having to think this hard. But at last, the answer dawned on him, and his mouth dropped in amazement.

"You're getting paid?!" He gasped. The necromancer nodded sheepishly, her greasy hair sticking to her face.

"I didn't know you could do that!"

"It's one hell of a loophole. Bet the bank is kicking itself for not thinking of it first," Cassandra said in what almost sounded like admiration. How could she not at least be impressed by someone who had cheated the system to such an extent? It may be a rather slow process, and was looked down upon as uncouth, but it was a somewhat safe and steady profession. Much safer than her own, anyway.

"So, what do we do?" Nate asked, flabbergasted that the fundamentals of their world could be outmanoeuvred and abused so easily. Cassandra threw up her hands, frustrated that the whole mission had been a waste of time after all.

"Nothing we can do. Technically she's not doing anything wrong." She looked over at the necromancer who now wore a relieved although still slightly nervous smile.

"I'm guessing the village folk are in on it?" Cassandra asked. The necromancer nodded.

"I give them a cut and they keep me fed and undisturbed. Well, they did," she confirmed, looking at Nate who still had his sword drawn.

"Guess that's it then. Job done," Cassandra said rising from her chair and heading for the exit with an annoyed huff. Nate, however, was still in awe and could not help but want to learn more.

"So how do you control the undead exactly?" he asked, certain it was something that would be worth knowing in future. The necromancer shook her head, wagging her finger to indicate Nate's ignorance.

"It's a common misconception," she sighed. "We don't actually control them at all. Bringing them back just makes them non-hostile, to the spell-caster anyway," she explained. "Makes them good guards and practice dummies, but not much else. That's how my partner got injured, got too close to one he hadn't brought back himself."

This time it was Nate's turn to shake his head.

"I still can't believe the bank lets you get away with it." The necromancer, now feeling somewhat at ease, giggled back.

"Oh, believe me, they're furious. They won't even let me open an account. They just drop the coins at my feet." This caught Cassandra's attention and she stopped, turning back to the necromancer.

"What do you mean? As in, when you kill something, the money just appears?"

"Yeah, exactly," the necromancer chuckled before her face became white, all the blood and emotions draining away until only one remained. "Exactly…" she whispered. Both she and Nate knew what was about to happen and yet could do nothing to stop it.

"Hand it over," Cassandra ordered coldly.

"What?" The necromancer replied, feigning ignorance. But Cassandra was not joking around, she took the necromancer by the hair, forcing her back onto her knees with a blade at her throat.

"The gold, where is it?" she spat.

"Cassandra stop!" Nate cried in horror, moving in to pull her away, catching only the hilt of her sword to his face as she pushed him back. Nate fell to the ground with a bloodied nose and split lip, barely recognising the woman who had been his companion only seconds ago. Something had come over her, something not unique to this world but ruinous, nonetheless. Greed filled her heart, the allure of the promise of paradise in exchange for shiny trinkets, not one easily overcome by even the most noble of souls.

"Please," the necromancer sobbed as Cassandra's grip tightened, the cold steel prickling against her soft, dirty skin.

"Just tell me where it is, and I'll let you go," Cassandra replied impatiently. The necromancer had both hands gripping onto Cassandra's wrist which pulled on her hair, her face streaming with tears. Her lip quivered at the thought of having to start this foul, arduous process all over again. But she had no choice.

"Over by the beds, there's a loose board by the divider," she wept. Cassandra turned to Nate.

"Go check."

"Cassandra, please, let her go."

"Just fucking go!" Cassandra replied so angrily that it came out almost as a squeal. Furious, but not wanting to endanger the life of the necromancer further, Nate did as he was told, making a point to nurse his bloody face as he made his way over to the beds. It did not take long to find the loose board, and upon prying it away, he found the woman to be telling the truth. There were four medium-sized purses bulging with gold. But that was all, maybe two-thousand coins at the most all together. Hardly worth the price Cassandra was willing to pay to get it.

Nate retrieved the bags and opened them, showing Cassandra the contents.

"Ok, so you've robbed her, well done. Now let her go," he demanded.

Cassandra chuckled softly, shaking her head and smiling in a way that left Nate deeply unnerved. She looked him dead in the eyes as she spoke, not once averting her gaze.

"You know what I find so strange about this place?" she asked rhetorically. Nate did not answer.

"Everyone is so obsessed with getting into Heaven. And yet nobody wants to die," she said as she slid the point of her blade into her victim's throat. The necromancer's eyes grew wide in shock and pain. Her mind filled with panic and desperation as she weakly struggled to free herself as she rapidly bled to death. Her mouth was soon filled with blood that cascaded like a waterfall of gore down her already bloody apron. Cassandra kept tight hold of her victim's hair as she struggled, all the while maintaining eye contact with Nate.

To Cassandra, Nate was pathetic, allowing himself to be moved by such trivialities as pity and empathy. Such things had no place in Purgatory. There was only one goal that mattered, and as far as Cassandra was concerned, there was only one way to achieve it. Ruthlessly. This was a lesson Nate needed to learn and, if she had to be the one to teach him, then so be it. When the struggling ceased at last, Cassandra threw down the limp body and casually approached her wide-eyed companion. Nate was stood frozen in horror, unable to comprehend the barbarity of what he had just seen.

"There was no need…" he began softly as Cassandra stooped down to collect the bags of coins. She quickly straightened up, a bag of gold in each hand, one of which she pushed against Nate's chest.

"Take this," she ordered. "She won't be needing it."

"I don't want it," Nate said, so angry that he began to tear up. Cassandra had no time or sympathy for Nate's sentimentality and pushed him against the wall, gripping the neck of his armour tightly. She looked into his eyes with a barely contained rage.

"Listen to me," she spat. "You think you're better than this, but you're not. If you were, you wouldn't be here." She lifted one of the bags to be level with Nate's eyes, jingling it like some cartoonish villain. "Do you know what that is?" she asked, knowing Nate would not answer. When her prediction came true, she continued.

"That's me being one-thousand steps closer to seeing my children again. One-thousand steps closer to getting out of this hell. I have no problem making it two, so take your half and stop being such a fucking pussy." Nate wanted to argue, to fight even, but all the strength and will had been sapped out of him. In the end he took two of the purses and stuffed them deep into his pack without a word.

Rather than head straight for home, Cassandra had another plan. The two returned to the village, where they would undoubtedly receive an unwelcome reception. Nate said nothing as they walked. He was too busy hating himself for not doing anything to help the necromancer. For taking the money. For being no better than Cassandra claimed. Unsurprisingly, the pub was empty save for the barman, the other villagers all out tending the fields or whatever else it was peasants did all day. As expected, the look on the barman's face as the pair returned was not a happy one. Nevertheless, he tried to be cordial, that was until Cassandra revealed her intentions.

"We slew the necromancer in the mine. You have no need to fear her now," she said triumphantly.

"W… what?!" The barman gasped with wide eyes.

"She confessed to holding you all hostage, forcing you to provide for her whilst she did her experiments," Cassandra lied.

"That… that's not… that's not what happened!" The barman spluttered, livid that his source of passive income had been forcibly extinguished.

"Listen," Cassandra interrupted before the barman could do anything with his rising anger. "We were charged with dealing with some undead. The job's complete, so now you pay us."

"Pay you?!" the barman cried in disbelief. Cassandra, however, was not intimidated. To make matters even worse, what she was doing was nothing less than extortion. The Guild had already been paid a posting fee, which the pair would be paid a share of upon their return. Customers were not expected to pay once the job was done. A rather curious way of doing business, but as there was no shortage of monsters to slay, it ensured timewasters kept away. However, in a tiny village such as this, it was unlikely anyone here knew that.

"Yes," she stated matter-of-factly. "And if you don't, well, let's just say the Guild does not take kindly to delinquents who don't pay their fees." As much as the barman wanted to fly into a raging frenzy at this arrogant woman, he knew he would come out worse off. Grumbling the whole while, he filled a purse with coins and tossed it at Cassandra who caught it deftly.

"Many thanks," Cassandra smiled as she turned to leave.

"Not going to count it?" The barman called after them mockingly.

"Don't worry, if it's short, I'll be back," Cassandra threatened, quickly erasing the barman's smugness. Nate had said nothing during the interaction, instead hanging near the door, hoping to leave as soon as possible.

"Come on then," Cassandra smiled, playfully squeezing Nate's cheeks as if he were a tiny child. "Let's get you home, Mr. Sourpuss," she cooed tauntingly.

Chapter 9

Catarah had always hated the city. The stuffiness, the people. But mostly the noise. She found herself forced to wear earplugs whenever going out in public, the only way to avoid being totally overwhelmed. She missed the bogs, the derelict towers and burned-out ruins she had for so long called home. That was until Adeneus had found her. He had sensed a massive concentration of magical energy, far too large to be natural, too much to ignore.

Stumbling upon Catarah as the unexpected source of the magical swell, he had been impressed by her arcane prowess. Especially after she had almost vaporized him with a bolt of lightning shot from her fingertips, a spell which he had later demanded she teach him. At first, she was not remotely tempted by his offer of joining the Imperial University as his understudy. She much preferred the solitude of the countryside, where she could practice whatever magic she wished. His repeated promises of unrestricted access to whatever tools, plus all the collected ancient and rare knowledge she needed, had won her over in the end.

As she paced the long road towards the University, which she now chaired, she found herself missing her old master. During their years together they had pushed their knowledge of magic further than either of them had ever thought possible. But it had been a long and painful road, the first few years being the most difficult. For centuries, the best and brightest magical minds had sought to earn their place as Adeneus' apprentice. Indeed, much of the current faculty had joined the University with the express objective of learning under him. Yet they had all been refused. Then Catarah had arrived.

A complete unknown with no academic titles or experience outside her own experimentation, she had drawn the entire

Imperial academic community's ire upon both herself and Adeneus. More attempts had been made to exclude her from the University than she dared count. But Adeneus had always come to her defence, whether she had genuinely deserved it or not, which was a whole other matter. She had indeed proved herself to be somewhat of a firebrand regarding pursuing new, often dangerous or forbidden, avenues of spellcraft. Flaunting well established safety procedures and offering little respect to those her senior.

Nevertheless, it had been this very refusal to submit to the established norms which had caught Adeneus' eye to begin with though, the pair had not always seen eye to eye. Her master had always been more reserved, unwilling to continue research if he believed it to be too dangerous. For Catarah, the more dangerous the spell, the better. This had put the two at loggerheads on multiple occasions, usually ending in screaming matches and slammed doors. Threats of expulsion or of leaving back to the wilderness of her own accord being used so often they lost all meaning.

Eventually, however, the two had rubbed off on one another. Adeneus eventually becoming more of a risk taker, willing to push a spell further than most would dare. While Catarah had become more conscious of the consequences of her wild experiments, resulting in a drastic decrease in lab assistant mortality rates, much to the delight of the first-year students who so often held these positions. In the end, Catarah could not help but feel guilt at her role in Adeneus' fate. If it was not for her, he never would have taken the Phoenix Project so far. He would still be here now, chastising her for not wearing her robe and threatening to explode faculty she disliked.

She had loved that old fool, more than she would have ever dared to admit to his face. Now that he was gone, she would never get the chance. This reflection had succeeded only in making Catarah sad, so she decided to focus her mind on something else. It was a beautiful winter's day. The sky was a bright, cloudless blue in which flocks of birds flew in all manner of directions. While her breath proceeded ahead of her, the sun was still warm and she enjoyed lifting her head slightly to enjoy its touch upon her face.

As she neared the entrance to the University campus, she could not help but admire its grandiosity. The campus itself was a large, ringed structure. Almost a city within a city, with only members being allowed access. On the outskirts lay the student's living quarters, an unhealthy number of pubs, and boutiques which sold everything a student would need. Otherwise, the remaining space was taken up by immaculate hedgerows, groomed and sculpted to perfection. Rows and rows of elegant and vibrant flowers of which Adeneus had known every type. And of course, marble statues, carved by hand over many years. Not the metal, animatronic creations he had so loathed yet seemed to be loved by everyone else.

This had been his creation, and possibly, Catarah thought, that of which he had been most proud. A lover of nature, Adeneus had hated with a passion the stone and brick which had smothered the campus when he was a student. Tearing down half the University as soon as he became Arch-sorcerer to make way for the sights and smells which Catarah enjoyed now. His reasoning being that bricks and mortar, the creations of man, could inspire no more than that which man had already accomplished. Only by being immersed in nature, surrounded by the majesty and supremacy of God's creations, could students begin to imagine and perceive that which had never been thought possible.

It was the University building itself, however, which Catarah and all others could not help but be left speechless by. One could easily mistake it for a cathedral, so similar were their designs. Although the Imperial University was far larger and older than any place of worship still found within the Imperium, a truly enormous structure, it was the largest building in the known world save for Tinelia's Citadel.

The circumference comprised of nine hexagonal hubs, each of which exhibited hundreds of dazzling stained-glass windows and countless spires and steeples in what Nate's world would have been considered a gothic style. Behind these nine, were a much larger six. Identical in all aspects other than their size. Each one containing more piercing spires, more magnificent windows and ever more intricate designs cut into the stone. This trend continued as six became three, and finally, three became one. In the very centre rose a tower of such magnificence and radiance, one could scarcely imagine it had been contrived by human hands, or even conceived by human minds.

The tower rose into the clouds and beyond Catarah's sight. This was the Arch-Sorcerer's tower. Her residence and seat of power. She could not deny it was a magnificent image, one that filled her with newfound determination with each fresh sighting, and even if it was a bitch to climb. With a wide and energised smile upon her face, the new Arch-Sorceress pressed on along the sweet-smelling path to where her work was waiting.

As she walked, despite not wearing her robe which denoted her prestigious position, all she passed bowed respectfully.

"Arch-Sorceress," and "Lovely to see you, Arch-Sorceress," being the two most common greetings she received. Catarah smiled and nodded her appreciation at the displays of respect. Reserving the largest, most satisfying smiles for those members of staff who had for so long tried to have her expelled. There really was nothing quite like seeing the hopes of your enemies so utterly crushed, that they now literally bowed whenever you so much as sneezed.

Leaving the throngs of noisy students behind, the Arch-Sorceress took one of the corridors reserved only for staff which allowed for swifter access to other areas of the University. These corridors reminded her of the ruins she used to camp out in, or at least how she imagined they would once have looked. Long and straight, the floors made of coloured tiles which crisscrossed in snaked patterns. The walls lined with statues of previous famous sorcerers who had studied in these very halls, no matter how briefly. Even in this rather disused path did priceless artworks hang, a reminder of how lucky the observing individual was to be in that very spot.

Nobody knew how old the University was exactly, but there were none in the known world who remembered a time before it. It had been a place of great evil at times. Such as when the traitor king Virion had resided here, many thousands of years before his defeat and the birth of the Dual Monarchy. That is where its history had been lost to the shifting sands of time, leading many to theorise that there were secret tunnels and sections of the University which too had been lost, just waiting to be rediscovered.

As Catarah entered one of the more central hubs, she pressed her earplugs in harder as she entered an unavoidable intersection which separated the more central and outer areas of the structure. Here, thousands of students and staff conglomerated either on their way to classes or returning home. These intersections were much smaller than the hexagonal hubs which contained the bulk of the University's functions, and the Arch-Sorceress had to hold her breath as she navigated them. Terrified that at any moment the mass of bodies would inexplicably merge together, crushing her under its suffocating mass.

Thankfully, one of the perks of her position was that people gave her a wide berth. Meaning her heart was not quite as far into her mouth as would usually be the case. She would need to pass through the final section of the University before reaching her own tower, that being the library. The Imperial University library was the largest in the world. Taking up the entirety of the three final, massive hubs which surrounded the central tower. No matter how many times she visited, no matter how many long nights had been spent poring over old texts via candlelight, Catarah could not help but fall in love with the place all over again.

The three branches which formed the library all had their own unique interior design. There was the west wing which the Imperial Palace library had based itself upon. With its grassy floor, abundance of resident songbirds and flora, this is where one could find students most interested in the natural world and its inhabitants.

The east wing was by far Catarah's least favourite. Made almost entirely of shiny, silvery, or bronze metal. Everything from the chairs to the floor, and in some cases, even the books themselves were made of the cold, unfeeling elements of the world. Between the thousands of bookshelves animatronic librarians whirred and hissed as their engines drove them on. Able to extend and retract their limbs to great lengths they could reach even the highest shelves with ease.

Furthermore, there were other animatrons which stood at the foot of every tenth row of shelves. These animatrons took the forms of historical figures and were programmed to answer questions students may have on certain topics. Of course, these were extremely rudimentary in their capacity for storing knowledge, staring back menacingly and in silence if asked a question it had not been programmed to answer.

It was not the sort of place one would go for a relaxing study session with one's friends. It was rumoured that the Lord of Embers himself had practically lived here during his studies, although no record of him ever attending the University existed. Nevertheless, it had its uses. Catarah could not help but feel the very essence of the place seemed to break down all the wonder and mystery of magic into little more than numbers and logic. How anyone could ever achieve any sort of progress with such a mindset was beyond her.

The north wing, where the Arch-Sorceress found herself now, was without a doubt her favourite. It cared far less for its own outward appearance, valuing instead the knowledge which could be found within. Indeed, it was quite an unremarkable sight, at least to those who had seen the wonders of the other wings or the palace library. But it was this rustic aesthetic which made Catarah feel so at home here, so relaxed and at ease. There were no ponds of colourful fish or damp, grassy seating areas circled by wildflowers, nor metal books with pages like razors and ominously watchful robots.

No, the north wing was little more than comfy chairs and long, wooden desks where people could sit and study in peace and quiet. Every so often there would be a well-shielded fire which warmed through to the soul. Especially appreciated on those cold or wet nights when homework was due the next morning or one just needed a place to relax. Catarah had spent many nights dozing off in the shadows of those flickering flames, a heavy book in one hand and a warm, spiced coffee in the other. If anywhere was truly home, this was it.

Catarah passed longingly through the library, reminiscing about simpler times. Times when all she had to worry about were deadlines and Adeneus' approval. Considering the enormity of the task ahead, she wished for nothing more than to go back to a time where she drank wine by the fire, while she and her master theorised their next breakthrough in magical theory. Alas, those times were gone. Memories would have to suffice as comfort, as there was neither time nor place for such softness now.

At the back of the library was a door to which only Catarah had the key. A door which led to the Arch-Sorcerer's tower. In truth, she could have bypassed this journey for a far quicker, more direct route. But she wanted to have some time to herself before work took up all her spare thoughts. Passing through the door, Catarah entered a wide, circular space which separated the tower from the library. Currently in a bit of disarray, the new Arch-Sorceress had ordered this area to mimic that of outside in homage to her late master. Therefore, what had once been a uniform floor of grey stone, was now a mixture of the former and freshly exhumed earth sprinkled with saplings and seeds. It would be a while before it was completed, but time well spent in Catarah's opinion.

At last, she entered the tower. The bottom floor contained a receptionist's desk, waiting room and many dozen other, smaller rooms with varying vocations. The tower had no other floors save for the Arch-Sorcerer's quarters and kitchens for her private retinue of cooks at the peak. Everything therefore had to be crammed into this rather limited space. Catarah did not mind this confined space, as it meant few people bothered her unless the matter was of great importance. Which it almost never was.

The reception desk was manned by a tall and gangly man by the name of Lento. With long, wispy hair the colour of straw, and a pale complexion after spending so many centuries without setting foot outside this very tower, visitors often mistook him for an undead. Catarah had always found Lento to be an amusing creature. A man so dull, so slow in speech and movement, that he had been hand-picked by the Arch-Sorcerer before Adeneus to serve at this very post. The thought of having to converse with this man, signing visitation forms and then waiting for hours with only his company, had proved enough to keep even the most persistent of nuisances away.

He sat on a tiny stool, comically tiny even. His long body and legs almost entangling themselves, like a giant spider balancing upon a pin. Many attempts had been made to acquire him a new, more comfortable chair befitting his size. Yet he always returned to his stool, claiming he just liked things that way.

"Morning, Lento," Catarah sighed, throwing a half-hearted wave his way as she made her way towards the thousands of stairs which would eventually lead to her quarters. It took so long for Lento to reply, that Catarah almost missed the words which would end up saving her poor calves from the pain she was prepared to put them through.

"They fixed the lift," he murmured in what sounded like a mixture between a yawn and a groan. Was this man so incredibly boring that he was in fact able to bore himself to sleep?

"Really?" Catarah gasped in delight. "Oh, thank God," she praised, stepping over to the wide, stone disk at the far end of the room. "What was wrong with it?" She asked, tentatively prodding the edge of the disk with her foot.

"Something with the pressure sensor. Maybe. I don't know. It was rather boring," Lento replied mournfully.

"Right," Catarah replied before stepping onto the square pressure-plate in the centre of the disk. As her weight pushed the plate down, cogs began to turn and soon the Arch-Sorceress was being whisked to the top of the tower. It was going slightly too fast as Catarah's body became increasingly more cumbersome to move. Nevertheless, she would happily be splatted against the ceiling rather than take the stairs ever again. It was funny, when she had started as Adeneus' apprentice, there had been an attendant whose sole role was to stand on the plate and bring you to the top of the tower. One too many strikes by the elevator operator's union, however, had swiftly seen an end to that profession. Now Catarah had to perform the menial task herself. Definitely a step backwards, she thought.

After only a few minutes, a welcome change to the hours the stairs would have taken, the Arch-Sorceress arrived at her quarters. She had made relatively few changes since Adeneus' death, although some minor alterations had been desperately needed. Anything even remotely taxidermised had been gleefully discarded. She may have spent centuries living in squalor, but that did not make her a psychopath. At least not enough of one to have stuffed corpses surrounding her day and night. What Adeneus had found so endearing about them she would never understand.

She had also replaced the curtains. What had once been old, moth-eaten rags no longer fit for purpose were now spectacularly expensive blackout curtains. Imbued with a spell that allowed them to trap even more light, these allowed for extended lie-ins when Catarah could afford them. She didn't care that the old pair had been the same curtains gifted by the very first Grand Seeker to the Arch-Sorcerer of the time. They were gross, and they had to go.

Immediately to her left upon stepping from the lift, there

was a wooden door that led to the kitchens. From within she could already hear the screaming of her head chef as he terrorised his poor employees. She could see steam escaping from the seams around the door and was caught in their allure. Whatever they were doing, they were creating something divine. Something beyond the realms of magic. Something so delicious Catarah's legs began to move towards the smell of their own accord. She stopped herself just in the nick of time. She may be the head of the University and the most powerful sorcerer in the Imperium, but in the kitchens, chef was king. He would not take kindly to her intrusion, and even she would not want to test his temper.

Despite the new curtains and distinct lack of dead animals in humorous positions, the quarters had remained unchanged. The room was very large, at least by the standards of the common man comparing it to his own quarters. But this was much more than a mere bedroom. It was a laboratory, a library, a lyceum. A place to ponder the wonders of magic, to experiment to the heart's content and argue with oneself for hours.

As one could have perhaps expected at this point, the immediate entrance to the quarters was a small, circular garden, flanked by two sets of stone stairs which led to the upper floor. This garden had not actually been Adeneus' doing. It had been a feature of the Arch-Sorcerer's quarters for as long as anyone could remember. A tradition the new Arch-Sorceress had no problem maintaining. There was a single, small tree, under which could be found only the rarest of plants and fauna. Rarely would even Catarah allow herself to pluck from this garden, as many of its occupants took many centuries to grow. The grief in waiting decades or even centuries for re-growth, no matter how close she thought she was to a cure for snoring, was just not worth taking the chance merely experimenting.

As she ascended the stairs, the branches of the tree reaching out to her like an old friend, the rest of the room came into view. The room had no definitive shape, additions having been made over the centuries to accommodate whatever interest the latest Arch-Sorcerer may have had. No bar though, a shame really. Although thinking about it a little more, perhaps unfettered access to alcohol and magical experimentation were not a wise mix.

A long, black and white chequered carpet led the way, splitting off in the directions of the room's different sections. Its final destination being the tall, teardrop shaped window at the far end of the room which offered an unrivalled view of the city. Catarah had spent countless hours staring out of this window at the world below. So tiny and yet filled with such mammoth grief and strife. It seemed so trivial from this God-like place in the clouds.

To her left was a modest alchemy lab. Hundreds of vials, some empty, others filled with different creations littering the space around the main workbench. A beautiful collection of instruments such as a marble mortar and pestle and bejewelled knives lay scattered about. Always at the ready should inspiration suddenly strike, as it so often did in the dead of night.

On her right lay one of her favourite places in the world. The spell-forge. The only one of its kind. The spell-forge was an octagon six feet wide which hovered just off the ground. A small but vital detail. Had this buzzing construct touched the floor, it would pull from it all the magical energy stored within. Although not much, touching the floor would have tainted the magical creation which had taken so much effort to make. At each point of the octagon was a small circle only a few inches across, within each of which a different gemstone hung suspended. These stones, while not rare themselves, were valuable beyond measure. They had been the very same used by Virion to conduct his experiments. Infused with an ageless, limitless power. The final gift of the last Dragon Lord before his departure.

The spell-forge allowed only the most powerful sorcerers to do what prophets and oracles could do with ease - create entirely new spells with the power stored within the surrounding gems. It was a dangerous and taxing process, yet the raw magical power was more addictive than any drug. To feel the indescribable rush as the language of creation flowed through your body, allowing you to manipulate the world to your will, there truly was nothing else like it. This was the closest one could come to mimicking the power of God. No wonder Virion had been so obsessed with it.

At the very front of the room, behind the stairs, was the rather limited library. At least when compared to the one only a lift ride away. Except this library contained books reserved only for the eyes of the Arch-Sorcerer. Indeed, there were tomes here that would make the professors below, so sure of their knowledge, blush with embarrassment. Even more tantalising, however, were those which being in the mere possession of, would earn you a date with the Grand Seeker himself. Almost guaranteed to be from atop a burning stake while he read out the charges of heresy against you.

Finally, by Catarah's reckoning, was the most wonderful place in the world. Near the tear-shaped window was her bed. It called to her like a lover, longing for her embrace. A call she was desperate to heed, but there was still much work to be done before she could reward herself with sleep. Plus, it was still early in the morning. The Arch-Sorceress could not be seen to be napping when war was so close at hand.

First, she needed a quick boost. She walked over to the very basic kitchen her chef had begrudgingly allowed, making herself a piping hot coffee. Taking a sip despite the heat she could not help but utter a loud sigh of delight.

"Ahhhh," she sighed. "Right," she said turning to where her work lay only a few feet away. "Time to earn that amazing government salary." Near the foot of her bed was yet another desk. Upon it lay a diorama she had painstakingly constructed over the last few weeks. It was a replica of the blueprints she had shown the rest of the Congregation before being appointed to the position she now occupied. The tower the focal point, which she theorised could succeed where Adeneus had failed.

In truth, she had not been totally honest with the Congregation when claiming her creation would definitely work. Truthfully, she had absolutely no idea. But there was no way she was going to be cheated out of her well-deserved promotion. Especially not by a Battlemage of all people.

The premise was simple enough. Atop the tower would be a huge collection of corite crystals, enough to harness the required levels of magical energy needed to control an entire army telepathically. These crystals would be connected to a main chamber near the summit of the tower. Here, an unlucky subject would find themselves strapped to a device which linked their psychic tethers to any nearby husks. This would be an extremely painful and taxing process, even for individuals of such power as prophets and oracles. Nevertheless, if they couldn't make it work, nobody could.

The only issue which remained, and continued to plague the Arch-Sorceress, was how to ensure compliance of the subjects. Should they suddenly decide to turn their new armies on the Imperium, there would be no way to stop them short of killing them. Luckily, she had quite accidentally stumbled upon a serum of Adeneus' own design which could render the target passive. Creating a vessel which Catarah, or anyone else for that matter, could control utterly with nothing more than their voice. Her experiment was nearly ready to execute. She was only missing two rather vital ingredients which she hoped would be delivered soon – a subject, and a few hundred souls to occupy the corite. One of these could be acquired rather easily. The other would be problematic, to say the least.

As she carefully fixed a small green ball of glass to the top of the tower, she could not help but wonder what Adeneus would have said. He had always expressed to her the importance of ethical boundaries with magic. Believing that progress was not always worth the price, especially if the cost was a human one. But seeing what had become of him, travelling to his fortress and witnessing for herself the cages filled with spent subjects, the surrounding villages laid to waste by his creations. She wondered if in the end, in those final moments where he was powerless to defend himself, if he still held firm in his old beliefs.

After a few more minutes of tinkering, she was finished with her diorama. She would present this rather lacklustre feat of engineering to the University Board of Scholars, along with her detailed plan of action. In truth, the replica she had spent so long working on was of little consequence, more for the benefit of those on the Board who were themselves bored easily. The meat of the plan came in the form of the hundred or so pages of calculations the Arch-Sorceress had written by hand. After this meeting, awaiting the beginning of the war, the Board would work to ensure Adeneus', and now Catarah's, mission could be completed at last.

This would not be the end of her endeavours for the day, however. She doubted she would ever be that lucky again. No, there were still endless meetings to be had, hundreds of documents to sign and letters to send. There would not only be one tower, oh no, Gaia would be filled with towers by the end. Imposing black pillars which would inspire both fear and awe from all those who bore witness. Every husk in the known world would become an instrument of The Emperor's will. It was not the type of work Catarah had ever expected to find herself pouring so much of herself into. Yet she could not stop now, she had to see if her towers worked, if all her efforts had been in vain.

Chapter 10

It had been a fortnight since Nate and Cassandra had returned from their mission, both with very different perspectives on the outcome. Cassandra had gleefully collected her share of the bounty from Marathel. Nate, however, with a face like a slapped arse. Marathel could not help but notice his sour demeanour and kindly attempted some reassurance, telling him that the first mission is always the trickiest but that he would soon get the hang of it. She did not know what had happened, and Nate was not about to tell her. He instead faked a smile and thanked Marathel for her help before returning home.

On that first night, he sat alone in his barracks for a while, staring at the two bags of gold he had taken from the necromancer. To him they were tangible reminders of not only his own weakness, being unwilling to risk his life for an innocent, but also of Cassandra's assertion that he was indeed no better than she. That after long enough here, he too would stoop to any low to get out. He didn't want to believe her, yet a small part of him could not help but be filled with delight at the sight of the gold, twinkling at him from the bulging purses.

It was this small sliver of his psyche which filled him with such anxiety. He had only been in Purgatory for just over a year, and yet he was already beginning to succumb to the desperate struggle to escape. He considered throwing the gold out, into the street, where someone untainted by their ill-gotten acquisition could make use of it. That thought lasted about two seconds as alternate, intrusive thoughts overpowered any noble intention. Leaving Nate believing that he may as well make use of his prize. After all, as Cassandra had rightly said, the necromancer had no use for it anymore. Plus, he had not been the one to end her life so violently. No, if anything, he *deserved* this money for standing up to Cassandra, no matter how token the gesture may have proven in the end.

Later that night Chen had arrived, throwing open the door with an exhausted yet satisfied huff. She immediately noticed Nate had returned, followed quickly by eyeing the bags of gold on the floor. "Nice catch," she praised, hopping her way to her bed, pulling off her muddy boots and tossing them in the general direction of the fire. "Didn't realise the Guild paid so well for undead," she continued.

"They don't," Nate had replied sullenly, falling onto his back, staring up at the ceiling.

A few days later he had given up wrestling with his inner demons and turned the gold over to the bank to be added to his account. An offhand comment by one of the Vault Keepers had vexed Nate slightly.

"There is no price too high for such a prize," it had hissed at him, almost mockingly. As if it knew exactly how Nate had obtained the gold and the inner turmoil it had caused him.

Now, two weeks after his return, Nate found himself somewhere he had hoped never to be again. While out for dinner one night, he had been approached by Chion, who had thankfully been absent from his life since finishing his training. Now, however, it appeared that he had returned. Only this time with a full set of gleaming white teeth, which were a drastic improvement from the asymmetrical mess they had been before. Sadly, though, the brilliantness of his teeth had not seeped into his personality. As rude as ever, he had informed Nate that Captain Ardell had summoned him to her fort for the following morning.

One pointless argument later, in which Nate asserted his independence from the army, he had found himself preparing for the meeting anyway. Now here he stood, alongside Marcus, in the war room of Ardell's fort.

"Any idea what this is about?" Marcus whispered.

"You're seriously asking me?" Nate breathed, gobsmacked

that Marcus would ever consider him to know anything. Marcus huffed and dropped his shoulders slightly. He too had hoped never to see the inside of this place again.

"I thought we were independent now. That Ardell couldn't boss us around anymore?" Nate complained. The risk of his face being slammed into something solid was always considerably higher around his former captain.

"Usually, yeah," Marcus confirmed. "But something's telling me that whatever Ardell wants us for isn't going to be usual."

"Fucking hell," Nate groaned. "I was just getting used to having a life." Before Marcus could reply, Chion appeared at the bottom of the set of spiralling stone stairs which led to Ardell's quarters.

"The captain will see you now," he sneered.

"She demoted you to personal assistant now?" Marcus grinned as he passed.

"It's an honour to serve, actually," Chion retorted with clear hurt and embarrassment in his voice.

"I bet she even has a bell for him," Nate added with a smirk as he too made his way up the stairs. Chion's face immediately turned a bright shade of red. It was all true. The captain did indeed have a bell she would ring, in response to which Chion would be expected to come running. But it would be a cold day in hell before he let either of these cretins know that.

Whatever sense of superiority that the pair felt after mocking Chion soon dissipated as they knocked on Ardell's door. They were met with the unchanged singular command of "enter," although it sounded far less surly than they were used to. Perhaps over the past year some form of miracle had occurred and the captain had mellowed out somewhat.

As the nervous pair entered, they found Ardell in her usual place. As beautiful as ever, with her raven-coloured hair spilling over her shoulders like a dark waterfall, her blue eyes seemingly gleaming in the morning sun which lit up the room. She was reclining on her chair with her feet upon the desk. In her hand she held aloft a large revolver which she admired with an endearing grin.

"I knew she was going to kill us," Nate whispered. Ardell's eyes flicked over towards her guests before turning quickly back to the gun in her hands.

"Nice to see you again, boys. How have you been?" she asked. The two men looked at one another hoping the other would have some idea of what to do in such a surreal situation. Marcus took charge as he realised anything Nate said was likely to result in the gun being pointed in their direction.

"N...not too bad, Captain...How are you?" Marcus replied sheepishly, pronouncing each word carefully, as if he were coaxing a bear.

"Good...good," Ardell whispered, having not heard a word of Marcus' reply, still fixated on the weapon. She turned it over again and again in her hand, her eyes glinting with delight each time the light caught it in a new way. It was not a weapon of exquisite beauty; in fact, it seemed quite common. A long, thick silvery barrel and a polished wooden handle were its only visible components. Yet Ardell seemed infatuated by it.

The room was silent for a while. The longer the silence dragged on, the more convinced Nate became that this was some sort of test.

"New gun, Captain?" he asked, not knowing what else to do.

"Yes, thank you for noticing," Ardell smiled, finally turning towards the two men. To their surprise, the smile remained.

"I need your help actually," she said, setting the gun down carefully on the desk while still keeling precariously.

"Whatever you need, Captain," Marcus replied tactically.

"I'm having trouble coming up with a name for my new friend here," Ardell sighed, once again picking up the revolver and turning it over in her hand. "I was hoping you could help."

Neither Nate nor Marcus bought this for a second. There was no chance in hell Ardell would suffer their presence unless absolutely necessary, let alone give a damn about anything they may have to say. No, something else was clearly on the agenda. But with nothing else to go on, they played along.

"I've been wracking my brain for days, and yet still haven't come up with anything even remotely decent," Ardell complained as the two men searched their own imaginations.

"Widow Maker," Nate declared triumphantly after a few moments of intense thought. Ardell looked at him in silence, her face expressionless before turning her attention to Marcus, awaiting his suggestion. Marcus continued thinking for a few more seconds before less enthusiastically suggesting, "Iron Rose".

"Iron Rose," Ardell repeated softly, as she eyed the weapon in her hand. "I like it," she smiled evilly.

"And Widow Maker, Captain?" Nate asked, slightly dejected. Personally, he thought his suggestion was much catchier than Marcus'. Plus, it seemed more befitting the absolute psychopath that was the weapon's master. Ardell did not look back to Nate as she replied, her eyes still running along the barrel of the gun.

"Nate, if you ever speak in my presence again, I will feed you your own teeth." Message received and understood, Nate thought as he stood there in silence, his lips pressed tightly together. Setting her new toy down for the final time, Ardell let out a loud mixture of a groan and a huff. Correcting her dangerous sitting position, she rested her elbows upon the desk, her hands clasped together as she eyed the men before her.

"Right," she began, the novelty of her new acquisition quickly wearing off, already dreading the journey this conversation was about to embark her upon. "There is another matter actually," she admitted at last, confirming Nate and Marcus' suspicions.

"You may be aware that relations between Tinelia and The

Imperium have been slightly less cordial lately." This was an understatement, both sides had been preparing for war ever since the empress was killed, and since Nate and Marcus had taken part in the attack on the Imperial City, neither could help but bear some responsibility for whatever came out of their actions, even if they were not the ones to drop the bombs themselves.

"Now," Ardell continued. "We don't know what they've been doing for the past year. They've been unusually cautious and tight lipped. Probably building up their armies in preparation to invade," Ardell said going off on a tangent. More so talking to herself now as she ran through the hundreds of scenarios she had mapped out in her head to explain the current situation. She quickly came back to reality, continuing her previous train of thought.

"Anyway, all of a sudden the whole country seems to have woken up and are wanting to take things in a direction even I didn't expect."

"What direction would that be, Captain?" Nate interrupted, quickly forgetting the Captain's warning.

"They're taking their case to the Judges," she revealed after a lengthy pause. This of course meant nothing to Nate, but Marcus could not help but be taken aback.

"Since when does The Imperium recognise their authority?" he asked.

"They don't," Ardell admitted with raised hands and shrugged shoulders. "But that crafty bastard Nestor must think they have an airtight case if they'd even consider putting themselves before the international community."

At this point Nate had been forgotten about entirely, the conversation now between the two people who somewhat knew what they were talking about.

"What would be the point? They've had all year to do whatever they wished, and only now they want to settle it in court?" Marcus pondered aloud.

"As I say," Ardell responded. "The rest of The Imperium may be filled with fanatics and lunatics, but Nestor is clever.

If he thinks he can beat us in court, we could end up with the entire known world united against us." Only now did Nate begin to understand the gravity of the situation. He had never wanted war, but the possibility Ardell had just raised had not occurred to him in even his darkest nightmares.

Marcus folded his arms, unable to believe what his former captain had suggested. He shook his head. "Our allies would never turn against us, not in favour of The Imperium anyway." This time it was Ardell's turn to shake her head.

"I wouldn't be so sure," she threatened without elaborating further. "Besides, it's not our allies I'm worried about. It's the powers in the east that concern me. They've played both sides for a long time, if push comes to shove, we may not like where they end up throwing their weight."

"Gods," Marcus whispered. As silent contemplation fell upon the room, Nate took this as his que to speak.

"Sorry, Captain, but how does this involve us exactly? Marcus and me, I mean?" That was a good point, one that Marcus had not yet considered and now he too was curious. Why would their former Captain impart such information on them of all people, being so far removed from any position which could be of use? Ardell could not help letting a thin smile creep across her lips. The kind of smile which indicated that she would rather be anywhere else other than having this conversation.

"The Grand Admiral is sending a delegation to Peace-Haven to present our case to the Judges." There was a painful pause as Ardell summoned the courage to say the following words. "He would like the three of us to be part of that delegation. Specifically, to protect our diplomatic representative."

"You're shitting me?!" Nate blurted out.

"I shit you not," Ardell breathed, taking a sip from a nearby wineglass.

Marcus said nothing. There was nothing he could say which would change what had already been decided. Instead, he closed his eyes and tilted his head back until he was facing the ceiling, his arms folded. This was not out of despair, however, not at all. Yes, the thought of travelling in a confined space with Ardell made him want to rip his own spine out, but being permitted to visit Peace-Haven was the closest thing to winning the lottery Purgatory had.

Ardell knew exactly what was running through Marcus' mind but decided not to quash his fantasies just yet.

"You will both be at the docks and ready to depart in two days. There will be no questions," Ardell added as Nate began to open his mouth.

"We should be gone for a maximum of ten days, so prepare accordingly. And whatever you do," Ardell said, raising her voice to indicate that if they had heard nothing else, they had best heed her current warning. "Do not tell anyone where you are going."

The two men nodded and left in a hurry as Ardell waved them away. They would need to leave tonight if they were to arrive at the docks on time. As they left, Ardell looked over towards her fireplace, above which Oath Breaker lay. She hated the thought of leaving it behind, even for a moment, but she could not take it with her. Not to a place like Peace-Haven. Not with the madness it carried.

Two days later

Nate could not help but feel a small rush of excitement as he stretched in the morning sun at the end of one of the dock's many piers. It had been a year since his first and only flight on an airship, and he was eager for another. The journey to Peace-Haven would take a few days, much longer than his previous flight, but he was not overly concerned. Why the Grand Admiral had chosen himself and Marcus for this mission, however, was a mystery. Even Nate with his planet-sized ego had to admit there were plenty of people better suited to the job. Nevertheless, he knew by now not to question the motives of those above him. Instead, he would simply enjoy the opportunity to get out of the city for a while.

As he twisted his torso and stretched his legs, Nate felt the cool sea-breeze wash over him. The distinctly salty, briny smell a comforting reminder of days long past spent on Welsh beaches. All around him were the expected sights and sounds of the docks, ships both arriving and departing for as far as the eye could see. Their colourful sails flapped gently in the morning breeze, while the dark shapes of their cannons protruded from their hulls like poisonous spines. Sailors bellowed at one another using language which would make even Ardell blush, unloading their cargo under the watchful eyes of their own captains. Meanwhile, armies of officials and busybodies made sure not a single item made it off the ships un-declared and un-taxed.

Nate wondered what it must be like, sailing the seas with no idea what may lie ahead. New continents and kingdoms overflowing with wealth they were willing to share? Or maybe island paradises the sailors kept secret amongst themselves? There was only one way to find out for sure. But Nate was quite happy with his life. He enjoyed having solid ground beneath his feet, of knowing what it meant to be dry, and having a diet which consisted of more than stale biscuits. The truth, he would be disappointed to learn if he had ever bothered to ask, was far duller. Very few ships dared risk travelling into uncharted waters. The danger of setting off with no destination in mind and only limited provisions was not worth the potential rewards for most.

There were, however, a few intrepid souls who did not fear starving to death on the open ocean. Yet that is what they were, few. Most with an unshakeable adventurous disposition preferred to join Lord Massah on his travels west. It was by no means glamorous, having that pompous cretin barking orders at you all day and then taking all the credit, but then neither was dying of scurvy without sight of so much as a pebble.

As Nate watched a pair of sailors accidentally drop a crate of bejewelled ballgowns into the sea, much to their captain's dismay, there was a sharp whack against the back of his head.

"Look alive wanker," Marcus chortled. Recently, before disappearing off the face of the planet, Joel had taken it upon himself to teach Marcus some of his favourite words. While not quite there yet, Marcus was certainly getting his money's worth out of them.

"Unnecessary," Nate complained, rubbing the back of his head.

"You excited for our trip?" Marcus asked, clearly trying to contain his own.

"It'll definitely be nice to get away for a while," Nate replied, distinctly lacking the sort of enthusiasm practically anyone else would be feeling in his situation. Marcus shook his head in amusement at his apprentice's ignorance. As that is what he still considered Nate to be, despite the fact he was now a monster hunter in his own right. Ardell had given Marcus a sacred charge over Nate, one that would last until one of them bit the dust.

"Believe me, once we get there, you'll change your tune. It's about as close to paradise as you'll find on Gaia."

Nate's interest was suddenly caught and he tried prying more information out of Marcus, who remained as stubbornly silent as always. His insistence on remaining tight-lipped, ensuring that the surprise would not be spoiled.

"We had best get aboard, don't want to keep the captain waiting," Marcus said after a few pleasant moments staring at the peaceful yet crowded horizon. Nate sighed in agreement, not yet willing to abandon this scenic spot for the dark and cramped belly of a ship. Their ship was located a few rows down from where they had been standing. Their vessel flew the Tinelian diplomatic flag beside the conventional flag displaying a white sailboat against a background of azure blue. This consisted of three different coloured roses held in the beak of a dove. A reference to how Arda Tinelia herself had supposedly been guided to these very shores.

This flag would inform any nearby vessel that under no circumstances was the ship to be halted, boarded, or attacked.

Pirates would patently not heed such warnings but, where they were headed, pirates would be the least of their concerns.

The ship itself was not much different from any other one might see at the docks. It utilised three tall masts to which the sails were currently furled. Its colour was a deep brown, partly due to the tar which was plastered across every inch to keep her waterproof. The only deviation from this were the planks which had been painted gold. These surrounded the outer edges of the captain's quarters, running down the stern and rudder, along the hull, and to the bow in two parallel lines three planks wide. It's only major difference to any other Tinelian ship was the presence of a second captain's quarters adjacent to the first. This peculiar design had earned the ship the nickname of '*Bucktooth*' among those who sailed her.

As Nate approached the ship, he incorrectly assumed that this second luxurious room would belong to Ardell. As the two were about to board, a man with a clipboard stopped them. He was strangely dressed, or at least so it appeared to Nate. He did not bother with the thin, open shirts, red or tan shorts and broad, square-toed shoes of the standard sailor. Instead, he wore a bright blue laced doublet, long red trousers, knee-high white socks, and polished leather boots. Upon his head he wore a powdered wig and a black tricorne to complete his livery.

Nate and Marcus both looked at him with a mixture of wariness and confusion. As if they expected him to at any moment break out into song or perhaps trap himself in an invisible box. This, however, was the ship's captain. And he was no greater fan of his ridiculous outfit as much as the gawping pair before him. It was a special occasion, however, and his yet to arrive honoured guest had insisted all the most trivial and out-dated ceremonial rituals go with it.

"You two must be Ardell's guys," he stated rather than asked, barely looking up from his clipboard.

"Is it that obvious?" Nate joked awkwardly.

The captain looked the pair up and down before replying, "Either that or you've just come back from finding your wives being ploughed by half the town. The expressions are very similar." Nate and Marcus looked at one another, unsure whether to be amused or insulted.

"You speaking from experience?" Marcus replied. There was a brief, tense silence as the captain's eyes darted from his clipboard to Marcus, staring menacingly before becoming relaxed. The captain could not help but grin and the three men shared a round of laughter.

"Captain Kellis, good to have you on board," he said shaking the pair's hands.

"How long before lift-off?" Nate asked, his excitement obvious.

Kellis shook his head.

"Won't be no lift-off I'm afraid. There's a huge storm coming our way, can't fly through it, so we will have to do it the old-fashioned way."

Both men's hearts immediately dropped at this revelation.

"Fuck me dead," Marcus exclaimed in surprise and disappointment. Nate and Kellis both gave him confused looks before deciding to ignore him entirely.

"Sailing will take us a few days extra, so I hope you two like biscuits," the captain added, his eyes returning to his clipboard. Nate's stomach turned at the words and just as he was about to suggest postponing their trip, a familiar voice spoke up sending a shiver down his spine.

"You two, here, now," ordered Captain Ardell who sounded even grumpier than usual. Nate and Marcus both obeyed, hurriedly turning and approaching their captain. She stood with her arms folded, a scowl etched upon her face, although her eyes were staring into the distance. It seemed, for once, the pair before her were not the source of her frustration. Nate and Marcus stood in silence, having learned long ago not to interrupt Ardell's brooding. Nothing good would come of it. Instead, they waited for her eyes to come back into focus and fall upon them, although her facial expression did not change.

When Ardell spoke, she did so softly, as if each word were

causing her physical pain, half her lip remaining clenched between her teeth.

"From this moment until we return, the man behind me is your god. You will do everything in your power to keep him from harm. You will do as he says unless I give you strict orders otherwise. You will lay down your lives for him without question. Is that understood?"

Nate and Marcus looked past Ardell to see a man approaching them. His entire upper body laden with luggage and bags for the journey ahead. He dropped them to the ground with an annoyed grunt before shooting a glare at Ardell.

The man was short in stature, perhaps four to five inches shorter than Ardell. His head contained only a few ragged tufts of hair, and his skin was a chalky white mixed with blotches of bright pink. A tell-tale sign of a man who lived a very luxurious and indulgent life. Upon his face sat a thick, black moustache, well-groomed and oiled. The complete opposite of his eyebrows which were wild and would have looked more at home upon an owl. He was also quite a large man. While he retained some stockiness and may have once been quite attractive, his years spent in extravagance had rendered him more round than robust.

"I'm not used to carrying my own bags, you should know," he fumed, pouting with his hands on his hips like a stroppy toddler. Supressing her desire to shatter his kneecaps, Ardell acted oblivious.

"My apologies, your Excellency. I was simply admiring your strength, a dainty woman like me could never hope to attempt such a masculine feat."

Marcus and Nate could see with their own eyes the physical pain it caused Ardell to say these falsehoods. She would have looked more comfortable chewing glass. Even they cringed at her forced, playfully soft voice. Nevertheless, the honeyed words worked and the man quickly blushed, a wide smile growing across his face as he puffed out his chest.

"No matter, my sweet, I shall go and fetch the rest," he began. Ardell, however, stopped him.

"My men here will take care of that, your Excellency. I see the captain is waiting, so why don't you go and talk with him over some wine rather than standing here with us rabble?"

The man nodded, offering Ardell the most miniscule of bows before pushing between Nate and Marcus whom he did not even acknowledge. They were beneath him, after all.

"Who's that charming fellow?" Nate asked with a sour tinge to his voice.

"Lord Ilrid," Ardell replied with an equally venomous tone. "Tinelia's finest diplomat, allegedly," she added as the three watched him greet the captain and saunter onto the ship without a care in the world.

"Marvellous," Marcus sighed sarcastically as the captain waved to them, signalling it was time to depart. As the three of them loaded the last of Lord Ilrid's belongings onto the deck, Nate could make out the shadow of approaching storm clouds in the distance. Like a wall of black and grey, they rumbled closer with each passing minute.

'How bad could it be?' Nate asked himself as he was led below deck to his home for the next week.

As it turns out, far worse than he ever could have imagined.

There was plenty of rum, but very little yo ho ho'ing to be had. Each morning Nate would wake after barely an hour's sleep to ankle-high water and a dark sky which knew no daylight. The rain was an endless, stinging torrent which soaked through to the bone, while the wailing wind whipped away one's words from their mouth. At night, the creaking and groaning of the ship as it was assaulted from all sides by mountainous waves were poor lullabies, leaving Nate rigid in his hammock, waiting for the sea to swallow him at any moment.

With no seafaring experience, Nate and Marcus were expected to spend their days and nights below deck, out of the way of the sailors. But this appeased nobody. Trapped in a soggy, rocking cage with no daylight, the pair quickly grew bored and irritable. A poor combination at the best of times. They would therefore venture onto the deck, only to be stared at with frustration and discontent by the crew. Why should these two not have to pull their weight? Instead, being allowed to pass their time resting, drinking what little rum remained. More than once tempers bubbled over, resulting in scuffles between the usually drunk Nate and Marcus and the crew.

Once Ardell had caught Marcus throwing drunken punches at the helmsman, she banished them to the lower deck until either the journey was over, or they sobered up. Whichever came first. In the dank bowels of the ship Nate and Marcus could do little but talk, doing their best to avoid any further confrontations with the crew. After a while, Marcus confessed an apprehension about their mission. Not that they themselves would fail at guarding Lord Ilrid, who had not once left his quarters since setting sail. They both felt an underlying anxiety at the prospect of how a war would be avoided.

A year ago, Marcus had considered war with the Imperium to be both inevitable and something to look forward to. Indeed, the delight on his face at the firestorm that engulfed the Imperial city was not something Nate would ever forget. But now he felt different. He had not just Nate to worry about, but he had become closer with all those who had survived their last mission. The thought of losing any of them was not worth whatever enjoyment he once found in battle. It had taken over eighty years, but Marcus now found joy in a quieter life. One that still involved hunting monsters, mind you, but which posed a far lesser risk to those he loved.

Nate of course laughed at this heartfelt revelation, called Marcus a pussy, and moved swiftly on. Although, this was only to hide his own fears he could not allow to be openly conveyed. He still had the occasional nightmare from their mission. He would see Said once again lying in that rocky alcove, torn to pieces, the fangs of the stalkers gleaming in the moonlight. He would imagine Marcus, skewered on the tip of May's sword, or worst of all, see Cassandra once again engulfed in flames while she screamed helplessly. Nate hoped more than anything that their latest mission would be a success. The last thing he wanted was to be sent back into the jaws of the Imperium, whatever the justification.

As he lay in his hammock, swinging gently from side to side and staring up at the dripping planks above him, he thought of Cassandra. Just as he believed their relationship had been starting to mend, she had shown another side of herself that Nate simply could not ignore. The way she had so callously and coldly murdered the defenceless necromancer haunted him. Yet he understood. And for that reason, he could not hate her or even hold a grudge for what she had done, no matter how awful. In the end she had been right. All that matters is getting out of Purgatory. Considering all she had been through, Nate could not blame her for what she had become. Although, he wouldn't be going on any more missions with her, if he could avoid it.

The next day, the sixth into their journey, Nate awoke to an unexpected sensation - the sound of silence. The thunderous roars of ocean waves and deafening drumbeat of rain had ceased. In their stead had come an eery nothingness. The wind had dropped too, and now his voice which had been strained for so long, felt loud enough to shatter the world around him like glass when he tried to speak. The rest of the crew could feel it too, this quiet seemed totally unnatural after what had become their norm over the past week. A fog of unease settled around them as they slowly and silently ascended to the top deck one by one. Nate was one of the last to brave the ascent and, once he did, he found the crew all gathered upon the port side, silent and motionless, staring off into the distance.

At first Nate wondered if perhaps they had at last arrived at their destination. However, he quickly dismissed this as they had been sailing against the wind for the last few days. It must be something else. But what could cause an entire ship of usually busy men to fall into such a trance? Nate was not sure he wanted to know. Nevertheless, he slowly gravitated towards the crowd, nudging his way forwards until he was staring out at the open ocean. At least, he assumed it was the ocean. Everything was deathly still, the sea like a pane of glass reflecting the dull, grey sky. It was a surreal sight to one who had not seen it before, one who had only known the sea to be a violent and unpredictable force. It was almost as if they had entered another world entirely.

But as the novelty soon wore off, Nate found himself confused at why the others, especially the hardened crew, continued to stare so intently out into this placid nothingness. He turned back towards the sea, wondering what he was supposed to have missed. But all he saw was the same tranquil waters as before. Then, he saw a shimmer. In the distance there was something disrupting the otherwise uniform stillness of the horizon. The longer he stared, the clearer it became until it was unquestionable. It was a ship, flying ripped sails and no flag, slowly gliding towards them. The water beneath it remaining completely still, as if the ship were hydroplaning above it.

The helmsman halted the ship as the ghostly vessel drew nearer. As it did so, its features became clearer, and Nate was horrified by what he saw. The ship itself was riddled with holes, as if she had barely survived a vicious battle. Broken planks jutted out into the water without disturbing it, and the whole thing seemed to be covered in thick green mould. It was the crew, however, which had Nate gripping onto the railings with both terror and dismay. The other ship was now passing close enough that the crew could be easily made out. They stood on the starboard side, staring back at the *Bucktooth*.

At first Nate believed the crew to be husks. The memories of his mission the year before now flooding back, filling him with fear. They stared back with their black, lifeless eyes, their emaciated skin, grey and paper-thin. He expected an attack to come at any moment. He reached for his sword and looked to those around him for confirmation of his suspicions.

It was the reaction of the crew that surrounded him which threw him into new depths of confusion. Many offered slow, mournful gestures from whichever faith they followed. Most remained deathly silent, not daring even to blink. The ghostly crew sailed by without so much as a whisper, their envious eyes filled with anguish not once diverting from the faces of their counterparts. At last, the ship vanished into a mist which quickly dissipated, leaving no trace of the vessel behind.

The silence which had remained unbroken for the duration of their encounter continued for a few moments more. Eventually, the crew slowly drifted away from the edge of the ship and back towards whichever duty was required. Marcus, with no work to attend to, remained a while longer, staring out into the quiet.

"What was that?" Nate whispered. Marcus looked sad, an unusual crease across his face, and a distant, thoughtful look in his eye. Clearing his throat, he turned to Nate at last.

"We call them Travellers," he said solemnly before giving a long pause. "If you've ever wondered why nobody dares kill themselves here, that's why. Stuck on a ship to nowhere for gods know how long." This was a huge and unexpected shock to Nate. Until now he had just assumed that if you found yourself in a difficult or hopeless position, you could just kill yourself for a re-roll of the dice. Not exactly a pleasant solution, but an easy one. Seeing now the consequences of such an action first hand, he was glad he had never seriously considered it.

"If you want to punish someone, and I mean really punish them, you don't execute them - you get them to do it themselves," Marcus added. Nate grimaced slightly at the barbarity of such a statement before spotting Ardell. She stood near the front of the ship, far away from the rest of the crew, her eyes still fixed on the spot where the Travellers had been. Nate then looked at the rest of the crew, all of whom went about their work in silence. This unwelcome apparition a stark reminder that not only were they here forever, but that there was no easy way out. With these thoughts swimming around his head Nate decided to get back below deck. If he was lucky, there might still be some rum left.

Chapter 11

After over a week of travel, Nate had never been so glad to see dry land. He was sick of being thrown from his hammock by rogue waves and feeling constantly seasick. He had heard the call from the upper deck and immediately dragged himself into the blinding daylight. It felt like months since he had seen the sun. For the last week his world had been nothing but an endless blanket of grey skies and lashing rain. As the warm, salty sea air rushed through his hair he turned his head skywards and took a long, refreshing breath.

He had hoped to have travelled by air, but the gathering storm on the first day of their voyage, the one which had persisted almost uninterrupted for the following week, had dashed these hopes. Nevertheless, it was all over now, they had arrived. Where exactly, Nate was still none the wiser. From where he stood on the top deck, he could see nothing but blue seas and sky. Although gradually, rising from the horizon like the stem of a flower, came the jagged tips of mountain peaks.

Strange, Nate thought, to have mountains so far out into the ocean. But as they neared, it soon became clear that these were no natural formations. They were four mighty spires, rising from a city of gleaming white against the sparkling blue backdrop of the ocean. At first, Nate thought they had turned back around and were witnessing the Citadel from a distance. But as they drew closer, it was clear this was no city in the normal sense. There were no defences, no high walls or thick gates, only the towers which shone out across the sea. Shining beacons beckoning them, their allure the inescapable siren song, pulling them towards solid ground beneath their feet.

The three smaller towers, which still measured many

hundreds of feet high, were arranged in a triangle. The greater fourth spire, which must have measured nearer to two thousand feet, stood in the centre of the others. The three outer towers were inter-connected at multiple levels by dozens of stone bridges and walkways, hanging over the city below like a spider's web glistening from the morning rain. Nate could not help but gasp as they finally drew into the port and the towers looked like the fingers of the world itself reaching to grasp the sky.

Ardell had been standing beside the ship's captain as he navigated them into port. She had been to Peace-Haven several times and no longer found any wonder in its beauty. Instead, she stared with angst at the other ships which had arrived a few days prior. Those from the far east were bunched together on the far end of the harbour. Their unique square design and lack of sails making them seem like floating fortresses, the unmistakeable property of the Eastern Defence Union, or EDU as they were commonly known.

Beside their own ship were moored two others from the Citadel Coalition. The rather flimsy alliance which had been cobbled together at the last moment to fend off the invading Imperium over a millennia ago. Both ships belonged to their ally Estrold. No ships having yet come from Gil-Ebrax it seemed. Not surprising really, she thought. Ardell doubted Gil-Ebrax's collection of so called 'leaders' had yet bothered to open Grand Admiral Lee's letter. If they had, they were probably still bickering over the generous terms by which they would attend.

Lastly, docked in the centre of the harbour, were the three ships representing the Imperium. The grandest came from the Imperium proper. It flew black sails and had an angelic bronze figurehead wielding a sword, watching over the dock with its unblinking eyes. The smallest came from the Order of the Seekers of the One. A token gesture really, trying to remind the wider world that they still pretended to exist as an independent entity. Lastly, came the most unique ship of all. It hoisted no sails and flew no flag. Made entirely of iron, it seemed more like the body of some monstrous beast than a vessel of men. It's only opening seemingly the reinforced chimney, silent now but usually bellowing thick plumes of smoke as its engines drove it forward. Ifritus, from whence the ship came, was not a place where man should dwell. Yet dwell they did, and from their dark forges spewed forth monstrous, aberrant creations such as the one before them now.

As the other groggy members of the crew hauled themselves above deck and readied the ship for disembarking, Ardell found Nate and Marcus preparing to do the same. They both immediately stood to attention upon noticing her approach before relaxing as she bid them at ease.

"Once we depart, we shall be asked to hand over our weapons. We shall oblige without complaint," she said looking at Nate as his face showed his unwillingness to part with his sword. "We will then be escorted to the central tower where we will be asked to change clothes and adopt masks."

"Is this part of a ceremony or something, Captain? If so, I'd rather stay on the boat," Nate quipped. Ardell suppressed her urge as best she could not to toss Nate overboard. Violence of any sort was prohibited in the strictest of terms on the isle. Anyone caught breaking this rule could find themselves and the nation they represented being ostracised from the international community. The last thing Ardell needed right now was to cause another incident with global repercussions.

"It is to ensure that the entire process is done fairly and without bias," she explained. "We shall all be asked to wear the same robes and face coverings. This ensures complete anonymity and the fairest possible outcome."

"Makes sense," Marcus added, folding his arms as he eyed a group of three robed figures approaching their ship. Ardell watched the two men's faces closely, looking for any indication of trouble to come.

"You are not to speak unless spoken to, and under no circumstances are you to mention anything which may indicate where you are from." Nate and Marcus both nodded in understanding, but Ardell was not convinced.

"Actually, just don't speak at all. I don't care if the Judges themselves ask you what your favourite colour is. You keep your mouth shut. Do you understand?"

The two men looked at one another confused. They understood Ardell did not like hearing them speak at the best of times, but the stress in her voice clearly conveyed the extreme importance of her instructions. What on Gaia could they possibly say which could cause that much trouble? Nevertheless, now with rather worried dispositions at their captain's seriousness, they nodded their understanding.

"Good," Ardell sighed, brushing her hair away from her face. Just then, Lord Ilrid emerged from his cabin. He was carrying a large folder of notes under his left arm, and he let out a loud yawn as he stretched in the morning sun.

"Oh great, his twatship is awake," Ardell cursed just loud enough for Nate and Marcus to hear. They turned to see the smiling diplomat waltzing towards them, as if he were not about to be thrust into the most serious political case of his life.

"Lovely morning," Ilrid beamed at the three of them who all replied with varying levels of false enthusiasm.

"Right," he said eyeing the welcoming party which stood only a few meters away at the end of the gangplank. "We'd best be off."

"Agreed," Ardell said showing Lord Ilrid the way forwards, not entirely convinced he could make it those few feet without falling off the ship and drowning. Nate and Marcus followed into the reception of the waiting welcoming party. The three men all wore different coloured robes. These denoted the Judge to which the individual served. Although Nate did not know this, assuming it was just another chance for these functionaries to show off the unmatched finery and wealth of the island.

There was a blue so dark and deep, it immediately brought back memories of the crushing depths of the ocean Nate had been so certain would be the end of his journey. The second was a dazzling yellow which seemed to twinkle in the light as if it were comprised of golden nuggets affixed to an underlying fabric. The last, a rather muted pink, as soft and gentle as the petals of a rose.

Lord Ilrid and the three men conversed with cheery smiles and polite courtesies while the other three stood there feeling ignored, as if they were unclaimed baggage. After far too long complimenting the weather and the improvements to the harbour since his last visit, Ilrid allowed himself at last to be led towards the central tower. This took the party down a well-kept road of grey brick, away from the harbour and into the city.

This city was unlike any Nate had seen so far in Purgatory, and was more like those from his own, more modern world. There were no walls or guard towers in sight, and the buildings were all rather tall and narrow, he assumed due to the limited room on the island. As they pressed on away from the harbour, the streets widened considerably, and their guides led them to the very edges where a narrower path from red brick was cut. The reason for this immediately became clear as they rounded a corner and saw queues of horse-drawn carriages and carts filling the roads from end to end.

"Must be rush hour," Nate whispered to Marcus who had no idea what that meant and continued walking without a word. Peace-Haven, also known as the Perfume or Blossom Isle, due to the large variety of cherry blossom trees which could be found there, had long been on Marcus' itinerary. Unfortunately, it was impossible to visit without an invitation, or if you were lucky, asked to be part of the staff which rotated each century. However, without an in-depth understanding of international law, it was unlikely Marcus would ever have had the chance to step foot on the isle.

As their guides led them through the busy streets and towards the central tower, Nate's mind began to wander. While enamoured by his surroundings at first, they soon became tiresome. Once you've seen one gargantuan structure reaching into the heavens you've seen them all he supposed. Instead, Nate found himself thinking of home. He wondered what that little restaurant he liked would be serving tonight. This served no purpose but to set his stomach rumbling as the imaginary scent of roasted meat filled his mind.

He then rather curiously, and unexpectedly, found himself thinking about Chen. He wondered what she was doing at this very moment, caring not that he journeyed towards one of the most important events for a thousand years. He wished she were here; she would have made the journey more bearable. Although anyone was a better sailing companion than Marcus The Perpetual Vomiter. He imagined her by the fire reading one of her books. He pictured in his mind an image of Chen resting her chin on her knees while the shadows danced around her. She was happy and she was safe, and that brought Nate an unexpected comfort.

Upon noticing the prolonged absence of Nate saying something moronic, Ardell turned her head and saw the distant look in his eyes, accompanied by a ghostly smile. She smiled herself, as she had seen that look plenty of times before. It was no stranger to her, and there was a time, long ago, that the same look had graced her own troubled and battle-weary features. But no longer. Now, when she pondered over past love, she felt nothing but a crushing guilt. Such guilt accompanied by a desire so strong that it took all her willpower to resist simply walking into the sea.

Before long they stood at the base of the central tower. Ahead of them a huge crowd had gathered. Legal experts from across the known world had made the journey to be part of this historic moment. The doors which led the way to the interior remained tightly shut. Ilrid and the other few diplomats had been led away to a separate building for the night, already informed that no deliberating would happen today. As expected, the doors were huge and obscenely decorated. They were tall and rectangular, their composition a dark, burgundy wood. Across the lower half, iron fittings had been fixed to form an intricate pattern of black vines which weaved their way to the outer edges.

All along its edge, carved into the stone, were beautiful depictions of ages long past. Beginning with the settling of the island during the Age of Subjugation, where great dragons with wings like ship's sails stood watch over the people. From there, flowing like a stream, the events through the ages played out. Until at last, on the opposite side, clearly depicted was the lady Arda Tinelia, stepping from her ship and laying claim to this land, the first in Gaia to bear her holy name.

Although it had been a long time since Peace-Haven had been considered a part of Tinelia. Now she belonged to no nation. The isle was a place of peace, somewhere for the great and powerful to gather so that they may chart a course for their world through dialogue rather than the sword. Each tower had its own name, denoting the role they played in upkeeping international law, while also representing the tenets on which Peace-Haven was founded.

Firstly, there was Peace, the servants of which wore the muted pink robes. Their job was to mediate disputes between nations and to ensure large-scale conflict did not break out. It was through this avenue that The Imperium had brought its case to be Judged. Then there was Prosperity. The dazzling yellow was their colour of choice, and they ensured that fair trade could take place between all nations and peoples. Their ultimate aspiration being that of a world united by the pursuit of wealth, rather than being separated by borders and ideology. The third tower was that of Order. By far the most shadowy and militant of all Peace-Haven's wings. It was their task to ensure that international law was heeded, and that the pestilence of anarchy did not spread unchecked. There were unconfirmed and harshly rebuked rumours that The Imperium had received their support during the peasant uprising of the previous century.

Finally, there was the largest tower of them all. That which stood greater than all the others and yet was inexorably linked - Justice. This was the home of the Judges. Where all rulings were made and the fates of nations decided. As Ardell awaited the ceremonial opening of the doors, she wondered if maybe, just this once, the powers gathered here could for the first time avoid bloodshed.

Nate, meanwhile, was busy examining the details of the tower now that they were finally close enough to properly see it. Overall, it was what he had come to expect of the afterlife. With nothing better to do, why not spend hundreds, if not thousands of years over-designing every inch of a building? Scrutinising the tower, Nate spotted something which caught his eye. Spaced equally apart from one another, around what he assumed to be the entire circumference of the tower, were countless gargoyles. Gruesome, spiteful looking creatures with narrow eyes and sneering snouts, they looked ready to swoop down at any moment. Their realism was unnerving, to say the least, and so Nate turned his attention instead to the crowd of people around him.

There did not appear to be anything particularly interesting about any of them. While many present held themselves in high regard due to whichever station they currently occupied, to Nate they were all the same. A collection of pompous leeches bloated with their own arrogance. He could tell from the way they held their noses up at their servants, and the way they paraded around flashing their jewel encrusted hats and doublets. It was clear for all to see that they believed themselves to be better than people like him. It was then that he noticed someone who stood out from the crowd. Dressed in full plate armour of an unfamiliar design, a man was walking in his direction, seemingly straight at him.

The man was of an average build, taller than Nate but shorter than Marcus. He wore a thick brown beard adorned with numerous braids held by golden beads and clasps. Clearly this was compensation for his head which was completely bald, a thin golden band its only protection. He walked with purpose, his strides long and heavy. His face was not that of a happy man. His features were creased into a deep

197

scowl, his usually dazzling yellow eyes were more restrained, like a flash of lightning behind the clouds. As the man grew ever closer, Nate decided to inform Ardell, just in case his intentions were as foul as his apparent mood. Surprisingly, she was already aware and approached the man with a wide smile and outstretched arms.

"Perm," she beamed as the man continued his approach, although his demeanour did not change upon being addressed. Both Nate and Marcus were twitching for their absent swords as they saw the man continue towards their captain with clear intent. Ardell, however, appeared to not be even remotely concerned. She kept her arms outstretched until Perm was upon her, lifting her into the air with both hands as if she were a child, before pulling her into a crushing hug.

Nate and Marcus both breathed a sigh of relief and allowed themselves to tentatively approach the clearly familiar pair. Neither of them had ever seen Ardell display such clear affection. In such uncharted territory, it paid to be cautious, and they kept a safe distance. Ardell, meanwhile, returned the embrace, wrapping her arms around Perm's neck before he gently placed her back upon the ground. Of concern, his scowl remained and he looked ready to break Ardell in half.

"Thirty years!" he cried with a thick Russian accent. "Thirty years since I have seen the twinkle of your starry eyes. Thirty years since I last looked upon this face as fair as the queens of legend, heard this voice as soft as silk and refreshing as the ocean breeze."

'*Oh, for fuck's sake,*' Ardell thought, as she rolled her eyes playfully. This is exactly why she hadn't visited for three decades.

"Still not married then?" She asked, placing her hands on her hips, to which Perm replied with a shake of his head.

"Oh yes, lovely woman, my dear wife. Tits like a heifer and a temper to boot. I'd leave her and my kingdom in an instant for you though, my dear Lady Ardell. Just say the word and we shall be gone by sunrise, just the two of us and our swords, into the wilds of the world to start anew."

Ardell shook her head and let out a forced laugh. She had nothing against Perm, he was a good man and a loyal friend. It was simply that his constant pursuit of her affection from the moment they had met had become tiresome after a century or two. She ignored his offer and gestured towards her companions.

"These are my men, Nate's the scrawny one, and Marcus is the one who killed Adeneus," she said, whispering the second half so only Perm could hear. Perm's attention focused immediately upon Marcus. He walked up to him and extended his hand, which Marcus shook.

"Good to meet you both," Perm smiled, his grip like iron.

"This is King Perm of the Styr Oblast," Ardell added, to which Marcus and Nate instinctively reacted with shock and quickly set about bowing. This caused nothing but a laugh from the King at their sudden awkwardness.

"No need to bow, lads. The title of king isn't what it used to be in Estrold, that's for damn certain." The two now thoroughly confused companions had no idea how to respond or behave and were thankful for Ardell stepping in.

"How are things in Estrold these days?" She asked. Despite being Tinelia's largest and most reliable ally, there was little communication between the two in times of peace. Perm shook his head and sighed.

"If I had a hundred years, I wouldn't be able to tell you. Every day it seems there is a new crisis. I'm thankful to you Tinelian's, actually. If you manage to kick off another war, Estrold might be able to pull itself together for five minutes."

"We were rather hoping to avoid another war, if I'm being honest," Ardell added, her tone now one of shocked concern which she tried to hide. If others in Estrold shared the same opinion, as Perm, could Tinelia count on their vote when the time came, especially when protected by anonymity?

As Perm was about to speak, there was a sudden shout coming from the direction of the tower. From an elevated lectern an individual wearing a white robe spoke, his voice amplified by some unknown magic so that it could be heard at the very back of the crowd with clarity.

"I'm afraid the opening ceremony will be postponed until the morning. I apologise for any inconvenience this may cause." With that, the man stepped down from the lectern and left. There was a sudden uproar amongst the crowd who had desperately hoped to get this matter resolved today. Yet their cries and noises of dissatisfaction went unaddressed. Ardell too was annoyed at the delay, but soon realised this could play to her advantage. She turned to Perm.

"We may not have a hundred years, but how about we get a drink, and you can make a start on exactly what's been going on back home?" Perm's eyes immediately lit up at the idea of a romantic candle-lit dinner with Ardell and its natural conclusion, once he had expended sufficient time and effort for Ardell to consider herself to be appropriately wooed.

"After you, my Lady," he cooed, bowing low and sweeping his arm aside. Ardell rolled her eyes again and turned to her subordinates. Her expression was as cold and sharp as steel as she pointed her finger at them.

"No stabbing, no shagging, no stealing. Do you understand?"

Nate and Marcus both looked at one another bewildered.

"So, what do you expect us to do?" Marcus cried, as Ardell walked off in search of a tavern with her new companion practically lapping at her heels.

It was still only early morning but Nate and Marcus both agreed that a drink was badly needed, and they too set off in search of a tavern. Unfortunately, as neither of them had been to Peace-Haven before, they had no idea where to look. After a good hour of wandering down immaculate streets, all the while being stared at by the locals as if the pair were creatures from another planet, they found a pub-like edifice. It was not the sort of place that they were used to. Rather than being old and beer-soaked, there were beautiful and stainless red velvet chairs and white tablecloths covering more than two dozen tables. Instead of a bar which looked to have had more skulls smashed into it than drinks served, there was a long marble surface, behind which full bottles of various alcohols could be seen.

The bartender, a thin and elegant man with slick black hair and a pointed nose, looked at them with nothing less than absolute disgust as they ordered two ales and threw themselves down into two unoccupied seats. Not five minutes had they been inside, yet already they had muddied the floor and creased the tablecloths. It was a good ten minutes before the bartender returned, apologising after being unable to find anything remotely similar to the apparent 'drink' they had requested. Still with a tinge of superiority to his voice, he suggested alternatives that these savages may instead prefer. If anything, he may be able to educate them, although he quickly dismissed this as an impossibility as he witnessed Nate pick his nose and wipe it on the underside of the table.

In the end, the two men settled for some wine with a name that neither of them could pronounce. A rare thing when considering that one of Purgatory's few benefits included the ability to see and hear everything in one's own language. This had therefore led to certain manufacturers plastering absolute gobbledygook on their products, all in the effort to appear more exclusive. Amused by the unlikely surroundings the pair found themselves in, they naturally took the piss, to the indignation of the few other patrons. Taking the most delicate of sips from their gold rimmed glasses, their little fingers held aloft as the pair drank and laughed. Unfortunately for the inhabitants of Peace-Haven, their presence would simply have to be tolerated. It was not long before the wine started to take its toll. Despite its fruity lightness, it was far stronger than anything the pair were used to, and after only three glasses their words were slurred and their limbs heavy. Nevertheless, the pair continued drinking and ordered some food to go with it.

Reluctantly, the barman obliged and returned soon after with tray after tray laden with the most finely crafted plates of food either man had ever seen. It had clearly taken an almost inhuman level of skill and finesse to create such wonders of the culinary arts. Skill which was entirely wasted on the pair as they began shovelling in everything within reach without so much as a glance. By this point some of the other diners began to leave in protest, their still steaming teacups now abandoned.

Marcus and Nate were in no way oblivious to the scene and aura of disgust they were creating. Rather they wholeheartedly revelled in it. Nowhere else would they be able to rub shoulders with such high society and get away with their uncouth behaviours. Marcus especially felt that it would do the high and mighty of Peace-Haven good to be exposed to such ruggedness every so often. After the pair had demolished every plate of food in sight and drunk the wine dry, they at last decided to call it a day. To the relief of the bartender, it seemed the monstrous pair were finally going to leave.

Stumbling towards the bar, Marcus and Nate both withdrew their coin purses, wholly prepared to be cleaned out for the meal they had very much enjoyed. But despite coming to terms with their imminent poverty, the barman simply stared at them with daggers in his eyes. He spoke slowly and clearly as his nose wrinkled at the sight of the gold coins the pair produced, as if they had presented him with handfuls of dung.

"There is no need for currency on the isle. I wish the both of you a pleasant stay," he said through teeth clenched so hard they may shatter. Nate and Marcus first looked at the barman as if he had gone insane, then at one another, their smiles growing larger as they realised the gravity of what they had been told. Hurriedly stuffing their purses back into their pockets, they quickly made for the door without so much as a thank you to their tolerant hosts.

As they emerged into the afternoon sun, they looked around as quickly as their drunk heads would allow. All around them there were amusements and activities with which they could entertain themselves. Activities which on the mainland would be locked tightly behind a hefty price tag. Giggling like schoolgirls, the pair ambled unsteadily towards the next place unable to refuse them patronage.

While Nate and Marcus terrorised the hapless inhabitants of the island, Ardell and Perm had also found themselves a pleasant spot to converse. Upon the Western outskirts of the city were a dozen vineyards which Ardell allowed her eyes to drift over while she ignored Perm's incessant torrent of compliments. With a glass of wine in hand, she took a deep breath and finally allowed herself to relax. Such moments of peace were exceptionally rare, aware she would be gaining nothing by not allowing herself to enjoy it. Unfortunately, there were important discussions to be had. War would not wait until Ardell had time to rest her legs and wash the sea salt from her hair.

Deciding she had best say something before Perm entered what was about to be his tenth minute of speech without so much as a breath. Ardell tilted her head back so rays of sunlight caught her face, their gentle warmth giving her the necessary energy to get started.

"So," she began, cutting Perm off just as he was complimenting with great excitement the suppleness of Ardell's thighs.

"So," Perm repeated, leaning forward in his chair, resting his head upon his fist as he stared into Ardell's tired blue eyes. From the moment they had met, Perm had been infatuated by Ardell's beauty. Her personality could admittedly do with some work, but he was sure those wrinkles would be ironed out after a few nights of animalistic ecstasy. It did not at all dissuade Perm that Ardell seemed about as interested in him as he was with his wife. It was the thrill of the pursuit which he enjoyed. Indeed, if Ardell were to give up now it would almost not have been worth it.

"Tell me of the situation in Estrold. Does Rex Broslig still rule?" Ardell asked casually. One would imagine the deposition of their closest ally would be the sort of thing the Tinelian ruling class would be aware of. However, Estrolian politics was far from simple and almost impossible to keep track of. So long as they swore friendship when the time came, that was all that mattered.

Estrold 'functioned', if one could call it that, under what was dubbed '*Dynamic Feudalism*' by scholars. What this meant, in layman's terms, was that any individual with enough wealth and power could declare themselves a Lord. A far cry from the usual process which would require royal approval.

The Lord with the most land within a region or 'Oblast' was usually granted the title of King. These kings would then form their own regional alliances and elect from among themselves a 'High King'. The high kings would then also elect the Rex, the supreme ruler of Estrold. However, due to the parameters by which nobility and power were measured, this resulted in an almost endless conflict between an equally endless pool of nobles, all competing for whichever title eluded them. Only through the sheer size of Estrold and its ever-expanding borders could such a system continue to function.

The Rex was not immune to this game of musical thrones either. Should another high king gain greater power and favour with his fellow nobles, he may choose to challenge the Rex and take his position.

Such constant chaos on their borders was of little concern to Tinelia. The monstrous size of Estrold meant half the country could be burning and there would still be more than enough men to overwhelm the Imperium. Still, Grand Admiral Lee's failed assassination of The Emperor had been met poorly by the nobles of Tinelia, none of whom had been consulted beforehand. The truth was that she was not ready. Even with the past year to prepare, it would be at least another three before Tinelia could declare herself ready for a campaign. Lee had taken a grave risk, and it was on the verge of blowing up in his face.

The thought that Estrold may use this opportunity to strengthen their own hand concerned Ardell greatly.

Unbeknownst to her, while she fought this political battle at the behest of her commander, Lee was fighting his own desperate battle at home.

Admittedly, neither Ardell nor anyone else was under the illusion that the morrow's deliberation would result in a satisfactory outcome which appeased both parties. War was coming. She could taste its metallic, bloody essence in the air, yet she would do whatever she could to avoid it. And if that was not possible, she would ensure Tinelia had the strongest hand when the shooting finally started. Perm retracted himself, disappointed Ardell would not humour him with even the most trivial of flirtations. He took a sip from his own glass before furrowing his brow and folding his arms.

"Barely," was Perm's reply. He ran his hand across his bald head, an unwanted nervous habit he could not shake. The truth was he had been desperate to take on this mission, anything to get away from the madness of home, even if only for a little while. He shook his head and let out a frustrated sigh.

"Damn fool has got the whole country on edge."

"How so?" Ardell asked taking gentle sips of her wine, her tone one of carefully constructed apathy, as if they were discussing something as trivial as the weather. Perm rubbed at his nose and sniffed loudly, pouring himself another drink.

"He's been talking some madness about reforming the whole system. Wasn't so bad at first, mind you. Mainly just silly things like creating an independent judiciary, things that don't really matter. But then he started sending auditors to each Oblast, making sure we were paying our 'fair share' to the state."

Ardell shook her head,

"Truly, he's gone insane," she said sarcastically, adding a smirk at Perm's indignation.

"But it gets worse," Perm added, unaware he was being made fun of. "Couple of days ago, a rumour came out of the capital that he had been discussing the abolition of the office of high king!"

"How to start a civil war in one simple step," said Ardell, her earlier amusement now replaced by yet more genuine concern. While wars between lesser Lords and kings were an almost daily occurrence in Estrold, a potential conflict between the Rex and the rest of the nobility had not been seen for centuries. Such an event would, without doubt, prevent them from coming to Tinelia's aid should war with The Imperium break out later.

At least now Ardell understood Perm's reason for coming here. He hoped a war abroad would prevent one at home. She could not blame him for wanting this, and had she been in the same position, she would probably wish for the same. Nevertheless, she could not allow the interests of even their closest ally to come before Tinelia. She must therefore do what she could, to ensure Estrold did not sabotage tomorrow's deliberations. But she now faced a sobering truth - either fight The Imperium with Estrold's backing or fight The Imperium alone.

She chewed on her nail for a moment while staring into Perm's eyes, allowing him to be drawn in before proposing her offer, which she was in no way authorised to make.

"If I can count on your support, I am sure I can convince the Admiral to spare a few dozen divisions to help back up old Broslig. I'll even lead them myself. After all, what are allies for?" This was of course a bare faced lie. There was absolutely no circumstance under which Tinelia would march troops into Estrold to meddle in their internal affairs. Nevertheless, she had to try something.

Perm smiled and shook his head, endlessly impressed by Ardell's scheming mind. It was by far her third most attractive feature.

"Then you'd end up facing me on the battlefield and, believe me, that is not what I imagine when I think of lying beneath you."

"Ah, so you oppose Broslig's reforms?" Ardell asked, disappointed in her old friend.

"He should know better. Our system has worked just fine

for thousands of years. I don't see any reason why anyone should go changing it now."

Ardell clicked her tongue against the roof of her mouth and raised her hand in a gesture indicating she was willing to negotiate.

"What can I do to bring you into my way of thinking?" she asked, making the excruciating decision to brush her foot slowly and gently against Perm's thigh. Perm could not help but snort so that wine trickled from his nose and onto his beard. Ardell knew one thing for certain which would convince him to change his mind, however, there was no way she was spreading her legs for him, even if it were for the rumoured fifteen seconds. Even if it saved the world.

Then, unexpectedly, Perm pushed her foot away and stood, a sad smile on his lips.

"Believe me, my Lady, there is nothing more in the world I wish for than your company." He turned his gaze out to the horizon where the vineyards were bursting with life and the gulls called faintly. His eyes hung there for a moment before focusing back on Ardell. "However, I serve my country as you serve yours, and I must do what is best for Estrold, not for Tinelia. Next time, I would advise your Grand Admiral not to start a war without thinking it through first." With that Perm bowed low and left, leaving Ardell to finish her wine with only her darkening thoughts for company.

The next morning Ardell found Nate and Marcus already at Justice's entrance when she arrived. They looked worse for wear, their skin ghostly pale, their eyes red and bloodshot. Clearly, they'd had a good night. She hoped for their sakes that they had obeyed her orders and not caused any trouble. Ardell's night had been less eventful. After finding a nice quiet hotel and a comfy bed, she had hoped for a peaceful night. Instead, she found herself unable to sleep. Her sleepless night spent running through every possible scenario and how she would respond should today end poorly.

"You two better not cause a scene," she said, eyeing them up and down with disgust. "If either of you even think about throwing up or passing out, I'll rip your legs off and beat you to death with them."

"Yes, Captain. Good morning to you too, Captain," Nate replied in the tone of someone doing their best not to be sick while swaying from side to side. Just as Ardell was about to chew the pair out further, a loud voice called out over the gathered crowd. The same individual from the previous day, dressed in his long white robe, called from his platform.

"My honourable Lords and gentlemen, the council will now convene. Please follow the directions once inside. The day's session will begin in one hour." As his words dissipated, the deafening sound of the tower doors being opened filled the air. Having been shut since the end of the Imperium's peasant rebellion, they were loath to open again without great protest. Suddenly, the crowd began shifting forwards, eager to begin. The sooner they began, the sooner they could get back to their wine and brothels.

"Where's Lord Ilrid?" Marcus asked, scanning the crowd for the man they were supposed to be escorting.

"Probably face down in a two-inch puddle," Ardell replied, as she too looked around with her hands on her hips. But their concern was unfounded as barely a few moments later His Lordship appeared from amongst the crowd by Ardell's side. He looked around at his companions, beaming like an idiot.

"Shall we be off?" he asked, "I'm ever so excited," he added, practically squealing. The others looked at one another, all sharing the expectation that the next few hours would be nothing less than excruciating. With Ilrid at their lead, the party joined the crowd queuing to enter the tower.

Upon entering, Nate was surprised by the interior. He had expected hundreds of floors, each with their own unique purpose, accessible only by a single incredibly tall staircase. Instead, there was no ceiling separating them from the next floor. In fact, the only other floor in the tower was at the very top. Nate was relieved to see no staircase, but instead dozens of fast-moving iron lifts.

As the crowd entered, they were each given a white robe

and mask. The mask was strange, having no holes for eyes or a mouth. Instead, it looked like a single sheet of oval glass. Upon bringing it to his face, Nate realised that it in fact acted as a one-way mirror. He could see the world from beneath the mask but, once wearing it, his face would be invisible. As the crowd continued to shuffle in, another voice called out with further instructions.

"You are to remove all items of clothing before adorning your robe and mask. Once you have done this, please step into an available lift which will take you to the council chamber."

Suddenly Nate felt extremely conscious of what was going on. He did not particularly fancy getting undressed around so many strangers. That was until he noticed Ardell, with her back to him, stripping off until she stood in only her underwear. Suddenly, he found himself caring very little for what those around him thought.

"If those are your eyes I can feel burning into my arse, Nate, I'm going to make sure it's the last thing you ever see," Ardell scolded without turning around. While Nate was weighing up whether this would be a worthy trade, there was a sudden smack on the back of his head as Marcus brought him back to the real world.

"Hurry up and get dressed," Marcus whispered as he pulled his mask over his head but left his face uncovered.

"You're going to need to give me a minute," Nate replied almost in a trance as he watched Ardell pull the robe over her chest. Once Nate was finally dressed, the four companions entered one of the lifts together and began their ascent. Once again, Ardell went over the rules with Nate and Marcus.

"Under absolutely no circumstance are you to speak or remove your mask. If you talk or remove your mask before being permitted to do so by the Judges, you'll be executed."

"Jesus Christ," Nate gasped. "Bit extreme, don't you think?" It was Ilrid who replied.

"It's to ensure absolute impartiality on the part of the Judges. If they recognise someone it could threaten the entire proceeding and, by extension, the world."

"Right," Nate acknowledged, as he prepared for the most difficult struggle of his life - keeping his mouth shut.

The lift reached the top floor in only a matter of minutes, and the now identical looking crowd were shepherded towards five doors, all of which led to the council chamber. Nate stuck with his group until the very last moment. The last thing he wanted was to become separated from them in this sea of anonymity. At each of the five doors stood a guard, dressed also in white robes but without masks. They inspected each individual as they approached, ensuring they had made no alterations to their attire which would allow them to be recognised.

The diplomats would be seated first, raising their masks so that only the guard could see who was beneath. The rest of the crowd were allowed to enter without confirming their identity as they were not permitted to speak anyway. Nate tried his best to remain close behind Ardell, but once she had passed into the chamber, she became impossible to distinguish from the others. Nate, therefore, had to take a seat next to, for all he knew, were three dogs sat on each other's shoulders.

The chamber itself was not as lavish as Nate had expected. There were two rings of seating. The much larger, outer ring where he currently sat could accommodate a few hundred. The inner, smaller ring could only seat a maximum of perhaps thirty. One for each emissary and their senior assistants.

In the centre of the room, surrounded by the inner ring, was a throne. Made of stone, it was in the shape of a pyramid. Three thrones attached at their backs to a central monolith. This is where the Judges would sit. Across from each seat was a wooden desk and, in neat stacks beside them, were the complete collections of international law. It is from these cumbersome tomes that the Judges would refer and ultimately make their rulings.

After roughly fifteen minutes of uncomfortable silence, as nobody was permitted to speak save for the diplomats who sat in the inner ring, a call came from one of the entrances.

"All rise for their illustrious masters, the Judges."

Nate obeyed the command and rose with the rest of the room. From three different doors came the Judges at last. Although, upon seeing them for the first time, Nate had to double check to ensure his eyes were not deceiving him. Dressed identically in purple robes with long golden sashes draped over their shoulders, the Judges entered and slowly crossed the room. It was not their robes which caused Nate to initially doubt his eyes, but rather their heads. They were huge, at least three times the size they should be. Moreover they were grey and their features unmoving.

It soon became clear by their slow, deliberate steps and the unnatural way by which their heads sat upon their shoulders, that these were not the Judges' real appearances. As the Judges delicately lowered themselves into their seats, Nate finally understood what he was looking at. Resting uncomfortably upon each of the Judges heads was a headpiece made entirely from stone. Their sheer weight and awkwardness forcing the wearer to take the most delicate of steps should the stone slip and break their necks.

As they slid themselves into their thrones, the weight of the headpieces were taken by two prongs which jutted out from the sides of the monolith at each seat, allowing for respite from the weight while maintaining the Judges' anonymity. Now that they were still, Nate could fully analyse and appreciate the headpieces themselves. Their likeness to life, the intricate lines on their foreheads, the curls of their hair, were so authentic it was no wonder he had been fooled at first.

"Be seated," one of the Judges instructed. As the room returned to their seats the Judges wasted no time starting the proceedings. The Judge seated on the far side of the pyramid from Nate, whom he could not see, spoke to those assembled. His voice echoing across the chamber.

"We are here today to hear testimony of unwarranted aggression and regicide. May the prosecution please present their opening statement."

Immediately one of the diplomats seated at the inner circle rose, bowing to the Judges, he began reading from a pre-prepared statement.

"One year ago, an unjustified act of terror was carried out upon a peaceful city with no warning. Hundreds were killed, including the sovereign of the nation in question. Since then, no official declaration of war or casus belli for said act was presented by the accused. We, who have been sent to represent the aggrieved nation, humbly request a judgment and ruling adequate in gravity to the crime committed."

With that, the Imperial diplomat sat once more. Only the Judges were unaware to whom they were speaking or of which nations were on trial, yet all three felt a tightness in their chests as they feared for their own former allegiances. When the international community and legal framework had first been formed, the position of the Judges had originally been taken by three individuals freshly arrived in Purgatory. While eliminating the issue of past allegiances. It had turned out not everyone was capable of learning and applying the complexities of international law. Hence the creation of this current, secretive system.

Next, another Judge spoke, this time instructing the defendants to present their own statement. This was immediately followed by the familiar voice of Lord Ilrid, reading from his own parchment prepared by his assistants.

"Your Illustriousness's," Ilrid began, stumbling over the word he had chosen when a bow would have sufficed.

"There is no doubt that an attack took place. This the accused does not contest. However, we object to the prosecution's use of the terms 'act of terror' and 'unjustified'. The act in question, which is claimed to have resulted in the death of the prosecution's sovereign, although no concrete evidence was presented for this, was in our view, entirely justified and within the law."

"How so?" One of the Judges asked. "It is generally accepted that an attack without prior warning is a crime."

"Indeed," Ilrid replied, his tone no longer noticeably

nervous, he was starting to get into it. "Although, the *Convention for the Standardisation of War and Conflict* states on page 206, section 3, that: *A state may embark upon pre-emptive military action without prior warning, if faced with imminent and severe danger or risk of military action by another state or non-state actor.*"

There was a brief silence as the Judges each raised a heavy tome from the pile beside them and placed it upon their desks. Carefully, they navigated to the section Ilrid had quoted and read it over until each was satisfied in their understanding. The Judge who was invisible to Nate on the far side of the monolith was the first to speak.

"The convention also states that for such parameters to be legitimate, undeniable proof of impending military action against the claimant must be presented. Do you have such proof?"

Ilrid nodded and beckoned for one of the Judge's assistants to come and take what seemed to be a small red notebook from his hand. As the notebook and two copies were presented to the Judges, Ilrid spoke once more. It was then that both Nate and Marcus, who were watching the unfolding events with uncharacteristic interest, held their breaths in shock. The journal the Judges were reading, originally belonged to Adeneus.

"Certain names and locations have been omitted to preserve anonymity. However, you can clearly see that the prosecution intended not only on war with the accused, but many other nations also."

At that moment the Imperial diplomat rose and spoke loudly and with clear frustration in his voice.

"The prosecution objects, this is an unfounded claim based on incomplete evidence." This was true, there were at least a dozen journals belonging to Adeneus which Tinelia had been unable to apprehend. However, the Imperials had not seen fit to bring any of these journals as rebutting evidence.

The Judges instructed the diplomat to sit until they had finished reading the journal, which took over half an hour.

Overall, they were not convinced by the journal alone. It was clear by the tone that the contents were only ever rhetorical. There was no concrete proof that this experimentation with husks was ever intended to be used to wage aggressive war.

At last, they allowed the Imperial diplomat to offer his rebuke of Ilrid's claims. This back-and-forth exchange of evidence and accusations continued for many more hours. The novelty soon wore off for Nate and he quickly found himself daydreaming of anything other than the dull events evolving around him. But there was one thought that kept coming back to him, that being the day they had passed the Travellers. Their haunted faces, devoid of hope and life, the ghostly grey sails in tatters carrying such wretched cargo. The very thought sent a shiver up his spine. To end up there, for eternity. He could think of nothing worse.

Nate was roused from his thoughts by the rising of those seated around him. Following suit, he caught the end of the Judge's statement.

"We must now retire for deliberation. The morrow's session shall commence at six-hundred hours." With that the three Judges were escorted from the room. Only after each had been safely returned to his quarters in each of the three other towers were the rest of the court attendees permitted to leave. The Judges were not allowed to sit and deliberate together anywhere other than the courtroom. Instead, they were forced to communicate their thoughts through highly reliable, incorruptible messengers who raced between the towers carrying the Judges words like holy texts. To interrupt or impede these messengers in any way was punishable by death by torture.

Once Nate was back on the ground floor, he returned his mask and robe before meeting up with the others. Ilrid was looking exceptionally pleased with himself while Ardell wore the same sour look as always. Clearly the two had very different perspectives on the day's outcome.

"I think that all went rather well, for the first day and all," Ilrid said stretching his legs after so many hours sitting.

"They didn't seem too convinced by our evidence," Ardell replied. "I'm no expert, but considering that journal was our key piece of evidence, I'd say we are on the back foot."

Ilrid shook his head while smiling smugly.

"My lovely Lady Ardell, there's no place in law for facts and logic. Often there is more significance in what is not proven than what is. It is by nuance and loopholes by which victory shall be won," Ilrid replied with a triumphant thrusting of his fist into the air. The others stared at him with varying degrees of disapproval. None shared his enthusiasm that victory was close at hand, even less so for the means by which he hoped to achieve it.

Nevertheless, a victory won by dishonourable means is better than defeat. Especially when defeat could mean the total ruin of their nation. Reluctantly, the three who were far more comfortable in battle than a stuffy court, agreed to dine with Ilrid that evening. Being a diplomat, he was provided an extraordinarily lavish room within Order, the tower reserved for the Citadel Coalition. From his balcony they could see the entirety of the island. They watched ships come and go, working hard at unloading cargo while they dined on crab and caviar.

Peace-Haven had no industry of its own other than a few vineyards. This meant it relied on supplies to be provided from the mainland all year round. Indeed, each nation was expected to provide one percent of their domestic produce to Peace-Haven each year. For free of course. International law was quite clear that the needs of Peace-Haven came before all others. For how could the world function without this great bastion of morality to twist its arm?

Dinner was by no means the relaxed affair that had been intended. Ardell could not help herself from re-examining every aspect of the case so far discussed and what was yet to come. Ilrid paid no heed to Ardell's concerns, dismissing her assertions with a flick of his wrist as he tore the legs off yet another crab, greedily gobbling the meat down in a very undiplomatic way. It was not often that a learned man such as himself would be given precedent over those in the military. A grave mistake in Tinelia's intricate societal fabric, he thought. He would not allow for his rare moment of recognition to be overshadowed or belittled by some uneducated simpleton, even if they were as delicious as Ardell.

Despite Ilrid's reassurances that all was going to plan, Ardell could not help but feel uncomfortable. A sharp, stabbing pain in her head at the notion that such an important event was being played out before her, without any way of influencing the outcome, was making her lose her appetite. Moreover, the fact that Tinelia's fate had been put in the hands of such an insufferable cretin as Ilrid made her doubt Admiral Lee's intentions. There were dozens of other diplomats who could have undertaken this mission. Men whom Ardell respected, who understood the law like no other, men who could eat a meal without wearing half of it. The rest of the evening was spent endlessly drilling Ilrid over every small detail of their defence, suggesting every trick The Imperium may try to get the upper hand.

While Ilrid had somewhat enjoyed showing off his knowledge of both the case and international law at first, he soon found Ardell's questioning tiresome. Her jabbing tone and narrow eyes, which seemed to doubt every word he said, soon bore into his patience. Even Nate, with his usual utter obliviousness was able to see the tell-tale signs of aggravation in Ilrid's body language. Yet for once, it was Ardell who was oblivious, and her barrage of questions showed no sign of stopping.

As she asked for clarification on a certain legal term for the third time, Ilrid lost his patience entirely.

"Will you shut up?!" He cried, slamming his palm onto the table, which caused the expected clatter of cutlery and toppling of glasses. He rose from his seat in an uncharacteristic outburst. Pulling his stained bib from his neck and tossing it with some force into Nate's unfinished meal, he glowered at Ardell intensely.

Suddenly, as he stared initially with intense animosity into

Ardell's eyes, he quickly shrank back into his usual meek self. The cold, lifeless stare Ardell returned being too unsettling for Ilrid to adequately hold onto his anger. There was an awkward silence as he tried to think of how to apologise while Nate and Marcus both prepared for the inevitable task of cleaning up a gallon of blood. Ardell stood, the scraping of her chair against the floor breaking the silence. At first she looked as if she were about to give Ilrid the dressing down he so richly deserved. However, her stance softened, and she instead stormed out without a word, leaving the three men to look at one another awkwardly.

Ardell did not attend the court's session the following day, or the day after that. This suited Ilrid just fine. He could get on with the job he had been sent to do without incessant nagging and pestering from someone who was little more than a glorified bodyguard. If Lee didn't speak so highly of her, and she wasn't so terrifying, he would have taught her some quick manners with the back of his hand like he did with his other servants. Nate and Marcus, however, grew concerned by the end of the second day with there being no sight or sound of her. The Judges were going to deliver their Judgment tomorrow, and depending on the outcome, they may need to make a hasty getaway.

Agreeing that if she was still missing the following morning, they would skip the joys of court and search for their captain. It was not a particularly large island after all, a trail of blood and guts shouldn't be too hard to find. Thankfully, their concerns were unfounded. Ardell reappeared at the base of the tower the following morning. She did not offer an explanation for her disappearance, instead being the one asking all the questions.

"Miss anything?" Ardell asked as the three of them ascended to the tower's pinnacle.

"I'm no expert, but I think it's three – one to them," Nate replied.

Chapter 12

As the trio ascended the tower and took their seats once again, they were each so nervous that their skin itched. Neither Nate nor Marcus fully understood what had transpired over the last couple of days, which only further frayed their worn nerves. The Imperial diplomat would stand and make a speech, usually followed by some evidence which the Judges would then review. This would be followed by Ilrid, doing his best to refute this evidence with his own. The day's proceedings would then be deliberated and on and on it would go until the sun had been pushed into slumber.

Ilrid had offered no helpful insight into proceedings either. Both days he had finished grumpier than before, muttering to himself while Nate and Marcus escorted him back to his quarters. If this was anything to go by, things weren't looking good for Tinelia, or her delegation. On the second day, the diplomat from Gil-Ebrax had arrived. His until now empty seat filled by another faceless figure behind a mask. Ardell sat beside Nate, tapping her thigh nervously as they awaited the Judges arrival. An arrival which was delayed by almost an hour.

When the Judges finally did arrive, once again sporting their excessively burdensome headgear, the collective feeling of unease in the room magnified tenfold. Even those diplomats who had presented such compelling evidence and arguments were visibly shaking, their robes jittering in the otherwise still room. This was an unusual situation for them all, even those who had been here on many occasions. This was the only time they could not use bribery, intimidation or outright lies to achieve their goal. Something many of them thought deeply unfair, these being all integral parts of the legal profession. They may as well be asked to juggle with their hands behind their backs.

The silence continued after the Judges had ordered everyone to take their seats. Rather than announcing their ruling immediately, they spent another forty-five minutes talking quietly amongst themselves. Their whispered words being relayed only to those sitting within a few feet by small brass tubes which circled the throne. This removed the need to move or the use of messengers who could distort the Judge's words. It seemed that there was a particular passage in one of their many books which was causing some contention, holding up their final judgment.

This eleventh hour deliberation did nothing to calm the nerves of the others in the room, all of whom watched with bated breath. This was extremely irregular. Usually a final judgment had been decided upon the night before, not before the twitching eyes and pounding hearts of the court. At last, a decision was made. The Judges slammed shut their dusty tomes which caused the entire room to collectively jump.

"Judgment has been passed," the three Judges said in unison. It would be the one who faced Nate and the two rival diplomats who would be the one to make that decision known. As he delivered this monumental, era-defining ruling, the Judge remained seated while the rest of the chamber stood, a small but clear sign of their place above the squabbles and concerns of normal men.

"After extensive and meticulous collaboration, we find the rule of law to be clear on this matter." There was silence for a moment as the Judge basked in the undivided attention of some of the known world's most powerful people. There was little opportunity for a man in his uniquely lonely position to enjoy the company of others. One could not blame him therefore, for wanting to be the centre of attention for once.

As she waited, imagining what horrors would be unleashed by the Judge's words, Ardell unconsciously gripped Nate's knee and squeezed with trepidation. While the fate of the world hung in the balance, at this present moment all Nate cared about was trying not to cry out, getting himself executed as a result.

"The case presented by the prosecution, while tragic, does not meet the criteria needed to justify a full inter-state conflict." There was an immediate uproar from across the courtroom, expressing their wildly varying levels of satisfaction seemingly far more important than the potential punishment it carried. Naturally, Tinelia's delegation was euphoric. If not constrained by her mask and being utterly repulsed by the arrangement of Nate's face, Ardell could have kissed him out of irrepressible joy. Those from the Imperial delegation, as expected, were furious. The two who sat beside the Imperial diplomat banged their fists on the table and gesticulated wildly in all directions. The Imperial diplomat himself, however, was emotionless, a fact which greatly disturbed Lord Ilrid who had contained himself until this moment.

There were multiple banging's of gavels until at last the room was quiet once again. The Judges were not used to being disrespected in such a manner. Recovering from his shock, the Judge who had delivered the ruling continued.

"We do, however, find the defendant guilty of regicide and mass murder. However, due to the evidence presented and unique circumstances which resulted in this action, we have agreed upon the following as a fitting punishment. Reparations to the victim nation equalling the total value of damage caused in the attack, and a fine to be paid to the international court equalling fifty million gold. Furthermore, a suspended sentence of eight years imprisonment for the ruler of the aggressor nation. To be served on Peace-Haven should they be found guilty of further illegal aggression."

While the Judges had expected this decision to be universally accepted and uncontested, this was not a day for meeting expectations. There was yet further outrage from whom they were still yet to learn were the Imperial delegation. The Tinelian delegation meanwhile could not believe their luck. A measly fifty million fine for mass-murder was nothing short of a joke. Made even funnier by the expectation that they would pay a single gold piece to the Imperium, or that Grand Admiral Lee would even entertain the idea of a jail sentence. Good luck dragging him out of the Citadel, was all they could think.

Ardell was beyond relieved. She had expected the Judges to rule in favour of the Imperium, in which case war would have been almost unavoidable. The Judges' clear ruling, however, waylaid these fears. It seemed her prayer had come true and, for once, the international justice system had actually worked. But then the Imperial diplomat stood. In his hand, a single piece of parchment which he had been instructed to present only in the direst circumstance.

"Masters, I would like to present to the court a writ on behalf of my monarch with the intention of withdrawing my state from the international community and all obligations membership entails." The uproar, which had continued unabated since the Judge's ruling, now fell into silence as each person in the court attempted to understand what such an act would achieve. Even Ardell was confused. Withdrawing from the international community would be of no benefit to the Imperium. Yes, they could declare war without being subject to the court's rulings, but that would only result in the rest of the world uniting against them, the exact opposite of what they had hoped to achieve in coming here.

Ilrid had gone pale, his hands beginning to shake, as butterflies fluttered madly in his stomach. For all his faults, he understood exactly what the Imperium was doing, and he was powerless to stop it. The Imperials had never intended to play fair should things not go their way. With this move they were not pandering to the rest of the world, but instead doing something far more consequential. They were threatening the Judges themselves with the only thing they cared about.

The upkeep of Peace-Haven was astronomical and, with one less member paying for that, more specifically one particularly very wealthy member, they would soon be forced to adopt a more reserved lifestyle. The Judges would be forced to live less lavish and in a less utopian manner than what they had come to expect. This would not just affect the Judges themselves, but the entire island they called home. Gods forbid they may have to go without, no matter how momentarily, something they desired there and then.

The Judges immediately recognised this threat to their power and, more importantly, their comfort. If one member of the international community were to leave and dare they say, even prosper, what was there to stop others from doing the same? They needed to do something, legal precedent or not, to prevent this. There were hurried, panicked whispers amongst the three of them as they tried desperately to save themselves. Loyalty to their profession and the rules-based order they so fervently upheld be damned.

Suddenly, an idea came to one which was quickly relayed to the other two. A few moments then followed where the Judges pretended to deliberate further, whilst investigating what they made out to be a particularly interesting clause in an ancient treaty which conveniently applied to this very situation. What they were so eagerly tracing with their fingers along the old, mouldy pages was in fact a law regarding fishing quotas for ships over a certain size. Nobody else needed to know that though.

"Ahem," the Judge who had delivered the initial verdict spoke up, admittedly rather shakily.

"There may in fact be a precedent, considering the gravity of the charges, where Judgment may be deferred to the court."

There was a chorus of gasps. The loudest of which came from Nate as Ardell's death-grip on his knee returned. This is exactly what the Tinelian delegation had hoped to avoid. The tables had been well and truly turned. Tasting the familiar sourness of treachery, Ilrid spoke up in a desperate attempt to save his case.

"May their Illustriousness's please name, for the benefit of the court, where said instance can be found?" The Judge waved him away.

"This trial has already progressed past its allotted time.

A vote will now be held on the matter, and I remind the defendant the gravity of questioning a ruling made by the Judges." That was Ilrid's final card played and defeated. All he could do now was raise his hand at the right moment and hope a majority of the others did the same. A tense silence gripped the room. A heavy, suffocating silence that could be felt in the back of the throat. An air of dread and apprehension so thick one could almost see it with the naked eye, hanging over the room like fog.

"The vote will be carried by simple majority," one of the other two Judges announced, as the rule of law gave way to partisan allegiances.

"All those in favour of upholding the initial Judgment of the court, please raise your hand," said the third Judge. To the utter horror of the Tinelian delegation, Ilrid was the only one of the ten total representatives to raise his hand.

"Oh fuck," Ardell whispered shakily, just loud enough for Nate to hear. Never had he seen Ardell worried by anything. But what gripped her now was a terror that seemed to spread from her touch upon his knee like a disease, seeping into Nate's very being. With the last hopes of peace nearly defeated, the court moved on.

"With the previous verdict overruled, the court will now decide the outcome of this case. Would the two parties please present to the court their own Judgments to be voted upon." It was Ilrid who presented his first, although half-heartedly, already knowing the outcome.

"The defence proposes further deliberations to conclude a fair and just punishment which categorically rules out the possibility of war."

"All those in favour," one of the Judges announced. This was it, the moment of truth. Where Tinelia would see whether her allies truly stood behind her, and what scheming machinations hid behind the mirrored faces of the representatives from the far east. In a logical world, the votes would have been split equally between the Citadel Coalition and the Imperium, with the Eastern Defence Union being the deciding votes. There was still a sliver of hope that the vote would be a tie, automatically and irrevocably finalising the original ruling as absolute.

This slight hope of peace was soon extinguished, however. In total, including Ilrid, only three votes were cast in favour of the motion he had put forward. It was now the turn of the Imperial diplomat to present his own proposition.

"The prosecution believes only one course of action to be both just and fair. That being a declaration of war by the international community against the offending nation." There was a tense pause as each voting member weighed up their decision with thumping hearts. It was one thing to promise action when it was merely an idea, far removed in the safety of an office. But to be actively responsible for what would inevitably be a horrific and destructive war was another exercise entirely. The permitted time for inner monologuing was brief, as the Judge spoke again.

"All those in favour." The hands raised slowly, but they came, nonetheless. Each one weighed down by the gravity this simple action carried. There were two abstentions, three objections, and five in favour. That was it. Decided by nothing more than personal and national interests, the fates of millions had been sealed. War was coming and, like it or not, Nate was to be thrust straight in.

Unsurprisingly, Ardell and her two companions made a hasty escape from the island as soon as they were permitted to leave. Ilrid had stayed behind with the other diplomats to finalise the terms of the coming war. Just because war was now reality, this did not mean it would be a lawless free-for-all. Restrictions on weapons, treatment of prisoners and the addition of third parties wishing to partake had to be discussed and agreed. This was a matter for the experts, however, not something Ardell and her companions were interested in.

As their ship sped away from the peaceful isle in the direction of home, Nate looked skywards. Against the bright blue sky flew hundreds of large, black shapes. At first, he assumed them to be birds, messenger pigeons carrying the dark news of the day's events. However, as the shapes grew closer, some flying only meters above the ship, their identities became clear. Tearing themselves free from their appointed positions upon Justice, countless hideous gargoyles glided through the air, their stone wings moving as gracefully as flesh. Their arrival upon the mainland meant only one thing. The Judges had spoken. The long peace was over. War had come.

Chapter 13

"I suppose that settles it then. The Imperium finds herself at war once again," Elias stated solemnly as he put down the letter, although inwardly he could not have been happier. The rest of the Righteous Congregation sat in silent contemplation in response to the Grand Seeker's words. Sir Bryce was itching to get out of this now defunct room, full of inconsequential men who no longer had any real impact. True progress would be made on the battlefield from now on. His armies were ready, they stood poised, prepared to march into the heart of Tinelia and rip it out.

Elias too was eager to get to work. Tinelia was filled to the brim with heretics and unbelievers, like a foul pustule ready to burst from its own vile, tumorous over-growth. If the fools in the west decided to fight alongside her, they too would feel the righteous fury of his holy order. The prospect of pyres for as far as the eye could see, lighting up the horizon and streets of the enemy capital like candles, filled him with a deep, unnatural delight.

They were the only members of the Congregation who viewed the war with such delight. The others all had their own unique obstacles to overcome. To them the war was nothing more than a distraction. The Arch-Sorceress had been hard at work, constructing the first of what she hoped to be hundreds of her dark obelisks which would carry the Imperium to victory. The Emperor was of course infatuated with only one thing - travelling to the deep, forgotten lands of the Great Wastes in search of the library the Lord of Embers had mentioned. And the ever-quiet spymaster, Lord Phillip Thorn. Well, what his motivations were, nobody could guess. Even Elias had completely forgotten about him now that his vote was no longer needed.

Nestor too, despite his support for the war, found the topic to be far at the back of his mind. Instead, every waking moment since the journey to Ifritus had been spent formulating a plan to uncover the potential traitor in their midst. He had a good idea of where to start. Whether his investigation would bear fruit or be his ruin, however, remained to be seen.

"Satisfied?" The Emperor asked rhetorically. He still had no interest whatsoever in the war, yet the clear delight on Elias' and Bryce's faces irked him.

"Have no doubt, Your Holiness," Elias assured. "We shall win this war. The Lord is on our side after all." There was a cruel glint in his eye as he revelled in images of torture and persecution, his tongue running over his dry lips unconsciously as he pretended to rub his lengthening stubble to conceal a smile.

"Indeed," The Emperor replied. Too often had he heard the overconfident proclaim such a statement, only to look so surprised as their heads were mounted upon their own city gates. "In which case, I expect the war to be won by the time I return with the Empress." The other members of the Congregation looked at him with surprise. None even remotely believed his quest to be anything less than folly. They were all shocked that he continued to entertain this delusion of hope, except for perhaps Nestor.

Despite his initial reservations, the Emperor had done a good job of convincing him that maybe there was indeed a chance of recovering their beloved Empress. The Lord of Embers had nothing to gain from lying or the Emperor's death. Slowly but surely, Nestor too had begun to believe in the potential hidden power of this library lost to time. Yet this newfound belief, as with all faith, was a painful one. So easily could it be expunged, plunging him once again into a deeper, renewed despair. He would rather abandon all hope now than suffer the pain of losing his Empress twice.

"You do not plan on fighting alongside us?" Sir Bryce asked, genuinely amazed that the Emperor was still entertaining the ridiculous idea that Sarah could be found.

The Emperor's presence would be invaluable on the battlefield, sowing fear and despair into the hearts of their foes. Traipsing around the freezing wilderness would benefit only their enemies.

"I remind you, Sir Bryce, that this war is your wish, not mine. I told you quite clearly that I would have no part in it." Sir Bryce rocked in his chair slightly, his face contorting into all manner of confused expressions as he attempted to fathom the Emperor's madness. He looked to the others in the room for some sort of support, a united front. However, at present, his only ally was Elias and he was likely to do more harm than good.

But then, the Arch-Sorceress spoke up. Much like her predecessor before her, she had taken little interest in the details of the meeting and had been busy making further notes related to her work. Yet upon hearing that the Emperor planned on leaving so soon, she realised she must say something so that her work may continue.

"Your Holiness, I apologise," Catarah began. As the eyes of the room shifted to her, they could see that for once, she had made an effort to appear presentable. She wore the official robes of her office, white cape and all. Her hair was tied into a neat bun, and clearly someone had done her make-up for her. Her lips were lusciously red, her eyeliner arranged as pointed black wings sprouting from the outer corners of her eyes. Not a man present could have denied that in this moment she looked uncharacteristically both beautiful and regal. Catarah paused momentarily as she felt the eyes of the room running over her. She was still not used to this level of attention.

"I can hardly forgive you unless I know what offense you may have committed, Arch-Sorceress." The Emperor replied. His tone was soft, almost warm. Catarah nodded, regaining her composure and stood to address her monarch.

"While I understand that no mission is of more importance than locating her Majesty, I must humbly request your assistance before you leave," she said with a slight bow. The Emperor raised his eyebrow slightly from beneath his mask.

"I'm afraid, despite my natural ability, I am not well versed in magic. I doubt I would be of any more use to your work than the common man on the street," the Emperor admitted. This was a matter of some personal embarrassment for him. Being a prophet, and an extremely powerful one at that, his potential magical ability exceeded that even of the Arch-Sorceress. Yet he had done almost nothing about harnessing this power he wielded, able only to perform the most basic of spells.

Catarah shook her head, indicating that the Emperor had misunderstood her request.

"Apologies, Your Holiness," she repeated, unsure why she was being overly apologetic. "But it is not with magic I am requiring aid." Catarah paused again, this time out of fear for how the Emperor may react to her request. A request which until recently had been assigned to Sir Bryce to complete. As much as she admired the man and his relentless, devil-may-care attitude, she knew that only the Emperor stood a chance of success.

"We need a subject to begin the last phase of the Phoenix Project. However, I believe only one person will do - the Oracle of Sundered Crown." The other members of the Congregation, who had very much forgotten about the vision of impending doom which had led to this mess in the first place, now began to nod as it came rushing back. Sir Bryce wore a look of offense.

"I thought you had already asked me to assist in this matter, my Lady?" he asked. The Arch-Sorceress nodded at Sir Bryce, apologising for the third time in a matter of minutes.

"I am sorry, my Lord. But in all honesty, you are no match for the Oracle. She could turn you inside out without so much as a word. I believe only his Holiness has the strength to defeat her." This admission, which the Arch-Sorceress had conveniently forgotten to mention when last discussed, filled Sir Bryce with mixed feelings. While he did not like being so easily disregarded as a threat to anyone, admittedly he was quite relieved at not having his insides become his outsides.

The Emperor remained silent for a moment, mulling the thought over. While finding Sarah was the priority, he had to admit there was little point in rescuing her if the world were to be destroyed soon thereafter. He nodded slowly, his fingers drumming against his throne. It had been a long time since he had crossed the Tinelian border. Even longer since his last meeting with the Oracle. Would she even recognise him, he wondered? Could she even in her wildest of fantasies have imagined what he would become when they had met so long ago? There was only one way to find out.

"It will not be easy," the Emperor admitted. "Sundered Crown is a fair distance from our borders."

"Not to worry, Your Holiness," Sir Bryce chimed in with a smile. "I have already arranged an appropriate diversion. Coinciding with attacks along the front, we should be able to siege the city within a few weeks should our initial advances be successful."

"And what chance is it that our initial push will be successful? As you well know, no plan survives contact with the enemy," the Emperor replied. This time it was the new Lord Spymaster's turn to speak. Although, even in the presence of the Emperor, surrounded by so many powerful individuals and holding such a vitally important role, he could not have sounded more disinterested in the goings on around him. He rubbed one of his golden eyes and then picked at one of his silver teeth before bothering to speak.

"My spies have reported Tinelian defences to be especially weak along the Ifritian border. Their main force is further north, and their reserves are waiting to be mobilised from the capital itself."

Sir Bryce could not help but interrupt. He usually had so little to say in these meetings and was desperate to make up for it. Lord Thorn didn't seem to mind, however, yawning before going back to inspecting his nails.

"If we concentrate our forces into two main thrusts to the

north and to the south of Sundered Crown, we can cut the city off from reinforcements. A smaller force can then siege the city while our main army continues their advance."

The Emperor took a heavy breath and leaned back in his chair. Everything was moving so quickly, seemingly against him, conspiring to keep him from his beloved for as long as possible. It felt like only yesterday he had woken from that deep, restless sleep. His body had recovered totally since his baptism beneath the palace, under the cold, stone eyes of his God. His mind, however, continued to suffer. A ceaseless, remediless exhaustion which no prayer or spell could heal. He must move quickly, before he fade away entirely.

"We had best move then. Every moment we waste here is a gift to our enemies," the Emperor sighed, rising from his seat. The rest of the Congregation followed suit, bowing before their monarch as he left, side by side with his new Arch-Sorceress as they discussed the details of her plan. Sir Bryce practically catapulted himself out of the room, desperate to begin the invasion. He was adamant to be the first to cross the Tinelian border. He did not care how the Emperor would scold him for putting the life of his greatest general at risk. He refused to send men into battle without being the first into the fray.

Now it was Nestor's turn to leave. He rubbed his forehead as he walked, still deep in thought. He had many loyal employees and friends he could rely upon to act on his behalf and in the greatest secrecy. But these were clerks or other administrative busybodies at best, not spies trained in subterfuge and espionage which he so desperately needed. Only complicating matters further was the fact his chief suspect, who stood only a few feet from him, had at his disposal an army of informants. Chances were that Nestor was being watched even now, as he exited the most secure room in the country. Nevertheless, the Emperor had given him a vital task to perform, and Nestor would not rest until a culprit had been found.

At last, as the heavy doors of the Congregation Chamber

slammed shut, only one man remained. Philip Thorn, who until now had appeared so docile, sprang into action. His formerly slow, dreary eyes burst into life once more, their brilliant colour like the sun as he scanned the room. He moved quickly but silently, like a shadow he glided across the chamber. At first he tried the obvious, closely investigating the treasures on show in the many locked display cases which encircled the room. There were indeed many magnificent artifacts, some which even he did not expect the Imperium to have laid their hands upon. At present only one treasure mattered, one that he could not find.

This was to be expected, however. An artifact of such immense power was unlikely to be kept in plain sight. No, it must be hidden. Thorn now began to search the room more carefully, keeping a keen eye out for anything that looked out of place. A hidden door perhaps, maybe a safe behind one of the many paintings. What about a button hidden on the underside of the Emperor's throne? All his theories proved to be baseless. It must be here, he was certain of it. Thorn's blood began to slowly boil with each wasted second. His cheeks flushed hot pink, his previously silent footfalls were now frantic stomps as he raced about the chamber.

Then a thought came to him. Such an obvious answer, he cursed himself for not having thought of it sooner. Of course, such an artifact would not be hidden by such primitive means. There was clearly magic at work, concealing this treasure from him. He need only cast a certain spell and the secrets of this room would reveal themselves to him. Yet, just as he raised his hand to cast such a spell, the door behind him creaked open. Thorn quickly spun around, bringing his raised arm behind his back as he tried to wear a look of disinterest at his disturber.

The intruder who had so rudely cut short Thorn's investigation turned out to be Nestor, returning after having left some ten minutes ago. Nestor could not help but be surprised to find the new spymaster still in the chamber. Standing beside a portrait of the late Empress, his cheeks hot and flushed, his breaths deep and controlled as if he had just been vigorously exercising.

"Are you okay, my Lord?" Nestor asked politely, drawing attention to Thorn's unusual state.

"Yes, quite alright, thank you," Thorn replied. Although his breaths were shaky as he tried to keep them under control. "Just admiring this portrait of her late Majesty," he added, hoping this would be an adequate alibi.

"I can see that," Nestor replied with a raised eyebrow. "I had just come to lock up. Must have forgotten earlier, a lot on my mind," he said giving a tired smile.

"Of course, of course, you're a busy man after all. Nobody could blame you for being forgetful of such menial things," Thorn praised. As weak as the attempt at flattery was, it could not help but bring a genuine smile to Nestor's face.

"We are all busy men, my Lord. Yourself more than anyone, I am sure. It cannot be easy after all, taking over such a large network of agents as the former Lord Rohm had cultivated." Thorn nodded his head and puffed out his cheeks in a show of agreement, looking at the room around him.

"It's certainly a culture shock after having spent the last few centuries hiding out in old crypts and underground safehouses."

"Well, at least you came into this already knowing the values of secrecy and discretion," Nestor added.

"That I did," Thorn bowed. But just as he was about to leave, Nestor made an offer seemingly out of nowhere, and quite an unexpected one at that.

"Would you care to join me for tea in the palace gardens later, my Lord? We have not had much chance to speak since your appointment. I believe it would suit us both and the realm itself if we were to get to know one another better." Thorn's initial, automatic response would have been to refuse the gesture, citing work needing to be done elsewhere. Yet, as he thought about it, he realised something. Nestor had been involved in the highest levels of governance for thousands of years, even before the time of the Emperor. If anyone could offer insight into the location of the artifact he so desperately coveted, it would be Nestor.

"That is very kind of you, my Lord, it would be my pleasure," Thorn responded with a genuine smile. Nestor, pleased by the response, bowed as Thorn left the chamber and returned to his office. Once he was out of sight, Nestor's smile immediately vanished, replaced by a scowl as he looked over to where Thorn had stood. The angelic face of the Empress staring down at him. This scowl followed him from locking the door all the way back to his own office, where now he had to organise an impromptu afternoon tea. The servants were going to love him for this.

Hours later, the sun had dimmed significantly, and Nestor found himself in the palace gardens. In his haste to draw Thorn into some sort of meeting, he had completely forgotten they were in the grip of winter. Sitting outside in the freezing cold amongst dead and dying flowers hardly seemed appealing. Instead he ordered their place be made in one of the small conservatories formerly used for birdwatching.

A pristine white tablecloth overlaid a rather old rickety wooden table stained with smatterings of paint. The chairs were in such a state of disrepair they were hacked apart and burned while more suitable ones were brought in from the palace. Thankfully, the conservatory itself did somewhat make up for the rather lacklustre sight on display through its floor to ceiling windows. Potted plants and raised flower beds encircled the room. Above them, suspended via hooks and chains were other, sweet-smelling varieties of vines which reached down to near head height, filling the room with pleasant fragrances.

Nestor had only been seated for a few minutes when Lord Thorn arrived, his signature black robes in stark contrast to the bright colours which surrounded them. Could the former Lord Rohm see how dull the current holder of his office dressed, he would just about spin in his cell. If there had been room, that is.

"Apologies for the delay, my Lord," Thorn bowed, as he

approached the table which was currently being laden with sandwiches and cakes. Nestor shook his head dismissively as he gestured to the empty chair opposite.

"You're right on time, they just finished boiling the kettle," he replied as he poured himself a steaming cup of tea. Thorn placed himself down and gratefully took a cup which he immediately sipped from. Neither wished to begin interrogating the other right away, instead playing at niceties and small talk until they felt their opponent had lowered their guard.

While this had all sounded very exciting when first invited and, with a pre-prepared script in his head, Thorn quickly found himself distracted. He had been back in The Imperium for over a year now, yet he still could not get used to the novelty of abundance which he had gone without for so long. With the Battlemages, every meal would be the same. Some form of highly calorific broth which would feed the fifty or so people sheltered within a safehouse at any given time. Their clothes would be plain and worn so that they did not draw attention to themselves. The only sights they would enjoy would be the dark bowels of crypts or whatever other hovels they had fashioned for themselves away from prying eyes. The Imperium was the antithesis to everything he had known these last few centuries.

Nestor could not help but smile inwardly as he watched his guest's attention be caught by the delights before him. Brightly decorated cakes, sugary jellies and freshly baked bread shouted up from their plates to be eaten. Their enticing designs and alluring scents creating the perfect trap for a man who had suffered much banality for so long.

"Is that … salmon mousse?" Thorn shivered, salivating like a dog as he extended a pointed finger towards the tray of sandwiches.

"On fresh rye sourdough bread," Nestor smiled, passing the plate over. For all his planning, all his scheming and rehearsing, Thorn was easily overcome by his most base desires. Loading up his plate until almost nothing was left for Nestor, he began wolfing his meal down in a manner very unbecoming of a Lord. Yet Nestor did not revile at his guest's animalistic manners, for this is exactly what he had hoped for. In such a frenzied state, Thorn would think little of the questions Nestor posed, even less so of the implications of his own answers. His mind would be too busy being assaulted by textures and flavours, smells and sights, which replaced any reminder of exactly why he had come here today.

As the new spymaster guzzled like an animal at a trough, Nestor inquired gently at first, with probing questions which meant nothing in themselves but would lead the conversation in the direction he so wished. He may not be a master spy, but he knew all too well how to convince someone to spill secrets they had sworn to protect. Yet the greedy Lord was not totally oblivious to his situation. Admittedly, he had allowed his guard to slip and had already revealed more to Nestor than he had ever intended. Between mouthfuls he had managed to pull back the conversation somewhat and gain some insight of his own.

They sat for hours, talking, sipping from cups which were refilled as soon as they ran dry, and now nibbling at whatever new delicacies were brought before them after their original meal had been quickly demolished. What had started out as a rout on Thorn's part, had stabilised into a calculated game of wordplay and analysis. By the time the third hour had elapsed, the pair were ready to call it a day. Both men had had an agenda coming to this meeting, yet for all their subtleties and tricks, neither went away satisfied with what they had learned.

Nestor had been quite open about his knowledge, or lack thereof, regarding magical items under the protection of the palace. According to him, there were indeed items which had been removed from the Congregation Chamber. But this had been some time ago, and he had never enquired as to where they had gone. He had always assumed it had been under Adeneus' directive, either to study the artefacts himself or to further protect them from those who would seek to use them for evil. Yet another obstacle caused by Thorn's failure to attain the office of Arch-Sorcerer. When Nestor enquired as to why exactly Thorn was interested in such artifacts, he was given some generic excuse about potentially using them for the war effort.

Now a new, painful task lay before the Lord Spymaster. That being to attempt what he had just done with Nestor, but now with the new Arch-Sorceress instead. An opponent he felt would not respect or care for the subtle intricacies this game required. Especially not with a man who had so recently contested her for the office which she now held.

Nestor too was disappointed. While he had learned a great deal from Thorn, without a doubt more than the Lord had ever intended to share, none of it was helpful. Not regarding his current mission anyway. Clearly Thorn had no interest in the position he had been awarded or in playing politics. No, his focus was on some kind of magical instrument he believed was in the Imperium's possession. What that artefact was, however, Nestor had not been able to uncover. This, along with everything else which had been shared, provided no evidence that it was indeed Thorn who was the traitor. If having ulterior motives to wanting a position of power was a crime, well, every government since the beginning of time would be guilty.

Ultimately, both men returned to their offices only slightly more informed than before. Although, both at least had a new line of enquiry to follow. Thorn would next target Catarah, while Netsor had his sights set on none other than Sir Bryce.

The next morning, Nestor found Sir Bryce with ease. With war now declared, the entire Imperial City had been turned into a fortress. Thousands more soldiers roamed the streets, and long caravans of supplies and military goods slithered their way through its suburbs. New fortifications had been erected also. As the city did not have an all-encompassing wall to protect it like the Tinelians did, fortresses and roadblocks ensured the people remained guarded from external threats. The Seekers too were out in force. Usually exclusive to their temples and parochial institutes, they now too prowled the streets. Working in conjunction with Lord Thorn's spy network, the sight of their crimson hoods and heavy golden pendants around their necks served as a stark warning to any enemies of their Order.

Much like they had done during the Emperor's illness, they went in search of traitors and heretics. The difference this time was they had specific targets in mind rather than simply terrorising the whole city. People cheered as their neighbours of many decades were taken from their homes, beaten, humiliated and sometimes summarily executed for treason. A word whose definition had been drastically stretched these last few days. While only a few months ago the possession of books critical of the Emperor or the Seekers would have been punishable by confiscation and a fine. Now they found themselves on great bonfires, along with their owners.

In the midst of all this, in a makeshift headquarters in the palace square, was Sir Bryce. In a striped tent of red and white, surrounded by guards and a mountainous collection of supplies. His own office was only a few minutes' walk from where he now sat, preferring to conduct his business out in the open. The war had barely begun yet he was acting as if the last one had never ended. Nestor found him barking out orders to a collection of sergeants and lieutenants, fistfuls of papers being bunched into their hands before they were sent away. Nestor stood watching for a moment. It had been so long since he had last seen Sir Bryce in his element, and he was soon reminded why he had been appointed to this position.

Already Sir Bryce had planned extensive operations across a multitude of theatres. Tinelia's allies were still yet to officially enter the war. Nevertheless, Sir Bryce had already prepared and planned for their eventual capitulation. There were maps upon maps with bold, black arrows thrusting in all manner of directions into enemy territory. Diagrams of defensible positions from the heartlands of the Imperium to the Western shores of Gil-Ebrax. There were even ongoing calculations attempting to discern the economic impact of blockades, and the impact food shortages would have on the campaign. Admittedly, it was impressive to behold. There were many who once considered Sir Bryce to be nothing more than a brainless dolt, revelling in violence and caring nothing for good strategy. Yet he still stood, while their heads had been taken long ago.

This theatre, this frantic showing of his military genius with such glee, only deepened Nestor's initially negligible suspicion. In truth, he had almost discounted Sir Bryce as a suspect entirely. But now he was not so sure. As he watched the burly knight stomp around, bellowing orders, he could not help but ponder to himself. Had the Emperor been slain, who would the people of The Imperium have turned to in their moment of need? As he watched on, only one name came to mind.

Sir Bryce was so caught up in the tasks before him that he did not notice the quiet man in the lime green robe idling at the tent's entrance. Nestor had to cough multiple times before he caught his attention.

"Put a bloody sock in it would you?!" the knight bellowed, as he looked up from his maps only to see Nestor stood before him. He wore a look of shock upon seeing his colleague outside of the palace. Like seeing a fish up a tree, he seemed so out of place surrounded by instruments of war rather than bureaucracy.

"Oh, my apologies, Nestor. I didn't expect to see you out here," he muttered, before quickly going back to his maps. But then he looked up again, almost immediately, a puzzled, suspicious look on his face. "What *are* you doing out here?" he asked. Nestor shrugged, pulling up a chair opposite Sir Bryce's desk.

"I was hoping we could have a chat," he replied casually. Sir Bryce, however, was not impressed by Nestor's relaxed tone.

"Sorry, my Lord, but there does appear to be a war on.

Can I get back to you? I don't really have time for 'chats' at the moment," Sir Bryce scowled at his colleague's apparent lack of urgency. Nestor smiled awkwardly and raised his hands in a defensive posture.

"Apologies, I chose my words poorly. I believe there is much we need to discuss if we are to keep the realm functioning on a war footing," Nestor replied. Sir Bryce remained dismissive.

"You stick to your job, and I'll stick to mine. Best way I see this working," he replied, scratching at the chin beneath his long, braided beard. The knight could not help but feel some degree of animosity towards his fellow Congregation members. For years they had dismissed his input and disregarded his concerns. Now that he was needed, more than any of them, suddenly they all wanted to hear what he had to say. All wishing to curry favour with the new centre of power now that the Emperor was overcome with mad, desperate grief.

Nestor began to shift in his seat uncomfortably, a hot flush running up his neck as Sir Bryce insisted on making his job even harder than it was already. He was not the kind of man who enjoyed playing the courtly arts of subtlety and discretion. No, Sir Bryce was about as discreet as a hammer to the testicles. This left Nestor feeling like he was already on his backfoot, at a disadvantage, not knowing how to play off his opponent to get the answers he needed.

But then a thought came to him. Nestor would have to be careful, frame his words in only the most hypothetical and devoted way, should Sir Bryce's apparent unshakeable loyalty appear to be genuine.

"The Emperor is clearly not well, still overcome with grief, allowing it to divert him from his duties," Nestor stated, his tone shifting abruptly to one of the upmost gravity. This immediately caught Sir Bryce's attention, and he lay down his maps and shifted his eyes over to his now, sober looking colleague.

"I am aware of this, but what of it?" he asked suspiciously, his eyes narrowing as he tried to make sense of what he had just been told, something which was apparent to anyone who had spent mere moments in the Emperor's presence. While Sir Bryce may have had a more positive opinion of Nestor than the other members of the congregation, that did not mean he trusted him. He too liked to play those silly cloak and dagger games, just like the rest of them.

Once again Nestor chose his words with the upmost caution and care. Making potentially treasonous statements in the presence of the Emperor's most trusted general in order to squeeze out some hint of betrayal, was a very dangerous game indeed.

"With his Holiness gone, the realm will suffer. We need a plan in place to ensure his absence does not further galvanise our enemies and weaken our own position."

While lying through his teeth was nothing new to Nestor, he found doing so to Sir Bryce to be extremely tense. Unable to work out what his opponent could be thinking, he waited. The knight was quiet for a moment, chewing the inside of his lip, staring intensely at the small man opposite. He nodded silently before moving over to the tent's entrance and drawing its canvas closed. A gloom settled upon the makeshift war-room as the knight returned, a haggard look upon his face. He sat across from Nestor, lowering himself carefully into his seat.

"Speak," he grunted. Before he did so, however, Nestor had to grip onto his knees tightly, finding himself to be literally shaking in the shadow of the imposing man before him. He could see this going one of three ways. Sir Bryce would either find Nestor's plan to be so treacherous, so cowardly and underhanded, that he relieved his head from his shoulders where he sat. This was, of course, Nestor's least preferable option. The second being that Sir Bryce still declared him a traitor but brought him before the Emperor for judgment. In doing so, the Emperor would be forced to explain the secret task he had bestowed upon Nestor. Saving his life but causing even more problems once the knowledge of the conspiracy was revealed.

The final option, and the one Nestor considered to be the least likely, even despite the obvious motives and potential rewards of Sir Bryce being the traitor, was that the knight would go along with Nestor's plan. This was not necessarily because he doubted Sir Bryce to be the traitor, but because he believed the knight to be far more intelligent than he let on. If he indeed was planning to overthrow the Emperor, Nestor doubted he would suddenly reveal his intentions to the first person to walk through the door. But Nestor had now talked himself into a corner. Hopefully, somehow, he would be able to talk his way out of it.

Nestor presented his plan with the cool, clinical tone of a doctor diagnosing an illness before presenting the cure. There was no malice in his voice, no hidden venom or constrained lusting for power. Only the innocent, cut and dry identification of their latest problem and the solution which he had devised.

"While I disagree with his Holiness' current trajectory, I understand that he will come out the other side eventually."

"He needs time to process his grief," Sir Bryce added with an unexpected softness and understanding for such a martial man. Softness and understanding which had been noticeably absent during the meetings of the Congregation, when he was still desperate for his war.

"As do we all," Nestor replied, before at last coming to what they had both been waiting for. "Unfortunately, his Holiness has chosen a poor time to embark upon this venture. The war, the Tinelians, will not wait for the Emperor's heart to mend before they strike at us with all their might." Sir Bryce nodded silently in agreement.

"We need someone to lead us in this war, someone the commoners and nobles alike can look to, someone who can take up the mantle of interim leader until The Emperor returns." There it was, Nestor's hastily constructed scheme laid bare for Sir Bryce to do with as he pleased. There was no doubt, what Nestor was suggesting was treason, and nobody could fault the knight for tearing the tiny man in half for the mere utterance of these words. Yet the burly warrior did not react with the sudden explosion of violence Nestor had expected. Instead, he enquired further.

"And who would you suggest as this interim, this placeholder emperor? And more importantly, what does his Holiness think of the plan?" Sir Bryce too chose his questions carefully. He wanted absolute certainty in Nestor's motives before acting. The last thing he wanted to do was act rashly should this in fact be part of a plan constructed by The Emperor himself. Nestor had gone slightly pale, his trembling having never ceased. Yet he answered with a calm, diplomatic air, as if it had never crossed his mind that the words he spoke could earn him a death sentence. As if what he said could ever be misinterpreted as anything other than fulfilling his duties to both his country and Emperor.

"I have not yet raised this with his Holiness. I did not see the point if you did not yet agree. You, of course, being my choice for the place of interim leader should his Holiness also agree."

Admittedly, the plan made perfect sense to Sir Bryce. An empire at war needed its leader to guide it. And he was, indubitably, the natural choice for the position. His martial prowess and the respect he commanded from all corners of the Imperium was second only to the Emperor himself. Yet the plan did not sit well with him, even had the Emperor been informed beforehand. Even if the Emperor commanded him to take the role personally, Sir Bryce would have been forced to wholly reject it. Not because he felt unable to perform the role or even that he did not want it, but he had sworn an oath.

When he swallowed the poison at the opening of Parliament the previous year, he swore never to betray his Emperor, to never subvert or act against him in any way. How would the magic contained within him know the difference between a voluntary, temporary transition of power and usurping the throne? Yet another reason for Sir Bryce to further detest magic in almost all its forms. Nestor conveniently had not been forced to partake in this ritual, meaning he could scheme and plot all he liked. Sir Bryce, however, was not about to risk a sudden, violent death for merely even entertaining the thought of taking power for himself. Even if it was only temporary. Even with the Emperor's blessing.

He conveyed his answer to Nestor, politely declining while explaining his reasons for doing so. The realm had managed to function under the congregation's rule during the Emperor's illness. They would just have to do it again, although admittedly under more dire circumstances than before.

This was not one of the three eventualities Nestor had prepared himself for, leaving him both shocked yet hugely relieved. Unbeknownst to Sir Bryce, he had managed to exonerate himself almost entirely. His concern about being struck down by the parliamentary poison showed that he was the only person in the Congregation unaware that it was little more than a mixture of various sour herbs. The man had spent the last century without literally a single thought which could be interpreted as treasonous entering his mind. A feat probably unobtained by any other politician anywhere ever.

Nestor ended the discussion by pretending to engage with all the points the knight had raised before bowing to Sir Bryce's clearly superior position. The Congregation would function as it had done before the war, simply having to shoulder the burden of an absentee emperor. Nestor's refusal to push back, to try and change Sir Bryce's mind on the plan, also worked in his favour. No longer did the knight suspect ulterior motives. The ease by which Nestor folded on his plan convinced him that he truly did have the best of intentions at heart.

The two parted ways after agreeing to continue with the current course of action. Sir Bryce immediately went back to examining his maps and barking orders at terrified subordinates. Nestor, meanwhile, left with the feeling of an anchor being lifted from his chest. If there had been one person he had dreaded the thought of turning traitor, it had been Sir Bryce. The others could all be dealt with without causing too much collateral damage. Sir Bryce, however, whether he knew it or not, could have turned half the country to his side should he have wished.

Chapter 14

News of the war had arrived home well before Nate. As their ship pulled into the docks, the crew could barely recognise the capital. They had already been delayed by the Tinelian navy, now out of port and forming a defensive perimeter around their coast. Despite their obvious naval ensign, they had been stopped and boarded before being allowed to continue. Now as they departed the ship, they were once again halted by heavily armed guards who demanded to see their diplomatic papers. This would not have been a problem if the crew had originally been given any before setting off.

What could have turned into a potentially ugly situation was thankfully resolved by Ardell, whom the guards immediately recognised. After a few not so thinly veiled threats towards the obstructing guardsmen, the crew were finally allowed to enter the city. Nate and Marcus, however, could not help but gawk in amazement at all that had changed in the short time since the war had been made official.

The labyrinthian walkways which crisscrossed the entirety of the docks were now each patrolled by squads of soldiers. What little remained of the beaches were now impaled by sharpened stakes which pointed out towards the sea. Coastal batteries of heavy artillery had been emplaced upon elevated points such as hills and reinforced rooftops. Huge, long-barrelled guns, which would not have been out of place during Nate's version of the Second World War. Then, in groups of four, were soldiers with rifles who patrolled the rooftops and other designated firing positions. Their weapons either slung across their shoulders or held firmly in their grasp as they stared out at the open ocean. Their fingers ready to jump to the trigger at any moment.

"This is all starting to feel a bit too real," Nate mumbled to Marcus as they passed through a checkpoint which would take them away from the docks and to the next layer of the city.

Ardell too felt the tension in the air.

"It only gets worse from here," she replied, scowling at a guard who had looked at her funny. With only the open road now ahead of them, Ardell turned to the two men she had forced to accompany her on their failed diplomatic mission.

"Listen," she sighed, placing her hands on her hips and looking upon the pair with what looked a lot like pity. "There's a good chance the two of you will be mobilised soon. There won't be many who escape it." Nate felt a stone drop into the pit of his stomach at the thought. "I'll see what I can do to make sure the two of you are kept together, under my command if possible. But I can't guarantee anything," Ardell said shaking her head. She knew in her heart that many hundreds, if not thousands, of people it was her duty to care for would soon be dead. There was little she could do about it, as such was the nature of war. Yet she would try to keep these two oafs alive if she could. After all, they were not too bad for company.

"Thank you, Captain," Marcus murmured. He truly appreciated the gesture. But even the mighty Ardell could not save them from an errant arrow or sorcerer's fireball. Their chances of death were too high for Marcus to even entertain the idea that they may see the end of this war. So, right then and there, he made a promise to himself, one that he had made over a year ago but this time renewed with clear understanding of what it would likely entail. He would keep Nate alive, the others too, if he had the strength, no matter the cost. Nate himself was too stunned to speak. He had gone deathly pale, his stare wide and far, as he struggled to imagine the horrors yet to come.

Ardell looked upon them with strong emotions of her

own. She cared deeply for those under her command, loved even, so long as they followed her orders. She did not wish to see harm befall even a single one of them. Yet she had a duty to perform, a duty which involved willingly sacrificing those she loved in mindless battle should those be her orders. She nervously picked at her nails behind her back while wearing a stern look. She could not have the lower ranks see how greatly the thought of war troubled her, as such a thing would inevitably lead to panic. No, she would continue to wear this mask of pitiless indifference for as long as it helped to maintain order and keep her men alive. However, offering some small token of reassurance would not hurt.

She smiled sadly, resting her hands upon their shoulders. "If you trust in the gods and one another, you might just live to see the end of this." This unusually warm gesture filled the men with a small degree of hope. Not enough to dispel the worries which clouded their minds, but enough that they could return sad, unconvincing smiles of their own. Ardell had never portayed herself to be a religious woman. That of course having a very different meaning in Purgatory as it would in the mortal world. No, everyone here accepted the divine as fact, but Ardell had never seemed like the kind to put much faith in them.

"Gods!" gasped Chen as Nate walked through the door. She ran over to him, dropping the pile of clean washing she had been carrying onto the dirty floor. She threw out her arms and pulled Nate into a tight embrace, so tight that Nate could feel his ribs crumbling like plaster. As Chen quickly pulled herself away, she viciously slapped the stupid smile off Nate's face.

"Ow!" He yelped in shock, stumbling back and holding his stinging cheek.

"Where the fuck have you been?!" Chen cried as she went in for another hit. Nate threw up his arms to defend himself as a flurry of blows landed against him. That's right, he had totally forgotten. Ardell had instructed them to leave without breathing a word as to where they were going. Chen had therefore awoken one morning to find Nate simply gone. The last few weeks on her part had therefore been filled with nothing but worry. She had searched every ditch and bar in the city for her roommate to no avail. Now here he stood, as if nothing had happened, with that stupid grin on his face.

"Stop, let me explain!" Nate protested as the blows continued to fall. Chen reluctantly pulled back her hands and stood awaiting what had better be a damn good alibi. "Ardell wanted me and Marcus for a mission. She told us not to tell anyone." Nate's admission did not convince Chen, however, who's face contorted into one of renewed anger.

"Bollocks!" She cried as she began assailing him once more. "You were with that whore Cassandra, weren't you?" She continued, now chasing him about the room, her hand raised. Nate attempted to retreat to safety, vaulting over a bed and then dashing over to the centre of the room where he successfully placed the dining table between them. All the while finding Chen's accusation extremely odd.

"What are you on about?" He panted from his new position of relative safety. Chen's jaw looked as hard as iron as she clenched it before calming down slightly.

"Listen, I don't care who you're fucking. Just tell me before you disappear for two weeks. I thought you were dead."

"I haven't seen Cassandra since we got back from our assignment," Nate scoffed at the absurdity of the accusation, although Chen still didn't believe him.

"Oh, then I suppose she's been singing your praises just because," Chen scowled, folding her arms across her chest. Now it was Nate's turn to scowl. He mirrored Chen and folded his own arms, demanding she explain just what the hell she was going on about. Apparently, for the last few weeks, Cassandra had been telling the whole Guild and just about anyone else who would listen, the story of their assignment. Or at least her version of it. A version where Nate had slain an entire hideout of necromancers without mercy or restraint. A version where he, not Cassandra, was the unhinged lunatic. The others at the Guild had lapped it up. Now just about everyone considered him to be a ruthless killer just like the rest of them.

Nate sighed heavily, dropping his arms to his side as Chen finished recounting Cassandra's tale.

"That's not what happened, and that's sure as hell not where I've been." Chen soon caught on to Nate's body language and adopted a less aggressive tone.

"Then tell me, and make sure it's the truth," she said, softer this time, although the threat of further violence was clear. Nate then spent the next hour recounting not only his mission to Peace-Haven, but the truth about the assignment with Cassandra. He spared no detail. From the wonderous sights of the few days upon the Perfumed Isle, to the revulsion he felt for himself as he watched Cassandra commit murder without remorse or consequence.

Chen shook her head as Nate finished his testimony, biting the inside of her cheek and staring off into the distance.

"I always knew she was a complete cunt," Chen grumbled. Yet even she was surprised by the barbarity Nate had just described in such detail. The sincerity in his words was enough to convince her that Nate was indeed telling the truth. She then made it abundantly clear that if he ever disappeared like that again she would kill him. Nate suspected that much of his roommate's anger came from the news that had been read out in every public square a few days prior. They were at war, and at any moment they could be sent to their doom.

Chen had been affected more than any other in their group by the attack on the Imperial City. Nate still remembered vividly the look of horror in her eyes, the crystal tears flowing down her face, illuminated by the burning city below. She had cried for days afterwards. Her anguish only made worse by the passing comments of others regarding the slow, painful end the victims of the bombing would have suffered.

In an attempt to avoid contemplating the inevitable, Nate suggested the pair go out for dinner. His treat for all the anxiety he had caused. Chen happily agreed to spend some of his money, and the pair found themselves at Nate's favourite restaurant that evening.

"Pedan would break your legs if he found out about this," Chen said without looking up from her plate, her cheeks stuffed with some pasta-like substance.

"Which is why we aren't going to tell him," Nate instructed, pointing his fork menacingly in Chen's direction. This threat meant nothing and Chen smiled, crossing one leg over the other.

"I'm not so sure about that," she teased, sharply sucking air between her teeth. "Dessert might persuade me though," to which Nate could reply with nothing but a smile. It did not take long for their relaxing evening to become undone. As the restaurant began to fill up, and new conversations arose, it was not long before the topic of war surrounded them.

Naturally, there was the usual chest-beating and enough regurgitated propaganda to make Goebbels proud. These could easily be filtered out and ignored.

It was the hushed tones and whispers of early defeats that lingered in their ears. The nervous, shaky voices which dared entertain that all may not be going according to plan. There was talk of an early offensive by the Imperium. One that had already broken through the Tinelian defences and was gaining momentum with each new day. There were rumours of sieges, of civilians and prisoners being hacked to death as they begged for mercy. Worst of all were the stories even the bravest only barely dared to whisper. Stories that an unstoppable, unkillable warrior was leading the Imperial charge. A man consisting of nothing but rage and bloodlust. A man one could safely bet was the knight Sir Bryce himself, keeping true to his promise of being the first onto the battlefield.

As Nate sat in his chair, staring sullenly at the bottom of his empty mug, Ardell's words returned to him. He may be drafted soon, and then he would see the truth of these rumours for himself.

It was only a few days later, after returning from a pleasant evening at Pedan's Inn, that Nate and Chen received the notices they had been dreading. Draft orders had been posted beneath their barracks door. They lay there menacingly, like venomous insects protected by their wax-sealed shells. The pair decided not to open them immediately, instead stoking the fire to life and making a pot of tea to calm their nerves. After nearly an hour of procrastinating in the gloom of their barracks, lit only by the flames of the fire, did they open their summons with trembling hands.

They did it together, breaking the seals with what felt like earth-shattering cracks as their fates were now loosed upon the world. There was a silence. An excruciatingly long silence as they quickly scanned the documents before going over them again more carefully. It was Chen who broke away first with a relieved sigh so heavy she nearly blew the building down. She twisted her hand to show Nate the contents of her letter. She had been ordered to patrol an area only a few days from the capital, far from the frontline.

Not only that, but she would not need to report for duty until the first rotation of troops in roughly a month. This was without a doubt one of the safest orders short from remaining in the city and was cause for celebration. But upon seeing the dismayed look upon Nate's face, and his even more vigorously shaking hands, Chen was filled with fresh fear. Slowly, as if he did not believe the words written clearly before him, Nate revealed the contents of his own letter. Both were stunned, aghast at what lay within. As clear as day, upon the parchment were Nate's orders to assemble as part of an army. Their mission, to break through the Imperial lines and relieve the siege of Sundered Crown.

"It's a fucking death sentence," Nate gasped. He had planned to remain strong, to appear stoic in the face of such hardship should this be his fate. But he had foolishly doubted such a thing could happen to him. Now that it had, with no room for misinterpretation, he found himself bereft of all strength and courage. He began to hyperventilate, slipping from his chair onto the ground beneath the crackling flames of the fire as he struggled to breathe. His hands shot out, in search of anything which could bring him comfort, yet found nothing but the cool stone floor. Chen soon bore down upon him, pressing Nate's face into her chest as she held him tightly. His hands still searched frantically, pawing at her but unable to form a grip.

"You'll be okay, you'll be okay," Chen cooed over and over, as she refused to let Nate out of her embrace. Her own heart was racing, a lump formed in her throat and her eyes filled with tears. She knew the likelihood of the fate which awaited Nate on the battlefield but refused to succumb to despair. With Nate now clinging to her like a new-born, Chen retrieved his summons which he had dropped to the floor.

"Look," she whispered, bringing the parchment within Nate's vision. "It says Ardell will be leading this mission herself. You're going to be fine," Chen whispered, as she once again wrapped her arms around her friend.

"It's going to be okay. You're going to be okay," Chen expressed in desperate consolation, as the darkness of night began to surround them.

There was no time to waste the following morning. Nate's orders had been clear, the mission ahead of him, one that would not wait. He had struggled to sleep that night as nightmares plagued him incessantly. His mind filling with images of a horrific and painful death before finding himself somewhere totally new. Somewhere alien and unwelcoming, with no friends to guide him, completely alone.

His hands were still shaking as he fastened his pack shut. Chen had tried forcing him to eat something but his stomach turned at the mere thought of food. What would be the point? Whatever he ate now would just end up spilled across some muddy field in a few days' time with the rest of his innards. Chen, ever the mother hen, continued fussing over him. It was clear she too was struggling to keep her emotions in check. She pulled at the straps on his breastplate to make sure they were tight enough. Continuing well after this had been confirmed, doing everything she could to keep Nate close for just a few moments more. She assured him that all would be fine, while barraging him with all manner of informative snippets she hoped may help keep him alive.

Nate heard nothing but a dull droning as his mind struggled to accept the reality of what was happening. Instead, he was focusing on Chen's face rather than her words. Her cheerless, moist eyes which remained glued to his own. Her pale lips, which he could see moving frantically, as if to a silent dance or some secret mantra. Her dark, unbrushed hair, which whirled about from her quick movements, catching her in the face with each turn of her head.

Nate threw his arms around her, pulling his friend into a tight embrace he desperately wished could last forever. Her babbling immediately stopped, as she pushed her face into Nate's chest to hide her tears. Nate rested his chin on her head, looking about the place he had called home for what he felt would be the final time.

"I'll walk with you to the gate," Chen sniffed, as Nate pulled away at last. But Nate shook his head.

"Stay here and look after Bob for me," he said, his voice cracking. Chen nodded solemnly, pulling Nate into a final, quick embrace.

"I'll see you in a few weeks," she whispered. Nate gave her one last squeeze before turning and exiting the barracks. As she listened to his footsteps retreat away, Chen could not help but be overcome with a deep regret.

Up until now, Nate had done a good job of keeping himself under control. But as he entered the makeshift stable he had constructed, where his four-legged friend stood waiting, he was overcome with grief. Like a damn bursting from the pressure of the emotions he had tried to contain, he wrapped his arms around Bob's muzzle, sobbing into her uncontrollably. Bob had no idea what was going on, but understood her master was leaving. And she sensed that she may not see him again for quite some time. She whinnied gently, offering whatever small consolation she could.

With all that now finally out of his system, Nate kissed

his old friend goodbye and made for the city gates. It was a nice morning, all things considered. The sun was warm and the smell of the lingering cold from the previous night's frost filled Nate with an appreciation for the beauty of the world around him. Far in the distance, the Citadel stood against the backdrop of a cloudless sky. Shimmering in the morning sun like the points of an icy crown. As his boots crunched upon the frozen ground, Nate kept repeating a mantra in his head - *Everything would be fine. He was going to be fine.*

Upon reaching the Vanguard's main gate, Nate presented his draft papers to a fully armoured adjutant. He even had the visor on his helmet lowered, as if he expected to be attacked, here of all places. Although admittedly, the area around the gate was a scene of carnage. Thousands had arrived at first light to present their draft papers. These were either the especially patriotic, or like Nate, the excessively terrified. Tens of thousands more would arrive throughout the day. These being less eager to spill their blood for Tinelia, but too afraid to refuse the summons.

There were of course those who had refused to answer the call of their nation. Many of them were currently in the process of being hunted down. They would be given the choice of enlistment, or execution for desertion. As Nate waited in line to turn over his summons, he watched with a pained expression as a conscript was beaten unconscious for spitting at an officer.

Nate had been unfortunate enough to be called up in the very first round of mobilisation, which everyone knew was the worst. It would be a while before the generals and their subordinates truly began to understand the nature of the war they would be fighting this time. With access to such a wide variety of weaponry, no war was ever the same as the last. The first round of mobilised recruits, therefore, were often little more than a trial run of how the rest of the war would be fought. At this point, the diplomats who had remained behind on Peace-Haven had yet to agree upon weapon restrictions which would apply to all parties. Horrendous casualties were, therefore, fully expected to be unavoidable.

After his summons were taken and stamped to show that he had indeed turned up, Nate was ordered to make for the city's lowest level immediately. There, apparently, Ardell had taken over a couple of fields and was assembling her forces. With a heavy heart and legs that felt like lead, Nate began walking down the dirt road out of the Vanguard. So far there had been no sign of Marcus. So much for Ardell's promise. On the final day of his journey to the furthest edges of the city, as Nate dragged himself along, exhausted and aching, there was a sudden slap on his back. Spinning around, he saw the surprising but welcome sight of Joel smiling down at him.

"Joel?" Nate asked, not entirely sure he believed what his eyes were telling him.

"Thought that sad looking sack of shit looked familiar," Joel laughed.

"What are you doing here?" Nate smiled, as the pair shook hands.

"Got called up by Ardell. I'm supposed to help with the rescuing of some lazy wankers sitting around in Sundered Crown." Nate's face could not help but light up at this revelation.

"Same here," he gasped. Admittedly, Joel was unlikely to turn the tide of the battle or make Nate's chances of survival any greater. Nevertheless, having a friend on this journey would make it considerably less terrifying.

"Chen did say I should find you moping about somewhere round here."

"You've seen her?"

"Only while I was looking for you. Guess destiny was on our side this time," Joel replied. But Nate furrowed his brow. While he considered Joel a close friend, they never spent much time together without Marcus making up their trio. He had no idea why Joel would have been looking for him specifically. It all became clear quite quickly, however, as the eternally grinning Aussie recognised the searching look on Nate's face.

"Been on a bit of a trek, I gotta say. Found this along the way though." As he said this, Joel withdrew a sword which had been wrapped in cloth across the top of his knapsack. He handed it to Nate who pulled the coverings back gingerly. As the blade became quickly familiar to him, he tore away the last of the cloth, a look of complete surprise and joy across his face.

"How?" Nate gasped as he held the sword upright. The same sword Marcus had presented him with over a year ago before setting out on their violent journey. The sword which had been taken from him after their group had been captured. Truthfully, he had never expected to see it again.

"Went for a little walkabout back to Adeneus' castle. Found Marcus' shield too, the clumsy bugger."

"I don't know how to thank you," Nate gushed. Joel waved his hand, instructing Nate not to be so stupid.

"How about you just make sure to stay alive. I don't want to have gone to all that trouble for nothing," he grinned. Nate grimaced slightly as he suddenly remembered their shared destination.

"Got anything easier?" He tried to joke, but Joel could see the worry on Nate's face plain as day. He shook his head, maintaining that characteristically reassuring grin of his, which had a way of downplaying any potential danger.

"You don't give yourself enough credit, mate. You're smart and you're good with a sword. If you can just learn to follow orders between now and the battle, you'll do just fine." Nate couldn't help but scoff at Joel's claim. Nevertheless, it did go some way in calming the swarm of bees raging in his stomach. With a familiar companion at his side, the remainder of the journey to where Ardell was mustering her troops went quickly. The pair laughed and joked but also shared any knowledge or strategy they believed would help see them through the coming conflict. Which admittedly on

Nate's part, was rather little. Although, he had learned the invaluable lesson that you couldn't cook a chicken rare.

The pair heard Ardell's camp before they saw it. The clamouring of thousands of voices all calling out over one another. The ringing of hammers upon steel and the crunching of thousands of armoured boots upon the ground. Cresting the small hill which had hidden the camp from their sight, Nate was amazed at the scene before him. He had never seen so many people gathered in one place, with one shared goal in mind. But that is not what surprised him. Rather, it was how well organised this deafening mob seemed to be.

There is something about loud, uneven noises which immediately conjures up images of anarchy, of disorder and chaos which seeks nothing more than the corruption and unravelling of that which surrounds it. Yet this is not what Nate found to be the case. Rather than chaotic, sprawling masses of men, caked in mud and seemingly wandering without cause. What lay below were hundreds of neat rows of light-brown tents, so straight they formed an illusion of being stacked on top of one another.

Between every fifth row of tents, a slightly wider space contained large fire pits and kitchens. While upon the outer edges of the camp lay the armourers, who continued to hammer away with vigour. This would be the last chance for the soldiers to maintain their gear. Nobody wanted to be the one going into battle with a chipped sword or wobbly helmet.

"Must be about ten thousand," Joel exhaled, also impressed by what he saw. He may have been around for a few centuries at this point, but still, never had he seen such a concentration of troops. Not belonging to Tinelia anyway. Joel's guess proved to be remarkably accurate. Ardell had been permitted exactly ten thousand troops for this operation. In the grand scheme of things, a tiny fraction of the total number of forces available. Nevertheless, that did not make the mission anything less than of vital importance.

The Imperium had managed to cut off the Tinelian army from its forces in the north, surrounding Sundered Crown as they did so. A second, southern offensive had failed to break through the Tinelian lines, however. This is where they came in. Ardell's forces would be split into three. Her army of four thousand would relieve the siege of Sundered Crown. While the other six thousand, would be split into two forces led by her most trusted officers. It would be their task to bolster the southern defence to ensure Ardell's relieving army was not cut off.

The war was barely a few weeks old, but already the stage was being set for one of its most decisive battles. Already cracks had begun to form in the Tinelian leadership. While the time for debating war was over, the Lords now found themselves divided in terms of strategy. Two factions had formed, which history would remember as the tortoises and the hares. The hares, led by Grand Admiral Lee, wished to launch a lightning counter-offensive. One that would push the Imperials deep into their own territory, where they hoped the rest of the war would be fought. This would be in conjunction with a vast naval blockade of the Imperium and its allies, starving them into submission.

The tortoises, however, rejected this strategy entirely. Believing Tinelia should abandon its empire, focusing all men and resources into the defence of the city itself. They hoped to bleed the Imperium dry until their allies in Estrold and Gil-Ebrax could join the war, overwhelming their enemies with sheer numbers. Such things, however, were both unknown and beyond Nate and Joel. Currently, the only thing they cared about was seeing another day in the same world they had spent the previous one.

"Suppose we best get down there," Nate sighed.

"Aye," Joel nodded, as they watched hundreds of stretchers and white cloths being loaded onto the baggage train.

Unsurprisingly, Ardell did not have time for just any idiot to come waltzing into her tent, expecting their orders to be hand delivered with all the niceties. They were quickly removed and pointed towards another, slightly less heavily armoured adjutant who would tell them exactly where to go.

This poor sod seemed to have been run ragged, having never had to work so hard in her life. She barely looked at them as they once again handed over their now stamped draft notices. They were each given a tent, an armband, and a slip of pink paper.

"What's this for?" Nate asked, twirling the bright green armband around his finger. The adjutant looked up at him as if he was an idiot.

"So you don't get stabbed by your own side. Although I'm happy to keep it if you want." Nate's eyes widened at the prospect as he wrapped the stretchy green material around his bicep as tightly as was comfortable. He had always wondered how armies back in the day had been able to tell each other apart. Hopefully, this tactic worked.

"And this?" Joel asked, holding up the slip of paper. The adjutant rolled her eyes in frustration as she once again looked up from her clipboard, filled with tasks yet to be completed.

"It's a token for a breastplate and your choice of either greaves or gauntlets. Go to one of the blacksmiths. The breastplate is *not* optional," the woman stressed as the pair finally left her alone. The blacksmiths were in no better moods. Having been hauled down from their shops into these makeshift forges barely fit for an amateur. They worked tirelessly to ensure each soldier in Ardell's force reflected the standards she had become known for. Every sword would be sharp, every shield sturdy. Their armour polished like mirrors, so the last thing the enemy saw was their own terrified reflection as they were cut down.

"I'm not really a fan of this heavy stuff," Nate complained as he tightened the new, steel breastplate across his torso.

"Leather is fine for monster hunting, when you can dodge and dive all you like. It won't protect you much from a thousand men charging straight into you though," Joel replied.

"And this will?" Nate said raising his eyebrow as he rapped the metal with his knuckles.

"No, but it cleans easier when you die," Joel winked. Nate

allowed his shoulders to sag as he let out a huff. He forced his mind to move on and now found himself staring at the rolled-up tent he had been given. He raised it slightly so that it caught Joel's attention.

"Any idea how this thing works?" Joel was silent for a moment as he stared at his companion, unsure if he was joking. When it became clear this was no joke, Joel made his thoughts known.

"I'm starting to understand why you get punched a lot."

Chapter 15

"Oh fuck," Nate whispered, his words trembling as vigorously as the rest of his body as he beheld the Imperial army only a few hundred meters away. The Tinelian force had taken a few weeks to arrive, not bad considering their number. The journey itself could not have been more uneventful. Even the most savage of creatures lurking in the woods would not consider attacking a column of ten thousand heavily armed soldiers. Only husks, brainless and far less prevalent than they used to be, had tried their luck with no success.

Instead, every day had been a repeat of the last. Ardell and her officers would wake the army before dawn, allowing a small window to eat their rations of bread and meat before setting off at first light. They would then march in formation until sundown. There would be no breaks, no stops for food or water. You ate, drank and pissed while marching, all in total silence. The stomping of twenty thousand feet could be heard well before being seen. Otherwise, the only deviations from this silence were the occasional coughs as cold air assaulted the lungs, and the almost synchronised sniffles of thousands of people simultaneously catching a cold as they marched in frost and the occasional light snow.

At the rear followed the baggage train. Manned not by soldiers but civilians or squires, anyone deemed unfit for fighting yet fit enough to work. They ensured the men and women of Ardell's army made it to their destination in good health, bringing everything they could conceivably need for the journey ahead. Nate had been surprised at the sheer number of livestock this relatively small army required daily. By the time they reached Sundered Crown, they had slaughtered hundreds of cattle and thousands of poultry.

Thankfully, their sacrifice was not in vain as the defenders of Sundered Crown still held the city, and their march had not been wasted. However, this meant that the battle would indeed be going ahead. The Imperials had pulled most of their forces away from the siege to face the oncoming Tinelians. While this gave Ardell's forces a slight numerical advantage, none were foolish enough to take up hope. This battle would still be a bloody one, and if there was one comfort it was that it would be over soon.

The battlefield itself, as Nate had pessimistically predicted, was a field roughly a mile from the city. The ground was frozen and white frost still clung to the tips of green shoots which had not yet succumbed to winter's grip. At the very least, he told himself, he would not have to worry about getting his intestines too dirty once they were ripped out. Both armies had made sure to position themselves clear of any forest or pockets of woodland. This would force any cavalry to appear in the open rather than hiding out of view until that crucial moment when they would crash into the enemy flank.

In the distance, Sundered Crown's cathedral and fortress could easily be made out. Both had suffered some superficial damage, and around them ascended columns of grey smoke as the Imperials halted their bombardment until the battle was won. The defenders at last had some momentary reprieve. The sun was dazzling as it bounced from the cold ground and frost-covered leaves, giving the impression that the day was much warmer than in reality. As the many thousands of soldiers formed their battle lines, most would be rubbing their hands together or hopping between feet to keep warm.

Nate, to his surprise, had been ordered into a unit of archers, roughly two hundred in number. This group was one of five, the remainder of the Tinelian force being infantry armed with spears. Usually archers would be found in the relative safety of the back lines, protected by their more heavily armoured comrades. Yet for some reason, Ardell had ordered Nate and the other archers to stand one hundred meters ahead of the infantry. From where he stood, Nate could see with almost perfect clarity those who would be his enemy.

The Imperial soldiers were dressed almost identically to their Tinelian counterparts. Most carried spears and round wooden shields as they too shuffled about within their lines to keep warm. This movement, with their spears upright, looked at this distance like the stems of tall, immature flowers swaying in the cold morning breeze. Their steel breastplates and helmets only magnifying the sun's presence until it too felt like a combatant, an overwhelming force which assaulted the eyes. The only difference Nate could see between the two forces were the red armbands of the Imperials compared to the Tinelian green.

Nate had expected an army in all black, heavily armoured and sporting swords as tall as he was. But from where he stood, the people he had been brought to kill would not have looked out of place in Pedan's Inn. Or even just walking about the streets of the Vanguard. It was strange, Nate thought. Considering the Imperium were the bad guys, they didn't look too different from anyone else. As the final preparations were made, and the last of the troops got into position, Nate's attention was caught by a horrifying sight.

On their extreme right, on the very edge of the Imperial flank, came hundreds of mounted men. They walked slowly, making their presence known. Their hope, to intimidate the Tinelian forces into quickly adopting a less rehearsed strategy. Each horse was covered head to tail by a coat, which already made them more suitably dressed than the soldiers of either army. While each coat was radically different, all were brightly coloured and stood out against the dull landscape around them. The men atop these steeds were all knights in the service of many different Imperial Lords. Today they shared one allegiance and one goal. In their hands, the knights held lances two meters long, also brightly coloured and engraved with all manner of crests and decorations.

The head of this cavalry contingent was a lesser Imperial noble. Not one of great worth or renown, nor did he have much experience of warfare. As he watched the Tinelians move their archers into such a ludicrous position, he could not help but feel temptation's soft whisperings begin to overcome him. One decisive charge. That is all it would take to wipe out their entire skirmishing force and effectively win the battle before it could even begin.

Ardell had taken a serious risk in not bringing any cavalry of her own. As she watched the Imperial forces finalise their positions from her place on a nearby hilltop, she could not help but tap her foot nervously. She had a plan, one that she had practiced too many times to count. Finally, only now would she have the chance to see if she really was as clever as she thought.

From north to south all Nate could see was a line of gleaming steel. Like a row of gnashing silver teeth, the Imperial army began to bash their shields with their fists or against the ground. Nate had always wondered how anyone could have ever found such a thing to be intimidating, but that was when he was watching a battle from the comfort of his living room. Now that he was on the front lines, he could swear that the ground itself was shaking. Soon after, his legs followed suit. The echoing metallic booming of the Imperial forces indicating that the battle was about to begin.

Nate had never been religious, and still wasn't, which is rather hilarious all things considered. But as he sensed yet another end drawing near, and with no idea what else to do, he crossed himself. All he could do now was hope that his efforts in battle would be enough to keep another excruciating conversation with Death at bay for a little while longer. Then came the signal. From the rear of the Tinelian ranks came the sound of a horn. Nate's company commander nodded to himself in understanding as he bellowed out orders to his troops.

"Archers, move up, seventy-five meters."

'*What*!?' Nate thought as those around him obeyed and began to move. This order was not followed without a great deal of apprehension. Even the company commanders felt their heart rates double as they ventured further from safety and into the jaws of their enemy. Enemies, which soon began to grow taller, their faces coming almost into focus, the points of their spears more menacing than ever. Additionally, at the back of everyone's minds, there remained the question of what the Imperial cavalry were doing. Should they charge now, the Tinelian archers wouldn't stand a chance.

Nate looked to his right as the company commander once again called out, this time ordering them to halt. The Imperial cavalry had swung out, revealing the true size of their host. Before them was a sea of unnaturally coloured beasts topped with silver, their lances swaying like treetops in the wind. The entire Imperial cavalry force was now facing the thousand exposed Tinelian archers, nearly two hundred meters from the safety of their own lines.

'*What the fuck are you doing Captain?*' Nate barely had time to think before a fresh blast of a horn brought new orders.

"Archers, take aim, one hundred meters, loose on my orders." Nate did as he was told but kept one eye on the enemy cavalry. There was a sudden *whoosh* in his left ear as the northernmost archer company released their arrows. Nate turned his head to see the arrows land amongst the thick lines of spears, seemingly to little effect as the Imperials raised their shields above their heads. There were three more volleys before Nate was given the order to release his own arrow. Each growing louder as they crept closer, like a screeching flock of birds as they rained down upon the enemy.

Nate expected this to continue for some time. Launching volleys into the opposing lines until either they ran out of arrows or the Imperials made a counter move. Of the two, it was the latter which he dreaded and, naturally, was exactly what happened. Just as Nate was preparing to release a second arrow, two conflicting sounds filled his ears. Both came from the blowing of horns, but he only recognised one. The other had come from his far right and was fainter than the others. He was prepared to ignore it, until his own orders made clear the situation.

"Retreat!" cried his company commander. Nate immediately checked the right flank and saw exactly what he had been afraid of. Hundreds of heavily armed knights charging directly at him. The Imperial cavalry commander, unable to supress his desire for glory, had initiated a charge without being ordered. Gripping his lance tightly beneath his arm as the Imperial banner flew above him, he was filled with mania as he imagined the honour about to be won. Likely imagining the recounting of his heroic victory years from now to captivated audiences filled with admiration and respect.

"Fuck fuck fuck!" Nate screamed aloud, as he sprinted his way back towards friendly lines. There was no order to this retreat, no sense of conformity, just a thousand poor sods trying to outrun the sound of thundering hooves growing ever louder behind them. If by some miracle Nate survived this, he was going to fucking kill Ardell. From the relative safety of her hill, Ardell watched the unfolding battle with glee. The enemy had fallen for her feint, now she just needed to close the trap.

As Nate ran for his life, his lungs threatening to burst as the freezing air rushed in, he could have sworn he was getting close to his own lines. But unless he had become the fastest man alive, there was no way they should be anywhere near their lines before the cavalry were upon them. Nevertheless, they were now only perhaps twenty meters away before he realised what was going on. The Tinelian infantry were rushing forwards! As the archers neared, the spear wall parted, allowing them to pass through thin corridors while maintaining a thick and rigid defence. While the Imperial cavalry had been focused on the seemingly suicidal actions of the Tinelian skirmishers, they had failed to notice the wall of infantry slowly creeping forwards.

The Imperial knights, realising what was happening too late, either crashed into the spears head on or into one another as they desperately tried to come to a halt. The Tinelian frontline held firm against the crushing hooves and thrusting lances and quickly threw off the aborted charge. Now entangled in a deafening mass of men and horses which cried out in fear, the cavalry attempted to turn back, only to find the final phase of the trap swinging shut.

As the cavalry attempted to retreat the way they had come, they found themselves surrounded by yet more Tinelian spearmen who had swung around, cutting off their escape. Some still attempted, of course. All attempts to try to hurl their horses over the rows of shields only resulted in both man and beast impaled. The rest remained in place, resigned to fight to the death, retaining any sliver of honour their actions had cost them. And fight to the death they did. Against the tides of the thousands of spears which jabbed at them from all sides, like thorns erupting from the undergrowth, the knight's lances could achieve little.

When the last knight had fallen, either pulled from his horse or skewered where he sat, the Tinelians hurriedly reformed their lines. The trap had been executed so decisively, so totally, that there was no feasible way for the Imperial to counter it. Their remaining infantry simply had to watch from afar as their nobles were massacred.

The Tinelian forces let out a resounding cheer at their early victory. A cheer which filled them all with much needed confidence, while simultaneously sowing fear into the remaining enemy ranks. But the battle was far from over and the real fight was about to begin as the Imperial infantry began their advance. The Tinelians too stepped forwards, clearing the space which was now littered with the corpses of man and beast alike.

Nate and the rest of the archers had reformed their lines behind the infantry and as the enemy approached, were once again given the order to let loose their arrows. They targeted the infantry at first, their volleys markedly more successful now. But quite quickly the enemy archers also began to shoot, causing Nate to curse every time he saw an arrow meet its target amongst the Tinelian lines. Now the two skirmishing forces were engaged in a competition of accuracy as they took aim at one another, hoping to whittle down their counterparts' numbers into irrelevance as the infantry closed in.

Once the Imperial forces were one hundred meters away, a deafening blast from a war horn filled the air. The sounds of arrows thudding into the frozen ground and the screams of the injured were drowned out as the Imperial forces began their charge. Even in his position of relative safety, Nate could not help but recoil and feel his whole body shiver with fear as the war cries of the enemy rang out while they surged forwards. Suddenly there was an almighty crash, as if the most tempestuous storm of Nate's life had suddenly erupted overhead. Shields smashed into one another with great speed and force. Bodies were thrown against walls of steel as cries of fury and soon anguish drowned out even one's own thoughts.

This was nothing like the movies, Nate thought, as the battle began in earnest. Men did not charge madly, without cohesion or care for their lives. Neither were there honourable duels between individuals as each man carved out his own arena on the battleground. No, nothing of the sort would be seen here today or on any battlefield thereafter. This war was real, and it would prove to be worse than anything Nate could ever have imagined.

Dense lines pushed against one another in a deadly contest of strength. Overhead, spears were blindly thrust downwards as heads were kept tucked behind shields. There was barely room to breathe as rows upon rows of steel-clad warriors pushed themselves and their comrades forwards into the madness of the melee. Any that fell, either through injury or mistake, met the same fate as they were trampled and suffocated by the boots of their own men. The screaming of the dying, the bellowing of orders and the raging cries of the infantry all mixed into one cacophony of madness. In this moment, all of man's virtues were lost. No honour or glory would be found here. No compassion or kindness, or even higher thought, as each man wrestled with only the most basic desire to survive. No matter the cost.

This pushing and shoving went on for hours as neither side was able to achieve a breakthrough. Nate had lost count of how many times his quiver had needed refilling. He could no longer feel anything but the intense burning pain in his arms as they begged for rest. The deafening cries of the melee remained, although less intense as more men fell with each passing moment. Without warning, Nate felt his heart jump into his throat as an arrow pierced the chest of the man beside him. Followed immediately by another which landed beside Nate's foot. He stopped for a moment, panting like a dog as his exhaustion caught up with him and he stared down at the body of his comrade. The pair had fought beside one another for hours, and yet not once had they spoken, or even shared a glance. Now they would never get the chance.

Nate quickly bent down and retrieved the fallen man's quiver which was still well stocked with arrows. Clipping it around his waist, Nate began to shoot once more. Not for a moment had Ardell looked away from the battle raging down below. She scanned each line, friend and foe alike, for any sign of weakness. Twice she had ordered reinforcements to bolster flagging units, and now, at last, the end seemed to be drawing near. She noticed the Imperial line on the far-left flank was finally only a few rows deep, with no reserves nearby. She called for a messenger who quickly rode down the hill to convey her latest orders to the company commanders below.

Ardell watched with morbid delight as her plans came to fruition before her very eyes. Bolstered by archers who had swapped their bows for swords, the Tinelian left flank broke through the final row of Imperial defences and began a rapid encirclement of nearby enemies. This continued down the line as Imperial units fell like dominos, gradually encircled by ever more Tinelians. As the Imperial soldiers began to realise their position was hopeless, their entire army broke at once. Disengaging from the melee they had been fighting so ferociously for hours, they turned tail and ran as fast as their exhausted bodies would allow.

The Tinelians, upon realising the battle to be won, let out a resounding cheer which filled Nate with a relief so fierce he almost collapsed. But the battle was not over yet. A final horn was sounded from behind the Tinelian lines. The order- pursue the enemy until none remained. What followed was no battle but a slaughter. Nate, while unwilling, was ordered to pursue the enemy with the rest of the Tinelian forces. Dropping his bow, he took out his sword and ran forwards, having to watch where he placed his feet as the cold, frosty ground gave way to a carpet of corpses.

The Tinelian lines now too were scattered, abandoning their formation as each soldier charged forwards, eager to avenge their fallen brothers and sisters. Nate, wisely, had no intention of engaging in close combat. Although he made sure to be relatively close to the front should a company commander see him wavering and label him a deserter even now, what Nate saw even after so many hours of intense combat shook him to his core.

Imperial soldiers unlucky enough to be caught by the pursuing Tinelians were ruthlessly cut down. Man or woman, hands raised in surrender or fighting to the last, it made no difference. Nate watched in horror as a group of five surrendered Imperials were rounded up and had their throats slit, their pleas for mercy going unheeded. He turned away from the grisly sight, only to be faced with a man, stumbling through the fog which had begun to settle at knee height, clutching at the bloody stump where his forearm used to be. Instinctively Nate moved in to help, but quickly noticed the red armband tied around the man's other arm. He simply watched as the wounded man, clearly in shock and no longer understanding where he was, was gutted by an approaching Tinelian.

The man fell to the ground, still clutching his bloody stump In his final moments he looked up at Nate, with much pain and confusion in his eyes. Nate's breaths were shaky, his right hand beginning to tremble, as he watched the man succumb to his injuries. Nate felt physically sick. His head was suddenly light as his stomach roiled, but he had to continue when he heard the voices of the company commanders approaching from behind. He dragged himself across the battlefield, his feet like blocks of concrete. No matter how much he wished, he could not lower his gaze should a desperately fleeing foe find Nate between themselves and safety.

He saw more acts of cruelty as he neared the edge of the battlefield, acts of such barbarism they did not belong even in battle. He saw a woman wrestling in the mud with another, before removing her helmet and crushing her opponent's skull with it. The victor then got up, moving on as if nothing had happened. The order then came to pursue the fleeing Imperials through the tall corn fields into which they had fled until the edge of Sundered Crown was visible. This was perfect, Nate thought. He would find a secluded place within the sea of green shafts towering over him until the horror was over.

The moment Nate pushed aside the first few stalks and entered the field it was as if a spell had been cast over the world. Everything suddenly became much quieter, the screams replaced instead with the gentle rustling of the wind as it navigated this maze. After a few minutes of cautious jogging to get away from the company commanders, Nate decided to rest. The sickness he felt had only worsened, and his head now pounded like the painful beating of a drum with each pulse of his heart.

He only managed to secure a few moments of relative peace before he heard it. A woman, shouting, pleading for help. Nate pulled himself from the ground and moved towards the noise, his sword at the ready. With the corn being so thick and tall, it was difficult to discern the exact direction of the noise. Nevertheless, Nate pressed on in what he thought was the right direction, hoping he would arrive before it was too late. The pleading soon became much louder, more frantic and desperate. While this indicated he was going the right way, he had no way of knowing what he was about to walk into. He gripped his sword tightly, in preparation for the worst.

He could soon hear movement nearby, the crunching of broken crops and the thudding and scraping of a body against the earth. Clearly there was some sort of struggle going on. As Nate drew apart the final stalks like emerald curtains between him and the desperate shouting, he expected to see someone locked in combat. The sight that greeted him, however, was infinitely worse.

Laid out on her back and desperately struggling to free herself, was a woman. What little clothing remained on her body indicated she was from the Imperium. Holding her down were three people in the Tinelian colours. A man sat on her arms which were stretched out above her, while a woman pressed a boot against her head, pushing the victim's face into the mud. The final assailant held her legs open as he undid his trousers.

"Aww, don't do that," he said to the female Tinelian. "I like it when they watch." The three attackers laughed while the woman began to shriek at the top of her lungs, calling them every name under the sun while struggling as hard as she could. Her face was bloody and streamed with tears, but these things did nothing to dissuade her attackers.

"What the fuck are you doing!?" Nate cried, as he burst upon this abominable scene, his sword at the ready. For a moment the soldiers stopped, afraid they had been caught by an officer or company commander. The punishment for rape was castration and hanging, in that order. The assailants breathed a collective sigh as they realised Nate was nobody important. The victim dared feel the flutter of hope for a moment before her attackers ripped it to shreds.

"Just teaching this Imperial bitch a lesson. You want a go?" the man struggling with the woman's flailing legs asked with genuine curiosity, as if it were the polite thing to do.

"Help, please help me!" the woman sobbed. The man

sitting on her wrists punched her in the face for her efforts, splitting her lip.

"Oi," the other man growled. "Don't do that. I can't do it if she looks like a punching bag."

Nate could not believe what he was hearing and pointed his sword at the man with his trousers around his ankles.

"Let her go!" he demanded, trying to sound authoritative and menacing. Nate was outnumbered, and his threats were simply met with yet more laughter.

"Unless you want to take her place, I advise you fuck off," the Tinelian woman replied, removing her boot from her victim's head and approaching Nate with clear intent. That was it. Nate was not about to just walk away as this woman was raped, enemy or not. He rushed forward with his sword at the ready. He doubted he could take on all three at once, but if he was lucky, he might be quick enough to deal with them one by one. Today, however, luck was not on his side and the Tinelian woman had quickly disarmed him, throwing Nate to the ground.

He now lay parallel to the still screaming and sobbing woman, the growing weight of a knee on his neck.

"Try not to enjoy yourself too much," the Tinelian woman whispered mockingly in Nate's ear as he struggled to no avail to free himself. The other two men went back to their sickening deed. Laughing as their victim screamed and struggled harder than at any point in her life.

Soon after they began, she fell quiet. Her earlier screams, pained cries which had died down into agonising gasps and croaks, signalling the pain too severe for her to summon anything more. She refused to give her rapists the satisfaction of watching their defilement. She turned her face towards Nate, as silent tears ran down her pained, bloody face as she was assaulted again and again. The pain she must have felt during this ordeal, the hopelessness which must have gripped her soul, Nate would torture himself over for the rest of his days. Not once did she look away from her would-be saviour.

She didn't even blink, while Nate was forced to watch as the last remnants of her humanity were forcibly ripped away.

Nate tried to free himself of course, thrashing as hard as he could, but it was no use. The pain in his head was like a thunderstorm in his brain and his vision was becoming fuzzy. At last, his little remaining strength left him, and the world around him grew dark. The sound of the soldiers laughing being the last thing he remembered before oblivion claimed him.

When Nate awoke it was dark, the sounds of clicking insects and other nocturnal creatures reigned over what had earlier been a rapturous battle. As his eyes slowly opened it took them a moment to focus. When at last they cleared, Nate recoiled in horror and pulled himself back. Across from him lay the cold, pale corpse of the woman he had earlier tried to save. Her eyes, which had conveyed so much pain and fear, were now glassy and lifeless. Across her neck she wore a red necklace of sliced flesh, a final parting gift from her assailants.

Nate pressed his face into the cold, frozen mud and sobbed, his fists balled with rage. It was too late, all the anger in the world would not bring her back, would not make up for his failure. Almost like a corpse himself, he struggled to his feet and shuffled back the way he had come. The battle was over and he would now be sent home for rotation. He felt strange as he stumbled away from the scene of depravity. His body was heavy with grief and guilt. He struggled to remain standing as the weight of his anguish pushed down upon him, heavier with each step. And yet he felt an unfamiliar lightness in his chest, a sense of having lost something vital which he had always carried but could not name.

As the field gave way and the torches of the Tinelian camp could be made out in the distance, Nate knew. He may soon be back home, but a part of him would never leave this place. A part of him would remain forever bound and thrashing in the mud as he bore witness to the worst humanity had to offer.

Chapter 16

From her room atop the cathedral, the Oracle of Sundered Crown could see the battle taking place barely a mile from where she stood. The two armies had only just begun their engagement, and it would be a while before either side claimed victory. She decided to descend the many steps from her chambers into the cathedral's main hall. As she did so, she ran her hand along the cool stone walls, a wistful, distant expression on her face. Her body moving of its own accord while her mind wandered elsewhere.

In the hall below, where once there had been long lines of princes and dignitaries desperate to meet the Oracle, now only scattered groupings of soldiers remained. Many were injured, all were tired and hungry. Despite their meagre training and woeful lack of supplies, the hopelessly outnumbered city guard had put up a valiant defence of the city. For weeks the Imperials had tried to break through, and each time they had been repulsed, although not without great cost.

The moment the Oracle entered the hall, her guards immediately appeared, surrounding her like a swarm of bees protecting their queen. She cast her sad, amethyst eyes over what had once been one of the architectural wonders of the world. Now, it was barely more than a ruin. The stained-glass windows created by masters long departed, lay shattered into colourful shards, like the petals of countless summer flowers. From these breaches, the bitter cold of the outside world slithered in. Many, especially the injured, lay under blankets, shivering as their breaths rose above them. Likely the only part of them which would escape this siege.

The statues too lay in various states of ruin. The animatrons, which had so gracefully glided above the heads of visitors for so long, now lay shattered upon the ground. One in particular, a Pegasus, lay on its side. One of its front legs slowly still treading the air, while its lifeless eyes radiated a deep sadness to any who looked upon them.

Despite this, however, there was still an element of hope amongst the beleaguered defenders. The enemy had yet to break through, and any moment now the relieving Tinelian forces would break the siege. Furthermore, even should the battle outside be lost, they still had the Oracle. While to strangers she may have appeared as little more than a girl, to the men and women of Sundered Crown, she was a beacon of hope. A reminder of what goodness remained in the world despite all they had suffered. Something worth defending, worth dying for.

If the Oracle had decided to remain in the secluded safety of her tower, none would have thought less of her for it. But that is not the kind of woman she was. She could sense the pain, the fear and suffering of those who had sworn to defend her city. She could not abandon them now, in their moment of greatest need. Taking her time, the Oracle patrolled the room. She would greet each soldier with a smile which warmed the chill from their bones. A smile which momentarily took them far away from the bleak circumstances in which they now found themselves.

With soft hands and gentle eyes, the Oracle would heal the wounds of those she could, before offering words of comfort and encouragement. They would do little against a blade or arrow, but against the weapons of fear and despair they would be mighty boons. Once completing her circuit, she ordered extra rations be brought out for the weary troops both within the cathedral and those still manning the walls. The effects of this would be twofold. It would bring some much needed warmth and strength to those who desperately needed it. But also, it indicated that the Oracle believed the siege would not last much longer. This would fill the defenders with renewed confidence that their plight would soon be over.

The Oracle then decided she would sit upon her throne a while. To allow her presence to be felt by the soldiers, so they knew they were not alone. As she walked to her seat, she stopped at the altar upon which the sundered crown rested. The four guards defending it were not her own and officially held no loyalty to her. None protested as she climbed the few steps to the altar and stood in quiet contemplation.

She thought back to ages past when she had first met Sabel, well before she became the famous queen of legend. She remembered how back then the struggles they shared seemed so great that they could never be overcome. Yet here she stood, five thousand years later as yet another war consumed their world. She wondered what that famous queen would have said to her now. Most likely something inappropriate the Oracle thought, smiling to herself. This quiet reminiscing of happier times was instantly shattered by a deafening explosion, followed by a rush of wind at her back.

The Oracle swiftly turned to face the onrushing gale but was immediately blocked by her guards forming a protective wall around her. There were desperate shouts from the recuperating soldiers, all of whom jumped to their feet, weapons in hand. Unable to see what was happening, the Oracle was quickly escorted away by her guards as the unmistakeable sounds of battle rang out across the hallowed hall. Without warning, a second explosion tore apart the far wall, taking down the Oracle's throne with it. This caused her guards to suddenly halt and tighten their formation until the Oracle risked being crushed between their steel plates.

As the sounds of battle grew louder, hearing the screaming of men and women in agony, the clashing of steel and spilling of blood, the Oracle began to panic. Packed so tightly between her guards that she had to fight for breath, she began pushing against them to afford herself precious room. Yet they refused to budge. Her heart was pounding now, her breaths mere gasps as she was roughly jostled about, as her bodyguards desperately tried to move her to safety.

Just as the Oracle felt her head lighten, the sound of

battle suddenly ceased, as if a switch had been flicked. In the silence she took her chance and gasped.

"I can't breathe." Her guards immediately loosened their formation, although without providing any greater vision of what was happening. Out of the silence a voice called out. This voice the Oracle had only ever heard once before, but one she immediately recognised.

"I come only for the Oracle. Stay back and be spared." The Oracle's eyes grew wide. The Emperor had come at last.

"Stand aside," the Oracle commanded of her guards. Yet they refused to move. They had sworn an oath to protect her. They could not abandon it now, even in the face of such hopeless odds.

"Step aside! Now!" the Oracle shouted with a voice far more commanding than her petite body seemed capable. Begrudgingly, her protectors parted and at last she could see the carnage before her. The cathedral doors and back wall had been blasted open. From the breaches, The Emperor's finest warriors, the Chosen, had poured through. The city guard, while brave, were no match for such an elite force. Most lay either dead or dying. Those few who still drew breath were huddled together in ragged groups, praying for a miracle.

At the head of this force stood the Emperor. Tall and radiant in his divinite armour, his face covered by a black mask. He stood motionless as he surveyed the carnage, flanked by the monstrous Chosen. It was a shame, he thought, that something so beautiful must suffer the effects of war. He shook his head and let out a sigh as he stepped forward. In the strained silence, slowly and calmly as he crossed the room. Passing by the altar as its four guards lowered their spears, still fully prepared to defend the crown to the death. The Emperor casually waved them away.

"I care not for your trinket. Keep your honour and your lives," he said, as he walked around them towards where the Oracle stood, still surrounded by her guards. At last, the distance between them was only a few meters, close enough so that the Oracle could fully appreciate the deific being that approached. For this was not the same man whom she had met so long ago. The man she had so erroneously informed would have such an unremarkable future to be unworthy of repeating. As she recalled, she had not even charged him for the reading, so banal had her vision been. Something had happened since then, something even she could not explain. But one thing she knew for certain, what stood before her now was no mere man.

She had seen much in her visions since those early days after his ascension to the throne. She had seen many futures, not all of them as terrible as the present they lived now. Yet none of these visions, no matter how vivid, could have prepared her for the real thing. The Emperor, he seemed to radiate something. Energy was too simple a word, too human, ugly and unrefined. It was a power, a majesty to which there was no compare. No other in the room was strong enough to sense it but the Oracle could feel it penetrating her skin, reaching with an intimate delicateness towards her very soul.

As she sensed and probed the power, she quickly understood that it was not his. Whatever power the Emperor possessed, whatever gave him such strength, it did not come from him. Without warning, the captain of the Oracle's guards stepped forward. A knight by the name of Vamir. A knight who had served the Oracle for centuries and would not allow any foe, no matter how mighty, to harm her. He cast aside his helmet from which his fair, golden hair spilled, putting himself between the Emperor and his mistress.

"Captain," the Oracle snapped, in no mood for honour and heroics. Too many had already died for such nonsense.

"I am, sorry my Lady," Vamir replied, his eyes fixed on the Emperor. "But I will not let him harm you." He raised his sword to shoulder height, pointed directly at his opponent.

"Don't be a damn fool," the Oracle chastised. "Put down your sword at once," she demanded. Vamir remained resolute and refused to move. Now it was the Emperor who spoke.

"I admire your devotion to your Lady, Sir Knight, but I advise you to do as she commands. You will win no glory here," his words cold and emotionless. Vamir bared his teeth at the insinuation.

"You think I care for things as trivial as glory?" he scoffed. "I swore an oath to protect the woman I love, unlike you, I intend to keep that oath."

The Emperor's jaw immediately clenched as a wave of silent, furious rage washed over him.

"Come then, Sir Knight, if you wish for your Lady to watch you die so badly, I shall not deny you this wish."

The Emperor reached down at his side and withdrew a large, golden flanged mace. Its head, set with eight large triangular flanges, surmounted by a final, small spike. It had been a gift from the last king of Gil-Ebrax upon the Emperor's ascension, and this would not be its first taste of blood.

"Captain! I am begging you, please lay down your weapon," the Oracle pleaded, trying one last time to save her friend. But Vamir ignored her. He could never have imagined what dark designs lay in wait for his mistress. It was exactly this fear which filled him with such determination to keep her from the Emperor's clutches. For centuries he had trained for this moment, for the day the forces of evil would seek to use the Oracle's gifts for their own ends.

As Vamir faced off against his opponent, he could not help but think back to those first days of his service. The fear that had filled him at the enormity of his task. The doubts which had plagued him regarding his own ability. His sleepless nights filled with worry as to whether he was worthy to take up such a mantle. More than once he had come close to resigning from the Oracle's service before even beginning. All these fears and doubts had been washed away as if they were little more than trivialities upon meeting her for the first time. With nothing but the kindness of her words and the sweetness of her smile, had she fostered a love within him which now burned as fiercely as the forges of Ifritus.

He looked back to her, to the shimmering amethyst eyes which had so securely bound his heart to her, and he smiled.

Filled with renewed valour, he charged forward. For how could the gods allow defeat to come to he with such a pure heart, acting solely out of love?

As Vamir neared his target, he pulled back his sword into the beginnings of a thrust aimed straight at the Emperor's torso. He let out a great cry as he channelled all his strength into the blade. His cry, however, was cut short as the Emperor brought down his weapon in a single crushing blow. The mace struck Vamir upon the top of the head and, so great was the force behind it, that his skull exploded into a shower of blood and brain matter. The rest of his body quickly followed suit. Bones splintered like dry twigs, until the former valiant knight was but an unrecognisable, shapeless heap upon the stone floor.

With that distraction dealt with, the Emperor stepped forward once more. Making sure to carefully step over the growing mess at his feet, he stood before the Oracle at last, her guards retreating and trembling before him.

"It is good to see you again," the Emperor said, trying his best to be polite. As if he had not just made a spectacle of brutally murdering one of the Oracle's closest friends. She looked up from Vamir's body with glistening eyes but did not say a thing.

"You know why I have come," the Emperor stated gently, like a doctor delivering bad news to a patient. The Oracle had a good idea. Nothing was certain of course, but all the signs seemed to be pointing in one direction. She did not respond, instead continuing to stare deeply, unnervingly into the Emperor's eyes. The Emperor let out a sigh. To submit the Oracle to what she was about to suffer felt cruel, yet he had been told it was necessary.

Frustrated but not deterred by the Oracle's eerie silence, he extended out his hand.

"Come then, let us not dither." At first the Oracle did not move, instead looking around with concern for the surviving members of her guard. The Emperor quickly did the same, promising no further harm would come to the defenders of the city should she go with him now. The Oracle nodded. She understood there was no escape from this fate. But before she left her home for the final time, she proposed a question.

"Do you really think you can find her?" The Emperor dropped his extended hand, surprised at how much the Oracle already knew. Did that mean she knew what awaited her? No, if she did she would never agree to come with him, she would have fought to the death, sacrificing every last one of her people to avoid such a fate. They shared a searching look which seemed to last for hours. These two strangers, now of nothing less than crucial importance to one another.

"I have faith," the Emperor replied cautiously. The Oracle gave a weary smile.

"Faith," she repeated, the word seeming to stretch on, filling the space between them, approaching The Emperor like mist rolling over the horizon. He did not understand why this filled him with such anxiety, but he knew the folly of questioning such things. The Oracle offered no resistance as the Emperor gently led her out of the cathedral and into the ruined streets where his airship was waiting.

*

When the victorious Tinelian forces finally entered Sundered Crown, they did not find the city to be as they had expected. There was damage of course. Many buildings had been reduced to smoking or charred ruins, the unfortunate victims of the at times, random aim of Imperial trebuchets. Surprisingly, most of the city remained intact. Even the outer city walls, which had been assailed numerous times by siege towers, had come away mostly unharmed. Indeed, it seemed that most of the damage had been superficial, nothing that could not be repaired with a bit of elbow grease and some peasants suitably whipped by an overseeing officer.

No, it was the people and the very air they breathed which seemed to be altered, unfamiliar and unpleasant. There were no crowds of ecstatic civilians and indebted soldiers, throwing themselves at the feet of their saviours. Nor was there any ringing of bells or triumphant cheers as the columns of soldiers marched through the streets. Instead, there was only a mournful silence which hung heavily over the city. Even the incoming soldiers, drunk off their earlier victory, were soon infected. They marched in silence. Their expressions pained and uneasy as they tried to understand for themselves the reason for their sudden, unexpected dourness.

Even Ardell could not help but feel a strange unwelcomeness as she halted outside the battered fortress. While this was something she was used to, she had not expected it given the situation. Her army had arrived in good time and saved the people of Sundered Crown from either slaughter or starvation. Even she, as realistic as she was, had expected at least a small modicum of fanfare to celebrate her victory.

Ardell's forces lined up in neat rows outside the fortress as they waited for the Lord of the city to appear. Their now muddied and, in some cases, tattered banners fluttering in the biting breeze. The silence was a tense one. The only interruptions were the coughing of the exhausted troops and the clanking of armour as the soldiers tried to keep themselves warm while they waited for an audience. From nearby windows came the shadowy, distorted faces of the locals. Those who had endured so many weeks of hardship, and yet they could only stare down at their liberators with disdain.

Many of the men could not help but feel a shiver crawl up their spine as they watched the multitude of watchful, distrustful eyes grow. Encircling them like nameless shadows in the dark. At last, the silence was broken by the loud creaking of the fortress doors being opened. From within came a half dozen men. At their head, the Lord of Sundered Crown himself. As they approached, Ardell gave a courteous bow. A far more pleasant and respectful reception than she and her men had received.

The Lord of the city stood, his nose upturned at the

forces gathered before him, his hands clasped behind his back. He and his bodyguards were all dressed in the finest of armours, although only the latter seemed to bear the scars of battle. Many were bloodied and bandaged, their expensive breastplates and helmets marred with small dents and lacerations. The Lord on the other hand, looked to have not once ventured from the safety of his fortress. There was not so much a speck of dirt or dust on the gleaming armour, on which Ardell could make out her own travelworn reflection. Upon his head was no helm, but an excessively large and colourful, flower shaped hat. Hardly appropriate, given the circumstances.

"Decided to turn up in the end I see," the Lord chastised.

"My Lord?" Ardell replied, baffled at the contempt aimed at both her and her men. "We won a great victory today and saved the city," she added, just in case the Lord so busy saving himself that he had misunderstood the situation.

"Yes, after we'd done all the fighting of course, convenient that," he replied spitefully. Ardell was forced to bite her tongue and tilted her head away from the smug look on the Lord's face. It was all she could do to contain her anger. Hundreds of her soldiers had paid the ultimate price in rescuing this city. To hear them insulted with such maliciousness stabbed at her very delicate and easily triggered temper. But the Lord would not relent or even tone down his tirade, despite the clearly diminishing patience of the weary captain before him.

"And if you think I'll be feeding and housing this rabble you've brought with you," he spat loudly, throwing out his arm, aimed towards the gathered soldiers in a threatening manner.

'You'll do what?' is what Ardell wished to say, and indeed would have done if one of her officers had not intervened.

"My Lord," he bowed. "I apologise for our overdue arrival. The Captain did all within her power to arrive as soon as she could. However, the battle is won and the city secured. Truly, I do not believe the Grand Admiral would be pleased to see us bickering amongst ourselves at such a time." The Lord was silent as he pushed his tongue against his cheek before scoffing.

"Bickering," he repeated, more softly than before, as if the word were alien to him. "Let's see what the Grand Admiral has to say when he finds out the Oracle is gone."

"What do you mean gone?" Ardell replied bluntly.

*

"Bollocks!" Ardell cursed as she stared down at the stain which had once been the captain of the Oracle's guard. Around her lay a scene of carnage. The hewn remains of the city guard littered the once holy hall, glass and rubble in such quantities one could not see the floor. Beside her, looking rather green as he too stared down at the former knight, was the officer which had prevented her earlier outburst.

"What do you think he wanted with her?" Ardell shook her head as she rested her hands upon her hips. Where this assumption that she could read minds had come from she did not know, but it annoyed her greatly. Especially when she was then blamed for not preventing an action she could not possibly have known about beforehand.

"I hear they're both avid chess players. Perhaps the Emperor popped round for a game," she replied sarcastically. Oblivious, the officer looked around once more at the destruction which surrounded them.

"I find that unlikely, Captain, given the circumstances." Ardell let out a sigh and rolled her eyes. She didn't have the energy to explain the subtleties of sarcasm to her colleague just now, she had far more important things to worry about.

"Fetch me some parchment and a quill, then get a fire going. There's someone I need to speak to." The officer nodded and quickly rushed off in search of the items his Captain had requested. Truthfully, Ardell did not know if Leridon would even get her message once she had cast it into the fire. She had heard worrying rumours of a schism within the Battlemages. Rumours of betrayal and slaughter, with the survivors retreating into an even deeper hiding. She had no way of knowing if he was even alive.

Nevertheless, Leridon had proven himself invaluable in uncovering the Imperium's plans for the husks. If anyone had knowledge of what the Emperor was up to and better yet, a plan to stop it, it would be him. That night, however, many hours after delivering her letter to the hungry jaws of the fire in her room, after painstakingly convincing the local Lord to allow her men to stay within the city, Ardell had heard nothing from her friend. She had hardly expected a personal visit, but the lack of even a scrap of paper to confirm his well-being concerned her greatly. She lay in her bed staring up at the ceiling, twirling her dark hair between her fingers, the snores of her exhausted men below rising through the floorboards.

Leridon or the Emperor. Right now she didn't know who she should be worried about more.

*

"I apologise for the unhappy circumstances of my visit, my lady. Even more so for the manner in which it was conducted," the Emperor confessed, as he passed the Oracle a glass of wine. The pair were currently high in the skies over the Imperium, the Emperor's personal airship carrying them towards the Oracle's final destination. The Oracle took the glass out of politeness but did not drink.

"You did not have to kill him," she replied sadly. Her only thoughts during this journey had been of Vamir. A knight of such great valour and renown, swatted away as if he were of little more consequence than an insect, buzzing annoyingly about the Emperor's head. Whatever horrors awaited her once they landed, surely, they could not be worse than the sight of someone so beloved being so remorselessly broken before her eyes.

The Emperor nodded.

"I am sorry, my Lady, truly, but I was given little choice." The Emperor spoke the truth, but that did not lessen the pain in the Oracle's heart. She looked out of the window of the

Emperor's quarters where they were currently seated. The ground was so far below that the green pastures and golden fields looked like little more than patchwork upon the land's surface.

The Emperor sat awkwardly in his chair, not knowing what to say in such a situation. He was taking an innocent woman to be tortured, all for the sake of averting a future he did not know was certain to pass. He scratched at the rim of his wineglass, second guessing both himself and the Arch-Sorceress. He wondered if he was taking things too far. Could the Lord forgive one evil to prevent a far greater calamity from taking its place? The Oracle interrupted this thought with a question. Finally deciding to brave a sip of her wine with a trembling hand, knowing there would not be much chance for more once they arrived.

"Tell me. In the end, which plan did you decide upon?" The Emperor looked at her, slightly puzzled.

"My Lady?" He asked.

"To avert your vision. Which action did you believe would be best? I have seen so many versions of this play out I am curious to know which in the end was right."

"You know of my vision?" the Emperor asked, suddenly filled with a rush of adrenaline. Perhaps there would be no need for the Arch-Sorceress' plan after all. Not if the Oracle had knowledge of the Emperor's vision which he himself did not possess.

"Oh yes, we discussed it at great length many times during your illness," she replied.

"Oh," the Emperor sighed, disappointed. His hopes of a new, less morally dubious solution to his plight already dashed.

"So?" the Oracle asked again. The Emperor sighed heavily, putting down his wineglass and leaning forward in his chair, his elbows resting on his knees.

"The Arch-Sorceress has…," he paused, not entirely sure how he was supposed to explain such a horrible truth. It was like trying to justify genocide to a child. "There is a tower," he began again at last, but the Oracle immediately cut him off, raising her hand to silence him.

"Enough," she whispered. These few words alone had been enough to confirm what awaited her. She turned to the window once again, her eyes now wide, although almost lifeless. Her stare far and searching as she wrestled with her thoughts. She could bring the airship down quite easily, killing them both. Saving her from what she knew now to be a truly dreadful end. Countless years roaming the ocean as punishment for such a deed, seeming of little consequence in comparison to the pain she would soon be subjected to.

She reluctantly decided against this, as ultimately she understood this was the role she was born to play. The Oracle was but a piece in a much larger game. There were other destinies intertwined with her own. Destinies which could only be fulfilled should she burden this sacrifice. She thought back to what she had seen in her visions, of the world that could be. Of the future that could be won should others follow her example. And so the Oracle accepted her fate, silently praying that others would face their destinies with the same courage and selflessness.

Despite accepting what was to be doing some small good in pushing down the rising tide of fear in her stomach, the Oracle soon felt it rise to new heights. As the airship began to descend, a shadow fell across the room. The Oracle stood, pressing her hand against the window as she stared out towards her destiny. Before them stood a great, dark tower. Its jagged points rising well above the treetops, loud crackles of magical energy ringing out from its peak like lightning. The world around the tower seemed warped, as if it were being pulled with great force towards its heart.

The Emperor too rose from his seat, joining the Oracle at the window. He spoke slowly, a clear regret in his voice.

"We are here."

Chapter 17

Catarah had been busy making final preparations for the tower's activation when she heard the airship approaching. It's arrival announced well in advance by the unmistakable throbbing of its propellors, their draught rushing through the nearby trees. She had chosen this location as ground zero for her greatest experiment to date with great care. Should things go awry, there was little nearby which would suffer the consequences save for those within the tower itself. A risk they were all more than willing to take to be the first to succeed in this combined feat of magic and engineering. With a loud, metallic clank she fastened the final piece of her apparatus into place and began an admittedly excited descent to meet her esteemed guests.

The tower had many floors, all linked by a spiralling staircase which hugged the wall all the way to the summit. Each floor had a unique function, each imperative to keeping the structure functioning as designed. As a result, there were just under fifty engineers and sorcerers working at any given time. The flowing robes and pointed hats of the sorcerers were in stark contrast to the soot covered, oily overalls of their more mechanically-minded colleagues. As Catarah descended the steps two at a time, she could feel her heart pounding with excitement and trepidation. So many great minds had spent centuries working on this very project. And she would be the one to finally flip the switch, to discover if all their toil had been worth it.

But as the Arch-Sorceress threw open the tower doors to greet the Emperor and his captive, she was caught off guard. The Oracle had no restraints upon her person whatsoever, not even so much as bound hands or a blindfold. Seeing such a powerful foe walking freely, Catarah instinctively positioned her hands for what she expected would be a cataclysmic and prolonged magical duel. A duel that even she would find to be a struggle to win.

It quickly became apparent that the Oracle was in no mood for a fight. The Arch-Sorceress could tell just by the way the Oracle walked, her feet dragging across the soft grass as if they were lead and by the way her eyes weakly drifted over the landscape, her face pale and drained. There was not so much as an ounce of resistance left within her. Whatever truths or trickery the Emperor had employed to render her into such a passive state would not last for long once she took her place within the tower. Nevertheless, the Arch-Sorceress approached cordially.

She bowed low as the Emperor and the Oracle approached, her arm sweeping out to her side while the other rested upon her stomach.

"Your Holiness, my Lady," she cooed, smiling. While she could not make out the Emperor's expression from behind his mask, the Oracle was clearly unimpressed by the performance. She hugged herself tightly, her gaze turned away towards the rustling trees and swaying blades of grass which surrounded them. But the Oracle could only distract herself for so long before she found herself once again gazing up at the tower before them. Her bright, colourful eyes now filled with reflections of dazzling green bursts of magical energy as they violently escaped the confines of their lofty prison.

It had begun to rain slightly. Not so much that it would have bothered most people, but the Oracle, still dressed in her thin, weightless scraps of silk began to shiver. Goosebumps soon broke out across her arms and shoulders as the cool raindrops burst upon her skin. Yet still she neither moved nor spoke, keeping her eyes fixed upon the ever-growing, roaring magical maelstrom above her. Catarah looked to the Emperor in a rare search for guidance as their prisoner continued to ignore her.

"Perhaps we should go inside, my Lady, out of the cold

and wet," the Emperor suggested softly. He felt truly awful for the part he was playing in all of this. A part far better suited to a remorseless servant such as Sir Bryce, one so blinded by duty that morality meant nothing so long as he was following orders.

"May we stay a moment longer?" the Oracle asked, her voice cracking and her eyes beginning to well up with tears as a lump formed in her throat. "I would watch the sky for a while yet." The Emperor and Catarah looked at one another hesitantly before the Arch-Sorceress spoke again.

"I will await you both inside," she bowed, for the first time feeling the stabbing pain of guilt upon her conscience as she retreated within her tower. The Oracle and the Emperor stood for a few minutes more in the open. The Oracle's eyes wide as she gazed directly upwards and into the heavens, trembling as the intensifying rain soaked through her clothes. The Emperor did not once interrupt her, offering all the time that was needed. They both knew there was no escape, the least he could do is offer her these last moments of peace.

When the Oracle knew she could stall no longer, she extended out a hand, her eyes still fixed upon the sky.

"Please, do you have a hood? Even a cloth would do," she asked. Puzzled, the Emperor realised he had nothing. Only a few freshly ironed handkerchiefs in the breast pocket of his doublet. He handed these over and watched as the Oracle tied them together into a single, long piece of fabric. With one final, sorrowful look into the cloudy sky, the Oracle shut her eyes before wrapping the handkerchiefs around her head, acting as a blindfold.

"I am ready," she said. She felt the Emperor approach, could feel the look of confusion upon his face.

"I would prefer the last thing I see to be something beautiful. Not the taunting walls of some prison." The Emperor nodded solemnly but said nothing. Taking the Oracle gently by the hand, he led her into the tower and up the spiralling stairs towards her destiny.

Catarah had awaited the pair two floors beneath the

tower's summit with a mixture of emotions. For so long the Phoenix Project had simply been a concept. Little more than theories and calculations scratched upon paper. Now it all felt so real. The moment the Arch-Sorceress had seen her test subject, supposedly the first of many, she began to question herself. For centuries she and other arch-sorcerers before her had wondered if the Phoenix Project could be made a reality. Now, as it approached the point of no return, Catarah could not help but wonder. Whether it could be done was not the right question, but rather, whether it should.

The time for self-reflection was now at an end as the door swung open, revealing the Emperor and his blindfolded captive.

"She is ready," he said regretfully, as he imagined the suffering this frail body beside him would endure. However, the guilt they felt at their actions was not so great as to alter their course. The work had already been done. Their goal was too important to be abandoned for the sake of one life. Catarah nodded.

The room in which the Oracle's journey would end was mostly bare. The only items contained within being instruments of Catarah's own making and what appeared to be intravenous tubes. The contraption which would be the centrepiece of the experiment looked much like an operating table. Suspended above it all by ropes and pulleys was a horizontal, human-shaped cage made of a dark metal infused with powerful magic.

With the help of two engineers, Catarah helped the Oracle onto the table before lowering the cage over her. It fit tightly over her body, allowing very little room to move while giving outside access to the subject's exposed skin. Once the cage was in place, it was further secured by being bolted to the table. The Emperor was under no obligation to watch this procedure, but forced himself to not look away. If he was the one giving the order, the least he could do was watch as it was carried out.

After fully securing the subject, Catarah brought forward

the various medical equipment. One stand held a large clear bag of white liquid. This was placed on the Oracle's left side, while the other, which contained a dark brown fluid, was placed on her right. As gently as she could, Catarah inserted a needle into each of the Oracle's arms which allowed the two liquids to flow into her bloodstream.

The white liquid was a strong painkiller. Something which would be desperately needed, and in huge quantities, should they wish the Oracle to survive this ordeal for more than a few minutes. The second, darker solution, was the truth serum Adeneus had modified during his own experiments. This would ensure the Oracle obeyed the Imperium's orders and not her own will. Lastly, a second device was lowered from above.

At first, the Emperor thought this to be a chandelier. It was smaller and carefully fitted around the Oracle's head by the engineers. This headpiece contained thick, magic-resistant wires which snaked up towards the ceiling, disappearing into the floor above. It was these wires which would transfer the Oracle's magical and psychic energy into the collection of corite crystals which sat atop the tower, already buzzing with power. There was only one more step to take - inserting corite crystals into the headpiece itself. Doing so would immediately activate the tower, connecting the Oracle's mind to any husk within a thousand miles. Or at least, that's what they hoped.

That is where the pain would begin. Catarah turned to the Emperor who remained standing in the doorway.

"You can leave the rest to me, Your Holiness. There is nothing else you can do here." The Emperor nodded in acknowledgement.

"I depart for the Great Wastes in a few weeks. Should I expect to see you before then?" The Arch-Sorceress looked down at the small woman strapped to the table, shivering like a wanderer caught in a blizzard, a single tear escaping beneath the makeshift blindfold.

"I would not expect so, Your Holiness," she replied. As

the Emperor turned to leave, eager to escape the grisly scene before the sound of screaming tore his very soul apart, the Oracle spoke to him.

"Is she really worth it? All of this?" She asked, her voice trembling with adrenaline as she waited for the agony to begin at any moment. The Emperor turned and looked upon the instruments of torture, the innocent victim he had taken, the uncontrollable shaking of her legs and fingers. There was a long pause before he replied.

"Yes."

The Oracle allowed herself to smile as she choked back her tears and fell into silence.

The Emperor slowly closed the door and descended the many steps with a heavy heart. A few seconds later came a scream. A scream so jarring, so piercing and terrible that the Emperor stumbled, slipping down a small portion of the stairs before righting himself. Just as each wail came to an end, another, more anguished than the last, took its place. Each new cry echoing through the structure like the rumbling of an earthquake. The Emperor increased his speed until he was sprinting down the steps and burst out of the tower onto the sodden ground.

As he sped towards his airship there was a great rumbling from high above. Turning back to face the tower, the Emperor could see the storm of magical energy at its peak growing ever more violent. Until suddenly, without warning, a great blast shook the ground. A bright green shockwave of crackling, sparkling energy racing out in all directions until it disappeared into the horizon.

The Emperor fell to the ground, such was the magnitude of the explosion. He was panting as he pulled himself to his feet. Quickly ascending the stairs to his ship, he took one last look at the tower before they set off into the air. Retreating into his quarters, the Emperor threw himself onto his bed, his hands wrapped around his head as the Oracle's screams rang in his ears.

*

As the door slammed shut behind The Emperor, the Oracle was at long last out of time. She could hear the discussion amongst the others in the room, their hurried yet purposeful steps as they prepared to take such a bold scientific step. Yet their words meant nothing to her. She knew little of science, even less so of the dark arts being practised here. She could tell by the shakiness of their voices that they were nervous.

It had only been a few moments since the drugs had entered her bloodstream, yet the Oracle was already beginning to feel their effects. At first, a gentle numbness began to spread about her body. Beginning in her arms before travelling down her legs and across her torso. This was not at all an unpleasant feeling. Rather, similar to that fuzzy sensation before the stinging of pins and needles would begin. No stinging came, but as the Oracle attempted to squeeze her hand into a fist, to prepare herself for what was to come, she found that she could not. It was not the case either that she simply could not feel her hand moving, but that her fingers would no longer obey her commands.

The Oracle's heart began to race much faster now, her breathing panicked and shallow. She could feel a presence near her face, inching closer until she could feel warm breath on her neck.

"Spread out your hands," the female voice whispered. The Oracle had no intention of doing as she was told, but that did not matter. She gasped in horror as she felt the fingers on both her hands spread of their own volition, against her own will. The Oracle tried to speak, the fear overtaking her earlier noble intentions. She wanted nothing more than to escape. She would do anything, promise everything. But it was no use. Her throat strained as she tried to form words, yet all she could produce was a muffled groan.

"Stick out your tongue," the same female voice commanded. Her eyes now streaming with tears, the Oracle felt her lips part and her tongue slowly slither out like a snake from its hole.

"Good, the serum is taking effect. We can begin," the voice said, directed at the others in the room. There was a loud creaking as what sounded like a heavy chest was opened, immediately following which came the sound of dim buzzing as three corite crystals were brought out. Even now, they shook with power, the souls within desperate to escape and re-join their host. So violent was their struggle that the engineer transporting them required thick, heat-resistant gloves. Otherwise, they would have burned his hands down to the bone.

The three crystals were carefully fitted into their reserved places in the instrument fixed to the Oracle's head. Their buzzing was almost deafening now, like thousands of furious bees swarming around her. The tips of magical bolts which shot out in all directions catching the Oracle's face like red hot stingers. This shock was enough to return some of the Oracle's faculties to her, but not much. Only enough that she was able to yelp out in surprise and pain as each new barb of magic caught her skin.

"Should we increase the sedative dosage?" a male voice asked. He was concerned that should these pinpricks be enough to warrant such a reaction from the subject, the procedure may kill her outright.

"No," came the voice of the Arch-Sorceress. "She's already at the maximum. Any more could stop her heart." The Oracle could hear little over the furious crackling and buzzing of the crystals around her. However, one thing she made out clearly, as the Arch-Sorceress prepared to flip the switch which would activate the tower, were her offered apologies.

"I'm sorry. I wish there could have been another way." With that she flipped the switch, and the Oracle took a deep breath, hoping to brave whatever was to come. As the collection of corite crystals at the tower's peak were joined with their power source, a surge of magical energy so strong that it could be seen with the naked eye, raced down the wires and directly into the Oracle's mind.

The pain the Oracle felt could be likened to that of being burned alive from the inside out. She let out an agonised, primal scream as she felt the magic course through her veins like liquid fire. Her body rocked and thrashed madly against the cage which contained it. The magic imbued within the metal bars dampening any spell she tried to cast in a desperate attempt to save herself. As she foamed at the mouth, screaming like a creature from the deepest pits of Hell, the darkness she had sought comfort in began to give way.

The nothingness of her makeshift blindfold suddenly became a blinding, purple light, and the Oracle felt herself being torn through the air with great speed. Faster and faster she sped until the light around her began to warp, like strands of multicoloured ribbon they formed a tunnel which spun around her. Within she saw the ages of men race past. Every act of love, every betrayal, every deed good and bad laid out like the web of some great blueprint. All in the form of this kaleidoscope of light which engulfed her now.

Then, without warning, the tunnel gave way, and the Oracle found herself somewhere new. Somewhere unknown and yet familiar. A forest in the opening days of winter. The trees were starting to be laid bare. Their leaves either having already fallen or close to doing so. The ground beneath her feet was cold and wet. Dew hung from the ankle-high grass and the heads of nearby flowers were encrusted with frost as they began to wilt. Had she escaped? Had she by some unknown magic transported herself away from that tortuous tower?

She looked down and found that her clothes were different. She appeared to be wearing some sort of uniform she did not recognise. It was a mixture of different shades of green, and in some places seemed to have large, red stains. But then she noticed something else. Her breasts were gone. Her chest as even as a shelf. She reached up her hands to unbutton her clothes and recoiled in horror. They were grey. The skin missing in some places, patches of reddish-brown flesh exposed to the open air.

The Oracle tried to scream, but from her throat came only a sickening gargle. She noticed now that not once since arriving in this new place had she taken a breath. She tried to breathe in, to take in the cool winter air to calm herself. Yet she could not. It felt as if she were trying to suck air through a stone wall. Just as she began to understand what was happening, she found herself being ripped at great speed through the tunnel of light once more.

At the same time, she remained in the forest. She could feel the cold air on her skin, could see the branches swaying in the wind. And yet, through the tunnel she travelled, it was as if she were in two places at once. Able to feel, to see, to act in one without influencing the other.

Then, she found herself somewhere new once more. A pebble bank beside a fast-flowing river which snaked its way through a rocky canyon. Upon the opposite bank a mountain goat sipped from the rushing waters. It's coat glistening from the spray, its eyes scanning for danger as its ears twitched doing the same. Again and again and again this process repeated. The Oracle would be pulled from one place to another, never staying for long, and yet never leaving.

Before long, she existed in over one hundred places at once. Each one as different as the new vessel she inhabited. The only constants being the rotten, grey skin which hung loosely from her bones, the agonising pain in her head continuing as her mind was continually torn into smaller and smaller pieces.

And finally, there was the hunger. A ravenous, ceaseless craving for sustenance. A hunger that somehow she knew, as if by instinct, no human food could sate. She needed flesh. The thought, no, the *need* for fresh, warm blood washing over her tongue. The sensation of muscle and skin being torn and shredded by her teeth having such a great hold over her that it caused her physical pain. As she continued being pulled from place to place, a voice, not her own, suddenly filled her mind.

"Return to the tower," it commanded. The Oracle obeyed, although through no choice of her own. Her now hundred strong and still growing pairs of legs set off at once. Pulled towards a single point somewhere far away. Not once through all of this did the Oracle stop traversing the tunnel in her mind. Finding herself in new places, only to immediately set off to assemble where she had been ordered. Throughout, she was still fully present and lucid within the tower where this had all begun. Still she screamed and writhed as the pain grew with each fragmentation of her mind.

Catarah looked down at the poor soul which had become the focus of her work and could not decide which emotion to feel. Already some nearby husks had arrived at the tower as commanded. Her work had proven to be a great success. Yet she could not help but replay the Oracle's final question in her head. She turned to one of the engineers who now stood idle.

"Draft a letter to the University and the Congregation. The Phoenix Project is a success. We can move ahead with the other subjects." The man did as he was told and hurried from the room, one of the first to witness the new age which had just been born. An age in which the strength of armies now meant nothing.

Chapter 18

Nate was surrounded. Nothing but a field of corpses lay in every direction. The dead were piled high, towers of rotten meat which reeked of decay. Swarms of crows filled the sky with their dark shapes, crying loudly as they dove like arrows into the mounds of flesh. Gorging themselves in a frenzy of tendrils and fluttering feathers, stabbing beaks and sharp claws. Nate looked on, breathless and full of fear. Choking on the vile stench he stumbled his way forwards, desperate to escape. Yet no matter how far he ran, how many corpses he clambered over, there were always more. The ground squelched and cracked with each step. Nate told himself these were just the noises of mud and twigs, but he did not believe it.

Suddenly, a hand shot out and took hold of Nate's ankle. He looked down in horror as the corpses around him came to life. Dragging themselves forwards with whatever limbs remained, they swarmed forwards like spiders. Clambering over one another in a desperate frenzy to reach their prey. There were hundreds of them, they snarled and growled as more and more hands took hold of Nate's clothes and skin. There were too many, he could not pull away or pry free no matter how hard he tried. Before long he was overcome. The rotting, stinking bodies piling onto him until he was beneath them. The crushing mass of writhing, wailing creatures pulling him ever further into darkness until the last glimpse of daylight melted away beneath this mass of undeath.

Nate screamed as desperately as he could, using what little room and strength remained to thrust his hand forward and emit a blinding blast of light. There was a great gust of wind and the lifting of a great pressure from his chest as the corpses were blast away, reduced to smouldering ruins or consumed by the light entirely. As Nate sat there, panting, sweating and exhausted he found he was no longer in the field of corpses. No, he was back in his barracks. Tables and chairs were either overturned or in splinters against the far wall. The fire had been blown out, while neat racks of weapons were now scattered about the floor.

This was what, the fifth, the sixth time this had happened in the past week? He pulled himself to his feet and immediately had to grab hold of the bedframe for support. His legs were weak, his arms trembling as he could not help but replay the events of the nightmare in his head. Deciding his best course of action would be to get away from the barracks, even for just a short while, Nate stumbled towards the door, not bothering to take his cloak. He mounted Bob who was surprised to see her master, although now somewhat used to the nightly explosions of magic next door. Nate hauled himself into the saddle and set Bob off into a reluctant run, he had no destination in mind, so long as it was far away from here.

It was still the middle of the night and Nate found himself entirely alone as he rode around aimlessly, trying desperately to rid his mind of unwelcome thoughts. It had been weeks since the battle at Sundered Crown, since he had been forced to watch his own allies commit acts of unspeakable savagery. Every night since had been beset by nightmares. Tame at first, they had intensified in brutality and vividness until Nate had been waking each night with uncontrolled bursts of magic.

Naturally, Nate's first instinct had been to go to the temple. But the priests had informed him that such sicknesses of the mind were beyond magic, that he would need the help of the gods. Nate tightened his grip around the reigns as he cursed himself, what the hell was he going to do? He reared his weary head and investigated the vast beauty of the sky. Tonight, it seemed, the gods were putting on a show. A vast spiral galaxy of blue and yellow sailed across the cosmos like a feather down a stream. Its many arms slowly spinning, making the surrounding stars seem like droplets flung from a woman's dress as she danced in the rain. Nate allowed himself a moment to forget his troubles and appreciate the view. These moments of peace were exceedingly rare nowadays, but they brought him the necessary, brief respite he needed from his troubled mind. All the while Bob had plodded on. Not particularly happy about being woken in the middle of the night when she had been quite comfy, she huffed and snorted to express her displeasure. Nate looked away from the sky at last to reach down and stroke his whiny companion.

"I know gorgeous, I'm sorry." Bob huffed again, fine. She would forgive him, but she would want some sugar cubes in the morning. Unknowingly, the two had strolled all the way to Captain Ardell's fort. The structure was somehow even more menacing in the gloom of night. The stakes which surrounded the outer edges of the moat, a recent addition, gave the fort the look of some horrible beast's head jutting through the ground. It's rows of sharp teeth daring any brave fool to come closer.

Stunned to realise how long they had been gone, Nate decided he had better go home, much to Bob's delight. That is, until he heard the unmistakeable ringing sound of steel and the crashing of bodies against the ground.

He doubted anyone in their right mind would try to attack Ardell's fort, even in the dead of night. However, curiosity got the better of him and Nate decided to investigate. Hitching Bob to a post, he walked around the stone keep and towards the yard at the rear of the fort. The clamour of fighting grew louder as he did so, forcing him to adopt a faster pace. Rounding the corner, he was surprised to see Ardell, surrounded by eight other individuals, sword in hand.

Instinctively, Nate went to draw his sword, only to find it absent from his side. He must have left it in the barracks along with his cloak. This was probably a good thing however, as it allowed him another few moments to observe the situation rather than charging straight in. It did not seem that Ardell was putting up too much of a fight. After all, Nate had seen her kill more people in less time than he had been stood there watching. Her opponents too were acting strangely, only approaching her one or two at a time. The reality of the situation soon became clear, Ardell was training with her bodyguards.

Nate hovered for a while, not wanting to draw attention to himself and the opportunity be lost. He had only seen Ardell fight once before and had been shocked by her brutality. But the sheer skill and swordsmanship she displayed was a sight which never grew tiresome, even more so as it was exceptionally rare. But Nate could not remain hidden forever and Ardell spotted him just as she was putting the captain of her guard on his head.

The fighting suddenly stopped, now only breathless panting could be heard as the crowd eyed Nate with both suspicion and surprise. Ardell looked bemused, Nate was as bad as, if not worse than Marcus when it came to being a lazy good-for-nothing. So, what was he doing here so late? She asked him directly, beckoning him forward into the light of the torches.

Ardell's bodyguards looked down at their guest with a mixture of annoyance and arrogance. Who was this rabble come to interrupt their training? Didn't he know this was going to be the night they finally got the better of their captain? Nate stepped forward rather sheepishly, the people around him clearly superior in every conceivable way.

As he stood before Ardell in the glow of the moonlight, he could not help but be captivated by her, no matter how much he loathed her. She wore an arrogant smirk, her chest puffed out, filled with her own hubris. But then, there were her enchanting blue eyes, soft, pale skin and hair like the woven night. He was doing it again.

"Damnit Nate, get a grip," Ardell snarled as she actively watched his brain begin to melt before her eyes.

"Sorry captain," Nate said suddenly snapping to.

"I asked what you're doing in my fort so late?"

Nate was reluctant to answer at first, fearing ridicule. But

Ardell's gorgon-like stare forced his capitulation in record time.

"Can't sleep Captain…" he paused briefly, feeling the eyes of those around him like needles in his skin. "Nightmares," he continued at last. To his surprise, there was no outburst of laughter at his weak resolve, not even from Ardell. She looked him over for a moment, filled with curiosity. She then turned to her bodyguards.

"Off to bed with you all, thank you for your efforts tonight." The eight bodyguards all bowed and returned to their barracks, bruised and exhausted. Nate and Ardell remained in place until they heard the keep door slam shut. While Nate kept his gaze fixed firmly on the floor, weary while still filled with shame and guilt. Ardell was examining the man before her. Perhaps for the first time, they may have something in common.

"You survived the battle near Sundered Crown then?" She asked rhetorically. Nate nodded without lifting his gaze.

"Although to be honest Captain, I almost wish I hadn't," he added softly. Ardell too, nodded. It had not been a particularly fearsome or brutal battle. It was in fact quite tame by modern standards and had all been over very quickly. Yet she understood what the unprepared mind could do to itself after witnessing even a small glimpse of the true face of war.

"Hmm," she said to herself as she turned and walked away. Nate was too exhausted even to stare at her backside as she did so, he really was suffering. There was a sudden *thwack* and a dull pain in his shoulder as Ardell threw a wooden sword at him. He looked up to see her twirling a sword of her own between her fingers. Nate's brain rarely fired on all cylinders, but even for him he was being slow, with a confused look on his face and narrowed, searching eyes.

"Come on," Ardell said gently stretching her arms and legs. Nate shook his head, trying to rub the tiredness from his eyes.

"Sorry Captain?"

Ardell rolled her own tired eyes. "Nothing puts the mind

at ease like a good sparring session. Let's see what Marcus has been teaching you."

Nate could barely believe his ears.

"You want to train with me Captain?"

Ardell laughed at the question. "This isn't going to be training. This is going to be me kicking your arse so hard that you sleep for a week." At first Nate shuddered at the thought of the beating he was about to receive. Then again, he could go for a nice relaxing coma right about now. He nodded and retrieved the sword, summoning whatever energy he had left in preparation. Thank God nobody was around to see this.

As expected, Nate found himself assailed by blows that seemed to materialise from another dimension. Every inch of his body stung from strikes by Ardell's sword, and yet he still had the overwhelming feeling that she was taking it easy on him. He had seen what she was capable of when she put her mind to it, and she was clearly far more sluggish and less refined with her movements now. Even so, Nate could barely see his opponent, she was but a blur of black against a dark backdrop. Just as he thought he may block one strike, three more would land across his body before he had been able to reposition his sword.

Yet the pain spurred him on, the relentless stinging of Ardell's blows and ease with which she overwhelmed him only strengthened his resolve to fight. After roughly ten minutes of constant physical abuse, Ardell knocked the sword from Nate's hand and struck the back of his knee before pushing him to the floor. Nate lay there panting and aching all over. He was going to look like an aubergine in the morning. Ardell stood over him, a strange look on her face which Nate did not recognise.

She grinned faintly. Oh great, she had thrashed him so hard he had entered another, insane reality. "I've fought champions who didn't last half that long," she said doing everything in her power not to sound impressed. Nate instinctively thought about making a lewd joke but reconsidered when noticing how close Ardell's foot was to his groin. Instead, he just continued to pant, waving his hand in the air in exhausted acknowledgement before letting it fall back into the dust.

Ardell then pulled her partner to his feet as if he weighed nothing at all. Prompting Nate to wonder where exactly she was hiding all that muscle. She did not say anything, instead examining his face. Her neck twitched as if she was about to say something, before quickly changing her mind. She patted him on the back and pushed him in the direction of home.

"Now get gone, I promise you'll sleep soundly tonight." Nate nodded and thanked the captain for her time. It was not often he thanked someone for beating the absolute shit out of him, but he knew that this was Ardell's own twisted way of being kind. The ride home was a blur. Almost as soon as he had left the fort his entire body began to fall asleep. It was a miracle he managed to drag himself through the front door without collapsing where he stood.

It was cold inside the barracks, and he was alone. Chen was still busy patrolling some backwater town behind the front lines and would be for the next few weeks. Nate shivered as he stared into the dark corners of the room, wary of what may be lying in wait. Cautiously, keeping one eye on his surroundings, Nate lit the fire once again before returning to bed. He rubbed his aching arms as he stared up at the ceiling, replaying the session with Ardell in his mind. Her movement, her skill was truly inhuman. He felt lucky to have been given the opportunity to train with such a renowned opponent, regardless of the outcome. But more than anything, he was thankful she was on his side. He pitied whatever poor fool mistook her for an easy target on the battlefield.

To Nate's surprise, Ardell had been somewhat right. He had managed to enjoy four hours of peaceful sleep before the nightmares had returned. With sunbeams now poking their way through the windows, Nate decided to wash and dress before facing the task of how to spend his day. With a war on, all Guild activities had been put on hold. He was also, as a conscripted man, barred from leaving the Vanguard without written permission from Ardell. He therefore spent his days repeating the same dull itinerary until he was given new orders.

He would wake and wander aimlessly around the town for several hours, before having lunch at his favourite little restaurant. That was half the day down. The remainder would be spent at the now almost deserted Guild Hall, either making use of their baths or training with the practice dummies. He had even taken up reading, so extreme had his boredom been. Although, one could only read so many almanacs on monster varieties before losing the will to live. The day would end with a drink or two at Pedan's before returning home, ready to repeat it all again tomorrow. However, since his unexpected excursion to Ardell's fort, Nate had a new item on the agenda. One that he actually looked forward to each night.

After being awoken by a fresh nightmare, Nate would travel all the way to his captain's fort to get his head kicked in. It did not seem to matter at what time this happened, if it was dark, Nate would find Ardell and her bodyguards already in the thick of a melee. This new routine continued every night for the next week. After resoundingly defeating her protectors, Ardell would order them to bed while she and Nate had a more relaxed (at least by Ardell's standards), sparring session.

After once again putting Nate to shame, Ardell called for a break. Something she had never done in any of their previous sessions. While she would never admit this for as long as she drew breath, Nate had improved immeasurably. So much in fact, that Ardell had only been able to knock him to the ground perhaps a dozen times. She was now out of breath, sweat glistening on her forehead as she wiped her face with a cool cloth. Nate was by comparison, paralytic. Lying on his back, breathing heavily, too tired to even open his eyes.

Smiling to herself, Ardell wrang a freshly wetted cloth over Nate's sweat-soaked face and chest, causing him to abruptly shoot upright.

"Come," she said, offering her hand which Nate gladly took. Pulling him to his feet, Ardell led Nate over to the keep where they sat resting against the wall. For a while the pair said nothing. Staring up into the starry sky as their breathing slowly returned to normal.

"You're not the only one," Ardell said cryptically, breaking the silence. Nate looked at her curiously, not entirely sure what she was talking about.

"The nightmares I mean," she clarified upon noticing the stupid look she was receiving.

"Oh," Nate breathed, returning to staring up at the sky, his head resting against the wall. He came here to escape the nightmares, and truthfully didn't fancy talking about them now. Although he appreciated Ardell's apparent kindness all the same.

"What are they about?" The Captain asked. Nate rubbed his eyes as he reluctantly thought back to those he had suffered the past few nights. He shook his head.

"They're just…. violent," he said at last. Ardell understood exactly what Nate meant, and her heart was heavy for him.

"Killing is the most unnatural, offensive act there is in the eyes of the gods. It's not supposed to be enjoyable," Ardell continued. Nate could not help but be amused at the claim, raising an eyebrow as he gave Ardell a smirk that indicated he did not believe her even a bit. Ardell too could not help but laugh as she shook her head.

"I admit I get carried away sometimes," she smiled before her face slowly became more serious. "But they stay with you. Every one." Nate's smile too quickly faded away as they both returned to silence. He picked at the dying grass between his legs before summoning the courage to ask a question which had been on his mind for over a year.

"Captain?," he began.

"Hmm?" Ardell hummed, her eyes closed, head tilted back slightly against the wall.

"There's something I've wanted to ask you, for a while now actually."

"If this is about to be your declaration of undying love, I advise you save your breath," Ardell grinned without opening her eyes. But Nate didn't smile, he bit the inside of his lip, wondering whether to continue. Curiosity got the better of him however, and he persevered with his question.

"Last year, with the Grand Admiral. Why did he call you Oath Breaker?"

Ardell's eyes opened slowly, not expecting such a personal question. She wrung her hands together between her thighs as she wondered whether to answer at all. Her grin had vanished entirely, any enjoyment gained from the night going with it. For a split second she felt herself growing angry, anger at the audacity of the question. Who was Nate to ask such a thing of her? But this anger subsided as quickly as it came, and she answered at last. Her words sinking like a stone from the weight of regret as soon as they left her mouth.

"A long time ago, I made a promise to someone… and I broke it." While this technically answered Nate's question, it did little to satisfy his curiosity.

"Care to elaborate?" He probed. Ardell let out a long sigh, she had opened a can of worms that would not be easily closed. To Nate's utter shock, Ardell reached within her breast pocket and pulled from it a single cigarette. She placed it in her mouth and lit the end with a flame which sprung to life at the end of her fingertip. There was a silence which even Nate dared not break as Ardell took long, thoughtful drags, blowing the smoke half-heartedly away from her.

"There was a woman," she began.

"There always is."

Ardell shook her head and smiled sadly as she thought back to those days which she refused to forget, regardless of the pain it caused her.

"This was the most beautiful woman you'd ever set eyes on. The most perfect, kind, loving woman you can imagine. The kind you'd sell your kingdom for if you had one. The kind you'd die for without a moment's hesitation should she ask it of you."

Nate nodded in silence, only now understanding what the captain had meant. She was not talking about a friend, a sister in arms or even a respected foe. No, this was someone who commanded something of Ardell which until this very moment, Nate had thought her incapable.

"Sounds like you really loved her," he said softly, wanting to show his captain that he was not as emotionally dense as most of the women in his life thought. Ardell scoffed at the feebleness of the word. At how little it encapsulated all she had been willing to lose, all she had sacrificed, all she had felt, how she still felt even now.

"I gave her everything I had, more than anyone could possibly imagine. More than anyone else would dare give. I promised that I'd keep her safe no matter the cost." Nate could hear Ardell's voice beginning to strain as she tried to stop it breaking. Could see the glistening of tears beginning to form in the corner of her eyes like diamonds protruding from the earth. He knew he should stop now, just leave the conversation here. But he had to know more.

"What happened?" He asked. He could feel the air around them growing colder, growing ever more tense, like standing upon a volcano mere seconds before it erupted. There was a long silence before Ardell finally replied with a voice like ice. She took a final drag from her cigarette before putting it out on the frozen ground.

"I killed her."

Nate was stunned into silence; he felt the world around him turn to ice. His organs froze, sinking with their newfound weight into the pit of his stomach. He felt suddenly overcome with a newfound fear. As he stared at the head of raven hair which now turned away from him to hide the crystal tears which ran down Ardell's cheeks, Nate no longer saw the woman. In her stead he saw a beast, a weapon, something truly dangerous, something, as he had always believed, incapable of love or compassion. He suddenly felt a sickness, but not physical, instead, a revulsion for his captain. He could not even for one moment imagine circumstances upon which he could bring harm to those he loved. He thought of Chen, of Marcus, of Joel, even admittedly, of Ardell herself. How he would do anything to keep them from harm, not once imagining the harm could come from him.

With this, Nate felt a strange sense of superiority over his captain. She may be an unparalleled swordsman, but at least he could say he would never hurt those he loved, not intentionally, as Ardell claimed to have done. But, as the sound of her sobbing finally broke through his own deafening thoughts, his heart softened. He reached out, placing his hand on Ardell's shoulder, but she quickly shot up, her back still to him.

"It's late. You may stay with my guard tonight, but after that I think our training is at an end." She made for the keep's entrance.

"C…Captain," Nate called after her, finally regaining his composure. But Ardell held up her hand, instantly reducing Nate to silence. She would hear no more. She returned to her room, a painful knot in her stomach as she pushed her emotions as far down as they would go. Nate stayed in place for a moment, allowing Ardell to put some distance between them before he too headed for bed.

While being permitted to stay within Ardell's keep was an honour awarded to very few. Nate did not feel the sense of pride that many others would have done in his position. He dragged his feet during the short journey into the keep and felt that usual, unpleasant chill down his spine as he ascended the stairs.

The bodyguard's quarters were located past Ardell's own quarters, and Nate could not help but have an insane thought as he came to her door. Perhaps he should go in, try to talk to his captain, act like a human with feelings for once. But in the end, he decided against it. Ardell may have allowed Nate a short glimpse beyond her rough exterior, but that was no invitation to go rummaging further. He was more likely to catch a dagger to the eye than a heart-to-heart conversation. Plus, the female emotional spectrum was far more advanced than Nate was capable of understanding, so it was probably best things were left where they lay.

Pushing on, Nate at last reached the second set of quarters near to the very top of the keep. He knocked, despite Ardell's permission. After all, how would he have liked someone to come barging into his room unannounced, regardless of who's permission had been given? The door was soon opened by a man Nate recognised as the captain of Ardell's guard. A title he felt only served to make things even more confusing, as he was by no stretch of the imagination of the same official rank as Ardell. No, in fact, most of Ardell's bodyguards weren't even members of the army when she had recruited them. Most had either been mercenaries or monster hunters who had impressed her in one way or another.

The man looked down at Nate with a furrowed brow, unsure as to what business he could possibly have here. He was tall too, having to duck beneath the doorframe slightly to answer it.

"Can I help you?" He answered gruffly but without hostility.

"Ardell, I mean, the Captain said I should rest here tonight," Nate replied sheepishly. He expected some sort of interrogation, to not be believed. But the man simply shrugged and beckoned him inside without so much as a disbelieving squint. The lack of suspicion was understandable though. After all, who in their right mind would lie about something so bizarre, just to risk Ardell's wrath when she inevitably found out?

"Zeiberg," the man said, holding out his hand once the door shut behind them. Nate shook it warmly, glad for what had so far been a much more pleasant encounter than he had expected.

"Find yourself a place and get comfy," Zeiberg yawned as he retreated to his own bed right beside the door. This room was perhaps three times the size of Ardell's, and unarguably, much cosier. Instead of being filled with beds, some tables and nothing else, the barracks was every grunt's dream. It had everything a tired and overworked soldier could possibly want. A large kitchen which was restocked daily. Separate bathing facilities in an adjacent room, private storage such as wardrobes or chests of drawers beside each bed. Each person had their own quasi-independent living space, decorated to reflect the personalities of the person who occupied it. There was even a bloody bar.

As he stood in awe, the others, many of whom had not even noticed Nate enter, went about dressing down and preparing for bed. Ardell's erratic schedule kept them all on their toes and rest would be taken whenever the opportunity presented itself. Noticing his obvious entrancement, one of the bodyguards approached.

"More extravagant than what you're used to?" She asked. Nate nodded.

"This is practically a palace," he gasped, finally turning his attention to the voice beside him. The woman was not at all the kind of person Nate would have expected Ardell to appoint to such an auspicious position. Slightly shorter than him, and much plumper. Her face was red and blotchy, her nose large and crooked, and her hair had both the look and feel of straw. Nevertheless, she was perfectly pleasant. Pointing Nate towards an empty bed, she then introduced him to those who had not already retired for the night, pulling large curtains around their beds for that rarest of privileges, privacy.

Despite being exhausted, most of the group were still too full of adrenaline to sleep. So, they, Nate included, sat and ate or drank, discussing quietly whatever came to mind. Most of the attention, however, was unexpectedly on Nate. Everyone had heard of his mission the previous year. The secret journey to Cotts, the discovery of the bewitched husks and slaying of Adeneus. And of course, the firebombing of the Imperial City. Most simply wanted a first-hand retelling of the tale. Others were more interested in Nate as a person, trying to work out what it was that Ardell saw in him worthy of keeping around.

Personally, Nate hated talking about the events of the previous year. He still found what they had done to the people

313

of the Imperium impossible to forgive, blaming himself for not doing anything to stop it. For now, however, he would humour his new friends and answer all their questions, only occasionally having time to ask any of his own.

As the night wore on and the adrenaline subsided, one by one the members of Ardell's guard retreated to bed. Nate was one of the last to do so, still buzzing from the night's excitement, but also in fear of what his dreams may bring. As he finally pulled the duvet up to his chin, he saw the woman from earlier. Hadilla, he thought she said her name was, pulling a heavy bolt across the door. Nate scowled curiously and whispered across the room.

"What's that for?" He asked. Hadilla paused for a moment before looking to Zeiberg who gave a cautionary nod. She whispered back, her voice stern and serious.

"Protection." The tone of Hadilla's voice was totally unexpected, leaving Nate with an unshakeable sense of foreboding. Shrinking down into his pillow as the last lamp was extinguished. *'What the hell does that mean?'* He wondered before at last falling asleep.

About an hour later, Nate was awoken by screaming, high-pitched, terrified screaming. At first, he expected to find himself in the midst of some new nightmare. But it soon became apparent that this was not the case. He was still in Ardell's keep, the other members of her guard either still asleep, or squeezing their pillows against their heads, trying their best to drown out the noise. Only one person was fully lucid. Propped up against the headboard smoking a pipe, Zeiberg sat motionless, taking in each fresh scream of terror as if it were a solemn duty.

He looked over at Nate who too had risen into a sitting position. Lighting a nearby lamp with his magic, Nate surveyed the room as the wailing continued unabated. Those woken by the noise no longer tried to ignore it, and sat or lay in their beds, as they did every night, waiting for it to end.

Nate of course, had no idea what was going on and pulled away the covers, swinging his legs over the side of the bed onto the cold stone floor. The screaming was unnerving yes, but what bothered him far more, was the response, or lack thereof from the others. Nevertheless, someone was clearly in danger, and it was his duty to face it, regardless of what others may do.

Yet before he could even stand, Zeiberg spoke up.

"Stay where you are," he ordered. Nate looked at him, still smoking his pipe, the same pained look on his face. Nate's brow furrowed in confusion.

"Don't you hear that?" He whispered, although he was not sure why. The screams continued, and they were clearly coming from below, further into the keep.

"Believe me boy, if you go out there, it'll be you screaming next. Just stay where you are. It won't last for much longer." Zeiberg took another puff from his pipe, the embers illuminating his face in this still dark section of the room where the lamp's light did not reach.

"What is it?" Nate whispered, his voice shaky, terrified even.

"It's the Captain," came a voice from the bed closest to Nate. Their tone was a pitiful sigh as they repositioned in their bed. Immediately Nate's thoughts shifted to scenes of torture. Imagining Ardell having her sick way with some poor victim, his mind thinking back to the vermin he had captured the year before. But these assumptions were soon quashed.

"And you thought your nightmares were bad," Zeiberg said through a pillar of smoke.

"What?" Nate whispered, but he had heard perfectly well what had been said. Zeiberg shook his head, his eyes burning like coals in the glow of his pipe.

"Whatever it is that can scare a woman like that," he said pausing for the screams which echoed off the stone walls, "I pray to all the gods I never run into it."

With this revelation Nate hesitated, staring at the door and wincing whenever a fresh cry erupted. Never had he expected such a sound to come from Ardell. One of such fear, of such helplessness that it shook him to his core. It was not long before he retreated to bed, the pillow pressed firmly against his ear. He thought about what Zeiberg had said. Wondering what could possibly transform a woman like Ardell into the screaming, crying infant he could hear echoing throughout the keep.

Chapter 19

At last the time had come. The Emperor now stood before the assembled Chosen outside of the Imperial Palace. After hundreds of hours investigating every whisper of a rumour of such a place, some of which dated back thousands of years, the new spymaster had managed to uncover concrete evidence for the existence of the library the Lord of Embers had mentioned. Now all that remained was to take the long and dangerous journey into the heart of the Great Wastes, a land where winter could last for years at a time. A place even the great powers had little interest expanding into. An already arduous journey which would only prove more difficult by having to be made almost entirely on foot.

The Emperor planned to take three hundred of his Chosen with him. Too many for the handful of airships in the Imperium's arsenal to transport at once. A vulnerability that was already well under way to being remedied but would not be ready for some months.

Nestor had suggested sending a detachment ahead of the main party to safeguard the area for his arrival. But the Emperor was impatient, wishing to set off immediately. Every moment wasted at home was a moment without his beloved Sarah. As his eyes rolled over the crowd gathered to watch his departure, he could not help but feel a sense of pride. The Chosen gathered before him were men of great honour and unmatched skill. To have such noble men sworn to defend him touched tenderly upon his heart.

Before they could depart on their mission, there was a very old, very important ceremony which must first be completed. Between the Emperor and his stout retinue, were three hundred women. They stood facing the Emperor, their arms interlinked, forming a great human chain across the palace courtyard. No two were the same. Some were rich, dressed in the finest silks and satins. The jewels that hung from their necks and ears worth more than a small kingdom. Others were as common as muck. Dressed in their work clothes which were stained with everything from flour to blood.

Never would you usually see such women cavorting, such polar opposites reflecting every rung on the societal ladder. Yet there was one thing these women all shared – a vocation of unique, unenviable privilege and sorrow. These were the wives of the Chosen. They had come, as they had done for a thousand years, to prevent the Emperor taking their men away to war, and certain death. This now honoured tradition had begun during the war which birthed the Imperium as it was known today. When the Emperor's armies had recruited by force, dragging men from their homes, off the streets, out of their very beds to serve at their new Emperor's behest.

It had been only five women originally, shielding their husbands with their bodies in the market square. They had called out their new monarch, challenging him to come and take the men himself after the city guard had failed, having been pelted with rocks by the riled-up crowd. Much to everyone's surprise, that's exactly what he did. The Emperor had approached these brave, defiant women and made them a promise, offering them the crown with which he was coronated as ransom for the safe return of their husbands.

Now he would do the same again, as he had done many times before. From his left approached Nestor, flanked by four heavily armed guards. In his hands, the coronation crown. This crown usually rested in the Hall of the Fallen. A sanctum dedicated to all those who had lost their lives in their Emperor's glorious service. Now the Emperor stood ready to take the crown, only to hand it over to the women who opposed him. A reminder of an old promise renewed. He lifted the crown gently from Nestor's grasp, turning with it held aloft, and slowly stepped towards the human chain which separated him from his Chosen.

No words were spoken. Instead, the Emperor slowly lowered the crown into the waiting hands of the wives' representative, breaking the chain. With this act, the Chosen were free to follow their Emperor. And he was free to lead them, down whichever bloody path he deemed necessary.

While this ceremony contained pomp and fanfare as one would expect, the emotions behind it had remained unchanged over the last thousand years. The wives, as honoured as they were to be part of such a display of culture, felt the same fear and heartache as their predecessors. They all knew there was a chance their husbands would not return. While in this regard they differed little from the average military wife, they knew in their hearts that their husbands would be facing dangers far greater than the average foot soldier. This was their honour, their burden to bear, until at last they returned home.

As the wives returned to their husbands, bestowing final loving words and embraces, the Emperor turned to Nestor.

"How goes your inquiry?" he asked softly. Nestor remained staring straight ahead, not wanting to give any potential watchful eyes a clue to his actions.

"I have learned much, Your Holiness. Although none of it helpful."

"Hmm," the Emperor replied, slightly troubled by this admission. "Perhaps your investigation has been uncovered?"

Nestor ran his tongue along the edge of his teeth as he considered the Emperor's suggestion.

"I don't believe so, Your Holiness. I have all but proven some innocence, others I have yet to question. But do not fret, I shall find you a traitor. You just focus on returning the Empress to us."

The Emperor raised an eyebrow from behind his mask.

"Come around at last, have you?"

Nestor could not help but smile, watchful eyes be damned.

"The more I think about it, the more convinced I become."

"Convinced of what?"

"That she was the only one among us with a lick of sense."

The Emperor too smiled at the statement.

"I'll bring her back, my friend. Then we can finally put all this madness to an end."

The pair ended their conversation, watching in silence as the women bid their men tearful farewells. While Nestor watched on with indifference, his mind focused on the next stage of his investigation, the Emperor's heart was heavy. Each of these men were risking their lives to return to him what they were willingly leaving behind. As he watched them kiss their wives' goodbye, wiping the tears from their cheeks, he felt the overwhelming weight of guilt upon his shoulders.

He imagined these same women, waiting day after day for news of their beloved. Unable to sleep, unable to eat for worry. Only to then receive that fateful knock informing them that their husband would not be coming home. Would they hold him personally responsible? Would they curse his name for sending their husbands to their deaths for his own selfishness?

The Emperor believed it cruel of Phalon to have demanded such a prerequisite before joining the Chosen. It was also perhaps the only time the Emperor and Elias had seen eye to eye, albeit for different reasons. Neither of them liked the idea of exclusively married men being permitted to join the Chosen. Elias claimed it would make them weak, split their allegiance and make them more prone to desertion. Phalon had claimed the opposite. Believing a man with everything to lose would fight hardest of all to keep it. Thinking now of what he himself was willing to do in the same situation, the Emperor could not help but be annoyed that Phalon had been right after all.

As the ceremony concluded and the crowds returned home, the Chosen formed into columns preparing to depart. The Emperor stood a while longer in silence, eyeing the men who would be accompanying him on this journey. It was them, for the first time, that he decided to try and keep the promise he had made to these women, which until now he had only meant to be placating words. He would do all he could to keep these men alive until they returned triumphant, back into the grateful arms of those who loved them.

As he waited, the sound of wheels against stone grew louder in his right ear until it was clear the source was right beside him. He turned to see the royal carriage, long held in storage, having been drawn out to take him. Led by no fewer than sixteen horses, the vehicle was a marvel to behold. Gilded with gold and adorned with countless intricacies and aesthetic features, the carriage was the only one of its kind. Many times longer than even its most luxurious counterpart in the Imperium, it was more of a moving palace than a simple mode of transport.

It was split into four, long, rectangular sections. each linked by a coupler. It was the closest thing in Gaia to one of the trains of old. At the front would be found the living quarters. Containing a few sofas and recliners, along with a stocked bookshelf to keep the occupants entertained. This is where the Emperor would spend most of his time. The second carriage contained the sleeping quarters. A double bed the only furniture.

The third carriage, however, was the most impressive. The largest of all, this was the kitchen, within which worked the Emperor's personal retinue of chefs. While it was basic compared to the marvels of the Imperial Palace kitchens, it was still better than anything they would find on the road. The last carriage was simply used for storage, mostly provisions, but also some of the Emperor's personal effects for which room could not be made elsewhere.

"Thought I'd get this old thing out. Wouldn't want your feet to hurt, after all," Nestor grinned, as he too marvelled at the carriage.

"A nice gesture," the Emperor replied, dismissively, "but I think I'd rather ride," he said as he mounted Legacy, who also in that moment had been presented by the Master of Horse. The look on Nestor's face was one of pure horror.

"Do you have any idea how long it took to get that thing

out of the stable? Some idiot had parallel parked it!" Nestor cried in anguish. The Emperor could not help but laugh.

"Oh, go on then, I might find some use for it," he winked before urging Legacy onwards.

As Nestor watched the Emperor ride away, his face sank at the apprehension of his next move. He returned to the palace, the guards taking note of his grim expression as they swept open the heavy doors before him. As he entered the main hall, he gazed up at the structure which surrounded him. The stone and marble seemed not like the rough, unrefined products of the land, crudely bent to fit man's need for shelter. No, the stone flowed like water, the marble dancing across the space above him like paint on a canvas.

Truly, this place was a masterpiece. And to think that so recently it had been little more than rubble. The broken, twisted shapes of men and women half-buried beneath, a sight Nestor would not soon forget. The screams, as those trapped were burned alive by the still unknown, sticky, black liquid the bombs had spewed forth, haunted his dreams still. Now he was to visit the man responsible for such destruction. The very thought leaving a lingering uncleanliness like oil over Nestor's skin. Nevertheless, his duty was to find the traitor. If he was lucky, one might lead him to another.

The Imperial dungeons were located about as far from the palace as possible while still being within the confines of the city. Certain prisoners, those deemed too dangerous or valuable to risk escape or rescue, were housed in the palace itself. Located almost directly beneath Elias' office, the singular iron entrance was watched over by a pair of guards armed with poleaxes. The approach to the dungeons was narrow, wide enough only for one man at a time. Nestor tightened his fists as he felt the grey stone barely centimetres from him on either side, his breathing shaky as the fear of being crushed began to take hold.

With no other rooms or functions nearby, there was only one reason someone would be heading this way. Therefore there was therefore no need for the guards to question Nestor as he approached. One guard withdrew a ring of keys so comically overburdened, one would expect to have to book an appointment weeks in advance just to give the guards time to find the correct key. This was a ruse, as only one key fit the door, and the guards knew exactly which. The giveaway, a fine cut along the body of the key, too small for a rescue party or frantic escapee to notice.

As the keys jangled and the clicking of locks echoed down the narrow passage, Nestor held his breath. This would be the first time he had seen Rohm since his arrest. Would he be able to contain his rage when faced with the traitor who had caused so much pain? He was soon to find out.

"This way, my Lord," the guard said, the one not holding the keys, taking up a torch and leading the way. Nestor could not help but be surprised by the man's accent, although he did not let it show. It was very distinct. In fact, he had never heard it anywhere other than the world he had been born into. Nestor smiled to himself as he followed the guard down this new, dark passage. What were the mathematical chances of running across a man from his own birthplace? Less than zero perhaps? The novelty was fleeting as he found himself once again pressed on all sides by immovable stone. The flickering light of the guard's torch his only lifeline in a tempest of darkness, which even in the stillness of the underground raged about Nestor's insides like a storm.

The dungeons were deep. Deeper even than the cavern where the Emperor had undergone his miraculous recovery. Down into the dark underbelly of the world Nestor descended, where only the most contemptible human refuse dwelled. There was no lift, only seemingly endless stairs. Stairs which in some places were so steep and shallow, Nestor feared one wrong step would send him to his death. The pair travelled in silence, the crackling of the torch and the armoured boots of the guard echoing down the narrow passage ahead of them. Nestor desperately wanted to shut his eyes, but the lethality of the stairs forced his keen attention.

After over an hour of increasingly heavy breaths and wild

imaginings of the excruciating nature of his death, Nestor finally arrived in the dungeon. How he had done this without fainting or losing his mind, he knew not. But he was here now, so he must continue with his mission. The dungeons were thankfully a single large cavern, the ceiling was tall and the walls far enough apart that Nestor could breathe easy. He wanted to get this over with and be out of this godforsaken place as soon as possible.

The guard beckoned Nestor to continue following, with which idea he was not about to argue over, he had the only torch after all. The cavern was cold and damp, the reddish-brown of the clay walls reflecting the light of the torch and casting a brown hue over the room. In the darkness, Nestor could hear murmurs, whimpering and, in some cases, sobbing. Nestor had expected more. To hear wails of madness and despair as men threw themselves against their cells in a futile attempt to escape. To have his very thoughts drowned out by the cries for mercy, promises of repentance.

Nestor expected these things only because he misunderstood what this place really was. He had no idea what it was like to be locked away in the cold and the dark, forgotten by the rest of the world and left to rot. This was not a place for those who still believed in the possibility of escape, nor in the concept of forgiveness and freedom, for those who still clung to the idea of sunlight. This was a place of hopelessness. A nothingness even the gods had forgotten.

In the limited light Nestor could make out some of the cells. Obsidian bars reflected the light of the torch beautifully from their smooth, rectangular surfaces. Like the lure of an angler fish they glittered, enticing Nestor to come closer, to put himself within reach of whatever lay beyond their allure.

"This way, m'Lord," the guard instructed. His already quiet words seeming to be absorbed by the walls themselves.

"You don't even know why I'm here," Nestor replied rather cautiously. The guard turned, the light catching only the left side of his face.

"Reckon there's only one person down 'ere you'd be

interested in seein' m'Lord. This way." The guard led Nestor to what felt like the rear of the dungeon. He had no way of knowing this for certain, but the air felt heavier, the walls closer and thicker. The guard abruptly halted, turning to his companion and handing over their only source of light.

"He's just ahead," he said before turning into the darkness.

"Where are you going?" Nestor asked, sounding rather more desperate than he had intended.

"I know better than to eavesdrop on Lordly conversations, m'Lord. Rather take my chances with those stairs in the dark." With that, the guard disappeared into the darkness, leaving Nestor alone with the most dangerous scum in the Imperium. Nestor turned back in the direction the guard had directed, stepping cautiously as the darkness gave way. Only a few moments later did he see the cell, and then what was left of the man within.

Lord Rohm had always been an excessively flamboyant sort of character. Far more suited to a fairy-tale full of gallant knights and fairy godmothers than the head of a vast spy network responsible for countless coups and assassinations. Nestor could not remember a single time in their long history where the Lord's outfits had matched. Nor an instance where the combined value of the jewellery he never wore more than once was less than that of a small village. Indeed, it seemed that Lord Rohm's greatest fear had always been that at any moment the fashion may change and he forever be labelled passe'.

Looking at him now, it seemed his fears had been somewhat misaligned with reality. His colourful silk robes were replaced with a large sack for holding grain. The glittering jewels, which so often hung from his ears and neck, shone no more. The flickering of the torch in his sad, hopeless eyes a taunting memory of whatever beauty they had once beheld. Rohm sat against the wall, motionless, unblinking, uninterested in this rarest of things - a visitor. For none dared come down here save the guards, eager to enact some extra-judicial punishment.

This is what he believed approached him now. He no longer gave his captors the satisfaction of either resistance or fear. They had done everything, taken everything, all that which could be taken from a man but his life. There was nothing anyone could do to hurt him now. His shock at the surprise was palpable, when he saw not his sadistic jailors emerging from the darkness but rather his old friend, the right hand of the Emperor himself.

Nestor had nothing left but hatred in his heart for Rohm. A man who had betrayed his Emperor and his country. And for what? Yet even his resolve faltered as he witnessed what had become of a once dear friend. Many times had Nestor counselled Rohm on the danger of his gluttony. Even requiring a specially made crane to be lifted from his bed had done little to sate his appetite. Nestor had always expected to hear how the spymaster's heart had simply burst one morning, most likely while struggling to sit upright before his morning banquet. But in the palace dungeon, there were no banquets. Half a loaf of stale bread and a cup of water every three days had taken its toll on the formerly jolly, fat man.

So rapid, so unnatural, had Rohm's weight loss been, that his skin had no time to catch up. It hung from him like sheets of grotesque, pale linen. His arms could have been used as both mast and sail should he find himself adrift. Even his face had not been spared. His formerly rosy cheeks were now jowls which collected in the hollow of his collar.

"A rather late rescue attempt but appreciated all the same. I would rise to greet you, old friend, but it seems my legs no longer recognise my authority." In this moment, all the animosity and venom which had been steadily building up inside Nestor simply faded away. He saw not a traitorous criminal receiving justice, but rather a once loved friend whose suffering he could scarcely imagine.

"I'm afraid you'll have to wait a bit longer for that rescue," Nestor sighed empathetically. He crouched down so that he was eye-level with the prisoner, the cold of the floor instantly breaching his trousers and spreading across his knee.

"Bugger," Rohm sighed in an amused tone. Nestor didn't see the humour in the response, scowling as Rohm turned his head away to rest upon the wall.

"I need to ask you something," he said, the words shaky as they left his mouth. Adrenaline began to course through Nestor's veins, unsure and afraid of what truths may come to light once he began. However, Rohm it seemed, was not in a talkative mood.

"You'll have to book an appointment, I'm afraid. My diary is fully booked with red hot pokers and fingernail extraction until at least next Thursday," he said, managing a weak wheeze. Nestor gave a scowl which could have turned the former Lord to stone had he been looking.

"I fail to see what's so funny," he replied.

"Do you?" Rohm shot back, turning his gaze back to Nestor as quickly as his weak body would allow. "Then allow me to elaborate," he continued, turning his head back to its resting place on the wall.

"You arrest the only man in the country with half a brain, torture him to the brink of insanity, and then come begging for his help when you realise how inept you all really are. Really, I'm surprised it took this long."

"Who say's I'm here to ask for help?" Nestor replied, clearly becoming frustrated at the man's arrogance, even now. The dishevelled Rohm could not help but smile, revealing how few teeth the guards had allowed him to keep.

"Come Nestor, I doubt you're here to see your dear old friend just for the sake of it."

"You're no friend of mine," Nestor spat in reply. "You betrayed your country, got the Empress killed."

"Is that what they say?"

"It's the truth!" Nestor raged through barred teeth, unable to contain his anger, some of it slipping out, his raised voice quickly swallowed by the walls.

"Indeed, how fortunate we are that the truth and gossip are so often one in the same. It truly did make my job so much easier. Frankly, I don't know why anyone even bothers with spies in the first place. You can learn all you need to know from the local fishmonger and his friends after a few drinks."

Nestor was once again filled with that same anger he had brought with him.

"You deny your actions even now, that you knew of the attack beforehand and did nothing to stop it?"

"Of course I deny it!" Rohm roared back, his eyes filled with the light of rage for the first time in over a year. "I sent no fewer than three letters addressed to his Holiness himself, each filled with the details of the Tinelians' plans."

Nestor didn't believe a word of Rohm's claims.

"Convenient that none of these letters arrived then," he said, raising his eyebrow to match his disbelieving tone. But now Rohm's eyes began to shimmer, like they would when he would impart information only he knew to the rest of the Congregation. With the little strength he had, Rohm pulled himself forward using only his hands. He stared deeply into Nestor's eyes, nodding slowly, a parched, purple tongue running over his dry lips.

"Yes, yes," he whispered, as he dragged himself forward like one of the undead. He reached the bars at last, wrapping thin, grey hands around them as he looked up at his old friend who had retreated slightly. "Convenient indeed," he wheezed, this short but trying journey having robbed him of any remaining energy. He nodded at the floor, lacking the strength to keep his head upright.

"That's exactly what I've been thinking from the moment they came for me. This whole situation is most convenient." Rohm paused as he tried to regain some modicum of strength, raising his head so that he stared once again into the fearful eyes of his former colleague. "But convenient for whom, I wonder. For me?" he asked rhetorically. "A man sentenced to suicide for his role in a crime he tried to prevent?" He raised a hand to show the rope he had been given upon his sentencing, to use whenever he saw fit. "Ask yourself this, my old friend. Who really benefitted from the attack which killed the Empress. Because I doubt it is the man before you now."

"You think you were framed?" Nestor whispered, the very thought being dangerous enough to grant him a cell next door and a rope of his own.

"There is no question, someone needed a scapegoat to mask their betrayal. If anything, I'm impressed," Rohm coughed as he attempted to chuckle.

"Impressed?" Nestor repeated. Rohm grinned ironically as he gave his reply.

"I always thought I was the clever one amongst our happy band. Clearly not clever enough," he sighed.

"Why didn't you say anything, try to prove your innocence?" Nestor asked, as he felt his heart begin to thump against his breast. If what Rohm claimed was true, not only was the architect of the Empress' murder still roaming free, but they had the resources and the cunning to outwit supposedly the most dangerous man in the Imperium. Rohm shook his head.

"What innocence?" he huffed. "My failure to warn of the attack was proof enough of my guilt. What good is a spymaster who can't even have a message delivered without it being intercepted?" Despite Rohm's convincing argument to his innocence, Nestor was not entirely swayed. After all, the last desperate defence of a guilty man is to claim conspiracy, to sow distrust and division amongst those loyal servants that remained. Nevertheless, he would take Rohm's claims seriously and add them to his already long list of enquiries.

"There is little I can do for you now," Nestor admitted. "But if you can help me, it may just be enough to prove your innocence and set you free." Rohm was not foolish enough to allow himself to be optimistic at his chances of freedom, but he would do anything to avoid the rope for another day.

"Very well," he sighed. "What do you need?" Nestor withdrew from his breast a neatly folded scrap of parchment and handed it to Rohm through the bars. With his weak and disused eyes, the former spymaster found it a struggle to read. Upon finishing the letter he quickly understood its importance, and its place in the grand scheme that was clearly underway.

"Someone intends to assassinate the Emperor," he stated.

"I believe so," Nestor nodded, taking back the letter. "I believed you to be a prime suspect, but..."

"But it would be hard for me to reach the Emperor from here."

"You're a resourceful man," Nestor replied.

"Not resourceful enough it seems, else I'd currently find myself somewhere entirely more pleasant."

Nestor rubbed his sweating forehead, a sign of the stress this task was placing upon him.

"My only other suspect is Cardinal Praxus, but news of the attack would not have reached him by the time this letter arrived in Ifritus."

Rohm raised a wispy eyebrow. "Your only suspect?" he repeated, disbelievingly.

"All the others have alibis. Someone could have forged the seal, I suppose," Nestor huffed. He had not wanted to entertain such an idea, a possibility which could extend his list of suspects to virtually anyone. Rohm shook his head, a disapproving scowl on his face, although it was hard to tell with all the sagging skin.

"If you so much as believe in that concept you've already lost," he growled, as his brain slowly kicked into action. "The seal cannot be forged. There is powerful magic protecting it. The Emperor would know a fake immediately."

"There is?" Nestor gasped, shocked. "Since when?"

"Since always," Rohm replied. "We aren't supposed to know about it, of course. But anyone using their own seal to create a forgery would mark themselves without even knowing it." Nestor wiped his brow again before letting out another huff, relieved.

"Well, at least that narrows down the suspects somewhat."

"To whom was the dagger delivered?" Rohm asked,

ignoring Nestor's meaningless comments which added nothing to his deductions. Nestor shook his head.

"We do not know. The courier who collected the dagger covered his face and claimed to be from the Imperial court."

"Yet he had the Imperial Seal as proof?"

"It would appear so," Nestor confirmed.

Rohm struggled to pull himself back, with great effort and much grunting did he position himself with his back against the wall. Nestor could see, even in this state, Rohm's mind was working like the tireless machine of old to unravel this mystery. He once again poked out his tongue while lost in thought. It wiggled at the corner of his mouth like a dried slug. An act Nestor had always found repulsive, even more so now.

"Have you considered?" Rohm breathed, as a thought came to him at last. "That it was the Emperor himself who ordered this dagger's construction?" Nestor was taken aback at the suggestion. Perhaps all this time in isolation had addled Rohm's mind after all. The old spymaster could see the confusion in his old friend's eyes and quickly offered an explanation.

"Imagine you're our beloved master. The love of your life has just been murdered and your dear friend Adeneus cut down enacting your orders. Then, your much loved and ravishing spymaster has been arrested for treason and it seems war is on the horizon. Treachery and danger are hiding around every corner. So, what better way to uncover any lurking foes than by creating a fake assassination plot? One any self-respecting traitor would eagerly jump upon?"

Nestor stood, stepping back and resting his hands on his hips as he entertained Rohm's words. He paced slowly, his thoughts tied in knots.

"But why ask me to go through all the trouble of investigating his own plot?"

Rohm could not help but flash a satisfied grin.

"Perhaps our dear Emperor does not trust you as much as he claims." These words looked to cause Nestor serious hurt as they reached him, his face twisting into a pained scowl. "A bitter truth to swallow, but one I certainly wish I had learned before now," Rohm added.

"I refuse to believe it; The Emperor would not do such a thing," Nestor stated confidently. This drew yet another smile from his imprisoned companion.

"Wishful thinking on your part perhaps, but no, I agree. I respect the man greatly, but such a scheme is beyond him, I fear."

Nestor let out another relieved, albeit slightly aggravated, sigh at the pleasure Rohm was clearly deriving from toying with him.

"So, what do you think? Do you have anything, any inkling as to what I should do next?" Nestor was beginning to sound dangerously close to begging, although he truly did not care. Any preconceived suspicions he may have had about Rohm's involvement in the plot had been dispelled. A man without the strength to wipe his own backside was unlikely to be coordinating an intricate plot to assassinate the Emperor from his prison cell.

Rohm fell to silence once again, shutting his eyes as he considered what he would do in Nestor's position. After a while, during which Nestor momentarily panicked that the old spymaster had kicked the bucket just at the wrong moment, Rohm opened his eyes.

"You're going to need to go back to the beginning." A pained sigh from Nestor accompanied by the dropping of his head to his chest indicating that this was not what he had wished to hear. A map to the signed confession of the traitor would have been preferable. Rohm continued.

"Ask yourself who had the most to gain from all this. Scrutinise everything. Believe nothing and trust no one."

"Not even myself?" Nestor interrupted, hoping this poor attempt at humour would relieve the tension from his shoulders somewhat. But Rohm replied with narrowed eyes.

"What an odd thing to say," he whispered.

"Just trying to be funny," Nestor apologised, sheepishly.

"Oh, is that what that was?" Rohm replied. Sensing the conversation to have turned sour, Nestor decided now would be a good time to leave. He could always return if he had any further questions. It was not as if the disgraced Lord would be going anywhere anytime soon. But as he left, returning his old friend to darkness and isolation once more, he offered some comfort.

"I'll see if I can get you some real food, for your help."

There was no response from the dark cell and Nestor, grateful but over encumbered by his task, returned to the surface.

Chapter 20

It was another miserable winter's night in Tinelia. Ardell sat hunched over her desk, the roaring fire barely keeping the creeping cold at bay. Outside, howling wind and rain battered against the windows, while darkness had arrived many hours earlier. It had been some weeks since Ardell had requested the aid of her old friend, and yet no word had come. Leridon may not have been the most punctual of people, but it was unlike him to ignore her messages entirely. Furthermore, she had learned nothing of the Oracle's fate. After being abducted from Sundered Crown, she had been seen flying towards the Imperium with not a peep nor sighting since.

The exhausted captain let out a sigh as she relocated one stack of papers on her desk, only to be replaced by another, taller stack. She reached for her cup and took a swig before recoiling and choking in disgust. Her tea was stone cold. She rose from her desk, cup in hand, the chair creaking as she did so. While she waited for the kettle to boil, there was a knock on her door. Strange, she wasn't expecting any visitors.

"There's someone here to see you, Captain," came the voice of Chion from behind the door. This gave Ardell some indication at least that it was nobody important that had come to see her. Anyone of relevance would not have bothered with such courtesies and just barged in.

"Who? What do they want?" She called back, not so much intrigued just yet as to be drawn away from her tea making.

"I…I'm not sure, Captain. He just said that he got your letter. He also mentioned something about making my head burst with his mind." There followed a short pause before Chion's squeaky voice came again.

"I'm actually quite scared, Captain."

Ardell pinched the bridge of her nose and smiled at Chion's pathetic, whiny voice.

"Send him in," she called back as she poured two fresh cups of tea and returned to her desk. Although the friendly smile the captain had planned to wear as Leridon entered quickly turned into a mouth agape at his battered and bloody state. He limped in, supported by a rickety wooden crutch under each arm, half his face covered by a stained bandage. Amused by his friend's shock, Leridon smiled.

"Don't get up," he teased. Immediately, Ardell jumped to her feet, helping her old friend into the chair opposite her own which he sank into with a grateful sigh.

"What the hell happened?" Ardell gasped, only now having the gift of speech returned to her, so severe had her shock been. Leridon first reached for the steaming cup of tea which had been prepared for him, the hot liquid warming his bones. Once his insides were sufficiently warmed, he wasted no time in getting straight to the point.

"I suppose you've heard rumours of conflict within the Battlemages?" he asked, steam from the cup rising in front of his face like the smoke of the figurative fires he had spent these last month's fighting. Ardell nodded in response but said nothing.

"More than rumours, I'm afraid," Leridon continued as he leaned back in his chair, letting out a pained grunt as he did so. "No, this is a full-on schism. We've had whole chapters turn traitor. Hundreds are dead, thousands more missing." His words were heavy with pain and regret. Clearly this betrayal had caught the veteran Battlemage unaware, and Ardell knew he would be blaming himself for all the damage caused.

"Is that how you ended up like this?" she asked, folding her arms as she began to include errant Battlemages in her calculations. Leridon nodded solemnly as he drained his cup.

"All these years and I've barely suffered a scratch. Then I turn my back on someone I once called friend for one moment and find myself down a pair of legs and an eye." Ardell grimaced slightly at the thought. Losing a limb was not a death sentence, but the healing process was far from pleasant.

"You didn't have to come all this way. A letter would have sufficed," Ardell scolded. But Leridon disagreed, shaking his head as he reached across the desk, taking Ardell's cup and draining it dry.

"Your letter worried me. You see, it's not just the Oracle of Sundered Crown who's gone missing. As many as seventy prophets and oracles have been reported to have disappeared. And that's just the ones we know about." There was clear stress in Leridon's voice, the kind you get when faced with a puzzle you simply cannot solve, no matter how hard you try.

"You think the Imperium is behind it?" Ardell asked.

"Who else?" Leridon grumbled, rolling his good eye. Ardell let the rudeness slide, the man was still in the process of regrowing half his body after all.

"But why? There was a time the Imperium wanted nothing more than to eradicate anyone with even a hint of divine power about them. Think it might have something to do with what Adeneus was doing?"

Leridon let out a loud huff to vent his frustration at not knowing the answer to Ardell's questions. An increasingly common, frustrating theme which had developed significantly over the last few months.

"I don't know what's going on," Leridon admitted. "I don't know where the prophets are being taken or why. I don't know what the Imperium is planning, I don't even know who I can trust anymore."

"So why are you here?" Ardell asked rather bluntly. As close a friend as Leridon was, she didn't have time for social calls. She had a war to fight. The battered sorcerer looked up, his eyes twinkling with hidden knowledge.

"I have managed to uncover something," he whispered. "Something which cost a great deal to get."

"What is it?" Ardell asked impatiently, returning to her seat and leaning over the desk so the two were nearly face to face.

"The Emperor is travelling into the Great Wastes, with only a few hundred men to guard him," Leridon breathed, as if he could scarcely believe his own words. Ardell pulled back, her face contorted into a disbelieving scowl.

"Why?"

Leridon hesitated, his eyes darting over to the window, expecting to see an unfriendly pair of golden pupils staring back. He licked his lips and his whole body quivered as he unloaded what he knew.

"They say there's a library, hidden deep beneath the frost. Within it, a weapon which will grant The Emperor victory in not just this war, but all others to come."

"Bollocks," Ardell laughed, leaning back in her chair. But the look on her friend's face soon made clear that he was serious. She leaned forward once more, now also adopting a look of grave concern.

"What kind of weapon?" she whispered. Leridon shook his head once again.

"I don't know. But whatever it is, the Emperor deems it important enough that he wishes to claim it personally."

"I see," Ardell sighed. "Well shit, do you know where this library is at least?"

Leridon nodded, his cold hands still clasped around the empty although still warm cup.

"That is why I have come," he admitted. "We know exactly where it is. There is a detachment of Battlemages there as we speak."

"Then why not retrieve the weapon yourselves?" Ardell scowled.

Leridon scratched his forehead in embarrassed discomfort before he spoke.

"We can't find a way in, and the locals refuse to help us."

"Locals?" Ardell repeated.

"There's a village, the people of which have safeguarded the library's existence for millennia. They refuse to aid us, claim the secrets of the library should remain so."

"Interesting," Ardell mused. "Although if the mighty

Battlemages are unable to unlock this library, who's to say the Emperor will have any better luck?"

Leridon raised his good eyebrow.

"Is that a chance you really wish to take?"

Ardell folded her arms and let out a long sigh, shutting her eyes as she thought about how much she would end up regretting her following question.

"What do you need me to do?" She asked at last. As she said this, Leridon's remaining eye shone with excitement.

"We have prepared an ambush for the Emperor once he has attempted to gain access to the library. Help us bring this war to an end, and I promise you and Tinelia a share of whatever secrets may be uncovered."

Ardell could not deny it was a more than tempting offer. She already knew Grand Admiral Lee would almost certainly agree to any plan which may result in the Emperor's death. A superweapon to go along with it would just be a bonus. There was one problem, however. Who could she rely on to ensure the success of such a perilous and yet vital mission? There was only one answer, a fact Leridon had been relying upon from the moment he had formulated his plan. Ardell would have to go herself.

While she did not like the idea of handing over command of her forces to another, especially during wartime, she could not deny that the success of this mission would be more significant than any other battle no matter how decisive.

"I will need to gain permission from the Admiral," she warned, acting as if it was in doubt. Leridon, however, knew as well as Ardell that the Lords would jump at this chance of an early victory. Ignoring this empty threat, Leridon continued revealing the details of his plan.

"I have an airship a few days from the city. It can only accommodate a handful of your men, however, so ensure those you bring with you are your best. They will need to be if they hope to stand a chance against the Chosen."

Ardell nodded in understanding. At last, she thought, a chance for her bodyguards to put all their training to the test.

"I will meet you there in just over a week," he continued. This drew the immediate attention of the captain.

"You're not coming with us?"

"I have some business in the city first, but rest assured I will join you for our departure."

Ardell pursed her lips and shook her head.

"I've read about sorcerers who leave their parties halfway through a quest. It always turns into an absolute clusterfuck. I'd prefer you stayed with us."

Leridon could not help but chuckle softly.

"I've told you to stop reading those books. They're not at all realistic."

"Either way," Ardell scowled, "I want you with us."

Leridon, however, was adamant. In the end, Ardell simply had to agree to his terms and hope he would not be delayed. Raising himself with a pained grunt, the battered mage bowed as low as the crutches would allow. He was truly thankful for Ardell's willingness to help in this endeavour, regardless of how she would personally benefit should they be successful. Before he left, he wrote down instructions on where to find his airship, the crew having apparently been aware of Ardell's arrival before even she.

As her friend stood in the open doorway, preparing to do battle with the narrow staircase, he turned. His eyes drifted across the room until they fixed themselves upon a particular spot, to the space above the fireplace where Oath Breaker lay in torturous slumber. He nodded gently.

"You may want to bring that," he advised with an audible degree of caution. Ardell did not shift her gaze, staring intently at the mage until the door closed behind him. As it did so, she let out a sigh and fell back into her chair. She then allowed herself to gaze at the weapon suspended only a few feet away. She understood the mage's advice but could not help from wondering if such a risk was worth it?

The captain immediately began composing a letter to her commander in chief, articulating the Battlemage's plan. She spared no detail, explaining fully the importance of this supposed hidden library and, more crucially, that the Imperium be stopped from gaining access to it. While Grand Admiral Lee may have a deeply held mistrust for the Battlemages, he trusted Ardell. She knew that if she recommended the course of action which had been proposed to her, he would order it so.

After attaching the letter to her favourite pigeon, she returned to her desk and waited. It would be a few hours before the message was delivered, probably a day before she heard anything back. Therefore, after signing and sorting a few more documents, Ardell reluctantly retired to bed.

*

Ardell found herself alone, surrounded by nothing but a thick, suffocating darkness. The air itself was heavy, difficult to breathe, and burning hot. As she tried to move, to escape this void, she found her limbs to be heavy, as if weighed down by something. With great effort she was still able to walk. Each step requiring the use of her arms, pulling herself through the darkness as if she were swimming. She had no idea where she was going, no idea if she were moving closer to safety or further from it, so she continued on.

She could not keep this struggle up for much longer, the weight of her limbs combined with the hot, grainy air sapping all her strength. She fell onto all fours and immediately felt a familiar sensation. The ground was wet, hot and sticky too. She pulled her hands away in disgust, the overpowering smell of iron following her movements making her gag. In her desperation she began to hyperventilate, although the air became no clearer, and Ardell began to panic as she felt herself suffocating.

Attempting to stand she fell onto all fours once again, desperately trying to control her breathing. But as she did so, a new torment rang out across the vast emptiness - screaming. Pained screams, screams of terror, of betrayal and desperation. They grew louder and louder until they were deafening. Ardell had before long wrapped her arms around her head and curled up upon the ground, caring not as the viscous substance which coated it glued itself to her skin. But no matter how hard she squeezed her hands against her ears, the screams only grew louder.

Suddenly, with no apparent cause, they stopped, and Ardell found herself in silence once again. Shaking, she pulled herself to her knees, sobbing as she wished for nothing more than salvation from this wretched place. But then a new sound filled the heavy air. Not screams but whispers, in a voice which Ardell recognised all too well. At first they were too ethereal for their words to be deciphered, suddenly shifting from one direction to another as if passing through the invisible walls of this reality. Again, they grew louder, but not so that they were deafening, yet inescapable all the same.

"Traitor..." the whispers began, finally clear enough to be understood.

"Betrayer...Deserter..." they continued.

"No," Ardell sobbed, as she once again curled into a ball, pressing her hands over her ears.

"Murderer..." the voice came again, echoing inside her mind.

"Stop!" Ardell screamed, but the voice would not relent.

"Deceiver...Kin slayer...."

Ardell's screams of protest soon devolved into nothing more than animalistic cries of torment as she tried to drown out the noise. It was no use. The voice kept repeating the same words, or variants of them, and all Ardell could do was suffer. After what felt like hours, the whispers faded away, and Ardell was left with a new sensation. She could feel a presence nearby.

She looked up, and breaching the veil of darkness which surrounded her, was a soft, almost heavenly light. Still sobbing, and with barely any strength left, Ardell crawled towards this vision of hope. As she dragged herself forwards, the ground itself seemed adamant on preventing her escape. It became ever stickier, ever stronger in its hold on her, as she groaned and grunted her way forwards. Eventually, Ardell did reach the light, this apparent tear in the fabric of hopelessness in which she found herself. Hovering above her as she lay almost prostrate, was her sword.

Summoning what little energy remained, battling against the ground which did not wish to let her go, Ardell pulled herself to her feet. The weapon remained inanimate, simply floating at eye level ahead of her, the source of this reassuring light. Believing this to be her escape, Ardell reached for the weapon, wrapping her fingers around the hilt. Immediately, the light dimmed, as if Ardell's touch corrupted it in some way, but it did not fade entirely. Then the voice returned.

"Oath Breaker…" it whispered. Suddenly the sword came to life. It's leather bindings wrapping themselves around Ardell's hand, burning as fiercely as a fire as they touched upon her skin. She screamed in agony, trying to release the sword and pull away, but it was too late. Oath Breaker had her in its grip, and it would never let go. The burning leather wrapped around her body like a snake, constricting, crushing her bones as she could do nothing but wail like an infant in its swaddle cloth. Like flaming tendrils, the straps covered Ardell's eyes as she let out one final, agonising cry. As she did so, they dove down her throat, choking and burning the life away from within.

Ardell awoke with a petrified scream, clawing at her face, clutching at her breast as her heart thudded against her ribcage. To her relief, she found herself back in her chambers. Awoken, she was far from the bed, lying upon the floor, her desk overturned. The neat stacks of papers she had spent all day organising scattered like leaves to the wind. This was not her immediate concern however, as she cast her eyes over to where Oath Breaker lay. She stared for a while as her heart drummed in her ears. The blade was still inanimate, posing no immediate threat. Yet still Ardell could hear its faint whisperings in the back of her mind.

One may wonder why she did not just sell the sword, or better yet cast the accursed thing into the sea or the bowels of a blacksmith's furnace. Oath Breaker would not fight back, could do nothing to prevent its own demise. No, it was Ardell alone that permitted for its continued existence. The guilt she felt, a noose around her neck. Oath Breaker, the whip with which she atoned for her sins. After all these countless years she still felt no closer to absolution, no closer to forgiveness. Clearly there was still much suffering yet to be endured before the end.

As Ardell turned her gaze away and picked herself from the floor, she was alerted by a faint cooing. She turned to see a pigeon, the same pigeon she had sent only that evening with details of the Battlemage's plan. Around its leg was a note tied with black and gold ribbon, a reply from the Grand Admiral himself.

Moving steadily, still not yet recovered from her nightmare, the captain approached the pigeon. She gently removed the note and offered the creature some seeds before placing it back in its cage. Not opening the message right away, Ardell first righted her desk before taking a seat. Clutching the tiny note with both hands as she unfurled it, Ardell began to read her latest orders with disbelief.

"Oh, you have got to be fucking kidding me," she sighed, running her hand through her sweat-drenched hair. She thought about writing another note, letting her commander know what she thought of his idiotic plan. It would be of no use. She and Lee were different in many ways, but one trait they shared was their stubbornness. She would have to do this his way, or not at all. Putting the note away in one of her drawers, Ardell considered what to do next. It was still pitch-black outside and she was exhausted. Her eyes stung and her limbs begged to be allowed to drag her to bed, to wrap herself in the soft sheets and rest. She looked once more towards Oath Breaker, her bloodshot eyes squinting as she calculated the risk before deciding against it. Sleep would have to wait another night it seemed.

*

"Any idea what this is about?" Nate asked the rest of the group, all of whom stood perfectly still and silent in Ardell's war room.

"No idea," Joel whispered.

"Not a clue," Kyle replied.

"Shut it, she'll be here any second" Cassandra hissed.

"Maybe we're getting promoted?" Marcus proposed rather optimistically, ignoring Cassandra's warning.

"Pfft, fat chance," Chen scoffed, as she flicked a speck of dirt from her breastplate.

"Must be something important to pull us out of our postings," Jin stated. On that at least, the party could all agree.

As they returned to silence, Nate's eyes wandered about the room. Very little had changed since the start of the war. There were maybe a handful more maps than usual, spread out across the large table in the centre of the room. Upon which, figurines representing armies were placed to visualise their current positions. But otherwise, everything else seemed the same as always. Banners fluttered gently above the quiet group, while the sound of soldiers marching could be heard outside.

It was strange, Nate thought. He had always been told that being summoned to a captain's quarters meant an incoming punishment of the worst kind. And yet he had spent more time in Ardell's chambers than anywhere else in her fort. So much so, that it was here in the war room where he felt more afraid of his captain than ever before. Suddenly, the sound of a slamming door echoed around the fort, causing the gathered group to jump to attention. This was immediately followed by the crunching of armoured boots against stone steps as Ardell descended.

At last, awaited by bated breath, Ardell emerged looking as lovely and terrifying as ever. Dressed in her signature black armour, sword at her side, she approached the gathered soldiers. She wore her hair differently today, collected into a twisted, messy bun. Her eyes seemed to shine, their natural brilliance accentuated by the dark rings that the others assumed were eye shadow rather than the culmination of many sleepless nights.

Clearly the captain had made an effort with her appearance, although the question now remained, why? She stood opposite her guests, sitting on the edge of the table, arms folded, one foot crossed over the other. She said nothing at first, eyeing up the specimens before her. Her expression clearly voicing her otherwise silent dissatisfaction. At last, with the energy to face what was to come, the captain clicked her tongue against the roof of her mouth as she began to explain the reason for this strange gathering.

"Before we begin, I want to make it absolutely clear that what I am about to say does not leave this room. The punishment for disobeying this order will be a painful, drawn-out death. Is that understood?"

The response to this threat was a series of nervous, 'yes Captain's' and nodding heads. Ardell paused for a moment longer, allowing time for the reality of her words to set in before she continued.

"You have been personally selected by the Grand Admiral for what could prove to be the most important mission of the war."

These words were immediately followed by the sharing of excited looks and smiles from some members of the group. While others were less thrilled, their expressions were serious and hard as they waited to hear more.

"Are there any questions before I continue?" Ardell asked. She was not used to asking for the thoughts of her underlings, but she understood that if this mission were to be a success, everyone needed to be on the same page. Naturally, Nate raised his hand.

"Why us, Captain?" he asked.

"Believe me, you weren't my first choice. None of you were," Ardell replied bluntly.

"The Grand Admiral, however, believes this is a perfect

opportunity to boost morale by expanding on the franchise of heroes you all apparently belong to."

Ardell was of course referring to the minor fame the party had accumulated after the discovery of their role in the slaying of Adeneus. While she understood Lee's thinking, she knew ordinary yet still living soldiers were worth far more than dead heroes. Yet this is what the party would likely become. She had wanted to take her own bodyguards but had been refused. Now she would be forced to lead this rabble into the most dangerous few months of their lives. It was almost unthinkable that any would survive. Against the Emperor and his Chosen, even she might struggle.

"So…what's the mission?" Joel asked tentatively. Ardell rose from her seat on the edge of the table, stepping forward so she could see if there was even a glimmer of weakness in the eyes of those before her.

"We're going to kill the Emperor," she said at last, her voice devoid of emotion. There was a sudden gust of quiet expletives as the party released their breaths at this revelation. Those who had previously been filled with excitement were now pale and shaken. Those who had before attempted to be more stoic, were now sweating and shaking at the knees. This definition of their mission was not exactly true, however, and Ardell admitted as much. She made it clear that whatever their actual objective, the conflict with the Emperor would be almost unavoidable and should be their only focus until she said otherwise.

"When do we set off, Captain?" Cassandra asked, she being the only person with even a hint of excitement remaining.

"Tomorrow, first thing. We can't waste any time with this," Ardell replied. Suddenly, Kyle spoke up, his tone quite clearly one of reluctance to partake in this quest.

"I'm sorry, Captain, but I really would prefer not to be involved in this. I'm a healer, not an assassin." Ardell stepped forward so that she was but a few inches from the lanky sorcerer. Her brow was furrowed, her lips curling into a snarl.

Kyle did not step back but retreated his head slightly as the captain got too close for comfort, so that he could feel her warm breath on his face.

"You are whatever the Grand Admiral commands you to be. Do you understand?" she growled.

"Yes, Captain," Kyle trembled. Ardell remained still for a moment, staring intently into the quaking man's eyes before returning to her previous position.

"I will say it again. I did not want any of you on this mission. Frankly, I don't think a single one of you will survive it. But even I must obey orders, and these are ours," Ardell stated with no small amount of frustration. All this honesty was hardly inspiring for her subordinates, occasionally throwing one another worried glances. But this was their fate, it had been decided for them and there was nothing they could do to alter it now. Taming her rising temper at the mere thought of how difficult the next few months would be, Ardell spoke again.

"As soon as you leave here, you are to go straight home and prepare your things for a lengthy expedition. Anything you do not yet possess, go and acquire it now. I shall meet you all at the southwestern gate in three days. Now get out."

The troops all stood to attention before preparing to file out. Before they did so, Marcus asked a question.

"Will we need anything specific, Captain?"

Ardell nodded, a tight grin forming in the corner of her mouth.

"We'll be travelling to the Great Wastes, so a blanket might come in handy."

Chapter 21

"Is it just me, or is everyone else really not looking forward to this?" Nate asked, as he waited with the rest of the group for Ardell to arrive. He was met with a collection of agreeing murmurs as everyone made final adjustments to their gear.

He placed himself between Joel and Chen, both of whom were sorting through their packs. If they had forgotten anything, it was too late to fetch it now. Suddenly, a slab of fresh meat wrapped in cloth was thrust under Nate's nose. He looked to whom the hand holding it belonged and saw Chen, her other hand still rifling through her things.

"No thanks, I'm full," Nate replied. Chen looked up, a look of bewilderment on her face.

"No, you idiot. I want you to freeze it, so it doesn't go off."

"Oh" Nate replied, his face flushing an embarrassed shade of pink. "Sorry, I don't know that spell," he admitted. Chen rolled her eyes.

"Fat lot of use you are. Kyle!" she called, to which the mage obediently shuffled over, still full of resentment at being forced to partake in this mission. A queue soon formed of people holding out their provisions while Kyle froze them with his magic. The party were not taking any chances. The Great Wastes were as unpredictable as they were dangerous, and as a result, almost half of the space in their packs was taken up by food.

"You've got your coat?" Chen directed at Nate, after finally being done reorganising her pack.

"Yes, mum. You watched me pack it, mum," Nate replied sarcastically. But before Chen could reply with a comment of her own, Marcus spoke up.

"What about goggles? Blizzards are a nightmare out there." Nate rolled his eyes.

"Yes, right here, father," he replied, slapping the front of his pack.

"What about…" Joel began before Nate cut him off.

"Sorry Uncle Joel, two overbearing parents are enough."

"We just want to make sure you're safe, sweety," Chen cooed mockingly, pinching Nate's cheek before offering it a quick peck.

"Piss off," he huffed, gently pushing her away as those around him laughed.

"Glad we're all in a good mood," came the sudden voice of Ardell at the group's back. They spun around, greeting their captain by standing to attention before she quickly bid them at ease. Ardell had come, as expected, in her signature armour. Her spider-hilted sword at her side. But this time something was different. Slung across her back, wrapped in cloth, was the unmistakeable shape of another sword. Oath Breaker, it appeared, would be accompanying them.

The captain did not look to be in the best of shape. Her eyes were dark, her shoulders slightly drooped, and there appeared to be streaks running down her cheeks. Having only recently dried, they were still noticeable. Nate could not help but grimace slightly at his captain's appearance.

"You okay, Captain? You look awful."

Ardell rolled her eyes skywards as she moved forwards to the head of the group.

"A lovely morning to you too, Nate."

As Ardell took centre stage, she inspected her soldiers and soon to be companions. Everything seemed to be in order. They all looked well prepared and had seemingly taken the correct precautions for such a dangerous journey. That was until she noticed one member of the group who stuck out from the others. A woman, blonde and beautiful, standing near the back of the group with wide, entranced eyes. However, this was not what made her unique from her companions. What was distinctly different was that her attire seemed to be wholly inappropriate.

The other members of the party had all donned thick leather at the very least. Even Marcus was wearing a set beneath his heavy steel. Thick cloaks or coats also adorned almost every set of shoulders, while others had clearly been packed for later use. This woman, however, despite Ardell's clear warning, was dressed in nothing but bronze and obviously not much of it. She had a breastplate which took its name literally, leaving her belly exposed to the chilly open air. Her arms were covered only up to her elbows by her gauntlets, while her boots only came up to her shins. Perhaps worst of all was the plated bronze belt, which was supposed to protect her groin, but that was all it barely covered while leaving her thighs totally exposed.

Ardell approached the woman curiously, not yet giving away how furious she was. Perhaps, just maybe, there was a reasonable explanation for this. Cassandra stiffened as Ardell approached, both in fear and admiration. Ardell was everything Cassandra aspired to be, epitomising everything it took to be successful as a woman in this world. To be personally addressed by her hero was nothing short of an honour.

"Apologies, my dear, I do not know your name," Ardell lied, rather softly and politely. She knew everything about everyone selected to go with her on this mission and so Cassandra's proclivity for walking around half-naked was well known to her. What Ardell had not expected, was for this apparent urge of Cassandra's to expose herself to every passer-by, to be stronger than the fear she should have reserved for her captain.

"C…Cassandra, Captain," she replied, barely able to hold back her smile.

"Cassandra, lovely," Ardell smiled warmly, sending Cassandra into a buzz.

"Erm…," Ardell began, her tone one of puzzlement as she made a clear point of looking the woman up and down. "There appears to have been some kind of misunderstanding," Ardell added, her voice remaining calm.

"Captain?" Cassandra replied slightly shakily, as she began to realise this was unlikely to be the pleasant chat she had hoped for.

"Yes," Ardell confirmed, taking a step back to appreciate the show Cassandra was clearly putting on. "You see, I distinctly remember advising you all that we would be travelling to the Great Wastes and to take necessary precautions. And yet," Ardell continued, "you appear to have come dressed for an orgy."

A stunned silence quickly overtook the party, not least of all Cassandra, who's jaw dropped at the statement. Ardell came closer so that she was whispering directly into Cassandra's ear.

"You have five minutes to find something else to wear, or I'm assigning you to battlefield corpse removal." Ardell began to walk away but then turned, her lesson not yet finished. "Oh, and you'll be docked ten percent pay for this mission."

"I…" Cassandra began.

"Make it fifteen," Ardell interrupted. With that, Cassandra took off, racing in the direction of anywhere which may be able to properly outfit her.

As the figure of Cassandra shrank into the distance and out of sight, Ardell turned to the rest of the group.

"Gather round everyone," she ordered, which the remainder of the group immediately obeyed. They formed a semi-circle, with Ardell at the front as she laid out further details of their journey. She detailed the exact route they would be taking out of the city, towards where Leridon had claimed his airship would be waiting. This trek would take them close to the scene of the battle at the smuggler's camp the previous year. The same place where Nate made his first kill, a place which still frequented his dreams. They would not pass through it but instead would take a quiet, although not abandoned, road to the northwest.

This road would take them through a small village called Porus. Here they would stay the night before completing their journey the following day. While it was not expected to be either an arduous or dangerous first leg of their journey, Ardell ordered them to be on high alert regardless. She was not so naïve as to think that if their own spies could uncover a secret plan of the enemy, that their enemy was not capable of doing the same.

With almost every horse in the city being requisitioned for use by the army, the party would be making the trip on foot. Wisely, before leaving, Nate had paid a generous sum to have Bob hidden away from the clutches of the military.

"Right then, no point in waiting around, we best be off," Ardell stated, taking steps towards the closed gate before them.

"What about Cassandra, Captain?" Nate asked.

"I'm sure she will catch up with us eventually," the captain replied.

Cassandra did in fact catch up with the party, roughly an hour after they had left the safety of the city. While they had been carefully and quietly traversing the bumpy dirt road, which bore the marks of centuries of similar adventures, she had come barrelling towards them like a bat out of hell. They could hear her heavy footfalls well before she came into view, and Ardell ordered them to stop, hiding at the edge of the forest which surrounded them.

Nobody had expected to be attacked this early, they were still in sight of the towering city walls after all, yet the sound ringing out behind them made it seem like an entire Imperial division was fast approaching. At the sight of Cassandra, now more adequately dressed for the task at hand in thick leather armour, overlaid by her usual bronze, Ardell ordered the party to reveal themselves. After chastising the red and breathless Cassandra further for her carelessness, Ardell ordered her to the front of the group where she would be the first to know of any incoming danger.

The party travelled in a tight formation. Ardell and

Cassandra led the group, while Nate and Chen covered the left flank, with Joel and Jin on the right. At the back, dragging his feet against the dusty road until Ardell threatened to do the same with his head, was the sulking Kyle. Marcus too kept guard at the rear, although spending more time ogling his newly returned shield than watching out for any potential danger. Joel had gone to an awful lot of trouble to retrieve said shield for Marcus. Braving the dangerous trek back to Adeneus' castle, he had found it abandoned, where only corpses remained now. Thankfully though, not the animated kind.

Joel knew the weight of the superstition Marcus placed upon that painted piece of wood. Any soldier who had spent enough time in the field developed their own superstitions in some form or another. Joel remembered one comrade long ago who insisted on circling his tent three times counterclockwise before setting down for the night. The claim had been that it prevented ambushes, and to the soldier's credit, not once had Joel been rudely awoken with a knife in his belly while in his company. A sudden falling tree, however, had proven immune to the ritual's power.

Most superstitions were relatively harmless, simply a way for people to feel more in control of the chaotic world around them. Marcus' beliefs however, verged on the detrimental or even dangerous. Believing oneself to be invincible in any capacity is a foolish delusion, even more so if that invincibility is entirely dependent on an item which could be so easily destroyed, or in this case, lost.

This past year without his beloved shield, Marcus had become a shadow of his former self. He had still been able to complete his Guild entrance exam without it, but his confidence had been shaken to the point of becoming a liability. Now, with his lucky talisman back in his possession, Marcus felt ready to take on the world. Although, admittedly, even with the shield, the challenge before them was not one he was eager to face.

Nate could not help but feel strange to be back on the

road again. It had only been a few weeks since he had travelled north to the battle of Sundered Crown. Yet the dusty road beneath his feet felt alien to him. It did not feel right, thrusting him into action so soon. He felt an itch under his skin, one that warned of imminent danger, that urged him to seek shelter and safety. As much as he would have loved to do just that, he could not. He had to keep his eyes and ears open, for the safety of his friends if nothing else.

As expected, the first day's journey was uneventful. A dog had crossed their path at one point, but that was about it. Unfortunately, Ardell was a very different party leader compared to Marcus. While Marcus had no problem with the company swapping tales and chatting so long as they kept their eyes peeled, Ardell suffered no such nonsense. She demanded they all march in absolute silence, shooting a death stare at Chen when she tripped to the ground with a loud clatter. This naturally left the group feeling tense as they settled down for the night. None of them were used to remaining silent for so long and were relieved when Ardell permitted them to talk once their camp was prepared. As long as they did so quietly.

The party made camp some twenty meters from the road, within an earthy alcove at the bottom of a small hill which descended into a thin valley. They had been unable to find any of the rest stops that were so prevalent on the more travelled roads. Overall, their current location suited them just fine. It offered greater protection from the elements and was hidden from any passing eyes. Nevertheless, Kyle performed his routine of casting an invisibility barrier around the camp just in case. This, however, was not enough to satisfy Ardell. She ordered Nate and Joel to stand guard atop the hill, directly above the camp. The invisibility spell would keep them covered while they surveyed the surrounding area until their shift was over.

With a groan and rumbling stomach, Nate accompanied Joel back up the hill they had just descended. The pair found a nice log they could rest against while maintaining a view of the road and the valley below. Resting his sword beside him, Joel sat upon the damp ground, stretching his legs across the prickly, frozen grass. Nate instead sat upon the log, peering into the valley from which the smell of food soon became noticeable.

"Congratulations, by the way," Joel said, rather randomly. It took a moment for Nate to realise he was in fact talking to him and not descending into hunger-induced madness.

"For what?" he replied, swinging his leg over the log so that he was straddling it.

"Your Guild entrance exam. Sorry I couldn't have been there to see it. Marcus tells me it was quite the feat."

"Thanks," Nate replied, lying back on the log. "Seems a bit of a waste now though," he added.

"The timing admittedly wasn't great," Joel grinned, to which Nate could not help but do the same as he stared up at the sky, already having abandoned his task of keeping watch.

"At least you got to have one little adventure before all this kicked off. From what I hear, you had a great time." Nate could tell from his tone that Joel was insinuating a very similar claim to the one Chen had hurled at him upon his return from Peace Haven.

"It wasn't as fun as you've heard," Nate replied, hoping this would be enough to keep Joel from prying further. Naturally, this only made him more curious.

"Care to elaborate?"

Nate let out a huff, trying to wipe the tiredness from his face with one hand while the other dangled aimlessly.

"Let's just say Cassandra has a tendency to embellish some details while forgetting others."

"I see," Joel replied curiously with a click of his tongue. "So, there's nothing going on between you then?" he asked suddenly. The question had been expected, but Nate was still unprepared when it came and couldn't help but laugh.

"Wouldn't touch her with a bargepole, mate. So please, be my guest."

"Got a thing against gorgeous women?" Joel teased, folding his arms.

"Got a thing against psychopaths," Nate replied coolly.

"If that were true, you wouldn't fancy the pants off the Captain," Joel laughed.

"Touché," Nate replied, unable to keep himself from smiling.

Deciding he wouldn't pry further, Joel returned to his seat and moved the conversation on. For the next hour they shared stories about their own worlds, Nate's being one of seemingly endless fascination for Joel. Nate by contrast, preferred to hear about Joel's many adventures in this world. Whether they be focused on his time spent aiding the peasants during their revolt against the Imperium, or more standard quests revolving around monsters and warlords, Nate did not care. It made more sense for Nate to try and understand as much about this world as he could rather than reminiscing over one he would never see again.

As the two chatted their watch away, the night growing darker until the world beyond the reach of their torch appeared to have been swallowed, there came a noise which caused the pair to halt their merry storytelling. Faint at first, like a whisper on the wind traversing eerily through the darkness, came the unmistakeable striking of chords followed by lyrics of an almost ethereal kind. The way they navigated the dense woodland, dancing over outstretched branches, the trees desperate to capture the melody for themselves having become sick of incessant birdsong. How they struck Nate's ears with such force and clarity that it was as if he were stood before their very source.

The two men turned to one another with uncertain looks upon their faces. Who in their right mind would be travelling the roads this late at night, and making such an obvious show about it no less? It could only be someone touched in the head, completely unaware of the danger their actions posed to themselves. Or someone without need to worry. Someone perhaps, with a much quieter, although more heavily armed group at their backs.

Erring on the side of caution, Nate and Joel dipped behind the log upon which they had sat, its primary function now being to shield these two from whatever may be fast approaching. This was perhaps an unnecessary precaution considering the invisibility barrier Kyle had placed around them, but old habits die hard. Peering over the cracked surface of the log, like sets of twin moons rising over the horizon, Nate and Joel's wide eyes strained against the darkness to locate the source of the still building torrent of music.

Just as Joel was considering carefully slipping down the hill to warn the others of this approaching tuneful doom, a figure at last appeared on the road ahead of him. Lifting each leg much higher than it needed to be, almost goosestepping along the road came a man, stumming what even Nate could recognise to be an Arabian Lute, so unique was its melody.

Even in the midst of night the pair could make out the strange man's vibrant clothing. A bright blue tunic held fast by a bronze belt, across his shoulders and circling his neck, a golden scarf which seemed to capture whatever light may have been lurking with such proficiency that the man seemed to be using it to light his way. The stranger had stopped singing now and was instead strumming his fingers against the strings of his lute and humming loudly.

The two men lurking not twenty meters away stared in amazement at the surreal spectacle presenting itself to them before Nate whispered.

"Idiot's going to get himself eaten."

Immediately as the words passed Nate's lips, the man stopped in his tracks, turning his head with laser like precision in the direction of the two gawking onlookers.

"No way he heard you," Joel gasped, as the men remained in place as if they had grown roots, their fingers which had slid over the edge of their hiding spot like cartoonish villains now gripping tightly into the sharp bark. Without hesitation. As if completely unaware of the dangers lurking in even this tamed part of the world, the man began walking towards them, a spring in his step and a wide smile on his face.

"He can't see us, right?" Nate panicked.

"We're invisible," Joel whispered in response, trying his best to sound confident. It was not that this individual was in any way threatening, rather it was the way he had so easily and unnaturally homed in on their position that filled the pair with fear.

"Good evening, friends," the man called out with a wave of his arm. The shock at being so easily discovered instinctively sent the hiding men diving towards the ground, bundling themselves against one another below the horizon of their previous cover.

"What. The. Fuck." Nate breathed as he reached for his sword. "You said we're invisible!"

"We are invisible," Joel growled back.

"Well, you better tell him that," Nate hissed.

"Evening," the man repeated, rounding the log so he could see the two cowering men more clearly.

"Aah!" both men cried, before jumping to their feet, hands on their swords.

"Who are you, what do you want?" Joel demanded, attempting to sound intimidating. Despite their attempts to at least appear hostile, both men were entirely caught off guard by their guest's appearance now that they could see him more clearly. He was, without a doubt, the most handsome man either of them had ever seen. He had a strong jawline, upon which perfectly symmetrical stubble was growing. His long, auburn hair seemed to flow like water in the night's breeze, while his golden eyes twinkled such to rival the most perfectly cut gemstone. He smiled at their questioning, his teeth dazzlingly white, and instantly both men felt at ease. Momentarily snapping out of the trance he found himself in, Nate tightened his grip on his sword.

"What are you doing out here, on your own, in the middle of the night?" Travelling alone was suspicious enough, but unarmed, as this man seemed to be, was even more so. An amusing situation if Nate had the time to think about it. That he was now so conditioned to be automatically distrustful of anyone not wielding a weapon, rather than the opposite.

"Could be a spy," Joel chimed in, to which the man could not help but laugh. A laugh which, while deep, felt to those who heard it as comforting as the first touch of a weary head upon a cool pillow.

"I may be. However, I would be a poor spy indeed, armed with not so much as a pencil and paper," the man replied. His cheery disposition not even remotely dampened by the two, armed men interrogating him.

Taking no chances, Joel searched the man, who raised his arms in the air gladly, not once letting the smile fall from his face. At first glance, the traveller seemed to have nothing but the clothes on his back and the lute he held aloft while Joel commenced his search. That was, until Joel had the man turn around, spotting a long object wrapped in cloth strapped to his back.

"Ah ha!" Joel exclaimed, taking hold of the object so that he could inspect it. Without warning, in a move so quick neither man captured it, the traveller spun around, wrapping his hand around Joel's wrist. Nate immediately drew his sword. He knew this encounter was too weird not to turn deadly. Surprisingly, the sudden descent into a duel both Nate and Joel expected never came. Instead, the traveller retained his smile, calmly offering an explanation.

"I will gladly show you what I carry. All I ask is that you do not touch it. It is extremely delicate, you see." Joel, filled now with adrenaline, slowly nodded in agreement. Still surprised at the sheer speed and strength of this placid wanderer. Releasing Joel from his grip, who then immediately stepped back while keeping his sword at the ready, the man gently lowered the object from his shoulder.

Carefully placing the object upon the ground, the traveller slowly pulled back the cloth. Nate and Joel stood looking apprehensively, expecting a weapon of some kind. A grand reveal of some dastardly instrument which would spell their doom. Yet were both surprised and amazed with what they finally saw.

Revealed to them at last, was indeed an instrument, a long trumpet of dazzling bronze. In the darkness of the night, the smooth surface seemed to give off its own, golden glow. Even though neither man was particularly interested in music, both were captivated by the beauty of the otherwise plain piece of metal. It bore no markings or decoration, its surface was smooth and unblemished. Yet this seemed to make it even more beautiful in its simplicity. Instantaneously, the world went dark once again as the traveller placed the wrappings back over the trumpet.

"You see," he said, carefully hoisting it back over his shoulders, "nothing to fear here." While this waylaid any expectations of conflict, both Nate and Joel were now thoroughly confused.

"What are you doing out here by yourself, carrying nothing but musical instruments? Aren't you worried about getting torn apart?" Nate asked. The man smiled and shrugged.

"Monsters don't seem to mind me. I leave them alone and they do the same."

Nate and Joel looked at one another, not sure what to make of the strange man before them.

"How did you see us?" Joel asked, suddenly remembering the strange circumstances which had got them into this situation to start with. The beautiful man squinted, as if he now was the confused one.

"I'm sorry, I don't understand the question."

"We were invisible," Nate added. The traveller upturned his hands, shrugging his shoulders.

"Perhaps you need to work on your spells. After all, you were perfectly visible to me."

"Bloody Kyle," Joel grumbled. "Well, you best be off then," Joel said, pointing towards the road with his sword.

"Oh," the man said in a disheartened tone. "I am quite tired now that you mention it, and hungry too."

"Join the club, mate," Joel replied sourly, suspicion and caution returning to his voice.

"Could I perhaps join your camp for a brief moment, just until my feet are warm?" At first, neither man liked the idea, but Nate eventually came around. The traveller had been nothing but polite and shown no indication as to being hostile whatsoever. Plus, he did not want the man's inevitable, gruesome death as he sang aloud in the middle of the night on his conscience.

"He's unarmed, let's just let him warm up and then he can leave," Nate suggested. Joel was less enthusiastic about bringing a stranger, no matter how courteous, into their camp. Especially considering that their mission and whereabouts were supposed to be of the greatest secrecy. Nevertheless, after a few moments of Nate's pestering and the puppy-dog eyes of their guest, Joel agreed to let him join their camp.

"Who the fuck are you!? Who the fuck is this!?" Ardell fumed as Joel, Nate, and another, unknown man entered the camp.

"Captain this is, er…," Nate began before realising he had not asked their guest's name as the three stepped into the light of the campfire.

"Gabriel," the stranger bowed. Ardell was red in the face with fury at this point, shaking with such rage she appeared ready to explode.

"I don't give a damn what your name is, I want you gone. Now!" She turned to the rest of the group. "Pack up your things, we need to leave, now."

This order was met with quiet grumbles and sighs, yet obeyed nonetheless.

"I promise you I am no threat," Gabriel said, stepping forward.

"Oh," Ardell chimed, feigning surprise. "You promise, do you?" She replied snidely. "And you two!" she snarled, turning her attention now to Nate and Joel. "What the hell are you doing? You're supposed to watch for danger, not invite it for bloody tea!"

"He seems harmless enough, Captain," Nate replied, although rather sheepishly.

"He may do, but can the same be said for his friends, who are probably watching us as we speak?" Admittedly, neither Joel nor Nate had considered Gabriel may be part of a larger group, intent on ambushing their own. At that moment, as hostilities towards their guest continued to climb, Gabriel stepped forward once again. Utilising a brief moment in which Ardell's attention was averted, he placed a reassuring hand upon her shoulder, once more reassuring her that he was alone, wanting nothing more than a place to rest.

Everyone watching this scene expected Ardell to react with great, sudden violence towards the stranger who had dared lay a hand upon her. There was a tense moment of silence as Ardell and the stranger's eyes locked. A moment where the air itself was a buzz of electricity awaiting the tiniest spark of anger to ignite it. Instead, Ardell's whole demeanour seemed to change, almost instantly. Her muscles could be seen to relax, and the furious scowl on her face fell away into a neutral expression. Ardell let out a breath, as if suddenly releasing all the tension from her body.

"Ok, fine," she tutted, her tone still one of mild aggravation, but no longer filled with fury. Confused by this sudden change in atmosphere, the rest of the group froze, unsure whether to continue packing away their belongings or not. Their question was quickly answered, as Ardell took a seat beside the fire, Gabriel taking another close by. Marcus looked first at Nate, then at Kyle for an explanation before shrugging his shoulders and returning to where he had been previously.

While Jin and Cassandra took the next watch, this time with the clear instructions not to bring anyone else back with them, Nate and Joel set about making their dinner. The rest of the group were naturally interested in their guest, not least of all for his seemingly inhuman ability to change their captain's mind.

Nate made Gabriel a fresh cup of tea, performing one of

his favourite party tricks by boiling the water with his magic as he handed the cup over. Although, to this day, he had yet to impress anyone but himself by doing so.

"Thank you," Gabriel said gratefully receiving the steaming cup and leaning back against the earthy wall of the alcove.

"So, what is it you do?" Chen asked.

"I'm a messenger," Gabriel replied with a smile that sent Chen's heart into a flutter as he took a sip of his drink.

"A messenger, without pen or paper, carrying only a lute and a trumpet?" Marcus queried, not entirely believing the claim.

"I must admit, you look more like a bard to me," Kyle added. He had become only more suspicious of their guest as time went on. The way he had altered Ardell's mind with just his touch screamed bewitchment, yet there was not so much as a whiff of magic about the strange man. That in itself was strange, as even the most magically inept individual had a certain magical aura that Kyle had been trained to sense. Yet Gabriel seemed to be akin to a black hole. Kyle sensed nothing, as if the man sat in front of him were not there at all. Gabriel flashed the curious sorcerer a smile, almost as if he could sense Kyle's thoughts.

"Ah, well I suppose you could call me that, yes. Although I prefer messenger. After all, what is music if not a message from one heart to another?"

"Gods," Marcus groaned with a roll of his eyes. Marcus enjoyed a good tune as much as the next man. What he couldn't bare were people that took music too seriously, interpreting it as more than what it was.

"Don't be so rude," Chen hissed, slapping Marcus' chest, having already planned in her head the finer details of her wedding to this handsome, wandering stranger.

"I could play you something, if you like?" Gabriel asked, bringing forward his lute. The party all looked at Ardell, certain she would refuse them should the music give away their position. However, to their surprise, she nodded, although making sure to add, "Just keep it down."

Ardell had retreated to near the back of the alcove, resting her hand against her head, as if she were suffering a migraine. Having been given the go-ahead, Gabriel began to strum the lute. After deciding on which song to start with, he began to sing. Immediately the entire camp was entranced. With unmatched skill, Gabriel's fingers would pluck and race across the strings of his instrument, producing melodies which even the greatest of musicians would have struggled to replicate over the course of a lifetime. This alone was a marvel to behold, the quality of the music being beyond compare. Yet even his playing seemed amateurish compared with his voice.

It did not seem to matter the tone or pace of the song which he sang, Gabriel's voice elevated it to new heights. Attaining notes few had heard before, giving such life to the music that his audience could feel it racing through their veins. It was like the first breath of air after a deep dive, the warmth of a lover's embrace, the indescribable exhilaration of victory. None of the songs were of the headbanging, mosh pit inducing variety which Nate had enjoyed in his old life. Nevertheless, he could not help but get swept up in their tune, tapping his palm against his thigh and his foot against the ground when the mood called for it.

The night began to wear on, yet none had begun to feel tired, despite their long journey that day. The music seemingly keeping them fresh and energised, with Gabriel showing no signs of stopping. Finally, Gabriel announced what was to be his last song, much to the disappointment of the crowd. He plucked a single note from his lute, the cry of which seemed to ring out like a warning. It sounded like the blowing of a horn to signal the beginnings of battle. Until now, the tempo of each song had varied wildly and they had all shared a jovial mood. Now though, the song which echoed across the landscape was sad and slow.

With a soft, mournful voice, Gabriel began to sing. A song

so beautiful, yet so sombre in tone and lyric, that it could reduce angels to tears.

It told the tale of a man, poor and dissatisfied with the peasant's life he had been allotted. How he would till the earth and toil away each day, dreaming of riches and adventure, far away from his boring life. The man had a wife, one he mourned to see living in such squalor, knowing in his heart how she deserved all the jewels and fineries the world could offer. So when war came, and the opportunity for plunder looted from foreign lands offered themselves to him, he took up his sword, determined to return with the riches he and his love so deserved for their years of hardship.

The song described the man's long journeys into the far-off lands he had for so long dreamt about. The friends and companions he made along the way, forever bonded by their spilling of blood together in pursuit of their noble cause. With each new verse the man's purse swelled with gold, although at the cost of a friend, until he was at last alone. Eventually the man was tired of seeing new, unfamiliar landscapes which would have once filled him with wonder. Now, they filled him only with a longing for home, to that which he knew and loved. Yet the war carried him onwards, further and further from familiarity.

Eventually, after an unknown number of years had passed, the war ended. And the man, wounded, haunted by the ghosts of the long dead, came home at last. Yet when he finally returned, his purse bulging with gold, he found no home waiting for him. Only the burned-out remnants of a familiar place he could recount only in his dreams. The woman he had left behind, her face now almost forgotten to him, nowhere to be found.

By the time Gabriel's song was finished, few had been able to retain their composure. Even Marcus was repeatedly rubbing his eyes, fidgeting to draw attention away from his screwed-up face. The song had brought home to many the realities of war. So far, they had all been lucky enough to avoid the worst of it. The conflict was still young however, and there would be much more pain to come before it was over.

As the last note from Gabriel's lute was carried away into the night, a tiredness settled upon the camp. Unable to resist its call, one by one the party fell into a deep, restful sleep. Even Ardell found herself enjoying her first good night in who knows how long. Only Gabriel remained lucid, smiling softly as he watched over the slow rising and falling of weary chests. Taking care not to disturb his sleeping friends, Gabriel prepared to leave the camp, knowing no harm would come to them tonight.

As he left, Gabriel could not help but look back one last time at the sleeping bodies. Within this small group lay such great destinies, such magnificent designs. He could only hope they had the stomach to see them through. With that final, pondering thought, the messenger disappeared into the dark. The ghostly tune of his lute like an other-worldly calling as it rose into the night.

Chapter 22

The next morning, the party were not surprised to find that their guest had absconded into the night. It was the fact that he hadn't stolen anything which truly caught them off guard. Nevertheless, after a quick breakfast they set off once again. It would take them the entire day to reach Porus, and that was in optimal conditions. As the snow began to fall and Nate's fingers started to go numb, he could not help but feel that conditions were far from optimal.

If there was one upside to the downturn in the weather, it was that the snow produced a pretty sight. The forest which surrounded them on all sides had always been a source of fear and anxiety. Within its shadowy domain often hiding potential danger, Nate had come to loathe anything more than a handful of trees in close proximity. Now, blanketed in white, the forest seemed almost inviting. The trees seemed to bow as the party marched past, weighed down by the already thick snow on their branches. While the ground too was mostly covered by this thick, cold blanket, there were still some who resisted. The colourful, albeit wilting heads of wildflowers poked out above what to them must have seemed like clouds.

Despite the chillier weather, the party were in high spirits. The good night's rest having done them all wonders. Even Ardell seemed to be in a good mood, permitting the others to speak as they journeyed. Not that there was much to talk about, of course. Their apprehension regarding the mission had formed into an unspoken rule where they would not mention it, even amongst themselves. This left little else but idle chit-chat about the weather, a conversation which was over rather quickly after Jin summed it up well with, "It's too fucking cold!" After all their collective grumbling the day before, the party soon found themselves back marching in self-imposed silence.

Despite trying his best to stay focused, Nate soon became bored staring at the same, unchanging view and decided to annoy Chen for a change. He produced a tiny flame in his palm, no larger than that from a candle. Slowly setting it adrift, like a ship at sea, into the space between himself and his companion. He did not need to worry about the falling snow dousing his flame, nor the occasional freezing gusts of wind which ambushed the party. It was sustained entirely by his own magical energy which, being a prophet, meant an almost unlimited reserve of.

Slowly, the flame crept forwards. Stalking its prey silently, like a cat on the savannah. Before long, and without detection, it had caught up and was ready to pounce. Rather than singeing Chen's hair until she noticed, which Nate admitted would be rather funny, he had another target in mind. Slowly, the magical flame drifted south until it arrived at its target. Barely an inch away from Chen's bottom, the flame did its work.

Being clad in steel and leather only amplified Chen's rapidly increasing discomfort. Assuming it at first to be nothing more than one of those occasional, nevertheless strange and seemingly pointless pains the body sometimes produces, she tried to ignore it. But as the heat lingered, the discomfort grew, so she began to shift her gait in the hope it would alleviate her pain. She wanted to do everything possible to avoid scratching her backside, simply because she knew Nate would notice and make some dim-witted comment.

After a few more seconds and with all her remedies thus far having been for nothing, Chen caved in and reached her hand to her backside, instinctively assuming that touching the problem would solve it. Immediately, she recoiled in shock, her hand having come close enough to the stalking flame to catch a brief bite of intense heat.

She spun around to see the magical annoyance and the

much larger, human one of Nate grinning like an idiot. Both the flame and Nate's grin quickly vanished, as Chen flicked her spear in Nate's direction, catching him between the legs with the blunt, wooden end. Taken completely by surprise, Nate took the full brunt of the hit, collapsing into the snow, groaning like a man on his deathbed.

"Prick," Chen growled, as she continued marching, contemplating to herself whether she should have used the other end of her spear instead. Nate had little time to feel sorry for himself as the familiar sensation of Marcus lifting him from the ground took over.

"You really do ask for these things," Marcus sighed, as he straightened his ward and helped him along, still doubled over.

"It was just a joke," Nate wheezed, sounding very close to being sick.

"Either way, you should probably keep the flirting to a minimum, at least while Ardell's around."

Nate rolled his eyes.

"Why? Think she'll get jealous?"

Marcus didn't even dignify the comment with a response and gently pushed Nate onwards, back into his previous position in the ranks. Ardell had in fact witnessed part of the drama whilst momentarily looking back to check on her squad. She had not seen what had led up to Nate being struck in the testicles, but naturally assumed Chen had a good reason and so said nothing. Perhaps a few more of those and Nate may be somewhere on the way to being tolerable. Sensing the space behind her to have once again been filled, Chen turned around, now walking backwards.

"Do something useful and give me one of those flames," she demanded.

"What?" Nate asked, his face scrunched up into a mixture of both confusion and lingering pain.

"I'm cold," Chen stated, as if the situation really needed explaining. Doing as he was told, Nate produced a flame like the last. This one would follow directly ahead of Chen, allowing her to warm her hands as she walked. This idea quickly caught on and soon everyone had a flame of their own. Kyle produced one for Nate's benefit, thanks to the annoying rule of spells not affecting their caster.

This was the only excitement the party experienced for the next few hours as they continued marching through the ever-heavier snow. Horses would have made the journey much simpler, including even just one wagon for them to dump their heavy packs onto. But as they were forced to go without, the weight of their provisions gradually began to take their toll. Eventually, the party were hunched over, forcing their bodies through the ankle-high snow. Nate had never seen weather decline so rapidly, eventually retrieving his heavy fur coat from his pack.

It weighed about as much as he did. But the difference in temperature as Nate threw it over his shoulders was stark. Those who had not donned their coats already, soon followed Nate's example as the snow continued to grow heavier.

"Well, at least we'll have some experience by the time we get wherever the hell it is we're going," Nate shivered. Chen scoffed at the naivety of the remark, having weathered a few postings to the far north herself.

"Please, this is nothing," she called back without turning her head.

"How much worse could it possibly get?" Nate asked, not sure he wanted his question to be answered. It was Ardell who replied, calling from the front in an amused tone.

"Put it this way, if we can still see that smacked arse you call a face, we haven't arrived yet." This was met by laughter from the rest of the group, although all were nervous about where their mission was taking them, some were simply hiding it better than others. Suddenly, Ardell ordered the group to a halt. She had heard something. The rest of the group instinctively took up a battle stance, preparing to be ambushed at any moment. They scanned the forest for any sign of danger. While the snow was thick and removed many of the darkest and most concealed of hiding spots, there were still plenty of areas it had not yet reached.

After only a few seconds of being motionless on the long, winding road, they began to hear it. Snapping twigs, the soft crunch of snow beneath feet. The crackling of frozen leaves like the deafening snaps of lightning in the otherwise still and silent forest. What soon followed was the sound of steel swords being pulled from their scabbards. Nate drew his own blade while preparing to use his left hand for any spells which may be required.

A thick tension soon rested itself upon the group, nestling amongst the layer of snow on their heads and shoulders. So far, they had seen nothing, but there was no doubt that they were being watched, hunted by something stalking the trees. As the group slowly tightened their formation, until they were back-to-back and facing all directions, something appeared on the road ahead of them.

At first glance, it could easily have been mistaken for a dog, especially at a distance. As the beast drew closer, it became clear it was not something Nate had ever seen before. While it certainly looked very much like a canine, with a long, thin body and a pointed snout. Its skin was pale, an odd yellowish-white concealing some rather unique and deadly defences. What Nate had at first assumed to be white fur, helping to camouflage the creature during the winter months, were in fact thousands upon thousands of overlapping spines. The closest comparison in Nate's world would perhaps have been a porcupine. However, unbeknownst to Nate, each of these creature's spines were filled with a poison which could paralyse and even kill those unlucky enough to come into contact.

The creature snarled as it came closer, stopping only a few meters away from the rigid formation of warriors. It struck at the ground with its front paws, as if it were building up the courage for what would be a suicidal charge. But this creature was not mindless. A beast, yes, but not without intelligence. It was attempting to draw the attention of its prey upon itself, while the rest of its pack, remaining hidden amongst the trees, closed in from the flanks.

Unfortunately for the hungry, slobbering monster, this was no band of helpless refugees. These were trained warriors and monster hunters. If these creatures wanted a meal, they would have to earn it.

"Ugars," Ardell growled. Despite not recognising the creature by sight, Nate immediately understood what to do next by the creature's name alone. Those boring afternoons reading in the Guild library were paying off at last. The party immediately turned their attention to whichever flank they were supposed to be guarding, knowing full well the tactics being employed against them. Sure enough, with some straining of the eyes, the party could see backs of bristling spines slowly shifting towards them, almost invisible in the deep snow.

"Keep tight," Ardell began, ensuring her squad were prepared for the imminent battle. "Don't let them get behind you, and don't touch the spines."

With a commanding bark from the pack leader, the ugars burst from their hiding places, launching themselves into the braced formation. It was times like this where Nate wished he bothered with a shield. However, a quick blast of telekinetic energy, casting two of the creatures back into the forest from whence they came, would also suffice. Chen was less elegant, skewering one of the creatures on the tip of her spear, then using her sword to finish off another which quickly came at her right side. She looked at Nate and gave a breathless smile.

"Well at least one of us is getting paid." In the heat of the moment, Nate had completely forgotten about the bounty for each monster he slew. A rather monumental gaffe when considering he was supposed to be a professional monster slayer. Not to mention that it was his only way out of Purgatory. He quickly remedied this lapse in memory, slicing through another ugar which lunged for his ankles.

The party weren't exactly having a great time, but they were holding together rather well. Their only issue was the seemingly limitless number of creatures which continued to hurl themselves at their rapidly tiring defence. No matter how many they cut down, or in Kyle's case vaporised, more would take their place. A relentless tide of ugars were emerging from the snow-covered undergrowth with snapping teeth and ravenous hunger.

Before long, the party were stood knee deep in ugar corpses. Blood stained the virgin snow around them while the stench of death and sweat filled the air. Even Ardell, who usually revelled in battle and bloodshed, found the affair to be boring and repetitive. There was no challenge in facing an enemy who relied solely on instinct. She therefore did not get her usual pleasure at the tearing of flesh and ending of lives, no matter how expertly she did so.

Without any warning, the balance suddenly shifted. Jin, who had been holding the right flank with Joel, suddenly tensed up. His body went rigid, frozen in place, before toppling to the ground like a felled tree. In his haste to see the battle over, he had left himself exposed and caught no fewer than three ugar spines in the calf. The poison acted immediately, paralysing Jin until he could do nothing but fall to the ground amongst the gnashing teeth and sharp claws of the enemy.

This chink in their armour allowed the ugar to rush into the space between the warriors, biting and scratching at whatever came nearest. Marcus received a vicious mauling as one of the creatures leapt upon his turned back, clawing and biting at his head and neck. Chen too felt the sting of a passing spine against her thigh as it penetrated her leather armour. Luckily, it was not enough to paralyse her whole body and she continued fighting, although now having to drag her left leg behind her.

Realising their formation was on the verge of collapse, Kyle reverted to a spell he hoped would end the battle here and now. There were still near to thirty living ugar assaulting the party, and Kyle knew the spell would be risky, but he had to try. With as much force as he could muster, Kyle slammed his outstretched palm against the frozen ground. The effect was immediate, although it took a few moments for the battered party to notice. The ugar had stopped attacking and were slowly being lifted into the air. Like puppets on strings, the creatures rose until they were at roughly double the height of the party members. Their flailing limbs and confused mix of barks and whines filling the air.

This did not just affect the living ugar either, but the corpses too, floating up as if they had themselves been called to paradise. While the party were now safe from the poisonous spines and sharp teeth, Kyle was bearing the full physical weight of his opponents upon his mind. The already weary sorcerer went red in the face as he struggled to maintain the spell. Once the ground was clear of anything even remotely ugar-like, he concluded the spell. Launching the creatures at great speed in all directions. Their high-pitched shrieks carrying over the treetops as they were hurled to their doom.

With the battle now over, Kyle, along with Marcus and Chen, collapsed to the ground. Nate immediately rushed over to the inanimate sorcerer. despite Marcus remained lying in the deep snow, drenched in his own blood from a deep bite wound to his neck. It pained Nate to leave Marcus where he was, especially considering the state he was in, but his training overcame his emotions. Sorcerers were the most valuable asset of any party, every effort which can be made to keep them alive should be made above all others. Thankfully, the other members of the group also rushed to the aid of their injured comrades.

Pulling Kyle into a sitting position, Nate gave his friend the once over. He didn't seem to have any physical injury, meaning it had been his spell which had caused him to collapse. Placing his palm over Kyle's face, Nate began casting a healing spell. Thankfully, it was not long before the blue glow of his magic receded, and Kyle's eyes flicked open. Upon seeing the face of his rescuer, the sorcerer smiled, patting Nate on the cheek.

"Thanks, chum," he sighed wearily.

"Call me chum again and I'll kill you myself," Nate grinned, releasing Kyle and working his way back to the other injured members of the group. By the time he did so, they were all up and about, as if nothing had happened. Thankfully, the party had brought with them ample stocks of healing potions. Exorbitantly expensive, but clearly worth it. Few parties were lucky enough to have two sorcerers accompanying them, so wearing them both out would be foolish. Even Marcus, still drenched in blood, his hair sticky and congealed, walked about with ease. The puncture wounds having entirely vanished.

Chen and Jin had been trickier. The healing potions had worked, although the effects of the poison would remain a while longer. Thankfully Chen was almost completely back to normal, the only lingering effect being a numbness in her toes. Jin was able to walk unaided, but was slow, his feet dragging, his shoulders drooped as he struggled with the weight of his own body. Ardell remained at the head of the group, peering into the forest, checking for any further danger before turning her attention back to her squad.

She placed her hands on her hips, an uncomfortable look upon her face as she surveyed the blood-soaked ground and her equally bloody comrades.

"We should have done better there," she stated. This criticism was directed at herself just as much as her subordinates. "If it weren't for our sorcerer, we'd probably be dead by now," she added. She let out an annoyed huff before turning back to the road ahead. "Porus isn't too far from here, we should be able to make it if we pick up the pace." The rest of the group looked at Jin with a mixture of doubt. He waved them away, sensing their eyes and Judgment upon him. He had made an uncharacteristic mistake. He would not do so again.

Despite Jin's dragging feet and the party's general exhaustion, they managed to arrive at their destination just as night began to fall. Porus was, just as Nate had come to expect of any small town outside the grandness of the capital, a bit of a shithole. A rotten and overgrown sign welcomed them into the bleakness of the town proper, with no guards in sight. Even though night had only just fallen, the place seemed abandoned. Virtually every house was dark inside, their wooden shutters banging in the wind. The town was still small enough that it had not expanded much further than the side of the main road, with everything being accessible without having to spend hours searching as one would in the capital.

As the group entered the eery stillness, not quite sure what to expect, they heard faint familiar sound. Further down the road, just visible were the dim lanterns of a tavern. The distinctive sound of laughter and general chatter spilling into the frigid night. Releasing a collective sigh of relief, the party dragged themselves towards the noise, like moths to a flame. Piling in through the door, the party were greeted by what seemed to be the entire town. There was not so much as a stool unoccupied, the fire in the centre of the room almost smothered by the volume of drying boots around it.

None of the locals paid their visitors much attention. Before the war it would have been a rare thing to have anyone at all pass through their quiet little corner of Tinelia. Now though, patrols and bands of mercenaries were almost a daily occurrence. Marcus got a few side-eye glances, which was to be expected seeing as he was still red from the shoulders up. But otherwise, the party made for either the bar or whatever space they could find uncontested.

The barman was a broad and stout man. Clearly, he had once obtained a rather impressive physique, his biceps as large as Nate's thighs as he busied himself pouring drinks and wiping mugs. Now, countless years spent eating well and moving little had taken their toll. A large, round belly was permanently squashed against the bar, no matter which way he turned. His hair was thinning too, although he made up for this with an impressively thick and bright orange handlebar moustache. He paid little mind to Nate as he attempted to order a drink. Regulars came first in a town this small, even if it was a captive audience.

This ignorance of his latest patrons was immediately dispelled as he heard a familiar voice. His ears pricked up, his eyes widened and his jaw at first dropped before turning into an awestruck smile.

"Bokear, you fat bastard," laughed Ardell, unable to quite comprehend the ballooned version of a once dear friend. Bokear could barely believe his eyes, feeling his way out of the confinement of the bar, not once taking his eyes away from Ardell. Caring little now for locals whom he had spent decades serving, almost squashing several of them as he pushed his way towards the captain. At last, he faced her, throwing out his arms and pulling her into a tight hug.

The years had not sapped Bokear's strength, and Ardell could still feel the old warrior buried deep within as she returned the embrace. He stank of smoke and stale ale, mouldy dishrags and low-quality tobacco. Nevertheless, it was good to see him again.

"It's so good to see you," Bokear breathed, his voice muffled by Ardell's armour which he had buried his face into, seemingly unphased by what must have been extremely uncomfortable. Despite weighing in at roughly a tonne by Nate's reckoning, Ardell was able to pull the clingy barman away with ease. She shook her head disapprovingly, although did not stop smiling.

"What have you done to yourself?"

Bokear returned a toothy smile, slapping his belly before letting out a hearty laugh.

"Too long spent in good company. I'm afraid my days on the battlefield living off rats are over."

"Your loss," Ardell smirked back. Resting her hand on his shoulder, Ardell introduced Bokear to the rest of her party.

"This is a dear old friend of mine, so I expect you to treat him and his home with respect," she scowled while also maintaining a smile. A skill uniquely befitting Ardell. While the rest of the group nodded, more interested in a soft bed and warm food than their captain's social circle, Chen stood in an awe of her own.

"Wait" she said, everyone's eyes turning to her. "You're not *the* Bokear, are you?" The others save for Ardell looked at her puzzled, ignorant of their own history. "The same Bokear that travelled with the Lady Arda herself, the person who planted the first Tinelian flag on the citadel?"

The rest of the group quickly shifted their gaze back to the overweight barman the moment Chen finished speaking. It was difficult to imagine the man before them climbing his own stairs, let alone being the first man to scale the citadel. The man, who to all intents and purposes, founded their country with his thrusting of their flag into that famous white stone. So, imagine their surprise when the old warrior blushed, bowing slightly in Chen's direction.

"So," Joel began, his tone one of someone piecing together a not so difficult puzzle. "After the Grand Admiral, you're the next in line to rule Tinelia. What the bloody hell are you doing here, you daft git?"

Ardell opened her mouth to chastise her subordinate for the insult, but Bokear beat her to it. He waved his hand in front of his face before resting it on his stomach.

"I gave all that nonsense up a long, long time ago." He swivelled slightly, holding out his arms. "This is the only kingdom I want to rule." In response, several patrons who had been listening in raised their mugs or gave muted cheers. "So, tell me," he continued, turning his attention back to Ardell. "What brings you out here after all this time?" Despite being one of the very, very few people Ardell trusted, she could not risk jeopardising their mission. She gave some story about being on patrol and moved on. Bokear didn't believe for one moment a captain of the realm would be sent on such a simple task, even in peace time, let alone now. But he understood that if Ardell was keeping something from him, it was for his safety as well as her own.

Bokear had no problem moving on and offering his friends, old and new, a place to stay for the night. An offer which was gratefully received. There were plenty of rooms available, so while the others either retreated to bed or sat together to eat their meal, Ardell joined her old friend in his room for a quiet drink. Despite being pitch black outside, it was only around seven o'clock when the party had arrived. This gave them ample time to relax and recuperate before they would have to set off again tomorrow.

Nate called it a night after only a few hours, dragging himself to bed while Joel, Marcus and Jin played a card game he had no hopes of understanding. As he topped the stairs, he caught sight of Cassandra just as she was about to enter her room. She heard him and turned her head, her golden curls bouncing like springs. She gave him a coy smile as she entered her room, maintaining eye contact until the door closed gently. Nate stood there for a while. He knew exactly what Cassandra was doing. Knew exactly what an idiot and pervert she would make him out to be if he came knocking. And yet, despite all his feelings towards her, his lingering anger and even fear, Nate's primitive brain was extremely convincing when it wanted to be.

"No, no, no, absolutely not," he whispered to himself as he practically head-butted the door to his room to rid himself of these unhelpful thoughts.

After a long conversation where the drinks and memories flowed like water, Ardell retreated to her room. She had missed Bokear terribly, letting him know as much as they reminisced about simpler times. Back when all they had to worry about was where their next battle would be, and which girl would warm their beds that night. But those times were gone, the weight of responsibility bearing down upon Ardell like a boulder. A weight which only seemed to grow with each passing day.

Perhaps Bokear had it all figured out, Ardell thought as she slid into a hot bath. No more wars, no monsters or bandits, or evil sorcerers hell-bent on destroying the world. Just a peaceful life. A quiet life surrounded by those they loved. Let other, younger fools do the fighting from now on. Ardell had done enough of it to fill a thousand lifetimes, perhaps it was time she too found some rest.

As she reclined in the hot water, steam rising into the air, dampening the already water-damaged ceiling, a knock came from outside her door.

"I swear if this is Nate," she whispered to herself. "Who is it?" she called.

"Ida, my Lady," a meek female voice called back. Ardell raised her eyebrow.

"I don't know an Ida," she replied.

"I'm Bokear's daughter." There was a pause before the voice came again, somewhat more nervously than before. "He said you might enjoy the company."

At first Ardell was suspicious. Bokear had made no mention of a daughter during their earlier catch-up, such a thing surely deserving of even a brief mention. Nevertheless, Ardell decided to take the risk.

"Enter," she called back rather half-heartedly, sinking further into the water. The door opened, indeed followed by a girl rather than a band of assassins. Locking the door behind her, the girl stood clutching a small bag, her eyes averted from where Ardell lay, her modesty preserved by bubbles alone. Ardell observed the girl for a moment before saying anything. She was not especially beautiful, not like the ladies Ardell had used to frequent before being banned from every brothel in the city. Despite being rather plain, Ida did have some natural beauty which caught Ardell's attention.

Her eyes were a stunning mix of green and orange, which even as she turned away seemed to twinkle like finely cut jewels. Her hair was long and blonde, Ardell's favourite, and even from here she could smell the mix of perfume she knew had been bought for occasions such as this. Mixed with the hot steam and the smell of the soapy water, Ardell could not help but imagine herself in the most luxurious spa. Fresh fruits and aged wines drifting right under her nose.

"What's in the bag?" she sighed contentedly, as she returned from her brief vision.

"Just some oils and lotions, my Lady," Ida replied sheepishly, her gaze still turned away. Ardell smiled, unable to help but find the girl's shyness endearing. Concluding that the girl posed no threat and enticed by the unspoken promises of what was surely to come, Ardell invited Ida closer.

"Well, you best come over here then," she said softly, her tone welcoming, not at all like some of the impatient and vulgar men Ida's father had used her to curry favour with in the past. Ida approached, at last meeting Ardell's gaze who was once again entranced by the girl's eyes. Unable to help herself, Ardell spoke.

"You have the most wonderful eyes I have ever seen," she whispered as Ida neared, kneeling so that she was level with Ardell who remained reclined in the bathtub. The girl blushed, once again turning her head away with embarrassment, she was not used to these kinds of compliments. She would be leered at and catcalled all day, a somewhat unavoidable consequence of being the only waitress in a small town. But the way this new guest addressed her, as battle-scarred and intimidating as she may seem, was with a softness Ida could scarcely remember experiencing before.

Ardell reached out, water and soap dripping from her hand as she held Ida's chin, turning her attention back to her.

"Beautiful," Ardell gasped, as she stared with the longing of a soul lost at sea witnessing an approaching ship.

"Thank you, my Lady," Ida whispered, herself now distracted. She had never been asked to perform these hospitalities on behalf of her father for another woman, and in truth had never stopped long enough to consider if she was even attracted to them. But the way Ardell's tired blue eyes stared back at her, screaming out for companionship, for comfort from whatever miseries lay behind them, compelled Ida to oblige out of a genuine desire to do so.

Concentrating back on the task she had been sent to perform, Ida reached into her bag and retrieved a sponge. She then carefully bathed the beautiful stranger, wiping away the blood and sweat accumulated after a hard day's travel. Her hands were rough from working the menial tasks required in a tavern. Not a quality one would usually look for in the assisted bathing profession. Yet Ardell did not mind it, there was something charming about it. There was an honesty to it, a feeling that nothing was being withheld or hidden as they ran over her shoulders and arms.

"So, tell me," Ardell sighed, thoroughly enjoying this unexpected experience. "Since when did my friend have a daughter? He certainly kept that hidden from me."

Ida smiled sweetly, something which Ardell was becoming a rather large admirer of, as it set off flights of butterflies in her stomach.

"I died about fifteen years ago. Not for the first time," Ida clarified. "Found myself in a temple, in a country I did not recognise. With no way of finding my way home, I wandered from town to town, taking whatever jobs I could. Fishmonger, cook, servant, but nothing ever compelled me to stay. Eventually," she grunted, squeezing the sponge before gently applying it to Ardell's face, where a streak of blood from her earlier adventure was soon removed.

"Eventually I found my way here and…well, it depends on whether it's me or Bokear telling the story," she grinned. "But he just fell in love the moment he saw me." Ardell raised an insinuating eyebrow before Ida laughed her assumptions away. "Not like that," she smiled, gently caressing Ardell's cheek with the sponge. "Said I reminded him of someone from a long time ago. Promised to keep me and look after me. It was the regulars that started calling me his daughter but seems Bokear liked the sound of it. Made it official and everything."

Ardell shook her head in awe.

"In all these years I never had that man down for a softy." Ida giggled, which drew a smile from Ardell.

"You've known him a while then?" Ida asked. Ardell nodded.

"We've been on some adventures together, I'll tell you that much," she said, resting her head back against the bath while Ida's hands, slick with a floral lotion caressed her neck and shoulders. "Does he not talk about his life before this?" she asked, intrigued. Bokear was a man with many accolades and stories to tell. She would be surprised if he had truly kept most of it to himself. Yet Ida shook her head. Screwing her face up slightly, as if wondering momentarily if they were talking about the same Bokear.

"He says he used to be a warrior, but otherwise he never brings up the past. Says some things are best left behind, where they belong."

Ardell nodded, pouting her lips slightly. It was a sentiment she wholeheartedly agreed with. Even if she was totally incapable of doing it herself.

"And what about you?" she asked, changing the subject. "Are you happy here or is there something more waiting for you out there? I can't imagine someone as charming as you wanting to stay cooped up in this dive of a town for long." As she said this, Ardell took gentle hold of Ida's right hand, stroking it slowly, hoping to make her intentions clear in case they had not been so already. Ida blushed, lowering her eyes out of embarrassment.

"You'll laugh," she smiled.

"I would never," Ardell gasped in mock surprise, turning around to face the owner of the hands which were sending shivers up her spine.

Ida sighed, summoning up the courage to disclose her dreams to this stranger. There was a moment of apprehension, fear of ridicule for what was undoubtedly a frivolous aspiration that even in her own mind Ida could not shake. It was best kept a secret, and a secret it would have remained had it not been for the disarming, soft stare of the beautiful stranger.

"I want to be an artist," Ida admitted at last, squeezing her eyes shut to save herself from the shame she would feel at watching Ardell attempt to suppress a laugh. But no laugh came. Admittedly Ardell thought it a stupid dream, a waste of time and energy. But she was not so emotionally inept as to actually say it, she was not Nate after all.

"What kind of artist?" Ardell asked, her tone clearly signalling her interest and desire to know more. Ida immediately picked up on this and a beaming smile burst across her face.

"I like to paint people," she said, her fingers curling over the edge of the bath, giddy with excitement as the women's faces inched closer. "So far, I think I've painted every person in this town twice over. But I want to go to school, to learn how to do it properly."

It was only now, behind the bright smile and sparkling eyes of the girl barely a few inches from her face, that Ardell noticed the portrait hanging on the wall. It was a man, a horrendously fat man with his arms folded and leaning back against the long surface of a bar, a dishrag draped over his shoulder.

If Ardell had been excited at the prospect of intimacy with Bokear's daughter a mere moment ago, she was suddenly less so at the thought of his unblinking stare observing every detail. Ardell's eyes then circled the room, noticing how upon each wall hung a minimum of three portraits similar in style, each worse than the last until they were almost painful to behold.

"You'll be painting royal portraits in no time," she grinned back, with only a hint of sarcasm she could not stop from slipping out. Thankfully, Ida did not notice, resting her chin on her fingers as she imagined her days spent as a renowned artist painting for the rich and powerful.

"I'm sure Bokear would be sad to see you go," Ardell added. But Ida shook her head, eyeing Ardell as one would after discovering a secret they were not meant to know.

"The old fool thinks he's clever. Hiding away some of the profits from the tavern. Thing is, I'm the one who does all the bookkeeping. How he thinks I wouldn't notice, I have no idea."

Ardell was confused at the sudden and seemingly random change in topic before Ida clarified.

"He's already saved up enough to send me to a university in Estrold. I heard from one of the girls in town that he's planning to give it to me once the war is over. Doesn't want me leaving while it's still so dangerous."

Ardell was both fascinated and even slightly emotional to hear of this seemingly new man her old friend had become. A far cry from the gruff, battle hardened one she once knew who cared for nothing but blood and mead. Right now, though, there was only one thing on Ardell's mind, and it was not her old friend.

Doing her due diligence, Ardell conversed at great length about every aspect of art with which she was familiar. Admittedly, this was not much, but it proved enough to whittle away their time until the water within which she lay was stone cold. Ida reached her hand into the water to confirm Ardell's claim for herself. In a calculated move, Ardell gently took the girl's arm and pulled her forward until only the sudden sensation of Ardell's lips against her own prevented her slipping head-first into the icy water.

It was not long after this that the pair found themselves drifting towards the bed, Ardell leading the way as she did with everything. Sometime later the pair found themselves in each other's arms, gently stroking and caressing one another's bare skin, both lost in thought as the sounds of merriment drifted up from the floor below, wondering if perhaps the other patrons had heard their own earlier exclamations of a similar kind.

Suddenly, disrupting the gentle stillness, Ida spoke, cuddling up to Ardell as she did so.

"I do wonder why these men feel the need to start all these wars. Sometimes I think they do it just so other people will be as miserable as them." Ida shuffled again, determined to find that comfiest of spots beneath Ardell's arm. "People should stop being so greedy and learn to appreciate what they have," she smiled, kissing Ardell's exposed side as she finally found her place to nestle for the night.

Ardell could not help but smile sadly at the naivety of such a statement. Spoken by someone with clearly little experience in either love or war. She replied softly, hoping to impart some wisdom of her own.

"You want my opinion?" Ida nodded gently, her cheek brushing against Ardell's side as she looked up into those now seemingly distant eyes which stared unblinking at the ceiling. "It's not greed, or jealousy, not even good old-fashioned hate that drives the worst of us. After all, I've killed enough tyrants, established even more. You'd be surprised how reasonable they can be. You can always offer more gold, more power to keep them on-side. Do you know what nobody can offer, what can't be negotiated away?"

Ida shook her head in silence, feeling the weight of Ardell's words press down upon her until she felt trapped against the soft, scarred skin beneath her head.

"Love," Ardell whispered at last.

"Love?" Ida repeated, somewhat surprised at such a romantic answer from so martial a woman.

"What can you offer he who fights for love? What good is gold compared to a wife's kiss? What comfort is power in an empty bed?" There was an audible lump forming in Ardell's throat and Ida could feel the increasingly heavy thumping of her heart beneath her ear.

"Greed and hate, they will give you evil."

Ardell paused, taking a shaky breath before continuing, her heart now a drum in Ida's ear.

"But only love will give you monsters."

A sadness began to permeate throughout the room the moment Ardell had stopped speaking. A stinging silence that even in her most optimal of positions, left Ida feeling uncomfortable. Not wanting to spend the rest of the night marinating in whatever feelings of regret Ardell was summoning, Ida reached up, gently placing her lips against Ardell's cheek.

"Very poetic, depressing, but poetic," she smiled. "Come," Ida invited, shifting into a sitting position, "let me massage your back." It was late, and Ardell was beginning to feel the call of sleep.

"I don't know, it's getting late," Ardell admitted reluctantly, not wanting this rare moment of happiness to end just yet.

"Oh," Ida's tone now one of disappointment and rejection. Had she just been used, to be cast aside now that she was no longer needed? This was something she had grown accustomed to and was usually grateful for. This time though, it hurt coming from someone who had shown her such genuine tenderness and affection.

Sensing the dejection in her voice, Ardell felt compelled to ease it despite the risks. She looked over to where Oath Breaker lay beneath the nearby window. Wrapped in cloth, it was silent, as it had been all day. This fact combined with the undisturbed rest she had been gifted the night before, convinced Ardell that perhaps Oath Breaker was dormant. Not knowing how much longer she would have to enjoy such a luxury, she decided to embrace it. She turned to face away from Ida, pulling her hair over her shoulder to expose her skin.

"Okay, but don't you dare put your clothes back on."

Chapter 23

Ardell awoke a few hours later to thunderous banging and shouting. So violent were the tremors that at first she believed she may be in the midst of an earthquake. She had been woken from a dream, a particularly frightening one, and for that she was thankful. A dream filled with blood and screaming, of snapping bones and unheeded cries of mercy. A dream she had fought desperately to escape. She reached her hand up to nurse her aching head, all the while the banging and shouting continued. Then she noticed something. Her hands hurt. She was still groggy from her awakening, not yet quite able to understand what was going on.

What had she been doing before she fell asleep? She remembered a bath, the feeling of smooth, silky skin against her own. And… a girl? Ardell's eyes grew wide, her breathing shallow, her heartbeat rapturous in her chest. All the while the banging continued, the door to her room shaking with each new blow. Muffled shouts came from the other side which Ardell could not make out. Ida. Where was Ida?

Ardell did not have to wait long to get her answer. The bright glow of the moonlight streaming in through the window laid bare a scene of carnage. Blood painted the walls of the room. Thick splattering's of crimson decorated every surface, dripping from the bedposts and ceiling. Clinging to the walls like ruby vines laying out a history of savage violence. Beside her lay the body of a woman, shattered and broken. Arms and legs were snapped in horrifically unnatural angles, bones protruding through the skin. Her face was swollen beyond the point of recognition. A deep mix of blues and purples as if she had been stung by a thousand bees.

In her time, Ardell had witnessed horrors beyond what most people could comprehend. Yet the situation she found herself in now filled her with a terror which gripped her very soul. She let out a blood curdling scream, falling from the bed as she desperately clawed at the sheets to get away. Away from the gruesome scene she herself had created.

It was only now, after the event had unfolded. After the tortuous screaming had filled the building. After Ida had suffered so greatly, that the door finally gave way. Coming free from its hinges and frame, slamming to the floor. Bokear and Marcus roared into the room, followed by the rest of Ardell's companions. The sickly silence that overcame each of them was immediate as one and all took in the scene before them.

Bokear approached the bed slowly, his feet like lead. He tried to speak, his lips quivering, his words incomprehensible stammers. His eyes, which had mere hours earlier been filled with indescribable joy to see his friend again, now swam with a pain few had ever shared. He fell to his knees at the bedside, his watery eyes nearly blind to what lay before him. He stretched out his hand but could not bring himself to touch what remained of his daughter. Instead, he floated just centimetres away. He began to sob. Deep, guttural sobs reserved for only the most heart wrenching of grief. The rest of the room was silent, unable to pull their eyes away from the mangled corpse.

As his sobs subsided, Bokear's mood shifted from one of pain to rage. His furious, streaming eyes darted over to where Ardell sat, bundled against the wall, wrapped in the bloody bedsheet. He pulled himself to his feet, moving far quicker than one would expect for a man his size. He charged over to where Ardell sat, wrapping his meaty hands around her throat and squeezing with all his might. His eyes were filled with madness as they stared down into the glassy, guilty blue of Ardell's.

"Not again," he raged through barred teeth, showering Ardell with spit. "Not again!" he screamed, as he summoned whatever remnants of past strength remained.

Ardell could have easily shaken Bokear off, torn him to

ribbons if she had truly wanted to. Yet she did not resist as he attempted to choke the life out of her. She simply sat there as her face turned blue, staring up into eyes drowning in rage. She had been here before. It took three of Ardell's companions to finally break Bokear's stranglehold over their captain. Pulling him free, as Ardell fell limply to the floor gasping for air, he began to roar with fury.

"Out! All of you, get out! I'll kill you all!" he continued to cry, as the party rapidly gathered up their things and ran out of the tavern into the freezing midnight air. As they passed out of the town a wailing curse followed them into the waiting darkness.

"You'll burn in hell!" Bokear cried, "Oath Breaker!" he boomed, before collapsing into a heap of anguish and despair. The journey that night was a long and uncomfortable one, filled with a silence so loud Ardell felt she was being deafened by the thoughts of those trailing behind her. They had stopped only for a moment while the party finished dressing themselves, half of them having fled the scene in only their nightclothes.

"Captain," Nate began.

"Quiet," Ardell snapped immediately.

Nate looked at the others, all of whom wore the same look of concern as they silently debated who would face the task of drawing answers from their blood-spattered leader. They all knew Ardell revelled in violence, yet none could seriously believe she would do something so horrific to someone so innocent.

"Please, Captain," Joel pleaded.

"I said quiet!" Ardell spat back, facing away from her companions as they finished preparing themselves for the long journey ahead.

"Why did you do it?" Chen asked, rather coldly.

Ardell span around, a look of constrained rage upon her face. She breathed heavily as she desperately tried to keep hold of her emotions. Her eyes were red and watery, clear streaks visible down her cheeks.

"It was an accident," she said trying to sound authoritative, yet it came out as broken sobs. None could truly understand how such a horrific crime could be considered an accident. Still, it was clear from their captain's distress that she was telling the truth. The others looked at one another once again, not sure how to respond, wondering if perhaps it would have been better to have said nothing at all.

Ardell turned away, biting her lip so hard that it bled, but necessary to hold back the pain she felt from spewing into the open. There had been a moment, as their captain had spun around, that familiar look of anger upon her, where Cassandra, Marcus, and even Nate had hesitantly placed their hands upon their weapons. Their captain could be terrifying and cruel at times, but, until now, had never made them feel a genuine fear for their lives. They watched on silently as she marched on without them, unsure what emotion to feel.

Leridon's airship was hidden somewhere roughly five hours to the northwest of Porus. There were a multitude of rivers in this area, upon any one of which the ship could be docked. Yet Ardell had been instructed to avoid the rivers entirely. Instead, she was to make her way to an old quarry, abandoned long ago, when the last of its gifts had been ripped from the ground. It was a curious order. As far as she was aware there was no ship which could traverse air, sea, and land. She trusted her friend without question, so pushed the party onwards in the frigid darkness of that winter's night.

As the moon began to shine with an ever-increasing intensity and warmth as the night grew into day, the party were struggling to stay upright. Even the most prudent of their number, those who had headed straight for their soft beds that night, had only managed a few hours' sleep before the sound of agonised screams had ripped them from beneath their sheets. All were exhausted beyond measure, Chen's spear dragging along the ground as she no longer had the energy to support it.

Ardell too was struggling to continue. Her eyes stung from the need for sleep, her usually immaculate posture reduced to a hunch. Just as the party were nearing collapse they came upon their destination. In the growing light of day, they stood upon the edge of the old quarry, its sheer walls plummeting for hundreds of feet below them. As they gathered rather precariously at the edge, they could see the shape of a structure, placed in the very centre of that deep hole in the world.

This structure was in fact the airship they had been searching for. Smaller than those in service with the Tinelian navy, with some rather ingenious modifications. From the base of the ship came four retractable metal legs. Two at the front and two at the back, allowing the ship to land almost anywhere. An invaluable asset for those whose specialty was stealth. Kyle could not help but make a passing comment at the obvious lack of an invisibility barrier. A rather rudimentary and costly mistake for such a supposedly elite force of magic-wielders.

From their vantage point the party could make out a handful of people around the ship. There was a small fire and at least two individuals were sat beside it. The others seemed to be patrolling the area, although with no clear pattern. Clearly these Battlemages were not used to the more basic concepts of security they were now forced to employ.

"Come," Ardell ordered, leading the way to the quarry's only entrance, a long slope which would bring them into the large open space at the bottom where the Battlemages were waiting. Before making the steep descent they were stopped at the quarry's mouth. Emerging from the dense woodland, before the barren stone began, came half a dozen more Battlemages. They held drawn bows, the tips of their arrows glinting menacingly in the still early light. The party threw up their hands in surrender, taken completely unawares. Ardell, however, kept her hands by her sides, an unimpressed eyebrow raised.

Despite being a mere twitch of a finger from an arrow to the eye, Ardell was unphased. The group surrounding them looked more like common bandits than the fearsome sorcerers they had expected.

"Put your weapons down before you hurt yourself," Ardell chastised. "We are here at Leridon's request."

The Battlemages looked at one another unassured. One of their number stepped forward. Pulling a heavy hood back with some theatricality, the Battlemage revealed herself to be a woman. A rarity, even amongst this most rare of secret societies. Her hair was a light auburn, falling freely over her shoulders. Her eyes a deep green, burning with pride as she approached the group currently at her mercy. She spoke with a clear sense of superiority, tilting her head so she was looking down her nose at Ardell.

"Leridon is not yet arrived, you are very early," she said with no small hint of both suspicion and annoyance. Ardell's eye twitched at the comment, her hand unknowingly tightening into a fist.

"We did not wish to be late," she replied, lifting her head from the sullen position it had sunk to. The woman was not convinced. She wanted proof before she would allow these strangers into the camp she had been charged to protect.

"Leridon said you would bring proof," the woman added. This was news to Ardell who was taken aback. Leridon had said nothing about needing to confirm their identities. Surely finding the hidden airship in the middle of fucking nowhere on the day they had agreed should be enough? The female Battlemage smiled thinly, sensing her guest's air of confidence to have faded. "A certain sword?" she added.

Ardell's body immediately tensed. What a foolish gamble Leridon had made, betting that Ardell would bring Oath Breaker with her. And yet, it was a gamble which had paid off. Slowly, and with every fibre of her sane mind warning her against it, she reached for the sword wrapped in cloth across her back. Her own party, which were by now well aware of the danger this cursed sword carried, watched with bated breath as Ardell handed it over. Still wrapped in cloth, she held the blade, the hilt within their interrogators' reach.

As the cocky Battlemage reached out her hand to remove the wrappings, Ardell gave a warning.

"I wouldn't," she stated, her voice devoid of all emotion. The Battlemage sneered with contempt before pulling away the cloth to reveal the weapon beneath. As soon as Oath Breaker was revealed, the sorcerer who had uncovered it found her mind bombarded with its cursed, unhinged rantings. She immediately fell back, clutching her head as she stumbled and fell to the ground. As Oath Breaker's voice grew ever louder in her mind, begging to be released, desperate for the taste of blood upon its metal tongue, the sorcerer cried out in fear.

Immediately believing themselves to be under attack, the remainder of the Battlemages loosed their arrows upon the party from point blank range. Kyle had pre-empted this, knowing full well the Battlemages would not take kindly to whatever effects were unleashed by the captain's insane weapon. He threw up a magical shield which deflected the arrows like twigs thrown against a stone wall. The rest of the party immediately drew their weapons, ready for a fight against foes they were not sure they could defeat. Yet Ardell remained calm, carefully covering Oath Breaker's hilt once more. Immediately the deafening whispers stopped, and the afflicted sorcerer was free from the curse's clutches.

Seeing their comrade slowly but surely returning to normal, the rest of the Battlemages halted. They too did not wish to engage in hand-to-hand combat with which they were unfamiliar. Struggling to her feet, grunting and latching onto the outstretched arm of a comrade, the formerly smug sorcerer stood to face Ardell once again. But this time, with far less hubris. It was difficult to feel superior to anyone after just pissing yourself with fear.

"I warned you," Ardell sighed.

"Come," the Battlemage gasped, "we will await Leridon below." With a collective sigh of relief, both parties joined together in their descent into the quarry. Ardell too was relieved, perhaps even more so than those around her.

Truthfully, she had no way of knowing what Oath Breaker would do once being revealed. Its full range of capabilities not known even to her. Frankly, the Battlemage had got off lucky, even if she did not realise it.

After a quiet and rather awkward descent, where one party pretended they had not just attempted to kill the other, they arrived at the airship. The other Battlemages paid their visitors little attention, more interested in keeping themselves warm by the small fire. Ardell's party joined them, taking up what little room remained. Ardell, however, wanted to speak with the person in charge during Leridon's absence.

She was led onto the airship where she met Leridon's second in command. A man, of course, clearly many millennia old. His advanced age was obvious based on his slow, deliberate movements. A man who had lived so long and seen so much that the rest of the world seemed to be racing ahead of him. This was despite looking no older than anyone else. With sandy-blonde hair and a large, hooked nose, his body mostly wrapped within his cloak. He sat at the captain's desk, slowly moving documents from one tray to another. A routine Ardell knew only too well.

The cabin was dimly lit, with only a few candles situated in the most strategic of areas. There was the lingering smell of smoke in the air, the taste of tobacco on Ardell's tongue as she entered. Off to her right was a large chest, its contents spilling out. Scrolls, potions, salves and alchemical instruments. Everything a group of budding young sorcerers would need on a dangerous venture into the wilds. And yet, so far there had been not so much as an inkling that the company with which she now kept had any knowledge of the arcane at all.

The Battlemages, despite their secretive nature, were unapologetically proud. Keen to show off their magical prowess to anyone who could stand to watch. She had once witnessed one be so lazy as to eat an entire three course meal with telekinesis alone, cutlery evidently being reserved for those little higher than animals on the social ladder. To find not even a whiff of magic about the camp was concerning to say the least. Had she unwittingly walked herself and her group into a trap?

Putting this thought to the back of her mind for now, Ardell wasted no time on pleasantries and immediately began barraging the man before her with questions of an operational nature. Questions which the old Battlemage was at first reluctant to divulge to an outsider. The pulsating aura of magic which surrounded Ardell intrigued him, enough to even reveal what was instructed to be of the upmost secrecy. Secrets to be defended with their lives if necessary.

Nate and the others were just glad to be sitting down once again. His eyes stung so badly he could no longer keep them open. He lay on the cold, perfectly smooth floor of the quarry, enjoying the heat from the fire on his feet. The silence between these two very different groups grew more awkward by the moment. The coldness between them even more fierce and uncomfortable than that of winter itself.

After staring into the flames of their meagre campfire for some time, Kyle was finally unable to contain himself. It was clear that the fire was real, not a magical manifestation. The way it flittered in the wind, weak and dying flames giving it away. Nothing like what he would expect of a member of the most powerful magical group on Gaia. He jumped to his feet, quickly bringing up his hand so that the fire exploded into a towering jet of flame three meters high.

All those around the campfire either rolled or dove for cover from the searing flames and the roar which accompanied it. Quickly bringing it back under control, returning it to a more acceptable size, Kyle called out a warning to his comrades.

"They're imposters!" he cried, instantly raising his hands into a battle stance. The others in his group, recovering from his seemingly random outburst, all jumped to their feet, drawing their weapons and retreating into a tight formation. None knew what had caused Kyle to suddenly reach this conclusion, yet they trusted his judgment and prepared for a fight. Kyle was cursing himself, he should have realised something was wrong when their ambushers chose bows rather than magic. No Battlemage would risk their reputation for something so beneath them as physical combat.

The imposters, their ruse discovered, did not suddenly attack. Instead they cowered at the sight of these clearly skilled warriors threatening to butcher them. Barely a couple of them had the nerve to reach for their weapons. Just as the battle-ready party began to suspect that Kyle may have been jumping to conclusions, a shout came from their rear.

"Oi!" came the furious voice of Ardell, ringing out across the barren landscape. "What the fuck are you doing!?" she cried, as she furiously stomped towards them. Followed closely by the woman who had accosted them earlier, Ardell approached her companions looking less than thrilled. Kyle rushed forward.

"They're imposters, Captain. They can't even do magic!" he gasped. Ardell rolled her eyes before dropping her shoulders. She was too tired for this. Admittedly, she herself had only become privy to the answer to Kyle's concerns mere moments ago, but he didn't need to know that. She was the captain after all, all knowing and all powerful as far as her subordinates were concerned.

"They're being tracked, you idiot. One spell from any of them and the entire Imperial army will know where we are."

"Tracked?" Kyle stammered. "How?"

"Dyad gems," voiced the woman who stood behind Ardell, her voice sheepish, embarrassed even.

"What's one of those?" Joel asked, the first to sheathe his weapon. It was Kyle who answered.

"It's a stone infused with a geo-location spell. When split in two, it points the user in the direction of the other half. But only if magically charged." While this all sounded very logical at first, the question remained. If two stones were required, why were the Battlemages holding onto theirs?

This very question was then posed by Nate who felt he was clearly missing something. Everyone else, including Kyle, had been wondering the same thing. The Battlemage shook her head, smiling slightly at the stupidity of the question.

"We can't get rid of the stones because they're inside us," she stated with clear annoyance at having to spell out the obvious.

"I knew they had something up their arse," Marcus whispered to Jin, who then struggled to contain his laughter.

"Inside you?" Kyle repeated, perplexed. "How did that happen?"

"The traitors crushed the stones into powder, mixed them with our food," came the despondent voice of another Battlemage. "Now, if we cast even the simplest spell, the dyad dust in our blood will tell the traitors exactly where we are."

"Well, that's less than ideal," Chen sighed.

"Then why are we here? What's the point in mages that can't use magic?" Cassandra huffed, annoyed that their tiring journey had been for nothing.

"Enough!" Ardell snarled. "You're here to obey, not to question," she snapped, scanning her subordinates with piercing eyes. "You're to keep quiet and out of trouble until I say otherwise. Is that understood?" she barked, the stress of the last day finally beginning to overwhelm her. She was met with grumbled agreement before she returned to the airship. There was still much planning to be done, much discussion to be had, before their mission could begin. Much of which could not be done without Leridon's presence.

Ardell's companions went back to their awkward sitting around the fireplace in near silence, although Kyle's outburst had ignited some conversation between the two groups. By the time Leridon arrived that afternoon, the parties had developed a somewhat cordial relationship based on mutual respect. Nate and his friends admired the mystique and infamy of the Battlemages, while the Battlemages themselves were impressed by their counterpart's ability to survive using only the most primitive of means. It was hardly the basis for a strong alliance, but it would suit them for now.

Leridon was surprised to find that Ardell had beaten him to their rendezvous, but was glad he would not have to sit around for hours with that boring old fart which was his second in command. He wasted no time, immediately meeting with Ardell to discuss their plan of action before relaying it to the troops later that night. Leridon stood at the edge of the airship, supported still by two crutches. He looked down upon the gathered forces below. Despite his rather ragged state, he still gave off an aura of authority. A sort of reassuring warmth fell over all those who took in his words, a sense that whatever danger was to come, Leridon would lead them out of it triumphant.

A sharp wind descended into the depths of the quarry, harassing those foolish enough to be stood out in the cold. Yet the gathered men and women did not flinch, they latched onto the piercing green stare which watched over them from the ship. The fierce gaze like a ghostly light guiding them through the tempestuous seas of uncertainty and fear.

"We are embarking upon a mission with no great chance of success. In truth, it is unlikely any of us will return once we depart," Leridon boomed over the wind.

"Great start," Nate whispered to Chen.

"Very reassuring," she replied with sigh.

"Hey," Nate whispered once again. "If you die on this mission…, can I have your bed?"

"Piss off," Chen growled, stomping onto Nate's foot with her own.

"Shh," Cassandra hissed at them both as Leridon spoke once more, having given time for the gravity of his words to set in.

"It was recommended to me that you not be informed of our mission. So vital is its secrecy. Yet I believe that should I ask you to lay down your lives, you deserve to know why."

"How thoughtful," Nate whispered once again before Marcus jabbed him in the ribs, signalling this was not the time for jokes.

"The Imperium has found something. A great subterranean library, built by the old gods themselves," Leridon revealed.

"The old gods?" Nate asked.

"Dragons," Chen clarified with a clear hint of both wonder and trepidation in her voice.

"We do not know what secrets lie within this library," Leridon continued. "But whatever it holds, the Emperor himself has seen fit to claim personally."

This was immediately met with a rush of murmurs as this unexpected revelation washed over the crowd. Why would the Emperor travel all that way for a library? Would he bring his Chosen with him? What was their plan? Leridon hushed the now energised crowd with a raised palm before offering further explanation of their task.

"Our initial plan was to ambush the Emperor and kill him once he arrived at the library's location." This sent shockwaves through the crowd. Kill the Emperor? Had Leridon finally gone insane? It had already been attempted once and look how that had turned out.

"However," he called, once more bringing the noise to a halt. "We have since concluded that the contents of the library are too valuable to be left to chance. We will secure it, retrieve whatever it is the Emperor has set out to find, and return it home. Where hopefully, we can use it to bring this war, and the Imperium itself, to an end."

"And what of the Emperor?" called a concerned voice from the crowd, its origin unclear. It was Ardell who stepped forward to answer.

"The Emperor is not our priority. Obtaining the knowledge held within that library is our objective. However, should we be unable to complete our mission undiscovered, you are to show no mercy." The cold, calculated manner in which she had said this clearly meant she thought this to be the most likely outcome. A battle against the Emperor himself, the most powerful individual in the known world. And that was without the legion of Chosen he was bound to have protecting him.

"We depart for the Great Wastes at nightfall. The journey should take no more than a few days, weather permitting," the helmsman added. With that, Leridon returned to his cabin, while the rest of the Battlemages began to whisper amongst themselves. Ardell descended the gangplank to address her comrades who now also huddled together in quiet discussion, separate from the Battlemages.

"How are you all feeling?" she asked, with that most rare of emotions, genuine care.

"I think I may have shit myself at the '*show no mercy*' part," Nate joked, doing a terrible impression of Ardell's gruff tone as she had given that very instruction. Ardell ignored him and looked to someone more able to gauge and represent the overall feelings of the group.

"Marcus?"

All eyes turned to the weary legionnaire as he gave his thoughts.

"I don't know, Captain. There aren't enough of us here to take on the Emperor *and* his Chosen. Seems like suicide to me," he admitted solemnly. Ardell nodded, hoping to offer some reassurances to those under her command, all of whom were visibly shaken by the revelation of their orders.

"There is a detachment of Battlemages preparing the ground for us at the library's location. Don't worry, we will have more than enough firepower to deal with the Chosen should we need it."

"And the Emperor?" Jin asked. In truth, this was the part which gave the party the greatest cause for concern. Ardell ran her tongue over her teeth from behind her lips. Even she was unsure how a confrontation with such a foe would end. She had seen her fair share of God-sent heroes and champions, none of whom had lived up to their legend. But if the Emperor truly was what he claimed, even she could not guarantee their safety.

"Should it come to it, leave the Emperor to me."

What had been a reassuring attempt at downplaying the danger was instead met by an almost contemptuous laugh from Marcus.

"Come on, Captain, you don't really expect to be able to face him?"

The others were admittedly surprised by the bluntness of Marcus' statement, even if they did agree. Ardell scowled and gave her response calmly, yet with the gravitas of a seasoned military veteran.

"I cannot guarantee victory. But should the need arise, I shall face him nonetheless."

With that, she turned and rejoined Leridon in the captain's cabin. The others stood there in silence, processing all they had just heard.

"She's so cool," Nate could not help but chime.

Chapter 24

For nearly three months the Emperor had followed the Forked Rivers towards its source deep into the far north, barely a day from the wild and unknown Borderlands. What had begun as a thick, foreboding woodland flanking his left side, the rushing water securing his right, had slowly given way to empty tundra as the Great Wastes neared. The border was still a few days travel from where they stood now, yet the distinctly fresh chill in the air and the hardness of the ground was unmistakeable. The Great Wastes had a unique taste to them. The air there not having been spoiled by the thousands of years of industry which had come before the Emperor's time.

Even now, nearly a century after the last remnants of those times had fallen silent, the southern air still retained a distinct, acidic taste to those unfamiliar with it. There was still plenty of greenery surrounding the Emperor's cohort as they travelled. Indeed, the ground seemed to be blanketed with strange, colourful, moss-like growths the closer they came to the border. The distinct lack of trees or grass was unsettling, however, for those who had never left the South.

At first the Emperor had enjoyed travelling in his carriage once again. It was not as comfortable or spacious as a ship, but it brought back happy memories of countryside tours before the rebellion. Yet nostalgia could only endure so much, and soon the Emperor became aggravated by the bumpiness of the road. Extended time collecting dust in the royal stables had left the carriage's suspension dangerously worn. So much so that the Emperor swore he could feel every twig they passed over like a jab along his spine.

It had therefore not taken long for the Emperor to abandon his carriage during the day, deciding instead to mount Legacy and travel alongside Phalon at the very front of the column. Phalon had argued against this, citing safety concerns. The Emperor had ignored him, as he had expected he would. In truth, Phalon was glad for the company. At first the pair had reminisced over old glories. Battles won, enemies conquered, riches acquired. Yet these victories now felt hollow as the sound of marching boots and clopping hooves echoed ever louder into the growing emptiness around them.

Neither of these men were foolish enough to believe that peace would have lasted. In truth, neither of them had wanted it to. Yet the circumstances by which it had ended were worse than either of them had ever dared imagine. When tales of times long past had run dry, the pair fell into contemplative silence. Both worried over the days ahead, over the challenges they were yet to face. The Emperor could not help but think of Sarah, where she was, what she was doing at this very moment. He prayed that she was safe. Somewhere quiet and boring, where the spectres of war did not haunt, and she could be at peace until their inevitable reunion.

As the formation passed through a valley, tall, emerald and ruby cliffs covered with thick moss rising above their flanks, they spotted something. In the distance, rising from beyond the valley's narrow exit, came a thin plume of smoke. Not enough to warrant concern, but instead an indication of habitation nearby. Phalon checked his watch.

"Perfect timing," he said to himself. The Emperor nodded in approval.

"You've got the men drilled to perfection," he praised.

"It's what you pay me for," Phalon smiled cheekily in response. He turned his head to face his friend, hoping to share a laugh. Only a cold, unmoving mask met him. The Emperor's gaze completely empty and devoid of joy. Phalon quickly turned away, nodding in the direction of the settlement as it came into view.

"We will set up camp just outside the village. I'll have the mayor or elder, or whatever it is they have out here, brought to you."

"Very good," the Emperor agreed, as the boom of metal boots descended upon the defenceless village.

The mayor was a pleasant enough man, the Emperor thought. Not too filthy and with an acceptable, but not pathetic level of grovelling as he was brought before his monarch. Although, now far from the safety of the Imperial City, the Emperor went under the disguise of a minor Lord, out to patrol the countryside for enemy agitators and spies. This ruse would not have fooled anyone who had ever set eyes upon the Chosen before, their distinct colours and aura of dread which permeated them making it clear that these were no ordinary soldiers. To those far enough away from the capital that it may as well be a myth, who had never seen their own Lord let alone their Emperor, the lie was enough.

Naturally the mayor agreed to provide whatever comforts he could to the hundreds of heavily armed men who had descended, rather unexpectedly, upon his meagre village. In return, the Emperor assured that his men would cause no trouble, and that the villagers would receive a generous sum should they prove to be kind hosts.

That night, sick of being hunched over in his carriage, the Emperor ordered a tent be erected. Placed in the centre of the makeshift camp, it dwarfed those belonging to his Chosen. Here the Emperor could at last relax. Reclining beside the fire, he carefully analysed the pages of an old book given to him by the Arch-Sorceress. She had found it amongst Adeneus' personal collection. A lover of ancient history, he had acquired many rare texts that shed light upon unknown areas of the world. This one in particular had been written barely a millennium after the beginning of the Age of Liberation. As close as one could find to a first-hand account nowadays.

It detailed many aspects about life under dragonic law, none of which were of interest to the Emperor. The intricacies of a long dead society, holding no intrigue, and having little impact upon his own life. What had piqued his curiosity, and indeed that of the Arch-Sorceress, was a short chapter detailing the author's investigation into what he referred to as both '*vaults*' and '*repositories*'. Created by the dragon overlords and used to both store and safeguard their most valued treasures, but also to act as impenetrable refuges should the need arise.

While the author had never actually ventured into any of these vaults, he had visited many, noting their locations, claiming that they could only be opened by those deemed worthy of the contents within. This had not stopped him from theorising what the dragons had been hoarding. Everything from magics deemed impossible or blasphemous by modern circles, to technologies which would allow man to shape the world itself to his liking. All of it fanciful stuff. The kind of thing the universities would include in their course descriptions to attract students, before they ended up sitting in dark rooms trying to interpret the meaning of a single sentence in an old book, like the thousands of students who had come before.

None of this was truly of any help to the Emperor, however. Even the noted locations of other vaults, should this one prove to be a failure, were useless. The Emperor knew for a fact that either most did not exist at all due to their location now being situated at the bottom of the sea or, in one case, inside a mountain which no longer stood. Or they were in parts of the world unknown to science, places the dragons had ruled from afar which could not be found on any modern map. Nevertheless, his eyes were glued to the old, musty pages as he searched for answers. The sounds of merriment outside as his men enjoyed the town's hospitality only acting as taunts as he struggled to find anything meaningful within the countless, rambling words. Gradually, the sounds of laughter grew louder until they were directly outside the Emperor's tent. Suddenly, pulling back the fabric came Phalon, wearing an unimpressed scowl.

"What is it?" the Emperor asked, noticing the mixture of anger and disappointment in his friend's hard eyes and pursed lips. Phalon was silent for a few seconds more, searching for the correct words which did not give away his frustration, not realising his face had already done so from the moment he had entered the tent.

"Some of the men, they've…" he began before falling silent again, huffing at how his own men would embarrass him so. His eyes searching the area, as if they may find the words he sought arranged in the folded fabric of the Emperor's travel clothes lying upon the bed, or in the reflection of the crystal decanter which held no more than a swig of wine. The Emperor found Phalon's uncharacteristic hesitation unnerving, quickly becoming concerned that the Chosen had commit some terrible, inexcusable act in their revelry.

"They've what?" the Emperor asked, closing his book and rising slightly in his chair. At last Phalon surrendered, sighing and letting his shoulders drop slightly, unable to think of how to more tactfully describe the situation.

"They've brought you a gift."

"A gift?" the Emperor replied in a wary tone, wondering why such a thing would cause the captain of his guard, the most capable man he knew, such distress. Phalon wondered if he should have stopped there, simply told his emperor that his men were merely drunken fools and would be punished for the disturbance they had caused. In truth, he knew he should have turned the men away the moment they stumbled their way from the town, giggling amongst themselves at the favour their prize would win them.

Yet he had allowed the situation to progress this far, despite his better Judgment. Why? Was he becoming soft, holding such love for his Chosen that he dared not rebuke them for behaviour not befitting men of their calibre? Or was it, despite the love he held for the late Empress, his unwavering loyalty to his Emperor, for whom he would travel far longer and more dangerous roads than this. That he truly believed that maybe this is what the Emperor needed, this seemingly crude gift which could in fact possibly break the stranglehold of grief which gripped the monarch's heart so tightly. Such stranglehold the depths of which drove him to lengths as seemingly suicidal as march into a desolate wasteland in search of fairytales.

This is exactly what the Chosen, who now wished to present this gift, had thought. There was no malice or insubordination in their actions. They had done this purely out of love for their Emperor. Brought forth from the pain it caused them to see him suffer so greatly each day. Now standing before the Emperor, Phalon began to doubt that the gift would bring them the reaction they had hoped for.

"Well, bring it in," the Emperor ordered, interrupting Phalon's contemplation, thus ending any hope that what came next could be prevented and forgotten. Phalon nodded and returned to the tent's entrance, poking his upper half through the fabric which fluttered in the cold night's wind. He ordered the gift to be brought forwards and he returned to his master. Behind him, followed a woman, her hands clutched together, her head bowed towards the floor.

As the two approached, it did not take long for the Emperor to understand the nature of the gift. He stood to bid his guest welcome, his gaze following her intently as she stood partly hidden by Phalon's frame, her head still bowed. He looked at Phalon and the two spoke without speaking. He understood the Emperor wished him to leave. Although he still as yet did not know whether this gift had been gladly received, he understood he would full well know the outcome in the morning. He bowed low and wished the Emperor a pleasant night, giving the woman only the slightest of unsure glances as he left.

As Phalon returned to his own tent, the Emperor turned away from the woman, walking towards the table which held the almost empty decanter.

"Would you care for a drink?" he asked. The woman did not reply, to which the Emperor turned and upon further examining her clearly scared and nervous fidgeting, poured her a drink anyway. He approached, holding out his hand which held only a half-empty glass of wine. For the first time, the woman looked up, and immediately returned to staring at the floor, shaken by the frightening image of the smooth, featureless black mask staring back. She had no idea who she stood before. The closest she had ever come to nobility heretofore was the knight who collected the town's taxes. And he had not been as remotely terrifying as the huge, imposing figure which towered over her now.

The Emperor was not used to being ignored, and with impatience but not anger, took the woman's hand and curled her fingers around the glass. Even after hours spent by the fire the Emperor's hands remained cold. This was but a taste of what was yet to come for the border, where the temperatures would suddenly plunge as if they had slipped off an icy ravine, was still days away.

"T…Thank you, m'Lord," the woman trembled, her arm rigid as it kept the glass at a safe distance. Overcome with such fear that she dared not drink, should it be some cruel test she had so often heard the nobility played upon the lower classes. The Emperor stood close, watching with curiosity at the woman's behaviour. After a few seconds of silence, interrupted only by the crackling of the fire and the raging wind outside, these two opposing forces battling to be heard over the other, the Emperor spoke.

"Drink," he commanded. His voice was soft, inviting, but it retained the authority necessary for the still petrified woman to understand that she had no choice in the matter. At last she raised the glass to her lips, lifting her eyes in the same moment, eager to see her compliance acknowledged. Eyes which unexpectedly caught the Emperor off-guard. They were a beautiful, dazzling green which captivated him, shimmering with apprehension, as they beheld his own, frozen blue.

Her eyes at that moment, as the light of the fire caught them, reminded him of the palace gardens. Of the grass freshly cut on a hot summer's day, the smell of flowers in bloom, of the hot air which clung to one's skin. He saw and felt it all, as if he were there now, transported through time by some beautiful magic. Then the light would shift, waxing and waning in its ceaseless battle with the wind, those bright green blades becoming a dark forest surrounding the Emperor on all sides, smothering him with the weight of their closeness. What he felt now he had not felt in a long time, and had feared to never feel again. In these brief moments, where only these wide, flourishing eyes seemed to exist, he felt Sarah's presence once again.

Instinctively entranced, he reached out his gloved hand, gently brushing the woman's cheek with his fingers, expanding his view to encompass her whole face. He had given her features little attention until now, expecting just another country girl, differing little from the millions of others scattered about his empire. Yet this one was different, without doubt fairer than any lady he had seen at court. Her hair was like spun gold, soft and silken, as the Emperor ran his hand through it. Her cheeks rosy from the cold, her lips plump and slightly parted, as involuntary aroused breaths escaped while the Emperor delicately stroked her hair.

The woman knew exactly what she had been brought here to do, exactly what was expected of her. Yet as these lightning bolts of pleasure shot down her back and arms at the Emperor's touch, she felt herself freeze. Too often did men rush into the act, unable to suppress their animalistic desires. There was little time to cherish, to savour and explore. It was now her turn to be caught off-guard, not at all expecting such gentleness from a man of such obvious strength. From the way he played with her hair, caressed her soft skin, she could feel how easy it would be for him to overpower her, to leave her utterly helpless and at his mercy. The fact that such displays of strength clearly did not interest this man, excited her even more. Her fearful trepidation, which had only moments before paralysed her, now replaced by a shameful lust.

The Emperor, now locked within this spell, said nothing. He stared intently, caressing with such softness and tenderness this increasingly vivid vision of his wife, growing clearer with each passing second. His heart wept as she smiled at his touch. Her twinkling eyes connected with his own, like binary stars trapped in one another's orbit, brought together by powers beyond their control, beyond understanding. Had he done it? Had he found love once again, near the edge of the world, beyond which lay only misery and death? Then, the Emperor felt something, ripping him from his trance like a newborn pulled from the womb. That safe, loving embrace he had known for what felt like so long, now suddenly replaced with the chill of an uncaring world where love was a prize to be won and lost, not a right guaranteed.

The woman, doing nothing more than playing the part she had been given, returned the Emperor's touch with one of her own. An intimate touch, one which laid bare her intentions with no room for interpretation. What else could she have done with what she knew? She did not know whose hands lay upon her. What tormenting apparitions appeared before the Emperor's lovestruck eyes as his heart reached out with tenderness, eager to be matched. Perhaps if she had, history would have taken an altogether different course. Then again, how long would the spell have lasted? How long before the Emperor looked down to find not his wife, but a stranger, and all that lost agony came flooding back, propelled by fury at her unknown deceit?

The woman smiled suggestively as she caressed the Emperor, yet the smile he had worn behind his mask vanished. At last he descended the pinnacle of his heart's desperate desires with an inevitable crash. The visions melted away entirely until he was left with the truth. The woman who faced him now, her eyes burning with passion, her heart finally unafraid, was not Sarah. Not the wife whom he adored so completely, but a cheap copy. A poor imitation who expressed love like a common whore, an offense to the Empress' very memory. The idea that his Chosen could, in this peasant woman, see even the most remote reflection of his beloved wife filled him with an anger he had never felt before.

He was breathing heavily now, struggling to contain the

hatred rising within him. Pure hatred. This was no mere anger brought on by grief or disappointment at the dissolution of the trance which had kept him captivated until now. This was a personal, directed hate at the woman whose unworthy, adulterous hands lay upon him now. How dare she try to trick him, to sully his marriage, with her shameless guile. Attempting to emulate something so far beyond herself that she ever thought this deceit possible.

The Emperor brought his hands down slightly, taking the smiling woman's face into his hands, directing her gaze at his eyes which seemed to tremor. Then, for the first time for what felt like an age, The Emperor spoke in a whisper as gentle as a lover's breath.

"For so long I have wondered. Wondered what it is that makes you women so different from us men. What innate part of you harbours this seemingly limitless capacity for love which we neither share nor comprehend. How jealous we are, to share the world with creatures which see it in a way we never could."

The Emperor lowered his hands slightly, gently running his fingers around the woman's neck while her sparkling eyes opened and stared back at him, shimmering like the jewels within in a kingly vault.

"So long have I wondered what it was that made you so special in the eyes of God, that he would bless you with such a mastery over the ways of love and gentle kindness. But now, at last, I think I know," he breathed, as knowledge long sought was finally delivered.

"What?" the woman whispered gently in return. "What makes us special?" she asked, her body trembling with aroused excitement as the Emperor's hands continued to gently caress her skin.

"Absolutely nothing."

With these words, the Emperor snapped the woman's neck like a twig, her body collapsing to the floor like a ragdoll. His heart raced, his hands shaking as he stared down at the lifeless corpse beneath him. Upon hearing the familiar thud of a body hitting the floor, the guards stationed outside rushed in. They said nothing as they stared into the lifeless eyes of what had only moments ago been an innocent and seemingly sweet girl. Neither did they say anything as they dragged her body from the tent and rolled it into a ditch barely a mile from the camp.

The following morning the Emperor and his retinue departed the village, thankful for the hospitality they had been shown. True to his word, the Emperor gave the mayor enough gold to see everyone in the village through the next few winters. And all it had cost them was a few barrels of beer and a nameless nobody who would not be missed.

This final stretch of their journey was by far the most uncomfortable, forcing the Emperor to retreat to the relative warmth of his carriage as they passed the border into the Great Wastes. As they left the green and fertile lands of the south, it appeared as if a line had been drawn across the land itself, marking the end of plenty and the beginnings of hardship. Where there had once been bright coloured moss carpeting the ground upon which they walked, there was now only snow and ice. Ahead of them raged a blizzard. Unseen to the eye, its roar over the snowy hills and through the icy valleys was their unmistakeable tumultuous welcome to this new land.

It was just before crossing this threshold that the Emperor and his retinue changed out of their southern winter attire, which even in the most southernly and temperate regions of the Great Wastes would have been considered a death sentence. The Emperor quickly changed out of his more regal and comfortable winter coats and thick trousers made from creatures more suitable to such climates. For the remainder of their stay, as long as it may be, he would wear his divinite armour. Out here the beasts were hardier, their skin tougher, their claws sharper. He would take no chances, not when success seemed so close.

This was the very armour forged by the Lord of Embers as part of their agreement, upon the completion of which, he would be set free from his fiery prison. There was not another set like it anywhere else in the world.

The colour of the sun, the armour shone with the brilliance of the heavens which had proclaimed the Emperor their champion. Its many overlapping protective plates giving the appearance of feathers sprouting from its surface. Across his breast were etched runes, ancient magic which would protect him from all but the most heinous and wretched of dark spells. His head was covered by a great helm, his piercing blue eyes staring out from the otherwise dark slits. Upon this helm's summit was a crest of two wings which pointed skywards, towards the authority for whom this great warrior-king fought. Finally, sprouting from the lower neck came three golden disks which sat behind the helm's crown, each adorned with ancient proverbs and words of divine wisdom. The Emperor stood now in full regalia, looking like an angel descended upon the world to enact divine Judgment.

Even with such protection, the journey across this tundra would be far from simple. Lacking in shadowy forests from which foes could launch an ambush, the deep snowdrifts often hid bottomless ravines which offered no shelter and would prove to be challenging obstacles. Ahead of them lay nothing but a blanket of white. Its unchanging landscape able to easily discombobulate even the most seasoned of adventurers.

That is not to say that the Great Wastes were unpopulated, avoided at all costs for the difficulty by which life clung on here. The truth was in fact, quite the opposite. The Great Wastes housed cities in every way as magnificent as their southern counterparts. Countless villages and townships were scattered around this seemingly inhospitable hellscape, not only surviving but thriving. This land, as bleak as it was, offered that which the south did not - freedom. True, the borders of the southern empires stretched far beyond where the Emperor now stood, only ending many thousands of miles away at the Borderlands where an almost impassible range of mountains and volcanoes stretched from coast to coast.

Yet the grip of the south was weaker here. No levies had been raised amongst the people to fight in the southerners' wars. For many here in the north, they were not even aware they were at war with their western neighbours with whom they traded daily. Even tax collectors rarely made the perilous journey, knowing it would take an army to ensure their cargo's protection over such a great distance. Therefore, the lands north of the border were treated more like colonies by their overlords in their summer palaces many miles away.

As long as they proved beneficial to upkeep, providing rare materials and herbs which could only be found within the icy caves and occasional volcanic springs, these absent kings were content to leave the freezing and barren lands to their own devices. The foolhardy belief that the north could not differ so greatly from the south had cost lives beyond count. It was not enough to simply wrap up warm and hope for good weather, which was rare enough as is.

No, life in the Great Wastes required an entirely different skillset. It required a mind geared for survival at all costs, for ingenuity with only the most basic of tools. It would not be hyperbole to claim that the average southerner would not last more than a few hours should they find themselves lost in this unforgiving and barren landscape.

There were no roads between towns and cities, as the snow fell faster and thicker than it could be cleared. Instead, the locals used skis for fast and efficient transport when travelling individually, making use of sleds drawn by local domesticated wildlife when needing to transport cargo. This wildlife often consisted of two distinct species, popular in areas where the weather was often not as harsh. Locals preferring to utilise a species similar to reindeer.

These northern creatures were much larger, their white coats invisible against the snowy backdrop which surrounded them at all times. Their antlers too were different, beginning as straight shafts before curling into two large rings roughly a meter above their heads. Scholars had long argued the practicality of such seemingly useless defences. That was until they had been observed using them to plough snow, forming dens from the tonnes they so effortlessly shifted.

Despite their size, these creatures, known as Cekey, were extraordinarily light. Where the Emperor and his men struggled on with ever more theatrical grunts, a Cekey could stand with ease without sinking into the cold depths. They did not like to be ridden, however. And only the most skilled of the northern people could ever claim to have ridden one for more than a few minutes before the proud beasts threw them off.

Further north, where the snows and temperatures sank to equally frightening depths, even the Cekey would not venture. This father distant area required an altogether different type of beast to traverse effectively. The far north was so alien, so fanciful to the people of the south, that all manner of rumours and stories had arisen. The main culprits of fanciful tales often being traders who had experienced no more than a moderate sprinkling of snow and who then claimed to have survived the edges of the known world.

In the learned places of the world such as the Imperial University, it was common knowledge that the people of the far north utilised trained bears to haul their cargo. While you would find not so much as a research assistant who could claim to have seen this for themselves, it was only natural that such a perilous land would require an equally dangerous solution. One could only imagine the immense disappointment, including the amount of credibility which would be lost by so called 'experts', should the truth become wildly known. In truth, there were no bears so far north, as even they could not survive the inhospitable temperatures.

One could only imagine the blustering, red faces of renowned professors and academics should you suggest to them that the main mode of transportation was not bears, tamed and subjugated by men equally as wild. Savages who were rumoured themselves to be in possession of magic allowing them to transform into these very same creatures. If any ever dared to venture out from their cozy, warm offices to the frozen edges of their world, they would see for themselves not mighty, hulking beasts with teeth like fence posts and claws like axes but hares. Hares so large that at first glance, in a blizzard, from a distance, at night, one could indeed mistake them for the creatures they were rumoured to be.

Yet these peculiar oddities were of little interest to the Emperor and his men as they trudged with difficulty through the now compact snow, which quickly turned to ice beneath their boots. Their destination was far removed from any city or major town. They were truly heading into the wild, where no help would find them. Despite all their intense preparation, their rigid and meticulous training for this journey, none in the party were truly prepared for what they would face.

Most had expected ambushes. Glorious clashes as the howling wind whipped around them, throwing up cries like it were itself a participant in the melee. Virgin snow, red from a gluttonous appetite for spilled blood, the ringing of steel echoing unobstructed for miles across the empty land. Yet there was not a soul to be found as they held their hands aloft, shielding their eyes from the snow which bit any piece of exposed flesh like the tiny stingers of countless, ravenous insects.

Those too who had looked forward to testing their mettle against the nightmarish creatures rumoured to stalk these forsaken lands came away disappointed. The only enemy they had faced so far was the very world itself, which was determined to make these men into warnings to all those foolish enough to dare cross the northern border. And if you had asked any one of this unfortunate company, even the most stoic and proud amongst them, none would have wished for any greater challenge than they faced now.

There is no place for ego when one's flask is frozen solid for days on end, where even the warmth of a fire cannot force the surrender of more than a few drops of water from ice so cold it hurts one's insides to drink it. When each mile travelled seemed no different from the last, with no indication you were any closer to your destination than when you had set off. All the while the wind screeched in your ears as it raced over the snowy hills, deafening you from the words bellowed by the man stood beside you. The snow came down in an endless avalanche from the heavens, so you could not see your own feet when you looked down to ensure you had not strayed from the path. And when night came, the torches of one thousand men could not have pierced the total blackness which engulfed them. The darkness so absolute that even sound seemed to be greedily gobbled up as soon as it left the tongue.

It was under these conditions that the Emperor and his men travelled for weeks, making camp wherever they could. Their rows of off-white tents slowly dwindling in number as more men fell victim to the elements with each passing day. What a fool he was, the Emperor thought to himself as he shivered in his tent, every spare piece of fabric wrapped tightly around him. He should have listened to his advisors. He should have come by airship once the area had been cleared. Now here he sat at serious risk of becoming a permanent feature of this accursed land. His heart bled for his men too. Men who had trained for centuries in some cases, brought down not with honour by the blade of the enemy but by the unforgiving elements which cared nothing for their honour or mission.

The royal carriage had long been abandoned after slipping into a ditch from which it could not be recovered. It would not have mattered regardless, as there were no longer any horses left to pull it. All having succumbed to the elements well before any of his own men. Only Legacy had survived, and the Emperor was doing all he could to ensure this remained so. Even should it mean his own men suffered the cold more acutely as every spare blanket was piled onto the animal to keep him warm.

More than once, Phalon had suggested turning back, returning to the Imperial City where they could travel by airship and recoup their losses. Yet the Emperor, unretractable from his goal, was stubborn, determined to press on despite the risks. With each passing day, each weary footstep, he could feel the library getting closer. He could feel Sarah's presence growing like the heat of a fire, reinvigorating him with the will to continue.

After more days of hardship, more days of suffering the biting cold and the now familiar pangs of hunger as their rations slowly dwindled, they came upon their destination. Rising from the horizon had come a thin trail of smoke. So used to the dazzling, uniform whiteness which had surrounded them for so long, the Chosen had almost forgotten of the existence of other colours. To see this, weak, grey trail of smoke rising skywards as the exhausted and frozen party watched on with mouths agape, one would have thought they had witnessed a miracle. Filled with a renewed drive, their stiff and frostbitten bodies summoned new energy, seemingly from faith alone. They pushed on at their fastest pace in days, desperate to have their resolve rewarded at last.

As the Emperor and his men scrambled over the final hilltop, which hid the source of their excitement, their faces lit up with jubilation. Below was a village. So tiny and insignificant that, had they been in the Imperium, it was unlikely it would have been included on a map. Yet for the exhausted men who stared down at it now, it was as if they had stumbled upon a palace from their dreams. Despite the barely contained joy of his men, Phalon remained composed. Forever a soldier, not even allowing himself to enjoy this one moment after overcoming such difficulties to get here.

He ordered his remaining men into three columns. With himself leading and the Emperor at his side, they would march into the village and make themselves known. If they were lucky, they would find the people to be cooperative. If not, well, a compromise would be reached one way or another. As the Chosen descended in formation towards the tiny settlement, the people, far more than would have been expected in a place so small, came out to meet them.

The locals were all dressed in a similar mix of dark greys and browns. Their thick coats and cloaks stacked upon their shoulders until they looked to be twice their actual size. All wore masks too, although not of the extravagant type like the Emperor's. These simple masks were made of cloth, wrapped tightly around their heads to protect their faces from the ever-present cold.

As expected, the villagers seemed surprised to see the sudden arrival of so many armed men at their village in the middle of nowhere. They gathered in the main square, where a fire was kept lit day and night, a final refuge should anyone need it, friend or stranger. As the Chosen moved into the square, they suddenly halted, their boots stomping to a halt which echoed in the morning air.

Phalon approached the gathered village people. The Emperor remained a few steps behind, seated atop Legacy, as he surveyed the crowd in silence. After Phalon had declared their mission to the people, he humbly requested aid in their endeavour. Promising riches in return, he asked that all able-bodied men support them in any labour that was required, while also asking for anyone with information on the hidden library to come forward.

There were uncertain murmurs from the crowd as they quietly discussed amongst themselves the implications of their guests' arrival. Finally, a man stepped forward. At least he was assumed to be a man. His whole body was covered head to toe in thick fur and leather making whatever lay beneath impossible to distinguish. Only his eyes were visible, a bright green which stood out against the bleak backdrop of grey, churned up snow and dull wooden houses. Aided by a crutch, he approached not Phalon, but the Emperor, who looked upon him with curiosity, his head held high.

"It is an honour to serve you, my Lord," the man began, bowing as low as his clearly painful leg would allow. Raising himself up, clutching onto his crutch for support, he continued. "I am afraid that the library is locked. Has been for longer than anyone can remember. Yet I swear we will do all we can to aid you. All I ask is that your men remain clear of the site. It is a holy place after all, and we would not want it spoiled by having an army stationed upon it." The man's eyes darted over to the columns of gathered Chosen, filled with mistrust, his hand tightening around his crutch.

The Emperor shifted in his saddle, leaning forward so he may address the man respectfully, as he had been.

"I appreciate you and your people's aid in this matter, friend. You may rest assured that my men and I will cause no trouble here, you have my word. Although I must insist, they always remain by my side, for my own protection." The man said nothing, bowing once more to show his understanding before slowly backing away. The Emperor called upon him once again, stopping him in his tracks. "And what do they call you? I would know the names of my friends. Especially those who showed such willing selflessness to support me on my holy quest."

The man looked up into The Emperor's bright, blue eyes. Eyes like ice, which seemed to freeze the very blood in his veins, piercing his thick coat more than any harsh winter wind.

"Leridon, my Lord," he replied.

Chapter 25

"Fucking hell, it's cold!" Nate shouted over the deafening rush of wind which accompanied their rapid journey through the air. He attempted to pull his coat around himself but found it would go no tighter. Chen ignored his insightful comment as she leaned over the side of the ship, hoping to catch a glimpse of the world below. For hours the view ahead of them had been nothing but a blinding blizzard, each snowflake the size of a fat bee, whizzing past them at great speed. Although the view below was no better, just an endless expanse of white, impossible to differentiate between the ground and the maelstrom which engulfed them.

"Let's go inside!" Chen cried, although her words were instantly whipped away, much like her hair which seemed adamant to detach itself from her head and set off on its own adventure. Nate shook his head, unable to hear a word his companion was saying.

"I think we should go inside!" he called back, his arms wrapped so tightly around his waist that even the gentlest of course corrections by the helmsman nearly sent him flying. Above them, the rotor blades which carried them forwards at such great speed were shaking and rattling unsettlingly. Nature, it seemed, was not impressed by their intrusion into her domain, and was doing all in her power to cast them from the sky. Each new gust of wind hit the ship like a cannonball. The whole structure would shake, and those within the confines of the hull were forced to hold onto whatever they could to avoid being tossed about.

Within they found the rest of the crew. Battlemage and soldier alike, huddled together around a magical flame suspended in midair.

"Oh, thank the gods," Kyle huffed, his breath a plume of icy cloud which raced ahead of him. "Your turn," he directed at Nate. Immediately understanding what Kyle had meant, Nate produced his own magical flame from which Kyle could at last leech some heat.

"How much longer?" Cassandra shivered, beyond thankful for Ardell's prior insistence she acquire more suitable clothing before setting off.

"Just a few more hours, if we're lucky," Ardell replied.

"Ah yes, lucky, that's us," Nate replied sarcastically. Although, from the collection of frowns and grimaces thrown his way, his attempt at humour had clearly not been appreciated.

"Can you stop trying to be the comedy relief for five minutes?" Chen grumbled, snuggling up as close as she could to Ardell, determined to steal some of her body heat. Usually, Ardell would have at least offered some resistance, either verbal or physical to such a violation of her personal space. Yet the circumstances were extreme enough that she would allow it. Besides, she was hardly repulsed by the idea of an attractive young woman in such proximity. She lifted her long, thick cloak which had been tightly pressed against her body, offering Chen a place beneath.

After a brief moment of hesitation as she tried to deduce her captain's motive, Chen quickly found herself in the crook of Ardell's arm, the cloak wrapped snugly around them. Ardell could not help but catch Nate's eye, offering him a smirk. He quickly turned his gaze away. Instead, Nate turned to Kyle, deciding he would brush up on some of the spells that they had been practicing before this whole mess kicked off.

Ardell was, as usual, correct in her prediction. The half-frozen party had arrived at their destination roughly three hours later. Emerging from the bleak belly of the airship, hands were quickly thrown upwards to shield unprepared eyes. The blizzard had subsided, and now the sun shone brilliantly upon a calm and picturesque landscape. The reflection from the snow being so bright that most walked with their heads facing the floor, trusting others to lead them.

Only a few hundred meters away from the landing site was a village, the dark brown of its buildings stark against the snowy backdrop. From the centre, a thin trail of smoke rose, a welcome sight for those who had spent so long in the cold. As the ship was slowly emptied, like hibernating creatures emerging from their burrows to face the spring, Leridon addressed them.

"The village before you is under our control, so do not fear having to keep your identities secret. We have a few days before the Emperor is supposed to arrive. In that time, we shall prepare our defences and await their coming."

"What of the library?" Ardell asked. Leridon nodded, speaking only to her.

"I shall take you there soon. We already have some of our best minds working on a way to open it. If we're lucky, we may not need to wait for the Emperor at all." There was that word again, *lucky*. As much as she hated Nate's inability to take anything seriously, Ardell could not help but dwell on his comment. Luck did indeed seem to be noticeably absent from their arsenal as of late. While Ardell pondered, Leridon turned back to the gathered crowd.

"Make sure you have all your provisions and then make your way to the village," he ordered. "The airship will be departing and will not be returning." This revelation surprised the party, not least of all Ardell who scowled at her old friend.

"And how are we supposed to get back, to escape if we are discovered?" she queried. Knowing how often schemes which relied so heavily on the element of surprise failed, she would have expected a robust and expedient getaway plan. Leridon returned a scowl of his own, surprised he was needing to explain something so basic to someone with the reputation of a tactical genius.

"Come on, an airship isn't the kind of thing a village like this would have just lying around. It's best we do all we can to look the part."

"Even if that means being captured, brutally tortured and executed?" Ardell demanded crossing her arms, clearly not convinced. Leridon did not try to argue, simply waving his hand, clearly stating that the matter was settled. Ardell could argue all she wanted, it would not change anything. By now Ardell and Leridon were the last ones off the ship, having gathered their belongings and were now walking a dozen or so paces behind the rest of the group.

Already Ardell was nervous. The Emperor was days away and there seemed to be so many holes in this plan which had sounded so foolproof in her quarters. She analysed her surroundings, looking for something that they could use to their advantage over the Emperor and his Chosen. The surrounding terrain bore nothing of value. Only deep, flat snow and hills could be seen, which became one with the horizon due to their fluffy camouflage.

Quickly abandoning the idea of a pitched battle, she briefly considered guerilla tactics. With so many sorcerers in their ranks, they should easily be able to disappear and reappear in the enemy flanks and rear. Promptly she abandoned this plan too. While it was the most promising of the two, they had no time for a prolonged campaign waged in the shadows. With no shelter for hundreds of miles and the traitorous Battlemages knowing their location the moment they cast their first spell, they may enjoy some initial successes. But exposure and the arrival of a battalion of sorcerers would quickly turn the tide against them.

Then, of course, there were the villagers. She had been told there were roughly one hundred people whose sacred duty was to keep safe the library. All it would take is one of them to let slip, either intentionally or by accident, what was going on. The ambushers would be dead before they even had a chance to fight back. Currently, this was the most pressing and difficult obstacle to overcome. Hoping her allies had thought of a way around this, she sought reassurance from her friend who limped on through the snow.

During the journey, Leridon's eye had at last healed, allowing him to see clearly once more and do away with the bandage covering half of his face. Once again his emerald eyes shone with vigour, with determination to see the mission through and bring an end to the Imperium's evil once and for all. When Ardell inquired about the villagers, the light in his eyes faded, as if passing behind clouded thoughts which had travelled from his guilty conscience to the surface.

"Don't worry about the villagers," he grunted. But Ardell could simply not let go of the thought of the easy with which their plan could come undone.

"But what if they talk? What have you done? Bribed them, bewitched them?" she asked, her incessant questioning boring into Leridon's temple like a parasite.

"There are no villagers!" he hissed, quickly spinning around to face the torrent of questions being spewed at him. Ardell froze, looking into her old friend's quivering eyes but saying nothing. "It was abandoned when we got here," Leridon added, before turning back to continue towards the village. A hand shot out, taking him roughly by the forearm, dragging him backwards until he was facing Ardell once more, only inches away from her face.

"What have you done?" she whispered, her voice somewhere between fury and disbelief. Unable to fathom what she believed Leridon was alluding to. The Battlemage said nothing, unable to break free from Ardell's grip. He stared into her eyes in total silence. Under her gorgon-like stare, he broke. Casting his gaze away he admitted to his part in the atrocity.

"We had no choice. The risk was too great. It was the only way," he said wracked with guilt, his voice breaking. Ardell immediately released him upon hearing this dreaded admission escape his lips. Leridon stumbled, falling back into the snow while Ardell made no effort to help him. Her face was twisted into such a mix of anger and betrayal that she would have looked more at home amongst a company of gargoyles.

She approached her former friend, still on his backside, the snow quickly melting and seeping through his many layers. He extended his hand, expecting aid, but was offered none. Instead, Ardell took him roughly by the back of the neck, pushing his gaze downwards which produced a pained gasp from the sorcerer. Ardell came close, the side of her face only centimetres away from his own, her eyes fixed on the gradually shrinking group ahead of them.

"Once we are done here, you can consider this partnership at an end." Ardell thought about leaving it at that, but the barely contained anger within her demanded more. "And if you ever set foot in Tinelia again, I'll treat you like the monster that you are." With that, she gave one last, painful shove of Leridon's neck and continued on without him.

The weary Battlemage remained there for a few moments longer, watching the angry figure of Ardell stomping away. When he felt enough distance had been put between them, he struggled to his feet, using his crutch as leverage. He understood Ardell's reaction. Indeed any sane person would have reacted the same way, but these were mad times. Never before had the world's freedom hung by such a delicate thread. The fires of the Imperium burned hot, threatening to engulf them all. If he were to be remembered as a monster for preventing this, then so be it. He would wear the badge with pride.

The village itself, despite being occupied entirely by Battlemages, was no different to one you would find anywhere else. It had numerous houses with strong wooden walls, the thatched roofs being thick and well insulated. Elsewhere there was a town hall, small yet functional and situated at the furthest end of the village from where the newcomers arrived now. There was only a single shop, however, an all-encompassing general goods store which held whatever was required to survive in this unforgiving climate. There was little need for fancy boutiques or parlours out here.

Thankfully, shining like a beacon in the darkness, there did in fact seem to be a tavern. Although out here, they were referred to as mead halls and were generally far less rowdy than their southern counterparts. When every day was a struggle just to put food on the table, the last thing anyone wanted was to be sat somewhere surrounded by noise and violence. Indeed, the far north was in fact far more civil than the snooty academics who sat in their ivory towers would have the world believe.

Despite the desperation of Nate and his companions to put their feet up and enjoy a well-deserved pint, they were instead summoned by Ardell. She gathered her forces on the outskirts of the village, the rather nervous figure of Leridon hunched at her side.

"Come, we're to investigate the library at once," she ordered. The others could not help but voice their dissatisfaction with a collection of groans and sighs. The weary captain could not hold back her temper and spat venomous words at her subordinates. "Shut it! You're here as soldiers, fucking act like it!" she fumed before storming off, expecting them to follow without question. The party shared curious glances. Ardell was rarely in a good mood, but something had clearly burrowed its way under her skin. Not wanting to tempt fate further, they followed without further complaint.

The now silent Leridon led Nate and the others out of the village, passing the town hall and further to the north. Expecting another long trek, the party steeled themselves for the unavoidable frozen limbs and numbness which seemed to creep into their very bones. And this was all in some of the calmest weather one could expect to find this far north. Their surprise and relief was palpable when Leridon led them for perhaps no further than a mile. Rounding a particularly steep hill, they saw before them what was undoubtably a gate.

This gate, however, was huge. Not at all like one would expect to lead to a library of all things. It reminded them of the gates which separated each ring of Tinelia. As wide and tall as two modest houses, the black metal from which it was made glaringly sticking out amongst the surrounding countryside. A contrast to such an extent that it was a wonder it hadn't been picked clean a millennia ago. But this gate was not simply standing out in the open on its own. It was built into the side of the hill and seemed to be slanted at an angle, as if it were slowly being claimed by the countless centuries which had passed without a visitor.

This was not all, however. Before you came to the gate there was a flat expanse of grey stone, upon which the party now stood. Assumed to be intended as a sort of ancient reception area, where scholars and students would congregate before being permitted inside. Now, long since abandoned to the tempestuous whims of nature and the apathetic annals of time, it lay host to this rag-tag band who came in search of its secrets.

Curiously, the rather unremarkable stone did not have so much as a speck of snow upon it. Even as the wind raced over the hills causing tiny avalanches upon its plain surface, the snow would disappear in an instant. Marcus was the first to notice this, instinctively placing a many times gloved hand upon the smooth surface. As he had expected, although still to a great degree of surprise, he found the ground to be warm to the touch. Not hot, but enough to be pleasant, to reach through his many layers and plant a kiss of warmth upon his skin.

"Weird," he said to himself, before thinking nothing more of it. The others had either not seen or did not care about Marcus' strange act, following behind their captain until arriving at the gate itself. Already gathered there were a group of Battlemages. They reacted cautiously at first as these strangers approached, thinking maybe the Emperor had arrived earlier than expected. Once they saw the familiar figure of their leader hobbling towards them, they became more relaxed.

"Any luck?" Leridon asked, breaking off from the group. He was met with disappointed shakes of heads and harsh stares aimed at the ground. For weeks now the Battlemages had tried every non-magical theory their collective minds could summon. Yet not a single one of them had come even remotely close to opening the gate. "Shit," Leridon whispered. He had sorely hoped to gain access to the library before the

Emperor's arrival, leaving his enemy to find nothing but an empty ruin, picked clean by his superior foes.

Their original plan would have to do it seemed. They would have to wait to see if the Emperor did indeed possess some innate ability to access the vault. If so, that would be most excellent. The Battlemages would eradicate him and take the secrets for themselves. If not, well, as far as the Emperor was concerned, his fate would remain the same.

Naturally, the burlier and less intellectually gifted of the group tried simply forcing the gate open with their bare hands. The Battlemages watched on in amusement. What oafs to think it would be that simple, wilfully neglecting the fact this had been the first tactic they had tried also.

After realising that he had little chance of shifting a two-hundred tonne slab of metal, Marcus looked for an alternate solution. He ordered Joel to circle the hill from one side while he traversed the other. What he was looking for was a secondary entrance, a secret tunnel or escape route which he naturally assumed existed. When he and Joel met around the hill's rear, they were disappointed to have found not so much as a burrow piercing the frozen surface.

Ardell was more than happy to let her people use their own initiative. It kept them busy and, most importantly, away from her with their agonising questions. Kyle and Nate being the only two people around capable of using any advanced magic, approached for an attempt of their own at opening the gate. Of the pair, only Kyle really had any hope of even coming close. Nate would simply watch, studying his teacher, trying to emulate and understand the spells he was casting.

At first Kyle ran his fingers along the metallic barrier, hoping to get some sort of sense for what type of magic kept the gate shut. Strangely, he felt nothing. Not so much as a light humming of magical energy as he tapped into that which surrounded him. And yet, he could feel in his bones the power which radiated from what was kept hidden beneath. Like the endless churning and crashing of the sea could he feel the waves of magical energy washing over him, over the entirety of the surrounding area. It was accompanied by a pull, like a stone tied around his feet, as if he was being dragged towards the cold ground. A sense of a relentless, unstoppable force which threatened to drown him in this swirling, bubbling cauldron of raw magic.

Nate could feel it too, this almost irresistible siren song which urged him to follow. Down into the depths of the unknown dark, where all his wishes were promised to come true. While Kyle did his best to resist whatever was calling him, trying to overcome his senses, trying new spells without pause, Nate embraced it. He approached the gate, a howling bastion of nothingness amongst this magical hurricane, its silent screaming louder than any blizzard or battle cry.

In a sort of trance, where the words of those around him were absorbed by the ever widening, gaping maw of silence, Nate reached out his hand. With a profound gentleness, as if he were afraid the lightest touch would cause the hillside itself to cry out in pain, he caressed the void-like surface of the gate. His black gloves disappeared against it, as if he too were now an integral part of its being.

Suddenly, there came the sound of rushing wind, filling his ears as if it were a liquid poured from a cup. Louder and louder it grew, until Nate's own thoughts were drowned out by the deafening howl. And yet, from within this senseless, shapeless noise Nate heard a voice. He could not make out the words but could distinguish this ordered, intelligent design amongst the random chaos which filled his mind. He tried his best to focus, to understand the words being spoken to him, words he could feel in his heart were of some vital importance. Yet no matter how much he strained, the words remained elusive, as if they were spoken in a foreign language.

As suddenly as the noise had appeared, it stopped. The onrushing wind and deep, cautious voice which had called out to him ending abruptly before Nate could discern their meaning. Released from his trance he turned to Kyle, eager to share what he had heard if the others had not done so for themselves. Indeed, the others were still going about their own, fruitless business. None of them had heard the voice. Kyle, however, had sensed something change. He turned to Nate, who in that moment smiled, releasing a relieved breath that he was not going mad.

As Kyle's face fixed on Nate, his expression soured. At first his eyes narrowed, as if he were unsure what he was looking at. But then, as it became clear, he dropped his hands from their spell-casting stance and rushed over, a grave look upon his face. Nate was confused, knitting his eyebrows together, as Kyle seemed to run towards him in slow motion, his footfalls against the still stone like drums in Nate's ears. Nate tried taking a step forwards, to assure Kyle that all was well. But as he did so, his legs buckled, and he fell to the floor.

His vision was blurry now, his hearing almost non-existent save for a low droning which drowned out any of the frantic shouts of those around him. Sat upon one leg which had folded beneath him, Nate tried to look around but found he could see little more than what was directly ahead of him. The swirling of his head made him feel sick and he looked to the floor to steady himself. As he did so, he saw a strange mark. Standing out against the dull stone was a bright, singular drop of something red. He reached out a shaky finger to touch it, but quickly found it accompanied by another mark nearby. Then there came another, and another. Before long the ground beneath him was carpeted with this red substance he could not place.

Nate felt something latch onto his shoulder tightly, and suddenly his vision was filled with the blurry outline of Marcus' face. Nate could see his lips moving, the wide, panicked look in his eyes, but could hear nothing of what was being said to him. He felt himself being lifted off the ground with ease. Just as Marcus had done on Nate's first night of freedom in Purgatory, yet that felt so long ago now. As he was hauled over a fur-laden shoulder, Nate could make out other figures approaching rapidly. He never saw the terrified faces of his companions rushing towards him as he slipped away into a silent darkness.

Nate awoke the following day in a dim room lit by a single pair of candles. He was lying in a large bed blanketed with thick animal pelts. To his right, placed upon a nearby table, was a half-empty mug of water and a damp cloth. With parched lips and a still weak hand, Nate reached over and took the mug. Draining the now stale water in one satisfying gulp, Nate gasped and relaxed back into his previous position.

He was surprised to find this bed to be extremely spacious and comfy, far more so than the glorified cot he called his own back at the barracks. He made a mental note to put in an order with the villagers before he left. With aching limbs, he stretched before rolling onto his side, almost jumping out of his skin when he saw that he was not alone. Slumped in a chair nearest to the bed, her feet resting upon a nearby table where a vase of purple flowers had tipped over, was Ardell.

She was asleep, her eyes twitching unnervingly beneath their lids as she battled some new horror in her subconscious. Yet she was not the only one. Towards the door, asleep in another armchair, was Marcus. His entwined hands wresting upon his stomach which rose and fell with the calm of a man at peace. Lastly there was Kyle. Lying beneath the table upon which rested Ardell's feet, the now empty vase positioned directly over his head, an empty bottle of something strong in his hand.

Just as Nate had thought of something funny to say to wake his guests, Ardell ruined it. She awoke in a panic, practically ejecting from her seat as her eyes opened, thrust back into the real world without warning. She gripped the wooden arms of the chair so tightly they cracked, and she panted like a woman hunted to the edges of the world. Nate too jumped back in shock but had no time to say anything before Ardell had come around and woken the others.

"Took your damned time," she huffed, brushing away a strand of sweaty hair as her eyes darted about the room, as if checking for some lurking danger which had followed her into the waking world. Her voice caused the others to quickly rouse, rising from their resting places, Kyle unsure why his face was so wet.

Whatever Nate had heard came from the library, of that they were certain. What it all meant was another matter entirely. Had it been a warning, some sort of magical intruder alarm set to dissuade anyone from entering? It was possible, but in which case why had they not all heard it? Why had only Nate been affected?

All manner of theories were proposed, some more fanciful than others, some downright terrifying. In the end, they all agreed on two things. Firstly, there was no way to know exactly what Nate had heard. Therefore, they would exercise extreme caution. The library may have been sealed for eons, but there were clearly still powerful forces at play here. Forces they would do well to avoid, and at the very least, not antagonise. Secondly, they would await the Emperor's arrival before going any further. Better he suffer the consequences of trying to breach this magical shield than any of them.

According to his companion's claims, the door had momentarily begun to open at Nate's touch, slamming shut again the moment he lost consciousness. Leridon and the other Battlemages had desperately tried to convince Ardell to surrender Nate to the effects of the gate, so that they may gain momentary access, but she had angrily refused them. She did not care what treasures lay behind that accursed entrance. She would not sacrifice one of her own for it. Even if it was Nate.

If the Emperor was not able to open the gate, they would allow him to depart. Slowly learning the secrets of the library and how best to unlock it without bringing any further harm to Nate. At that moment, as the four of them agreed to their plan, an unexpected sound rang out. Echoing across the village, the unmistakeable thundering of hundreds of armoured boots marching their way.

Chapter 26

Back out into the cold, Nate and those who had watched over him donned their heavy coats, obscuring their faces with cloth masks as they greeted their visitors. Like a line of ants, the Chosen had emerged from the south, cresting a tall hill before descending in a thick column upon the village.

Nate watched with both extreme caution and interest as Leridon addressed their guests. The Chosen were far more intimidating than he had first imagined. Even after their long march, which had left them battered and exhausted, Nate did not doubt for a second that any one of them could still cut him to ribbons with ease. He was further surprised by their unique and vibrant armour. A far cry from the dull, identical brown leather and silver steel worn by virtually everyone else. They were like a rainbow painted against a blank canvas as they lined the path into town.

There was one individual who caught Nate's attention more than any other. Sat atop a horse as black as midnight was a man resplendent in gold. The feather-like plates of his armour and the halos formed by the three ascending rings of metal resting behind his head giving him the perception of one of the archangels themselves. At long last Nate beheld the Emperor with his own eyes. A man he was duty-bound to kill, a man Nate himself had caused so much pain with his part in the attack on the Imperial City. There was an inward battle currently going on inside Nate's head. Was the Emperor, this man who sat before him now so regally and godly, truly the monster Nate had been told? Or had Nate, through his own actions, created such a monster? Was he just as much to blame for all that had happened as the Emperor himself?

There was no time for further contemplation, as the apparent leader of the Chosen, a strong, stout man with a bald head which was kept exposed to the cold even now, bellowed out an order. The Emperor, it seemed, was not willing to wait another moment before entering the library. Ordering to be brought to it at once, Leridon led the Emperor and his Chosen towards the black gate. As Nate and the rest of the supposed villagers attempted to follow, they were halted by a vanguard of Chosen left behind to block their path.

Naturally, this threw a rather large spanner in the ambushers' plan. Some considered attacking now, throwing off their disguises and bombarding their sworn enemy with a hail of magic so fierce not even dust would remain. Yet a mixture of fear and uncertainty stayed their hands. Instead, the ambushers simply watched as their leader led the Emperor and most of his Chosen towards the library. With no other plan immediately formulating and disseminating itself amongst them, the Battlemages retreated into their commandeered homes.

Nate too, his sleeve tugged gently by a suddenly appeared Chen who he had not recognised amongst the identical crowd, was directed into the town's only inn. Once inside and away from the eyes and ears of the Chosen, Ardell began to furiously pace as she tried to come up with a plan, and quickly. While the others pulled away their masks and hoods so as to be identifiable, they gathered around their captain in a semi-circle. Not daring to disturb her, they sat or stood in silence, nervously awaiting the unarguably genius plan about to be revealed to them.

There were, however, some unexpected difficulties to overcome. Firstly, they were outnumbered, far more heavily than they had expected too. Perhaps three to one. Even the skills of the Battlemages would be hard-pressed to wrest a victory over the Chosen given such odds. Secondly, they had allowed the Emperor to leave their sight. This meant any attempt to get at him now would mean going through the Chosen blocking the way to the library. This would negate what was currently their only advantage, the element of surprise.

Lastly, Leridon was now, by all intents and purposes, a hostage. Even if the enemy did not realise it. These factors did not leave much room to work with. A fact which was increasingly growing on Ardell's nerves as every new plan had to be discarded as soon as it had been thought up. In the end, there seemed to be only one option remaining. They would have to wait for the Emperor to find whatever it was he was looking for, and then attack him as he prepared to leave. As far as plans went, it wasn't the best, but it was currently all they had.

This was, of course, assuming their enemy could in fact gain access to the library. This plan presented its own unique set of challenges. If the Emperor, his mission having failed and deciding to return home, would the Battlemages really be able to let their most hated enemy just walk away? Would Ardell?

Slowly word had spread that Ardell had taken charge of the operation, and more and more Battlemages began to trickle into the inn to hear her plan. It was hardly the mind-blowing stroke of genius which had been expected, but in the end was agreed to be the best course of action. While it was risky to permit the Emperor the chance to obtain what he sought, it was their best chance to kill two birds with one stone.

The ambushers set about preparing for the inevitable conflict to come. When nightfall came without sight nor sound of the Emperor or Leridon, the ambushers began to whisper amongst themselves. At first it was harmless things, theories that the Emperor must still be searching the heart of the hill. Or perhaps he had been refused entry and was still there, banging his head against the gates until they opened out of sheer embarrassed pity. But these theories quickly gave way to more dangerous conspiracies.

Nate did not know who had started it, but by midnight the inn was drowning in rumours of the Emperor's departure. Some claimed, with no proof of course, that the Emperor had already found his weapon and secretly slunk away into the night. Naturally this rumour grew until it was all but established fact. Another, the Emperor had somehow discovered their plan and any moment now the Chosen would burst through the doors of the inn and put its inhabitants to the sword.

Despite Nate knowing these were nothing but rumours, concocted by nervous and frightened minds, it was difficult to shake them off, especially when those repeating them did so with such certainty. Ardell did her best to quiet these pessimistic murmurings, but it was an impossible task while Leridon and the Emperor were still absent. At roughly quarter past one in the morning, a figure emerged from the cold, dark night into the warmth of the inn, his face illuminated by the fire whose shadows danced upon the walls.

It was Leridon.

While there was undoubted relief to see him unharmed, he was quickly set upon by a frenzied crowd demanding answers to all manner of questions. Pushing his way to the centre of the room, he was soon followed by any Battlemage who had not yet joined their brothers in arms at the inn. Taking centre stage, stood on one of the few tables, he addressed the room. He did so quietly, as the enemy were still close. And while he had no reason to suspect they were at all under suspicion by their guests, he did not want to take the risk of being discovered by shouting his plans for all to hear.

It seemed that the Emperor had indeed managed to gain access to the library, and without suffering the same ill effects as Nate to boot. However, despite this initial obstacle being overcome, there was another which even the Emperor could not defeat single-handed. Beyond the gate there was a tunnel, which they assumed led further into the library. This tunnel, however, was blocked. An earthquake must have caused the ceiling to collapse and there was now an unknown amount of rubble separating the library from the surface.

The Emperor, frustrated but not deterred, had ordered that from tomorrow, all able bodies in the village were to help clear the blockage. Overall, this was quite good news for the hundred or so people who had spent the last few hours sick with worry. Therefore, after consulting with Ardell, Leridon quietly announced their new plan.

They were to do as the Emperor ordered, clearing the rubble from the tunnel entrance until a way forward could be found. Until then, they were to keep a low profile and avoid confrontation of any kind. Seeing as the Emperor was undoubtedly able to unlock the gates without incident, it would be foolish to squander this opportunity by killing him too soon.

While this plan sounded far better than getting mercilessly slaughtered, as had been assumed by most for the last few hours, none were looking forward to the task ahead. Clearing the tunnel should have taken no more than an hour with so many master sorcerers in their midst. However, without being able to use any magic whatsoever, the task was a daunting one. As Nate looked around at the Battlemages who surrounded him, he could not help but wonder if any of them even knew how to use a shovel.

That night was a restless one as the party prepared themselves for the coming day, they had no idea of the magnitude of the task which lay ahead. As they dragged themselves from the comforting warmth of the inn the next morning to their new lives as labourers, they soon found out.

"Oh, fucking hell," Nate grimaced at the sight before him. The way to the library lay open, the huge gates parted to allow entrance. Before the gathered mix of Battlemages and Chosen lay a tall, dark tunnel blocked entirely by rubble perhaps no more than six or seven paces past the entrance. While there was no way of knowing exactly how long the blockage extended, nobody was under any illusion that this would be a quick and easy task.

After being asked whether there were any sorcerers amongst the 'villagers', the answer to which was a resounding no, shovels and pickaxes were handed out. Some rocks were small enough to be moved by hand, but most were large or medium sized boulders which would need to be broken up first before they had any chance of being moved. They worked in shifts, rotating from dawn till dusk to move the seemingly insurmountable obstacle which halted their progress. They started at the top, not wanting the whole pile to collapse upon them by removing anything holding the whole thing up.

Nate had climbed almost to the ceiling, swinging a pickaxe with increasingly sore limbs. His only reward for all his efforts, a chunk of stone no larger than a football breaking free and tumbling to the ground below. Those on the ground did not fare much better either. Waiting for a chunk of rock to fall before hurriedly gathering it up and moving it to a slowly growing mound clear of the gates. After each day of back-breaking work, Nate would collapse into any available space within the inn to seek solace in sleep.

The Chosen had occupied the other buildings in the village, the Emperor taking up residence in the town hall. This meant the hundred Battlemages and Nate's party had to squeeze into the inn while the work continued. Furthermore, with the arrival of so many extra mouths, the village food stores were being rapidly depleted. Resorting now to rationing, Nate felt weaker and emptier each day as what had begun as filling meals of meat and vegetables gave way to bread and soup. Before too long they had been forced to surrender the last of the bread to their guests too.

Thankfully, the Emperor did not appear to be a slavedriver, allowing the workers to stop once the sun began to depart, all work resuming early the next morning. This was not out of any lack of drive to see the rubble cleared, but through understanding that rested workers were effective workers. Nevertheless, by the third day, little visible progress had been made. While a gap had opened near the ceiling, beyond it lay only a fraction of free space before the rubble continued.

On the fourth day, the Emperor ordered his Chosen to cease guarding the village and to aid the 'villagers' in their task. Frankly, Nate was amazed that the ruse was still succeeding. Anyone who didn't spend most of their days in luxury would soon have seen through the Battlemages' disguise. The fact that it took some instruction on how to swing a pickaxe, and the excessive strain upon their faces as they used long forgotten muscles for the first time in centuries, being dead giveaways that these were no peasants.

Nevertheless, either through unwavering dedication to the task at hand, or simply sheer ignorance, the ambushers had yet to be discovered. Watching the Chosen work was a marvel to behold. Not one removed their thick, cumbersome armour while they hauled stones larger than the workers around them with ease. Not once did any stop for water or to rub their sore and aching muscles until their shift was over. As Nate watched with amazement as a member of the Chosen hauled a stone roughly the size of Marcus onto his shoulders, he could not help but feel butterflies in his stomach. After all of this, the heavy manual labour while surviving on scraps, was he really expected to fight these monsters?

After yet another agonising day of work Nate had tried to spend his whole life avoiding, he lay on the floor of the inn, as close to the fire as possible between all the other horizontal bodies. No sooner had he closed his eyes did he feel a gentle poking on his cheek. Opening only one eye, he saw Chen laying on her side, one arm tucked beneath her head as she gently prodded Nate with her finger.

"What?" Nate sighed, in no mood for anything other than lying there for the next eight hours with a sore back, trying in vain to sleep with a stomach containing nothing but spinach soup. But Chen said nothing, simply retracting her arm now that she had Nate's attention, placing it atop the other, as if it would make the floor any more comfortable. When no answer came, Nate sighed heavily, rolling onto his side to face his companion, now using his own hands as a pillow.

"What?" he repeated, this time making sure the annoyance

in his voice was clear. With her back to the fire, Chen was mostly a silhouette, the light spilling around her shape like a mould. Slowly, her face came into focus. She had a bruise on her forehead, a dark purple mark where she had caught a small stone while clearing the floor of the tunnel from debris. She had a graze on her chin too, obtained from struggling with a wicker basket usually used for carrying fur, but this time laden with rocks. One of which had caught her as she had tried to position it into a more manageable position.

Despite the exhaustion evident upon her face, the dark rings under her eyes and the creases which had formed across her forehead from so many hours of bodily strain, her eyes still shone beautifully. Nate could not tell if it was from the light of the fire or something else, but Chen's eyes sparkled like diamonds as he looked into them now.

"Are you ok?" he whispered, far more gently than before.

"Yeah… You?" Chen whispered back. This was hardly the thrilling conversation Nate had hoped for, especially considering he was now wasting valuable sleeping time. Yet no matter how much he wanted to just turn back over and shut his eyes, he couldn't shake the feeling that his friend needed him.

"Talk to me," he said gently, trying to coax out whatever Chen was bottling up. She shrugged in response, her eyes closing gently before coming back to meet Nate's.

"Just a bit scared," she admitted.

"Scared? You?" Nate smiled. "I didn't think I'd ever see the day," he sniggered trying to downplay her fears. Chen smiled too, but more out of not wanting Nate to think his efforts were being wasted than any actual comfort she may have felt.

"Why are you scared?" Nate asked, reaching out a reassuring hand and placing it gently upon Chen's arm.

"This isn't like last time. These aren't just husks or your average Imperial soldier. These are the Chosen, the best soldiers in the world. Not to mention the Emperor himself." Chen paused for a moment before continuing, allowing time for Nate to understand what she was hinting at. "I'm not sure we can win this one," she admitted at last.

Nate felt a growing weight in his stomach, and this time it wasn't the spinach. It felt strange to hear what he, and likely everyone else, had so far thought but not dared voice. Every day they grew weaker, and he worried that the time to enact their plan was well past. Yet there had been no indication from either Ardell or Leridon that this was the case. The plan remained the same. Not wanting to scare Chen further by agreeing, he smiled unconvincingly, gently rubbing her arm.

"They can have all the emperors they want. We've still got something they don't," he whispered.

"What's that?" Chen asked. "And if you say friendship, I'm going to stab you in the eye," she frowned.

"We have Ardell."

Chen smiled, for the first time with a hint of authenticity about it.

"You really think she can beat the Emperor?"

"I'd bet my left nut on it," Nate smirked. Chen rolled her eyes but admittedly felt better. While she had her doubts regarding their chances of success, Nate's optimism, no matter how misplaced, had rubbed off on her. She thanked him and turned to face the fire, finally ready for sleep, but Nate stopped her. Gently, he rested his free hand upon her face and, despite the risks it carried, healed her scraped chin and bruised forehead.

For a moment neither said anything. They stared into one another's eyes with tight chests and words of meaning hanging on their tongues. After a while Chen simply smiled, her eyes glittering like the sun across the sea before turning over once again. Nate did the same, although the weight in his stomach remained. As he closed his eyes he could not help but fret about tomorrow. Each day brought them closer to this inevitable, almost hopeless, battle. He just hoped he would be ready when the time came. And if not, that he would have no regrets. But already there was one weighing on his mind. Would he have the chance to correct it before the end?

Unbeknownst to either of them, Ardell had been nearby. Camouflaged by the same heavy coats as everyone else, making her impossible to distinguish with her back turned to them. She had heard their words - their worries, their doubts, and their hope. Hope that was misplaced, in her opinion, resting entirely upon her. She shifted from one uncomfortable position to another, under no illusion she would get any meaningful sleep tonight.

Oath Breaker lay hidden in another room, far enough away that its spiteful curse could not influence the minds of the others sleeping soundly. As Ardell lay there, nervously, unconsciously picking at her nails, she could not help but overthink everything. She thought of the Chosen, the sheer number of them and the skill each one possessed. While never afraid, she maintained a healthy scepticism in the ability of her forces to overcome such a foe.

Then her mind turned to the Emperor. The image of him standing there, radiant, seemingly invincible, turned her stomach. She imagined his blade against her skin, the sharp sting of its kiss and, for the first time in many years, felt something new - doubt. Perhaps this time, her own strength would not prove enough.

When Nate awoke the next morning, he was already drenched in sweat. He shot up from his place on the floor, his arms and legs flailing before being quickly caught by ready hands. As the waking world came into focus, Nate could see familiar faces staring down at him, all sharing looks of pity and concern. Marcus held onto his left arm which had struck out, and Joel held both his legs which had tried to leap from whatever dangers his mind had faced. Standing over him were Chen, Kyle and Ardell, who quickly helped him up once the danger of being struck had passed.

"You were having a nightmare," Ardell said, her voice filled with a familiar sympathy. Nate was still panting as he got to his feet, his body trembling as he wiped sweat from his forehead. He didn't say anything, just nodded in response to Ardell's observation.

"You okay?" Marcus asked, still supporting Nate by the arm.

"Yeah…" Nate gasped, the stale, sweaty air doing little to ease his racing heart.

"Come on then, let's get going," Ardell said as she headed for the door. While she shared Nate's struggle, she knew dwelling on nightmares would only make them worse. The others said nothing as they followed after her, each giving Nate their own sympathetic smile or glance so he knew he was not alone.

Kyle lingered behind, gripping tightly onto Nate's shoulder as he looked him deep in the eyes.

"Are you sure it was just a nightmare?" he asked, his words fast, frantic almost.

"What?" Nate asked, still not sure he was entirely lucid enough for such intense questioning. Kyle gripped Nate's other shoulder so that they were staring straight at one another. There was something about Kyle, something had seemingly overcome him, filling him with some desperate madness as he searched for answers in Nate's eyes. Nate could not help but notice those orbs staring so intently at him were bloodshot, twitching with feverous, uncontrollable jitters. His usually tidy, albeit pathetic beard was wild, his breath thick with yesterday's dinner and sour alcohol.

Nate pulled himself away, understanding what Kyle was asking, but unsure as to why it had such a hold over him. He looked around to make sure nobody was listening before whispering.

"It wasn't a vision."

"How do you know?" Kyle responded immediately, stepping closer once again. But Nate held out his palm and thankfully the sorcerer stopped.

"I just know. I can't even remember what it was about," he lied. A sudden calmness immediately took effect. Kyle seemed to be tamed once again, relieved at Nate's answer. But this did little for Nate who now wondered what the hell was going on, posing the very question.

Kyle rested his palm against his forehead while taking a deep breath before answering Nate's question.

"I'm sorry, Nate," he apologised, before taking a swig from a bottle hidden up his sleeve. Where Kyle managed to find all his booze continuing to be a total mystery. "There's just something about this library," he said, cutting off frustratingly, before offering any real answers. Nate was exhausted and didn't want to be drawn into a long debate when he had work to do, but he had never seen Kyle like this before and pressed further.

"I've been hearing a voice. No," he quickly corrected, should his words discredit him by making him sound insane. Although what he said next did little to help in that regard. "I've been *feeling* a voice. Pulling at me from within the library. It wants me to go deeper. I feel like a fish on a line. I've been trying to resist, but it's constant." As Kyle rambled this admission, Nate quickly began to think that he wasn't the one they needed to be worried about, but the erratic, twitchy sorcerer they had brought with them.

Nate assumed this was all a product of being overworked and underfed, with a dash of exhaustion to spice it all up. After all, once the gate had been opened, Nate had felt nothing. The previous chaotic vortex of magical energy swirling around them seemed to have entirely dissipated. Furthermore, none of the Battlemages were expressing similar concerns or symptoms. Why would the library single Kyle out, of all people?

Nate suggested that Kyle rest, nobody would mind if he took the day to sleep and recover when he was clearly unwell. Yet Kyle was adamant to continue, more determined to gain access to the library than maybe even the Emperor at this point. Unable to convince him to remain behind, Nate decided to bring up his friend's condition with the rest of the group later that night. Until then, he would keep a close eye on him while at the worksite.

The day started out like those which had passed before it. Rocks would be removed, boulders broken into smaller boulders and then hauled off. Today seemed like any other, where minimal progress would be made at the expense of maximum effort. To add to their woes, the day was uncharacteristically hot for this part of the world. It must have been at least two or three degrees above freezing, and many of the workers had done away with their thick cloaks and masks as their bodies sweated uncontrollably. None of the Chosen had seemed to notice that there were perhaps only half a dozen women in the entire village. Everyone was so focused on their shared goal that you could have slapped any one of them with a herring and gone unnoticed.

Unfortunately for Nate and his companions, the heat was unavoidable as they retained their weapons under their cloaks, prepared should their deception suddenly be discovered. Their progress, however, was too slow. It had been a week of hard labour and still only the first ten meters of the tunnel had been excavated. This had resulted in the Emperor taking further measures to speed up the project, measures which would soon make themselves known. At around three in the afternoon, while Nate was working hard to dislodge a particularly stubborn rock from his section near to the ceiling, he spotted something in the sky. A black dot, which seemed to be approaching with some speed.

At first, he assumed it to be a bird. Although he quickly corrected himself, as at this distance the bird would need to be the size of an airship to be noticeable. "*oh shit*", he thought, as the realisation dawned on him. The Emperor had brought reinforcements. As the now severely delayed ambushers watched with dismay, an airship flying the Imperial colours landed on the outskirts of the village, only reappearing a few minutes later after it had deposited its cargo.

At first some dared to hope it was simply a supply ship, here to top up their vastly depleted reserves so they may continue with renewed strength. This was partially true. Crates of food and other supplies were indeed arriving in reassuring quantities. The problem was the hands carrying them. At the head was the Emperor himself, leading a line of perhaps fifty individuals towards the excavations. These were evidently not Chosen, no. The reinforcements the Emperor had summoned were much worse.

The Battlemages had always been distinct for their bright blue robes, a sort of trademark which almost anyone could recognise. The men following the Emperor's lead dressed in very similar robes. These, however, were not blue but black. At this distance they stood out against the tundra like stalactites of darkness marching eagerly towards them.

It was at that moment a fear gripped the ambushers, spreading amongst them like a plague until all had fallen victim. The Emperor had summoned the traitorous Battlemages to clear the tunnel once and for all with their magic.

This unexpected and unwelcome complication totally upended any remaining semblance of a plan the ambushers may have had. They looked at one another desperately, hoping someone would know what to do. But even Leridon had failed to plan for what now seemed to be such an obvious possibility. He had expected this whole misadventure would have been over and done with days ago. In their current state they had almost no hope of success should they attack now. All they could do was hope to keep their identities a secret from their traitorous former colleagues until a new plan could be formed.

As the Emperor and his new cohort approached, they quickly began filtering out amongst the workers. They did not engage in removing the rubble straight away but were taking stock of the situation first. With no idea what else to do, and with no orders from their leader, the disguised Battlemages quickly donned their cloth masks once more, hoping to go unnoticed by their corrupted brethren.

Nate decided all he could do was play along and once again began striking at the boulder nearest to him. He could not help but be absolutely terrified at this new reality. If there was little chance of success before, it had all but vanished entirely now. He doubted even Ardell would be enough to secure victory anymore. Suddenly, as he allowed his mind to wander towards terrifying thoughts of imminent death, Nate struck a stone with his pickaxe which for the first time rolled backwards rather than forwards.

Sure enough, the stone, now heavier at one end, continued to shift backwards until it fell away entirely, leaving a hole which Nate could peer through. Expecting to find another tight space before yet more rubble, he almost fell from his perch when he saw the way to be entirely clear. While it was dark, the shaft of light piercing through the gap clearly showed a corridor leading to a set of carved stairs before trailing away into darkness.

Unable to contain his excitement after so many days of what he had fully come to believe would be an endless punishment, he shouted for all to hear.

"I've broken through! It's clear up here!"

Immediately everyone stopped and all eyes were upon Nate. It was as if everyone below had become frozen in time, staring up at him with disbelief. Only when he repeated the words did everyone suddenly come back to life. Everyone rushed forwards, filled with renewed strength and conviction that the end was close at hand. Picks swung madly, shovels struck the ground like rods of lightning as they attempted to break through.

Nate remained where he was, pulling away at loose rocks to make the hole bigger. Eventually it was large enough to squeeze through and he turned around in triumph to announce his success once again. The words never made it out of his mouth. He instead, nearly knocked himself out jumping in surprise as turning around, right beside him, was the Emperor himself. Stepping aside, his eyes wide and not once leaving the gleaming example of divinity before him, Nate allowed the Emperor to peer through the hole he had dug.

Below, people ran around madly, trying to shift every stone they could. Excitement filled some, dread others, as they imagined what would come after the way was cleared. During this mad rush, one of the disguised Battlemages tripped. He fell to the ground, his cloth mask untying itself and falling to the floor as he landed. Others noticed but did little to help as the Battlemage scrambled to get his mask back on before anyone could recognise him. But the damage was done. One of the newly arrived Imperial Battlemages had seen a glimpse of his face from a distance and was now slowly approaching.

The Battlemage who had fallen quickly attempted to get back to work. To mingle with the crowd so that he would be lost within the identical looking masses of masked people. The Imperial Battlemage, however, called out to him.

"You there! Stop!" he ordered.

The first Battlemage pretended not to hear him, heading back to the tunnel to gather more rocks. But the traitor had him locked in his sights and, upon approaching, took him roughly by the shoulder.

"I said stop, peasant!" he shouted, spinning the Battlemage around so he could see his face.

"Sorry!" The original, terrified Battlemage squeaked as he came face to face with his worst fears. He knew the man currently barking at him. The pair had been neither friends nor close, barely acquaintances when the schism split the order. The frightened and now trembling Battlemage could only pray his counterpart did not have a good memory for faces. Those Battlemages nearby who had some idea of what was happening began to slow their work, keeping an eye on the scene as it unfolded.

"Do I know you?" the Imperial Battlemage inquired, his eyes narrowing as he tried to place the top half of the man's face.

"Sorry, no. Never been to the Imperium. Sorry," the Battlemage spluttered, as he tried to push his way past his accuser and head for town. But the traitor would not be dissuaded so easily. He shot out his arm and took hold of the attempted escapee once again.

"Take off your mask," he ordered.

"What? No," the now petrified Battlemage protested,

as he tried to free himself from the iron grip. Furious, the Imperial Battlemage reached for the mask himself, but his opponent resisted. A small struggle ensued which caught almost everyone's attention. After a short bout of pushing and pulling, the Imperial Battlemage stumbled back as his counterpart shoved him. In his hand, the mask the Battlemage had been wearing.

Time once again seemed to freeze as the turbulent scene neared its climax. The now unmasked Battlemage stood still, his legs like ice, unable to move as he felt hundreds of eyes upon him. His opponent stared, wide eyed and open mouthed as it quickly dawned on him that he had been right. He did recognise this man. It did not take long for him to reach a final verdict. They had just walked into a trap.

Then all hell broke loose.

Chapter 27

In Nate's long, boring conversations with Kyle about magical theory, the Battlemages had come up often. Kyle, it seemed, was a rather keen admirer. Their disdain for any authority but their own, the dogged determination with which they pushed the boundaries of what was known to be possible were all traits he shared. Yet Nate had always wondered, other than a rebellious, Devil may care attitude, what separated the Battlemages from the average sorcerer, from him?

Finally, Nate got his answer. Although it came not from an ancient text or even a conversation with any Battlemages themselves. Instead, this knowledge was imparted upon him in the form of a telekinetic blast so strong, Nate feared his skin would be ripped from his bones. His identity discovered, their plan rapidly coming undone, the unmasked Battlemage had done the only thing that remained to be done. He attacked.

His Imperial counterpart, still holding tightly onto the cloth mask in his fist, was practically vaporised where he stood by the force of the spell which hit him head on. Nate had been perhaps twenty meters away, yet when the spell reached him, it was still strong enough to cast him like a stone. He slammed into the back of the Emperor, and straight through the opening which he had only moments ago uncovered.

Nate fell for a few seconds before skipping with great speed along the hard, rugged ground like a stone deftly tossed across a lake. He reached out his hands in the hopes of catching himself, of coming to a halt, but it was useless. He skipped across the floor many times, each fresh connection with the ground sending stinging pain rushing through his body, knocking any remaining air from his lungs. Echoing across the vast, empty corridor Nate could hear the crashing of metal against stone as the Emperor too was thrown violently forwards. All of this in darkness. As the breach Nate had so painstakingly uncovered was once again filled as the force of another blast had caused more rubble to take its place.

After many painful connections with the ground, Nate at last began to feel himself slowing down. This did little to help him in the moment, as his body continued to be battered with each passing second. But the fact it would be over soon was a small comfort. Now going at perhaps a tenth of the speed he had started at, he suddenly felt the hard, rugged floor no more. Suddenly, there was nothing beneath him at all.

Nate felt himself gaining speed. A lot of speed. The stale air tasted of decay as it whipped across his face and through his hair. As the seconds ticked by without the inevitable, painful crash into the ground, Nate's heart began to race with an ever-increasing urgency. It is a strange thing to wish for pain, yet Nate knew that each passing moment without that pain indicated his fateful meeting the ground below, which only decreased his chances for survival. He had lost count of the seconds since the beginning of this nonconsensual descent into darkness. A sense of dread overcame him. Would this really be his end, after every danger he had so far faced and somehow overcome?

These sorrowful thoughts were brought to an abrupt halt as his body finally crashed into the cold stone below. There was a deafening thud and a sickening snap which echoed around the chamber he now found himself in. Nate screamed out in agony, he was alive, but something had broken. And still in the crushing darkness he could see nothing, only feel the pain shooting up his body like the vines of some suffocating weed. His hands fumbled, trying desperately to assess his injuries while he sobbed and cried out in pain.

With trembling hands and shallow, rapid breaths as he went into shock, Nate gradually worked his way down his body. His torso and thighs felt fine, no cause for concern there. But his hands shot back, and he yelped in fresh pain as his fingers brushed against something hard and wet just below his left knee. Feeling around the wound Nate knew his flesh had been shredded and there was a good chance of a protruding bone. His head began to feel light and his eyes heavy as he turned his attention to his other leg. This time he managed to get all the way to his foot before recoiling once more. Unless he was mistaken, his right foot was facing backwards. And he was pretty sure it had not always been that way.

"Oh fuck," he groaned as he lay back upon the cold, dusty ground. Above him he could see nothing. Not so much as the flicker of a candle, or the glimmer of a single ray of daylight in this all-encompassing nothingness. Fear then filled him, like water it rose in his stomach until his lungs were filled and he was drowning in his own despair. He had failed, but not only that, he would die in agony in the dark, never to see any of his friends again. He thought of Marcus, of Chen and Ardell, of all the things he wanted to tell them before they were lost forever. But it was too late, the next time they saw him, he would be a corpse who spent his final moments scared and alone.

As Nate closed his eyes, the pain in his lower body forcing them shut, he heard something next to him. It sounded like a grunt, followed by stones being scraped against one another. Then he remembered. The Emperor! Was it possible he had survived the fall too? His question was soon answered as he heard another grunt before a ball of light suddenly materialised just a few feet or so ahead of him. In his state of shock Nate had forgotten all about magic and would have kicked himself if he didn't think it would cause his legs to snap off entirely.

The Emperor had indeed survived, seemingly without a scratch on him. His armour having saved him from injury. At first Nate questioned whether drawing attention to himself was a good idea, but if he didn't get help soon, he would be dead either way. Deciding he would prefer a quick death as opposed to slowly bleeding out in the dark, Nate called out. The Emperor immediately turned, the ball of light following as he searched for the cause of the noise. As he grew nearer,

Nate could at last assess the damage he had suffered with his own eyes.

His own prediction had been remarkably close. He did indeed have a protruding bone as his femur had snapped and now jutted out of his left leg like a stalk from the ground. His right foot was also broken, although it was only at a ninety-degree angle rather than a full one-eighty. The Emperor saw the injured Nate and crouched down beside him, assessing his injuries for himself. They were bad, but nothing he couldn't fix.

He looked at Nate and Nate at him. "This is going to hurt. A lot," the Emperor stated. Nate nodded and bit down on his armguard in preparation. With a final nod the Emperor placed his hand over Nate's broken foot. Nate shut his eyes as the spell did its work. There was another snap and a crunch as Nate's foot righted itself, the bones fusing back together in an instant. Nate shot up into a sitting position and screamed into his armguard for all he was worth, his teeth doing their best to reach the flesh beneath.

"Now for the painful part," the Emperor said regretfully, moving to Nate's other leg.

"Oh God," Nate gasped as he lay back down, his forehead streaming with sweat and his trembling worsened. The Emperor looked around, and saw nothing but darkness in any direction.

"I don't think even He can hear us down here," he said solemnly, before placing his hands at the ready. Healing this injury took longer than the first, the Emperor having to manipulate Nate's lower leg as the spell forced the bone back into his body before fusing them together once more. At first, Nate had begun screaming once again, but after a few seconds had gone silent, either dead or unconscious from the shock.

Once the injury was fully healed, the Emperor checked to see if his patient was still alive. He was, just about. After a few seconds of coaxing Nate out of unconsciousness, his eyes finally wrested themselves open. He was white as a sheet, but he would recover. Nate looked down at his lower body and was relieved to see nothing where it shouldn't be.

"Thank you," he gasped in a mixture of both semi-conscious exhaustion and lingering pain. Despite the events which had brought them here, Nate decided to continue playing the part of a dim-witted peasant. After all, neither man had actually seen the fight take place, and so the Emperor had no concrete reason to suspect Nate of anything more than being unlucky. Even if he did, Nate would hardly have had the Emperor shaking in his boots.

The Emperor helped Nate to his feet. He was unsteady, and each step caused fresh bouts of pain, but otherwise his legs worked like new. Nate thanked him for his aid, to which the Emperor nodded his acknowledgement and began to look around at the limited view his magic provided. Nate could have easily helped light the way, but revealing his magic now would definitely have earned him more than a couple of broken bones. Instead, he watched as the Emperor produced more floating balls of light until there were five in total.

The first he sent straight up, back the way they had come. The pair watched as the ball rose higher and higher until eventually locating the spot from where they had fallen. They seem to have slid off a walkway such a distance above them that Nate was unsure how he had come away with only broken bones. By all rights they should both be nothing but stains on the floor, demi-god or not.

"How the hell did we survive that?" Nate gasped.

"It seems the Lord still has use for us," the Emperor replied, equally as impressed by the survivability of his new companion, who, after a brief introduction, he discovered was called Nate. Nate felt uneasy at the thought of being thrown into the dark with such a dangerous foe for a higher purpose and was glad when the Emperor changed the subject.

"Well, we can't go back that way," he sighed. He turned around and directed his remaining orbs to travel in opposite directions until they had a clear view of what lay ahead of them. The lights did not have to travel far before the stone-lined emptiness was soon made clearer. From floor to ceiling for as far as they could see, the room was crammed with bookshelves. Each one bursting with tomes and scrolls until they disappeared into the darkness above and beyond. Nate gasped in amazement, but the Emperor began to scowl. The idea that the answer which he sought was hidden here, amidst these countless pages, shattered his hope of a rapid return of his wife. It would take years to go through everything in this room, even with the help of an army, and that was just what they could see with their limited light.

"Come," he growled in frustration with this new predicament. Nate obeyed and followed at the Emperor's side as they passed through the library. As they walked, the Emperor could not help but notice the similarities between this place and the palace library. The towering bookshelves, the smell of old paper and the feeling of inadequacy at being surrounded by the words of those with a far greater intellect than himself. Nevertheless, he did not have time to appreciate the beauty or antiquity of the place, he had a promise to fulfil. Nate, however, was transfixed. He had never seen anything like the place in which he now found himself.

He wondered how long it had taken to fill to such a degree, where each shelf looked ready to collapse with the weight of knowledge held within. He wondered what secret and ancient wisdom lay here, abandoned and forgotten by the rest of the world. If the Emperor had seen fit to travel here in search of something to end the war, what other calamities could be etched upon these innocuous scraps of paper?

The pair did not walk in silence. While at first being intimidated by his new companion, Nate soon fell into his old ways. Completely forgetting that he was speaking to royalty, he attempted to engage the Emperor in conversation. And not just idle chit-chat. Nate wished to learn more about the Emperor himself and any plans he may have which could help Tinelia in the future. If he managed to make it out of this mess alive that is.

While the Emperor was not used to speaking with

commoners, he found Nate remarkably tolerable. He was not at all surprised by his apparent lack of what would be considered basic knowledge about the Imperium. Out here news travelled slowly, and he appreciated Nate's clearly sincere condolences for the loss of his wife.

"Are you married?" the Emperor asked. Nate could not help but scoff at the thought, before quickly remembering who he was talking to and offering a reply. Upon hearing Nate's one word response, the Emperor could clearly tell that he was holding something back.

"Let me offer you some advice," the Emperor began, not once turning to face Nate, instead keeping his eyes fixed straight ahead as they continued down the ancient hall.

"This girl you are clearly in love with, whoever she is. Make sure you tell her. And once she's yours, do everything in your power to keep her safe. Otherwise, it'll be you wandering through the forgotten corners of the world searching for a way to bring her back."

The Emperor's words were heavy with grief, each one falling out of his mouth as if attached to great weights, dragging him down like a doomed mariner by the chains they wrapped around his heart. While to the Emperor they were nothing more than the confessions of his love. His words thoroughly confused Nate.

"What do you mean?" he began. "I thought you were here looking for a weapon, something to end the war?" Clearly Nate was not even trying to hide his identity anymore considering his new line of direct questioning. The Emperor simply laughed humourlessly in response, keeping his eyes facing forwards.

"I have no interest in war," he claimed. A claim which Nate immediately disregarded as a lie. "I am here for Sarah and Sarah alone. Be it spell or ritual, whatever the method, whatever the sacrifice, I am more than willing to pay."

Nate was not sure he believed what he was being told. But some innate part of him could not help but feel that the Emperor was telling the truth. The raw emotion in his voice was not something which could be faked, not easily at least. Now, for the first time, Nate felt conflicted about his mission. If the Emperor really was telling the truth, then why was Nate here, to steal the last rays of hope from a grieving husband?

He shook these thoughts from his head. No. He had seen what the Imperium was capable of, what they had planned. His mind went back to the events of the previous year, the glowing eyes in the living corpse of Adeneus which still haunted his dreams. Whatever it was the Emperor was truly here for, he could not let him leave with it. He would not sacrifice all those he loved, the world itself to these seeds of doubt his enemy had planted. With that the pair fell into silence, still with no indication as to where they were going, or even if there was another way out.

While the Emperor seemed uninterested in his surroundings, Nate craned his neck in vain to find the limits of the room. The only sounds which could be heard were the falling of their feet and the ghostly hum of the Emperor's orbs as they kept pace. They must have been walking for half an hour without any change in scenery whatsoever. Nothing but row after row of books and scrolls, each one adding to the growing weight of the task ahead in the Emperor's mind. Suddenly, the Emperor stopped. Nate did the same but wondered why they had done so, there was still no hint of an exit anywhere.

The Emperor remained unmoving, as if suddenly frozen by a spell. "What is it?" Nate whispered, slightly unnerved. The Emperor immediately raised his hand to silence him. The helm still hiding his features giving no indication as to his current mood or thoughts. Nate's heart began to quicken as he wondered what could cause the most powerful man in the known world to act with such caution. It was not long before he got his answer.

"There's something down here," the Emperor whispered. This caused Nate's already stressed heart to go into overdrive as it began to thud loudly in his chest. Despite not being afraid, the Emperor was still unable to retain the level of calm necessary to maintain his spell, the hovering lights which had guided their way blinking out one by one until there was only darkness once more.

Nate didn't dare move. His heart and mind ran rampant imagining what horrors could be waiting for them in the dark. He was desperate to see again, to prove that there was nothing there after all and that the Emperor had been mistaken. But with his stress levels nearing the heights he had tumbled from to get into this predicament, Nate could not have produced the smallest of magical lights to offer even the tiniest bit of reassurance.

The darkness suddenly retreated as light burst into life once more. At first Nate had assumed it was the Emperor's doing, but it soon became clear that this was not the case. Upon the sides of the bookshelves were torches, surely long burned out, they fought off the darkness once again.

Nate and the Emperor shared a look. Even in the gloom Nate could see the fierce blue eyes burning brightly behind the armour's golden glow. Both knew now that the Emperor had indeed been right. They were no longer alone, perhaps they had never been. Their silent stalker in the shadows only now choosing to make its presence known.

Nate instinctively reached for his sword, a detail which the Emperor gave little thought to considering the circumstances. The Emperor tried his best to remain calm. He had come this far, his god would not abandon him now. For a moment there was silence, broken only by the scorching of dust by the torches as they remembered their purpose assumed long since forgotten.

Just as Nate was beginning to lower his guard, there was another noise. Ahead of them came a loud rumbling like that of an earthquake, followed by a foul gust of wind which raced down the passage, buffeting them with the stench of age and rot. Nate threw his free hand over his face to shield it from the tempest, the Emperor meanwhile stood poised and at the ready. The rumbling came again and again until the very ground shook. Dust, undisturbed for eons, fell from the ceiling and books flew from their tight confines. The rumbling was getting closer, the foul wind following each rocking of the chamber.

Then it began to move. Circling the pair as they stood between the rows of shelves like a wolf circling its prey. With each new direction they faced, more torches would light themselves until they found themselves stood in an octagon of light, a clear break in the otherwise uniform design of the library. At last, the rumbling and the wind stopped. The sound Nate had dreaded to hear most of all took their place. A snarling, thunderous voice which had not seen use since darker days called out.

"We meet at last, dear friends." The voice echoed through the empty halls as if the world itself were speaking. Nate by this point was shaking in his boots and even the Emperor had placed a hand on his sword. Whatever this voice belonged to, it was huge. It only now dawned on Nate. He had been here before, had heard this rapturous voice echoing across these very same stone halls.

What a fool he was! So caught up in his mission, in the events going on around him, that he had not once paused to connect the dots. The dream, clearly now not a dream at all, but a vision! The one he had been so quick to try and forget, convincing himself it was nothing more than the overworking's of a tired and excitable mind. He scrambled to remember the events which felt like so long ago, desperately hoping they may be of some use to him now.

But Nate was not quick enough. The Emperor called out in response to the greeting.

"You speak as if we are familiar, yet this place had been forgotten long before my coming. Tell me, how can this be?"

There came another rumbling, but this one was different, the messy laugh of one who had long forgotten how.

"Have you forgotten me already?" the voice asked. "What a shame. We had such excellent debates," it continued. But the Emperor remained perplexed. Was this creature, whatever it may be, confusing him for someone else? He had never stepped foot anywhere like this before. But clarification soon came, carried by the rumbling wind.

"Your long sleep has addled your mind, my friend," the voice added. The Emperor felt a stone drop into the pit of his stomach. Yet another who claimed to have been visited during the Emperor's illness. And yet maddeningly, he could not remember even a scrap of these supposed meetings. Nate's hands shook as he turned to follow the voice which had once again begun to circle them, just shy of the light's reach. The Emperor, for now at least, remained calm, but was disturbed by this revelation.

"What do they call you, *friend*?" the Emperor asked of the darkness. There was a low, menacing grumble before the voice replied.

"I had a name once," it sighed, still circling. "But it has long since died from the lips of others, themselves long dead and nameless. This, at least, is a burden we share. Two nameless relics, unsure of our place in a godless world, our purposes long forgotten."

The Emperor did not like the tone, the familiarity with which the voice spoke. He tightened the grip on his sword, taking a single step towards the darkness, away from the safety of the light.

"You speak only of yourself. I have not abandoned my God," the Emperor replied in both accusation and in defence of himself.

"Perhaps," the voice whispered, which to Nate was somehow even more terrifying than before.

"But can he say the same of you?"

The Emperor began to feel the blood in his veins boil, filled with anger at the accusations being cast against not only him, but the Lord himself. As His representative, he could not let such insults go unanswered.

"Come, *friend*, show yourself," the Emperor demanded, eager to put this performance to an end.

"Very well," the voice replied with a hint of menace. Nate had been perfectly happy not knowing what eldritch horror would come skulking out of the darkness. Yet the Emperor was adamant to face this nameless threat, ready to draw Serpent's Bane and enact holy vengeance for its blasphemy.

The ground rocked as the creature approached, forsaking the darkness which had for countless years been its domain. Its movements were slow, and yet each step could be felt to cover a great distance. What they had thought to be so close was in fact not so, the thunder of its approach as the creature came close now deafening as at last it revealed itself.

Out of the shadow came the outline of a head. Huge, it was larger than any boulder which had earlier blocked their descent. It was smooth, lacking any horns or protrusions, or blood-matted fur of which Nate had been so expectant and afraid. Set within the head were eyes which hung like globes in the surrounding darkness. Vertical slits surrounded in a cloud of red and orange so fierce that one could almost feel heat radiating from the fire which surely raged within.

As the beast continued to slowly emerge from the void, its features became clearer. Two huge feet armoured in black scales glided across the ground, coming to a halt just past the border the torches had drawn. Each was as wide as Nate was tall, ending in four yellowed and stained claws which scarred the stone beneath as if it were butter. As the scaled head grew ever closer, a forked tongue quickly shot out before retreating within a mouth filled with rows of spear-like teeth.

Looking now upon the monstrous beast for the first time, Nate would have given anything to be back in that battle outside Sundered Crown. Amongst the reeking corpses, the helpless screams, the merciless slaughter. Anywhere other than where he stood now, petrified. The creature, amused at the reaction it had solicited by what was but a fraction of its form, pulled back slightly. Suddenly the room erupted with light. Every torch was now aflame, and the creature rose to its full height so the small men below could marvel at its majesty.

It stood on two, muscular hind legs, its body thickset, not at all like its long, slender neck, atop which that monstrous, snake-like head sat. As the light of so many torches caught its scales, they seemed to twinkle, like stars against a body as black as the depths of the cosmos. Finally, sprouting from the beast's back came two magnificent wings. As they slowly unfurled, they dimmed the room, so great was their span to block all light from passing.

"Is that... A dra... Nate blurted out, the only words he had managed since the beginning of this ordeal. However, the creature barred its teeth at the mere beginnings of association.

"A Zephyr." the Emperor interrupted, as he too marvelled at a creature long since thought lost to myth. The zephyr smiled at its own recognition. The humans still remembered. While the name no longer inspired the fear it once did, it was still spoken in hushed tones, should the mere repeating of the word loose them upon the world once again.

Despite the theatrics and clear warped pleasure the zephyr extracted from terrifying Nate, it did not pose an immediate danger to either man. For as bloodthirsty and ruthless as they could be, the zephyr were not mindless animals driven by instinct. No, they were the creations of the old gods. Birthed through long forgotten and blasphemous magic, the zephyr were extremely intelligent, more so than any man. They would not stoop to acts as base as violence without cause, preferring instead the arts of negotiation and intelligent conversation.

Try telling that to Nate, however, who's teeth currently chattered out of fear like a character from a children's cartoon. No matter the fortune he had enjoyed in getting this far, if this gargantuan beast decided it wanted a piece of him, no amount of plot armour in the world would be able to save him.

Having had its fun, the zephyr dimmed all but the closest torches once more, all but its head disappearing back into the darkness. It lowered itself to continue its conversation with the two awestruck men.

"What are you doing here, a zephyr, in a library of all places?" the Emperor gasped.

"I am the guardian," came the reply. "The last defender of

this holy repository. The final memory of a more enlightened age."

The Emperor was not sure he would call the enslavement of an entire species enlightened, but he moved past it. He had wasted enough time already on questions which ultimately did not matter.

"Do you know why I am here?" he asked. The zephyr nodded, its huge head fanning the air around them.

"Yes, we discussed it at great length. There is only one thing that would bring you here, to the dark, frozen edges of your world. You seek an end to the great struggle, to the suffering, to the madness that consumes you from within."

The answer, while cryptic to anyone else, could only have meant one thing to the Emperor. He stepped forward, his hands upturned, his arms raised at shoulder height as if begging for alms on the street.

"Please," he gasped. "Will you help me?"

"I can deliver what you seek," the zephyr replied. "But nothing from this library comes without a heavy cost. I am unsure whether it would be wise to pay such a price."

The Emperor, caring not for how he looked, what others would say could they see him now, fell to his knees.

"Please," he begged.

The zephyr looked down upon the small creature before him, its bright eyes seemingly scouring the depths of the Emperor's soul, burning away any deceit he may have kept hidden within him. Despite all the long conversations they had already shared, many on this very topic, the zephyr had always retained some doubts. For how likely was it that a man of such strength and power would care so greatly for one woman? Love so deeply that he would travel all this way for nothing but the chance to bring her back?

And yet, the zephyr knew it to be true. Its creators had not seen fit to imbue it with the ability to love, to care for another beyond the capacity of one's own self-interest. Nevertheless, the desperation it felt radiating from the Emperor now, this god amongst men who would throw it all away in an instant for love, filled the zephyr with envy.

After a short while, the creature bowed its head, knowing the Emperor's intentions to be genuine.

"Very well," it replied, somewhat solemnly. In that instant a scroll materialised within the Emperor's hand. Tied with a purple ribbon it looked no different from the millions of others that surrounded them. But this one *was* different. They all knew it.

The Emperor took a moment to fully register what was happening. All his efforts, all the death and struggle which had led him here. All of that brought to conclusion in a mere instant, in a single flash of magic so simple it felt almost insulting, trivialising all that had been sacrificed to receive the answer to his prayers.

"I... Wait... So... What is this?"

"Peace," the zephyr responded. Its words echoing, seeping into the men's very bones.

The Emperor could barely move, still on his knees he stared at the parchment in his outstretched hand as if he were looking into the eyes of God. Was this truly it, the end of his anguish? While he remained transfixed, Nate's sword hand began to itch, his heartbeat so frantic he thought he may faint. He had no way of knowing what was in that scroll, but the risk was too great, whatever it may be, he could not let the Emperor have it.

The zephyr now turned its attention to him, addressing Nate directly for the first time.

"We meet again," it said, greeting Nate as if the pair were old friends. "And why have you come all this way? What answers could you possibly seek? After all, you were so determined not to need my help the last time."

Nate was unable to say anything as the huge eyes pierced his soul with their stare, narrowing into orange slits like rivers of magma as they searched his heart for foul intentions. He dared not do anything. He had to, before the Emperor could unleash whatever terrible power lay within the banal off-yellow confines of the parchment he held, but his limbs were numb. He stared back at the creature, begging for some sign or direction of what to do next. The zephyr simply looked at him in silence.

Then came the sign. With a roar so loud and terrible that the world around them threatened to collapse, the zephyr began to scream.

Chapter 28

Like a star streaking across the night sky came a spear from the darkness. Its shrill whistling as it sailed through the air echoing across the otherwise silent library. With masterful skill it found its mark, piercing the zephyr's eye like it were a fish in a river. There was an explosion of blood and the zephyr fell back, its long neck writhing in pain. The ground shook as its body thrashed, desperately trying to find its feet, all the while screaming in agony. A scream so guttural, so animalistic, that anyone would have been hard-pressed not to feel the most gut-wrenching sympathy for the beast.

The spear seemed to have materialised out of nowhere, and both men were frozen with shock as they watched the mighty creature before them reduced to a screaming, writhing mass of blood-soaked scales, flailing limbs and gnashing teeth. The first to snap out of his trance, Nate realised this was his only chance to fulfil the mission, his whole reason for being here.

He reached forwards and snatched the scroll from the Emperor's open hand. The Emperor immediately turned, his body still stiff from the sudden shock. The two shared a look which seemed to drag on for eternity as their eyes conveyed everything words could not. The Emperor opened his mouth to speak. To beg, to plead with Nate to stop before he set off an unstoppable, ruinous chain of events. His words, however, were drowned out by the sudden roar of telekinetic force Nate unleashed upon him. The blast hit the Emperor head on, and he was flung like a stone into one of the bookshelves with the deafening crash of splintering wood.

As Nate watched on, not quite believing what he had just done, the bookshelf the Emperor had collided with began to collapse. Like a domino it leaned forwards, countless pages pouring from its slanted shelves like a waterfall upon the dusty ground so far below. As the bookshelf fell it collided with another, which in turn also began to fall, beginning an unstoppable avalanche of wood and paper. The ancient words of long-forgotten scholars floating through the air as their prison disintegrated.

Nate immediately turned to run, but in what direction? It did not matter. He just needed to get as far away from the Emperor as possible. He had barely taken a step before crashing into Ardell. She stood, wide-eyed, bloody and breathless. Her eyes were fixed on the spectacle of the writhing monster she had so deftly struck with her spear. In all her years she had never seen anything like it, and she began to wonder whether maiming it had been such a good idea.

Behind her rapidly approached the other members of the party, although they seemed to be dragging themselves onwards, most of them clearly injured. Not far behind, hot on their heels, stormed the Chosen. They were unlikely to take kindly to what Nate had done to their beloved monarch, sprinting forwards with relentless fury. Ardell gripped Nate's shoulder so tightly she drew blood as they locked eyes, hers full of manic frenzy.

"Run," was all she said, all she needed to say, to convince Nate to take off into the bowels of the library, further into the unknown darkness. The whole party were sprinting as fast as their legs would allow when a sudden, terrible roar shook the room and knocked them to the ground. They dared to look back, and saw flames, as bright and unstoppable as the dawn ripping through the room behind them. They could feel the heat intensifying on their faces as the flames fast approached. Ardell jumped to her feet and ordered the others to do the same, pulling Chen up by her hair and kicking Jin forward.

"RUN!" she screamed over the zephyr's furious roars and curses as it called after those who had so unjustly attacked, desecrating the eons-long sanctity of this holy place, now irreparably tainted. They all obeyed the captain, dragging their tired and bleeding bodies from the floor and setting off, away from the firestorm engulfing everything it touched.

No matter how fast they ran, the desperately fleeing party could feel the prickling heat of the flames intensifying upon their backs as they drew ever closer. Like a ravenous beast it pursued them, driven on by an insatiable hunger which could not be quenched until all was but ash and smoke. It was now, as their bodies struggled to meet the demands required of them, that one of their number made a grave mistake.

Kyle, his feet like lead, his lungs burned black from the smoke which smothered the air above their heads like a noxious blanket, tripped. He did not so much fall as crumple to the floor. Had it been a loose book which had caused him to stumble, his addled mind overcome by the poison he inhaled with each breath? No one would ever know. Arranged in a heap of scorched paper, singed clothes and ash, Kyle looked up at the rapidly shrinking figures of his friends leaving him behind.

Only one saw what happened – Marcus. In a moment of fear and desperation had glanced back to see how close the flames had come. He was met with the sight of Kyle, motionless upon the floor as the Chosen approached, the flames not much further behind. Marcus wanted to turn back, to drag his friend from where he lay, carrying him home if he had to. But it was too late, and they both knew it.

As Kyle turned to meet his fate, he heard a voice. The same voice which had plagued him for days. It filled his mind, whispering grandiose promises which even the most resolute of magical minds would have found near impossible to ignore. It would deliver unto him all the knowledge it possessed. He would become the greatest sorcerer who had ever lived. All he had to do was stay behind. He smiled as the voice, a soothing melody, drowned out the roars and the screams, the trampling boots and explosions which filled the world around him.

The Chosen, led by their Emperor who had pulled himself free from the rubble, ignored their fallen enemy. They had only one goal, to retrieve what had been stolen. There was no need to waste precious time when the firestorm was so close they could taste its sting upon their tongues. As they raced past, Kyle was met by a wall of fire so tall it licked the ceiling. Like a rogue wave of burning orange, it crashed down upon him. His final thought, how beautiful it had looked. That rising pillar of destruction given life of its own, its brilliant light reflected beautifully in his eyes, as it consumed him.

Tears filled Marcus' eyes as he turned away, his heart filling with self-loathing for leaving his friend behind. None of the others had seen what happened. None would lie awake at night, the final image of their friend annihilated without trace forever burned into their minds. They would soon notice, of course, once all of this was over that one of their number had not made it out. And they would grieve for a while, but in the end would fall back on those happy memories they had shared. This was impossible for Marcus now. He would only ever remember the look in Kyle's eyes as Marcus abandoned him.

Despite all their efforts, barely keeping ahead of their pursuers, the party seemed to have made little progress in their attempts to escape. No matter how far they ran their surroundings remained the same. Towering bookshelves illuminated by the inferno behind them stretched on for as far as their eyes could see, those ahead of them worryingly beginning to catch aflame from the embers which surfed the black waves of smoke suffocating the room.

Ardell led them, darting from one identical aisle to the next in the desperate hope of finding an exit, but now even she was beginning to tire. They had reached the base of the library via a set of stone walkways which criss-crossed near to the ceiling before spiralling towards the ground. The first of these being those which Nate had missed by mere meters as he skidded off the platform high above.

Now, however, no staircases could be seen. And the spiderweb of sandstone walkways which stretched on above their heads seemed to taunt them as they desperately searched for a way up. It was Ardell who first saw it. Off to their left, perhaps one hundred meters away, rapidly appearing and disappearing as they passed countless bookshelves, like an image from a flipbook, was a door.

Ardell darted towards it, the others following closely, renewed with hope as they too saw this potential escape for the first time. The door was small, at least when compared to the scale of the library itself. For all Ardell knew it could have been a broom cupboard, a revelation which would have proved fatal should it be the case. She did not stop, sprinting into the door shoulder-first. It swung open violently, colliding with the adjacent wall with such a thunderous crash that it echoed across the new chamber like thunder.

Thankfully, this was no broom cupboard, and when the last of her people were through Ardell slammed the door shut once more. This new room, while large, seemed to be almost completely empty. It was of equal proportions, roughly two hundred meters in any given direction. The walls on either side of them seemed to have channels carved along their base for their entire length. It was unclear what these were for, until suddenly they came to life, illuminated by flames which flowed like water until they reached the far wall.

Whether this was by design, or an indication of proximity to the chaos behind them, the party did not know and preferred to keep it that way. Otherwise, the large space between the now fiery edge was occupied by little more than a collection of rotten and termite-infested beds, tables and chairs. The room may once have been a barracks, or simply a social area for visitors to the library to congregate in. Such academic musings would have to wait, until they were free of the danger behind them and free from the enraged Emperor who they knew would stop at nothing to retrieve what Nate still clasped tightly in his hand.

The room, now filled with a soft, cozy light, revealed what the party had been so eager to see. At the far end, hugging the intersect between the left and back walls, was a staircase. Never had any of them been so overcome with joy to see a dusty, cobweb-strewn set of steep steps leading to the surface. Should this be their salvation, never again would they complain of tired legs and aching muscles after a steep climb or perilous descent.

Ardell immediately began to run for the stairs, escape being so close she could taste it. Whether the walkways would lead them to a secondary exit, or straight back into the furious, awaiting arms of the Chosen which stood guard on the surface, was something they could concern themselves with later. After covering roughly half of the distance, she was forced to stop. Her companions were lagging. Many had suffered injuries in the chaotic battle above and had done well to make it this far. Now they limped and gasped for air as their wounds caught up with them.

Even those who had managed to get away with only light scrapes and bruises struggled to keep up, their heads weighed down with hot ash nestled within their hair. Ardell waited for her companions to meet her, pushing them onwards, urging them to fight on for a little longer. As they passed, she did a quick headcount. Joel was badly injured, his sword arm hanging by a single thread of flesh, his face as white as snow. Marcus was practically carrying him at this point. Cassandra had a deep gash across her midriff and was almost completely doubled over, yet she still ran. Only one was missing - the ginger fellow with the funny voice. She shook her head, comprehending there was nothing anyone could do for him now. She only hoped his death had been quick.

As the last of her companions dragged themselves past, gasping and groaning with exhaustion and pain, Ardell too turned to run. Stunned, she was halted by the rapturous crashing of heavy steel against a hard surface. She turned back to see Chosen piling through the door they had themselves just come through. Black with soot, their eyes filled with bloodlust, the Chosen rushed towards their injured prey, hurtling with inhuman speed despite the weight of their armour.

There was simply no way the party would escape in their

current state. Ardell turned her gaze towards her companions, who were now perhaps fifty meters from the stairs. The Chosen would be upon them well before then.

"Shit," she said, snapping her head back in the direction of the enemy. She drew her sword and awaited the inevitable, taking deep breaths laced with adrenaline.

Nate was the last to reach the stairs, allowing the injured members of the group to go ahead of him, partially supporting Jin who had his right ear cut clean off and was now weak from blood loss. Chen had been waiting at the stairs, reaching out a hand to support Jin who struggled weakly upwards. The steep climb made harder as each step became increasingly slick with blood. Just as Nate too raised his leg to begin the climb, he noticed the shaken look upon Chen's face, the blood having drained from it almost entirely.

At first Nate believed she may be concealing some hidden injury, but a quick once over with his eyes confirmed this was not the case. Yet still she stared, as if shellshocked. Nate turned in the direction Chen was facing and immediately understood. Ardell had not followed them. She stood alone, sword drawn, the Chosen thundering towards her.

Nate instinctively stepped forward, ready to rush to the captain's aid. To drag her back by the hair if he had to. But Chen stopped him. She gripped his arm with a strength he did not know she possessed, her earlier trance broken, her frightened glare forced his eyes away. Neither of them said a word, staring intently at one another in a way neither of them had ever done before. Nate's erratic blue eyes now a cloudy, smoky grey. Chen's soft, warm gaze tearfully telling him there was nothing more he could do.

Now fighting back tears of his own, Nate gritted his teeth, turning his back on his captain and darting up the stairs two at a time. Chen followed close behind, making sure he did not attempt anything heroic. Nate cursed himself with each step. He was a coward, abandoning his friend to die just so that he may live. He bit down on his lip until it bled as he climbed the old, cracked and dusty stairs not daring to look back.

As Nate reached the top of the staircase he darted along the walkway until reaching the point where it exited the room, turning at a ninety-degree angle into the unknown. The others had already gone ahead, leaving a bloody trail in their wake. Only he and Chen remained. And Ardell. Despite every fibre of his being telling him not to, telling him that he would not like what he saw, Nate made one last look back at his captain. Hoping against all odds that she had abandoned her foolish heroics and followed after them. Unfortunately, his instincts had been right.

Ardell was no longer alone. The corpses of half a dozen Chosen lay at her feet. Yet in the time it had taken Nate to climb the stairs, the remainder of their number had filed into the room. They came at Ardell with a relentless appetite for death which she was only too happy to satisfy. With a final, silent farewell, Nate and Chen hurried from the room, leaving their captain to her fate.

The walkway took them through a passage, wide enough only for one. Nate led the way. It did not take long for them to catch up with the others, most of whom had collapsed, unable to make it any further on their own. The first they came to was Jin, the blood loss having finally bested him despite his admirable efforts to soldier on. Nate told Chen to continue, to check on the others while he stopped, kneeling beside the ashen looking samurai.

The distinctive armour, which Nate had never seen Jin without now that he thought about it, was painted in a thick layer of blood. It had been bent in some places, having caught heavy blows during their battle upon the surface. In other spots there were deep gashes, and it soon became clear that Jin had many more injuries than Nate first assumed. He set to work quickly, focusing at first on the most severe wounds, the worst of which was his missing ear.

Nate had healed plenty of minor cuts and scrapes before, but nothing as serious as trying to regrow an appendage. He looked further down the narrow passage where the others were either lying upon the ground or slumped against the walls. "Kyle!" he called, hoping the more experienced sorcerer could take over. When no answer came, he called out again. Growing increasingly frustrated by the silence that answered his desperate cries, he summoned a large ball of light, far brighter than he had intended, which illuminated the passage from end to end.

"Kyle!?" he called again. But as the sorcerer once again failed to make himself known, Nate began to understand. He could not see the familiar face or stark ginger hair against the blandness of the walls. He peered further into the passage, wondering if maybe Kyle had gone ahead, but then he could not remember seeing him since the main chamber. Nor could he remember seeing him in the group as they climbed the stairs.

A weight dropped in Nate's stomach, one so violent he almost threw up all over the unconscious and blood-soaked Jin. Kyle was gone. Now it was up to Nate to keep these people alive. With no time to think, to reminisce, Nate held his hand over the still spurting cavity which had once been an ear. Thankfully, the task was not as difficult as had first been expected. Being nothing more than cartilage, flesh and fat, the wound healed over quickly. The regrowing process would probably take a few hours, but the danger was past.

After fixing any other obvious wounds Nate moved on towards Cassandra, who lay slumped over against the wall. It was only a few seconds later that Jin felt well enough to stand, squeezing Nate's shoulder in thanks as he pressed on along the passage where Chen had found the other end. Cassandra's face was chalky and lifeless, her skin deathly cold. For a horrifying moment Nate thought himself too late, but he could hear strained wheezes coming from her cracked and bloody lips.

Cassandra's midriff was so drenched in blood that Nate struggled to see anything at all as he carefully displaced the arm which had for so long been held tightly around it. Upon moving the arm to the side, he recoiled in horror as steaming, pink intestines began to slide out of Cassandra's open torso.

Nate was dumbfounded. The fact Cassandra had run for so long, with such intensity and amidst such an appalling injury, earned her a morbid respect as Nate mentally prepared himself for what he had to do next.

He had remembered reading somewhere that somehow the intestines know how they're supposed to be arranged, and will move themselves into the correct position on their own. Theoretically, therefore, he should be able to just shove them back in and heal the wound, hoping the rest would take care of itself. One way or another, he was about to find out if it was true.

Holding his breath and unable to stop himself from grimacing, with one hand he held open the gaping wound, and with the other shovelled Cassandra's intestines back where they belonged. He had to keep one hand in place, holding the mass of warm, slimy flesh in while the other worked its spell. Sealing up the gash like a zip until not so much as a scratch remained. Gradually, the colour returned to Cassandra's face and her eyes began to fill with life once more.

She blinked slowly, re-emerging into this bleak and unforgiving world, seeing the relieved face of Nate staring back at her. Where had she been just now? She remembered somewhere warm and light, where the peach trees were laden with fruit and drooped from their weight. She had seen a house, small, basic, but homely and familiar, made of smooth stone with flowers guarding its perimeter. There had been a man too, handsome, although his features eluded her. And children. Had she heard the high notes of a small child. A boy? Playing excitedly, the soft barks of a young dog accompanying him.

But they were all gone now, the memories like smoke escaping through her fingers. She was back in the tunnel, deep underground, her body drenched in her own blood and sweat, the smell of which hung thick in the air. She grunted with discomfort as she tried to sit up, her stomach still agonisingly painful. Ignoring what had happened the last time he placed a hand on her, Nate helped Casandra into a sitting position.

This time she did not lash out. She sat for a few moments longer, taking in deep breaths as she collected herself. Nate stayed with her until she was ready to stand, pulling her to her feet. Cassandra said nothing, much like Jin, deciding to show her appreciation physically. Quickly, as if she didn't even want Nate to notice, let alone the others, she pecked his cheek before carrying on down the passage.

In any other situation Nate would have been dumbstruck, but there was no time. Marcus had managed to drag Joel out of the passage and into the next room where the others were waiting. The room in question seemed to serve no purpose any of them could discern. It was small, rectangular, and contained three other passages which they could follow. Chen set off down one of them while Jin and Cassandra scouted the others. In the meantime, Nate would look over Joel who was in a bad state. He had fallen unconscious some time ago, Marcus having had to carry him up most of the stairs now watched on, filled with worry.

"Where's the Captain?" his voice panicked having only just noticed her absence.

"She stayed behind," Nate choked, as he tried his best to focus on Joel and not imagining whatever had become of Ardell. Maybe she was already dead. Marcus didn't say anything in response. Instead he turned away, staring down the tunnel from whence they came. Nate assumed this was to see if their captain had managed to escape and catch up with them. But in reality, it was so he did not see the tears leaving long streaks down Marcus' ashen face. Even Marcus could not have imagined the disaster this mission had turned out to be.

Joel, similarly to Cassandra, was covered in blood. His right arm having been ripped to shreds. While the top half seemed to only have suffered minor lacerations, the underside was missing almost entirely. Only a single, shattered bone, of which there should have been two, kept his arm attached to the rest of his body. Half of his hand was missing too, leaving only his thumb and forefinger, the flesh around them torn like paper.

This would be far trickier than anything else Nate had attempted so far. Re-growing bones could take days, time they simply did not have. But the wound needed to be sealed now. Every second it was exposed to the open air carried the risk of infection. Nate made the decision to close the wound without attempting to re-grow the bone. This would stop Joel bleeding to death and mitigate the risk of infection, which was currently Nate's primary concern. Joel would have to simply put up with only being able to use one arm until they could get to safety.

Under Nate's spell Joel's flesh began to mend, his broken bones snapping back into place before fusing together. It took many agonising minutes before he could safely say the procedure had been a success. Joel's missing fingers were now small lumps of smooth skin, while the underside of his arm was whole once again, albeit practically useless. Tearing some cloth from the inner lining of his cape, Marcus fashioned a sling which he tied around Joel's neck to keep his arm supported.

"Good job," he praised, laying his hand gently upon Nate's shoulder as Joel roused to life. After the initial shock and some choice but apt words about the state of his arm, and the situation in general, Joel was helped to his feet. Thankfully, in that time the correct passage they needed to follow had been deduced. Chen's investigations had led her right back to the space above the library where the flames still spread wildly. Cassandra had fared no better, being led to a set of living quarters and, ultimately, a dead end.

Jin's passage, however, was much more promising. It had taken him a long time to return, but when he did, he triumphantly proclaimed that he had found the way out. All were cautious about allowing themselves to become optimistic at their chances of escape, but a way out was a way out. The now mostly intact party followed Jin along the narrow, winding passage in single file, their way lit by

Nate's spell. Gradually, they could feel the incline growing with each step until, rounding a sharp corner, the blinding rays of daylight lit up their weary faces from less than one hundred meters away.

As soon as the end was in sight, the party stopped. They stared ahead as if that small opening radiating bright, white light was the messiah himself, come to lift them up from the darkness. With renewed energy they surged forwards, tired legs finding new strength as salvation seemed so close at hand. Bursting from the ground like water from a dam, the party fell into the open air, collapsing onto the deep snow which surrounded them, gasping as the fresh, freezing air filled their scorched lungs. Marcus was the last to emerge, having remained behind for as long as he could, waiting, praying to see that long dark hair and furious scowl of Ardell's emerging from the tunnel.

Alas, she never came, and Marcus was forced to tear himself away and join those who remained, now on the surface once again. He found the rest of his party collapsed, panting and coughing, relieved to be delivered from that vision of Hell. Marcus took no time for himself, instead assessing the area. They had emerged some distance from the main entrance to the library, now on the edge of a dense forest of firs and pines.

Yet they were not safe yet. The smoke from the town, whether it be from their battle or that which remained lit in the town's centre could be seen not too far away, behind a few hills and snowdrifts. Not far enough for the party to consider themselves to have escaped their enemy just yet. Now, out in the open, those who had not done so already, made the realisation that two of their number were missing. Their earlier relief and jubilation at having escaped the library, no matter how minor, was instantly swept away by grief.

There was no time to mourn. They were in hostile territory, with no provisions, not even a map, and a long, long way from home. As the party hauled themselves up and scattered

into the forest ahead of them, their greatest test it seemed
still lay ahead.

Chapter 29

In the depths of the library, flanked by fire as the room slowly filled with poisonous black smoke, Ardell fought alone. At first the Chosen came at her like waves breaking upon the shore, a relentless, unstoppable force of nature. Yet break them Ardell did. Her muscles burned, her lungs screamed out for rest as each breath grew ever more strained, each swing of her arm extracting a punishing toll on her already weary body. Yet she fought on. She would hold out for as long as she could, as long as it took for this steel tide to overwhelm her, washing her away into the awaiting arms of oblivion. She fought masterfully, her skills pushed to their very limits as she cut down each man foolish enough to challenge her. Yet she was under no illusion. There could be no victory here.

As the fifth opponent tasted the kiss of her blade, they changed their tactics, no longer rushing headlong into battle with total disregard for their own lives. Instead, the Chosen attacked in groups as a seemingly endless number continued to trickle into the room through the single, small door, now reduced to splinters. This made little difference to Ardell. The Chosen were extremely well trained, perhaps better than any foe she could recall, yet they still fell in droves. Their skill was simply no match for her own, and even the mighty Chosen were by now beginning to fear that their opponent was something more than human.

The way she moved, ducking and dancing between swinging blades and mighty axes, the sheer speed and strength possessed by one so frail, they had never seen anything like it. These men had each spent centuries honing their craft, but their opponent, she had perfected it. While they had shaped themselves into mountains of muscle and raw strength, immovable objects in the face of the enemy, Ardell was like water. With speed and grace, she seeped through the cracks in their defences, exploiting weaknesses they themselves had not once considered. And one by one these mountains crumbled before her like a wrathful god set loose.

Only when a pile of corpses of once proud foes surrounded her, their extraordinary armour sundered under her fury, their menacing weapons scattered upon the ground like discarded tools, did the carnage stop. A voice called out. A voice of authority which echoed across the room, drowning out the sounds of clashing weapons and cries of anger. A voice the Chosen immediately obeyed without question.

"Stop!" it had cried, its echo rebounding off the walls until it seemed the room itself had demanded an end to the bloodshed. Ardell quickly found herself alone once again. Her enemies having retreated towards the other end of the room. As the steel tide receded, Ardell could now see who had given the order. At the head of his host stood the Emperor. His armour, previously dazzling gold but now more muted, bearing scorch-marks and a heavy layer of ash, still magnificent, but otherwise unharmed from his altercation with Nate.

"There will be no more of this. I will not have you die for me," he said solemnly to his men as they retreated behind him. The Emperor looked upon those Ardell had already slain and felt a great weight upon his heart. He had promised these men that they would return to their wives and enjoy peace once more. Now they would not return at all. He felt an anger rising within him. The sight of his men slaughtered like animals, and the scroll growing ever further out of reach, was too much to bear.

And yet by the time he spoke, addressing this mysterious woman who had so bravely remained behind so that her comrades may escape, the anger quickly receded, washed away by fear. A fear that with each passing moment, the chances of Sarah being returned diminished before they would fade entirely. His voice was not one of regal authority, but of agonising desperation.

"Please," he began, the events of the day overwhelming him so that he could not properly express all that his heart was desperate to convey. "You don't understand…You took her from me…I just want her back…."

Ardell, however, could not hear the Emperor's pleas. Perhaps if she had, the world could have been spared so much grief. But upon sensing the arrival of such a formidable opponent, Oath Breaker, which had remained slung across Ardell's back, erupted into a chaotic discord of screams and insane screeching.

"Slaughter!" it cried out, the word ringing inside Ardell's head like a bell. She tried to tune the voice out, to focus on the insurmountable trial which lay before her. Yet Oath Breaker persisted in its attempt to drive its master berserk, into the very arms of death which stretched out ahead of her in a dazzling array of glittering armour and pointed steel.

"Blood! Pain! Death!" it screeched relentlessly. Ardell tightened the grip on her sword, wincing as she tried to overpower the cursed weapon with her own will, to push the voice out. She allowed herself to hesitate. She looked up at the foe which faced her now, his words still unintelligible from the deafening cries engulfing every thought she could muster until only Oath Breaker's remained.

The Emperor stood tall and strong, his divinite armour reflecting the light of the flanking fires until he seemed to be bathed in it. Until even Ardell could not help but momentarily question the scene before her, as she eyed the glowing halo behind his head. Had this man truly been sent by Heaven? Even as he begged for peace, Ardell could feel an inhuman power radiating from him. It filled the room like the creeping heat of the sun until nothing and no one could escape it, could not deny that he was no mere man. Ardell was physically struggling to contain Oath Breaker's will, and as the Emperor stepped forward, she felt her hand reaching behind her head. Could she really hope to defeat such a foe without it?

"Death!" the cry continued. Her hand grew closer to the smooth leather of the hilt, her fingers mere centimetres away.

Ardell's heart was pounding, the sound of blood rushing through her ears as she inched ever closer. All the while Oath Breaker continued to shriek until it felt as if Ardell' skull would crack open, and the deranged demands of this ancient, cursed sword would be loosed upon the world.

"*Death! Death! Death!*" Oath Breaker cried, it's maddening screech reaching a rapturous crescendo as at last it sensed its time had come. A time of pain. A time where the fields of corpses would smother the world with the stench of death and rot. A time where the virtues of mercy and honour would be forever lost, discarded into the annals of history as relics no longer fit for purpose in the world it would create. At the last moment, Ardell regained her senses and pulled her hand away quickly, as if she had reached it into the cage of some wild and unpredictable beast.

"*Traitor! Murderer! Kin-slayer!*" the furious weapon spat, its insidious, demonic hiss demanding payment for old sins before its voice faded away into nothingness. Having finally emerged victorious, albeit barely, from this battle of wills, Ardell focused on the Emperor once more. While at first he had been diplomatic, hoping to explain himself so that further misunderstanding and bloodshed may be avoided, he was now visibly incensed. He had attempted to create a dialogue, to reason with his enemy so that they need be enemies no more.

Yet her clear scorn for his words, for his attempt at peace, not once responding to his questions or even attempting to negotiate, it was no less than an insult. Breathing heavily as pure fury coursed through his veins, the Emperor at last abandoned the ways of peace. If this woman, whoever she was, wanted blood, she would have it.

He took another step forward, and, deciding he would waste no more words, reached for his sword. The very sword gifted to him by Heaven itself. That which had cast the Fallen One from paradise, which had safeguarded mankind from evil since their creation. The sword which, until this very moment, he had never used in anger. Even when he had overthrown the Republic, never had he felt the need to use this divine weapon for anything more than cementing his image as the Lord's champion. There had always been others willing to commit violence on his behalf. Now, at last, it would taste human blood.

Serpent's Bane would be unleashed.

He took another step forward and at last, pulled the sword free from its scabbard for the first time in over a thousand years.

A great beam of pure, white celestial light wrapped itself around the blade like a cloak as it cut through the air. With it came a great noise, like that of a thousand heavenly trumpets which shook the ground as it tasted freedom once again. Immediately the entire chamber was illuminated in a light which obliterated any pretender to its rule over this new domain. As the shadows retreated in fear, even the smoke which hung above their heads evaporated into nothingness.

Many of the Chosen fell to their knees in reverence. Before them was the reward for their unwavering faith, the undeniable truth that their Emperor was indeed the divine champion he claimed. Even Ardell could do little but stand in awe. Slowly, as the Emperor held the sword aloft, the light receded, spinning at great speed around the body of the blade until it erupted into a flame of indescribable purity. Even at her current distance Ardell recoiled at the intensity of its heat, a fire which seemed to pass through all physical barriers until it left her very soul exposed.

Ardell felt naked in the presence of this mighty weapon. As she stared into its radiant light, she swore she could feel it staring back. It looked right at her, right through the sweaty and bloody skin with a familiarity, as if it knew everything about her. Everything Ardell had ever done, everything she had ever been, everything she would ever be. Yet it did not Judge her sins. Bizarrely, despite being drawn with the sole intent to kill her, she felt reassured by the blade's presence in a way she could not explain.

The Emperor began walking towards her, eager to end this

facile defiance and retrieve that which he had been gifted. His boots crunched loudly with each new step, heavy with the weight of destiny. Serpent's Bane remained at his side, permanently scarring the impure ground as it passed by. Finally, they had come to it at last. Ardell closed her eyes and took a deep breath. She held her sword tightly in her right hand, so many thoughts racing through her mind. She could run, there was still time, get to the stairs and out, away to safety.

No, every second she caused the enemy to delay bought her friends more time. This sudden, new thought at what those annoying underlings had undoubtably become, tickling her until she was forced to smile to herself, surrounded by the calming, swirling darkness behind her eyelids. But the time for these thoughts was past. As Ardell raised her sword, she could only hope she had done enough to secure their safety.

As the crunching boots grew ever nearer, like a steady drumbeat leading to her own execution, as she felt the heat of that unnatural fire intensifying upon her skin, Ardell's eyes shot open. She was greeted by the figure of the resplendent demigod marching towards her. All around him was darkness, Serpent's Bane appearing to consume nearby light like a black hole, drawing it in, growing ever more powerful.

With no time left to feel fear, to ponder with regret the choices which had led her here, filled now with thoughts only of battle, Ardell sprinted forwards. The Emperor, taken aback by such suicidal recklessness, took a defensive stance, more than happy for his opponent to appease whatever idiotic bravery she thought she possessed.

With a pounding heart and a grip of iron, Ardell came storming towards her opponent like an avalanche, the very ground quaking as each thunderous step echoed across the chamber. Her sword still glistening with blood as it hovered just above the ground behind her. As she gained speed, the stale air whipped through her hair until it pursued like hounds on the hunt. As the distance between the two combatants rapidly closed, both readied themselves. The Emperor tightened his grip, placing both hands around his weapon, strengthening his stance for the inevitable clash.

There was no time left for doubt as now only a few meters separated the two. These storybook heroes carrying so many futures upon their shoulders, these opponents of such skill and power that it was inevitable only one could survive their fabled clash. Suddenly, Ardell leapt into the air, her sword raised, its black body invisible against the shadowy ceiling above. In this final, seismic moment, Ardell channelled all that she had. All her remaining strength, all her ferocity, all her hate and anger into this one, cataclysmic swing.

Letting out a ferocious cry which tore through the resolve of even the mightiest of the Chosen, a cry which would echo through the ages and haunt the most terrible nightmares of those who heard it, Ardell descended with all the unstoppable burning might of a falling star. The Emperor raised Serpent's Bane above his head to catch the incoming strike, the flames licking at the air as they hungered to purge the evil and the damned. At long last, the blades met.

And Serpent's Bane shattered.

It exploded into a million shards against the force of the incoming blow as if had been glass all along. The pieces cast off at great speed in all directions, tumbling down like razor sharp rain. At that moment, the world seemed to slow to a fraction of its normal speed. Ardell and the Emperor's eyes met, both wide in disbelief, neither able to comprehend the impossible event they had just partaken in. The Chosen, watching on with feverish excitement, were immediately filled with horror. Their mouths hanging open as they watched on helplessly.

Its opponent unexpectedly defeated, Ardell's blade continued its trajectory, cutting through the Emperor's divinite armour like paper, embedding itself deep into his left shoulder until it came to a halt, just centimetres from his heart.

A deafening silence filled the air, broken only by the sharp ringing of shards of broken metal hitting the ground.

The sickly silence of over one hundred men, who had just witnessed the faith to which they had pledged their lives, disproven before their eyes. It rained down around them, catching their exposed flesh, opening new physical wounds over an already mortal spiritual one.

The weight of the blow had forced the Emperor to one knee, one hand placed firmly against the floor to keep himself steady. His head was bowed, blood dripping from the inside of his helm. His blood. The Emperor felt dizzy, the view of his lower body blurry, swaying from side to side with no form, as if he were in a feverish dream.

He felt something. Pain. No. Yes. But something else, something with no physical source, something he could not place as his weakening grip on reality worsened. There was an emptiness, a coldness within. He scoured his memory, as far back as it would allow as he sought a parallel to this sensation. While he could find nothing in the depths of his past, he suddenly knew. His soul instinctively knowing what he felt, reserving it for what appeared to be this very moment.

This was defeat.

With raspy, pained breaths the Emperor summoned the last of his strength, looking up at Ardell who still held a firm grip on her sword embedded in his body. She was just as surprised as anyone else. She had expected a prolonged battle, one worthy of re-telling in song until the end of days, one she could not hope to win. She had expected death, had accepted it even. Yet now here she stood, as victor. A king-slayer.

"How?" the Emperor gasped, in a voice full of confusion and pain. He had been chosen. Why would the Lord abandon him now? Then a truly terrifying thought filled his addled mind, one which in a thousand years he had never once considered before. Had it all been a trick, a scheme by some great evil, to raise him to such heights, only now to cast him down at his moment of greatest need? But this was a question which Ardell could not answer.

She said nothing, and in a single motion wrenched the

sword free, spinning in a full circle from the force required to retrieve it from the Emperor's shoulder. There was a sickening squelch as flesh tore, as blood spurted from the wound and the Emperor let out a pained cry. As Ardell came around to face her defeated foe once again, she pulled Steel Rose from its holster on her left thigh, the muzzle resting against the Emperor's helm. There was a single moment of hesitation, the two weary pairs of eyes conversing beyond the limits of words as they accepted what must come next.

Ardell fired a single shot. The bullet shattering the Emperor's helm like it were made of porcelain, bursting through his head in a shower of blood and gore. He fell onto his back with a deafening crash which could be felt in one's very bones.

As he lay there in absolute darkness, his eyes wide but perceiving nothing of the world around him, the Emperor could make out only the faintest of sounds. A sudden shout, the turning of one's heels as they scratched against the floor, their thudding growing fainter as the owner sped away. Then the stomping of what sounded like hundreds of hooves, racing in his direction, animalistic cries creating a swirling, tempestuous sea of torment as the thunderous steps came to a halt around him.

Then the silence came. And the Emperor felt nothing, saw nothing, heard nothing as he breathed his final breath, slipping away without resistance into the dark.

End.

9 781835 635070